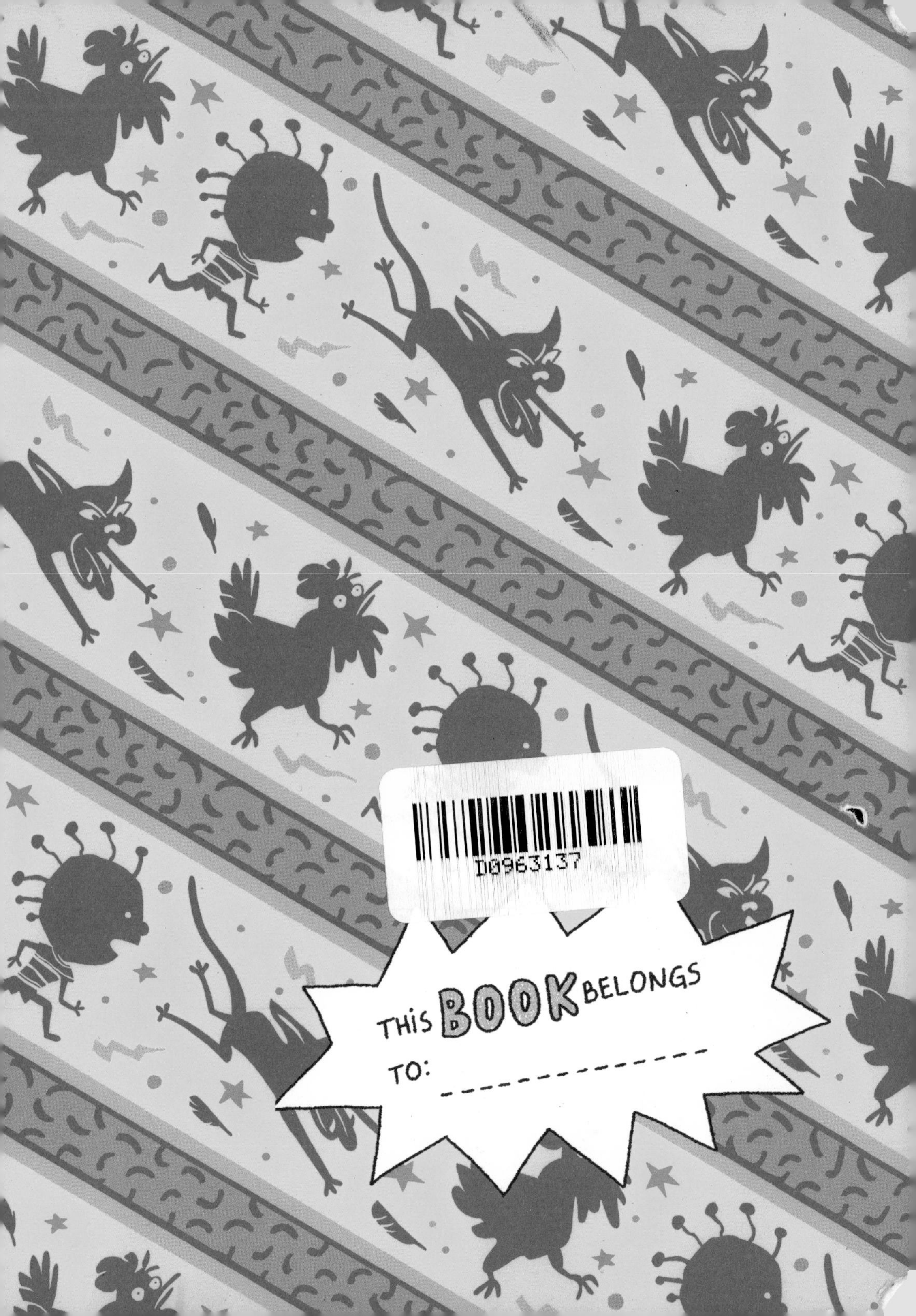
THIS BOOK BELONGS
TO:

First published in English in 2020 by Flying Eye Books,
an imprint of Nobrow Ltd. 27 Westgate Street, London E8 3RL.

Akissi 7: Faux Départ, by Marguerite Abouet and Mathieu Sapin© Gallimard Jeunesse, France, 2016.
Akissi 8: Mission Pas Possible, by Marguerite Abouet and Mathieu Sapin© Gallimard Jeunesse, France, 2018.
Akissi 9: Aller-Retour, by Marguerite Abouet and Mathieu Sapin© Gallimard Jeunesse, France, 2019.

Published in agreement with Éditions Gallimard Jeunesse.

Inspired by the graphic universe created by Clement Oubrerie.

Text by Marguerite Abouet. Illustrations by Mathieu Sapin.

Marguerite Abouet and Mathieu Sapin have asserted their rights under the Copyright,
Designs and Patents Act, 1988, to be identified as the Author and Illustrator of this Work.

Colours by Clémence.

Translation by Marie Bédrune.

1 3 5 7 9 10 8 6 4 2

Published in the US by Nobrow (US) Inc.
Printed in Poland on FSC® certified paper.

MIX
Paper from
responsible sources
FSC® C001693
FSC
www.fsc.org

ISBN: 978-1-912497-41-6
www.flyingeyebooks.com

Abouet & Sapin

Akissi

EVEN MORE TALES OF MISCHIEF

FLYING EYE BOOKS
LONDON | NEW YORK

INTRODUCTION

Initially, Akissi was born out of my desire to tell the story of my homeland and the happy memories of being a young Ivorian girl, who would leave her home too soon and head for France without her parents. Akissi was also a product of wanting to show a different view of Africa than the one we are usually shown. An Africa that is full of life, rather than sorrow. The Akissi stories are above all about the need to not focus – like most children's books and animated films do – on the folktales and legends that come from Africa that don't represent the actual day to day lives of modern Africans.

The character of Akissi is just like me when I was young. The whole neighbourhood was my playground and the people that lived in it were my family. With her braids and cute, expressive face, Akissi encourages her friends and all the local children to become urban explorers. She shows that kindness and courage are what is needed for forging friendships and taking on everyday challenges. Akissi treats everyone just the same, without any judgement or prejudice regarding race, religion, ability, gender identity or age.

The stories I tell simply show Africa through the eyes of a child that has grown up there. The characters are positive-minded for the most part. They are full of imperfections at times but always joyful and lively, and children from all across the globe can identify with them.

Come on board and visit a welcoming and fun-filled land and discover an Africa that is so close, and yet so far.

Welcome to my childhood!

Marguerite Abouet

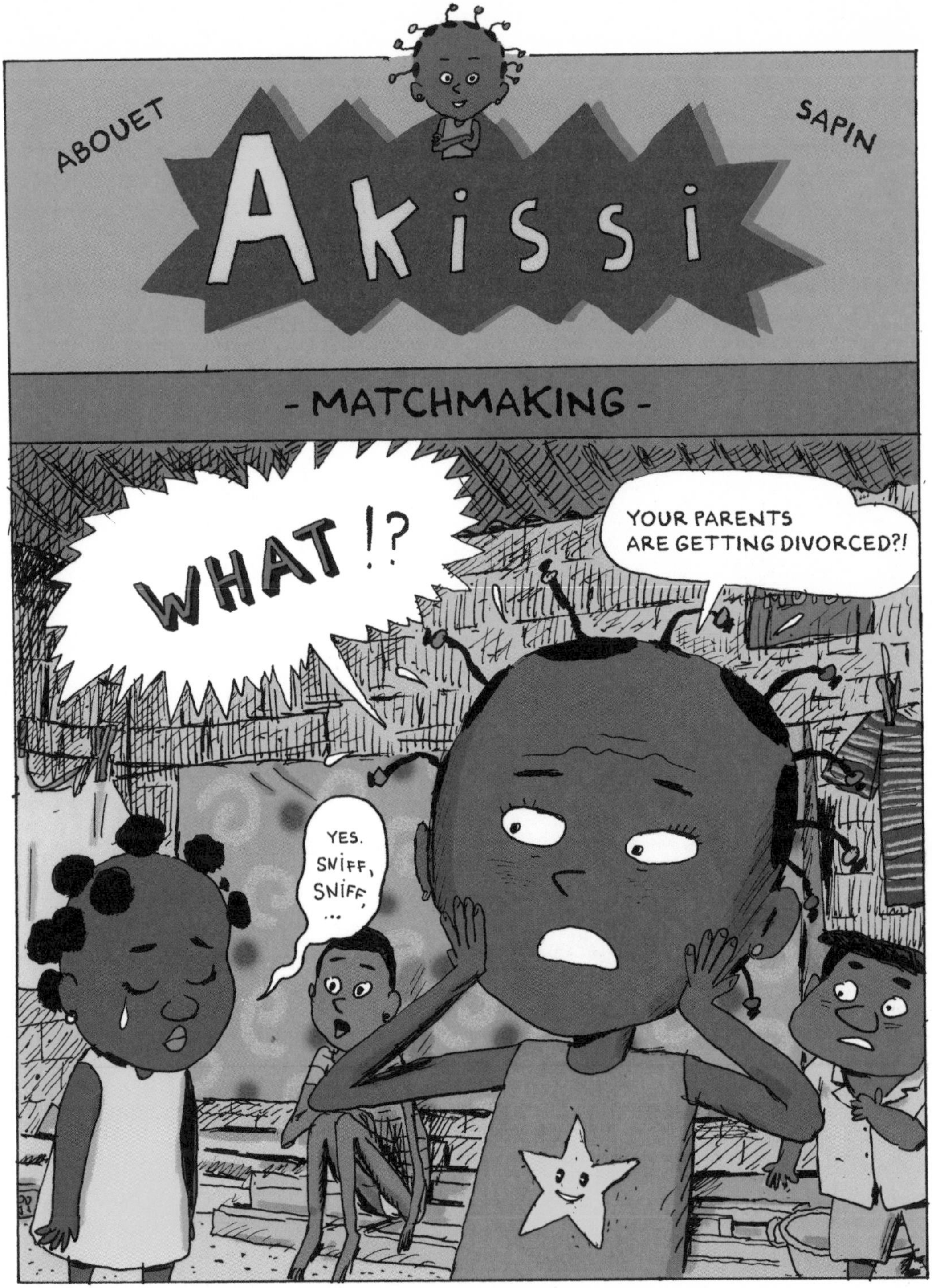
ABOUET
Akissi
SAPIN
- MATCHMAKING -
WHAT !?
YOUR PARENTS ARE GETTING DIVORCED?!
YES. SNIFF, SNIFF, ...

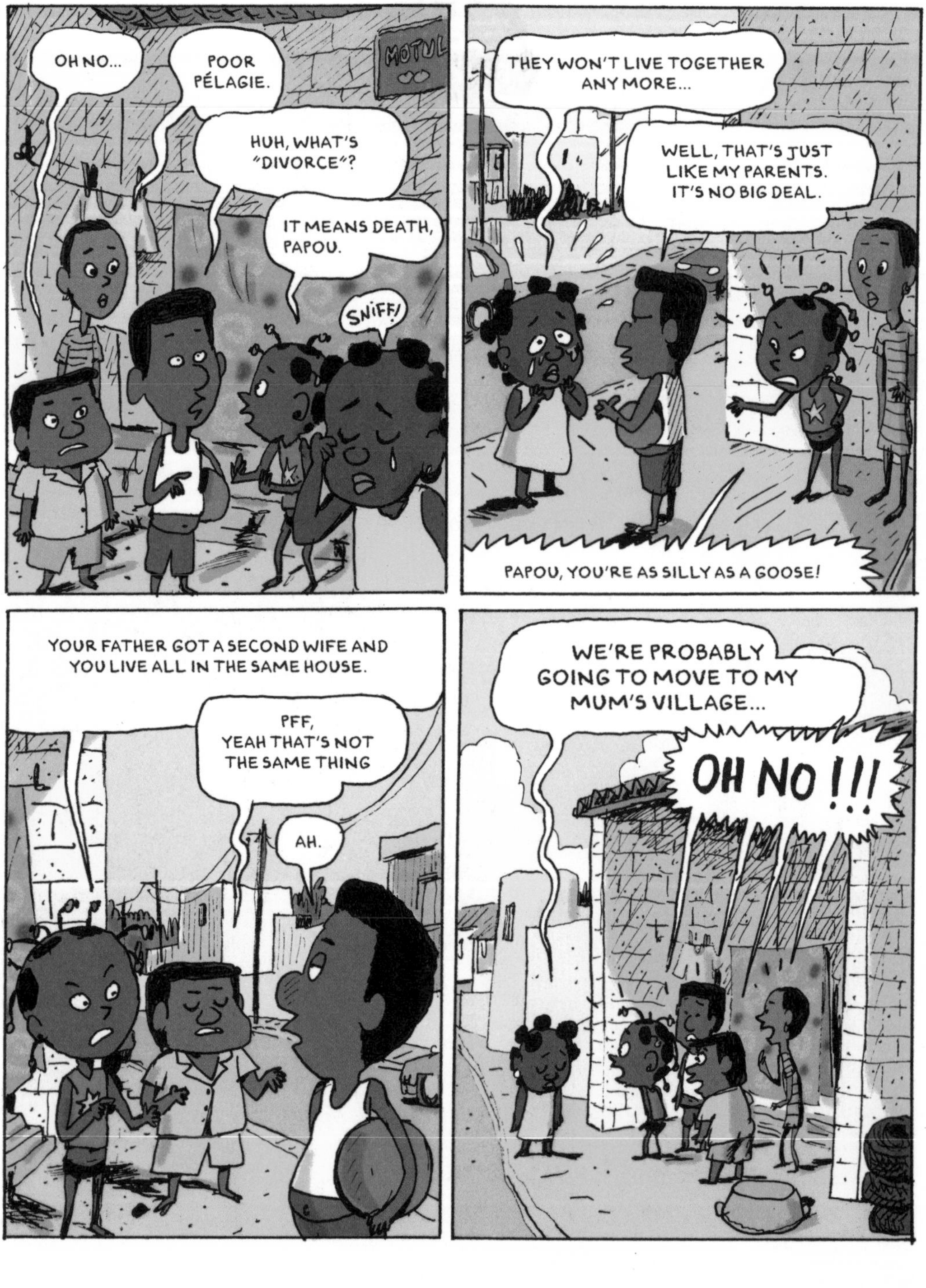
OH NO...
POOR PÉLAGIE.
HUH, WHAT'S "DIVORCE"?
IT MEANS DEATH, PAPOU.
SNIFF!
THEY WON'T LIVE TOGETHER ANY MORE...
WELL, THAT'S JUST LIKE MY PARENTS. IT'S NO BIG DEAL.
PAPOU, YOU'RE AS SILLY AS A GOOSE!
YOUR FATHER GOT A SECOND WIFE AND YOU LIVE ALL IN THE SAME HOUSE.
PFF, YEAH THAT'S NOT THE SAME THING
AH.
WE'RE PROBABLY GOING TO MOVE TO MY MUM'S VILLAGE...
OH NO !!!

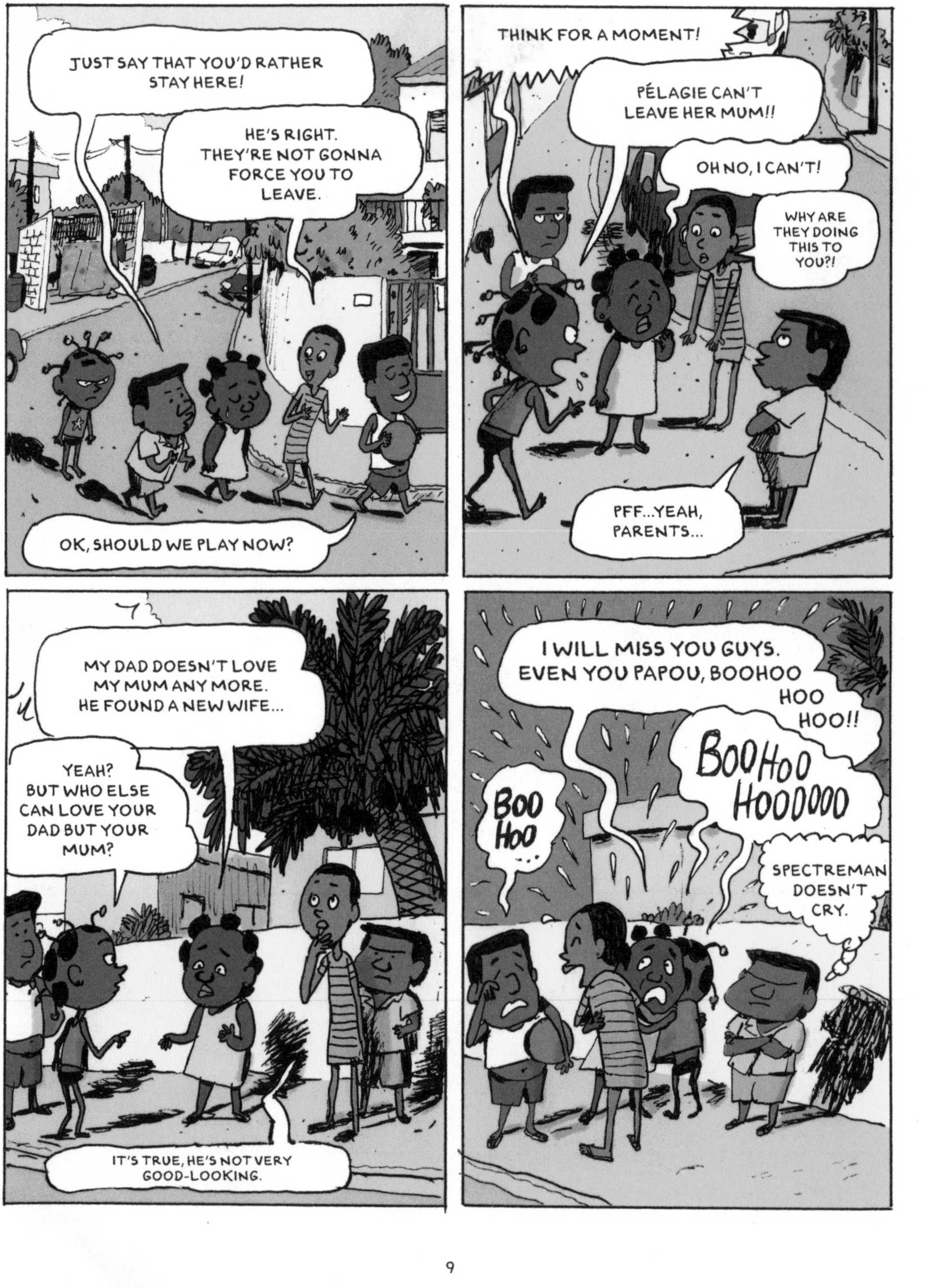
JUST SAY THAT YOU'D RATHER STAY HERE!
HE'S RIGHT. THEY'RE NOT GONNA FORCE YOU TO LEAVE.
OK, SHOULD WE PLAY NOW?
THINK FOR A MOMENT!
PÉLAGIE CAN'T LEAVE HER MUM!!
OH NO, I CAN'T!
WHY ARE THEY DOING THIS TO YOU?!
PFF...YEAH, PARENTS...
MY DAD DOESN'T LOVE MY MUM ANY MORE. HE FOUND A NEW WIFE...
YEAH? BUT WHO ELSE CAN LOVE YOUR DAD BUT YOUR MUM?
IT'S TRUE, HE'S NOT VERY GOOD-LOOKING.
I WILL MISS YOU GUYS. EVEN YOU PAPOU, BOOHOO HOO HOO!!
BOO HOO...
BOOHOO HOOOOOO
SPECTREMAN DOESN'T CRY.

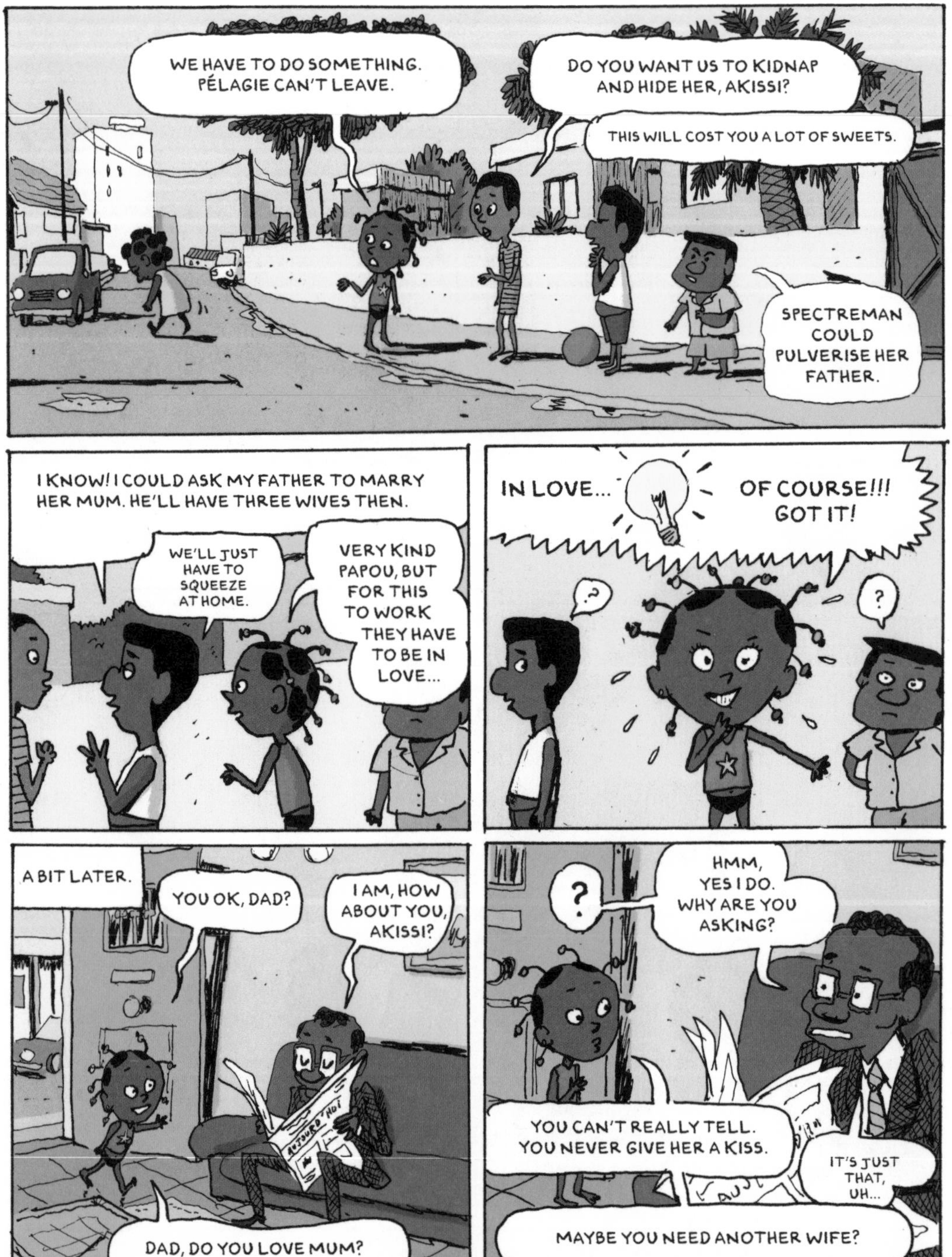
WE HAVE TO DO SOMETHING. PÉLAGIE CAN'T LEAVE.
DO YOU WANT US TO KIDNAP AND HIDE HER, AKISSI?
THIS WILL COST YOU A LOT OF SWEETS.
SPECTREMAN COULD PULVERISE HER FATHER.
I KNOW! I COULD ASK MY FATHER TO MARRY HER MUM. HE'LL HAVE THREE WIVES THEN.
WE'LL JUST HAVE TO SQUEEZE AT HOME.
VERY KIND PAPOU, BUT FOR THIS TO WORK THEY HAVE TO BE IN LOVE...
IN LOVE...
OF COURSE!!! GOT IT!
?
?
A BIT LATER.
YOU OK, DAD?
I AM, HOW ABOUT YOU, AKISSI?
DAD, DO YOU LOVE MUM?
?
HMM, YES I DO. WHY ARE YOU ASKING?
YOU CAN'T REALLY TELL. YOU NEVER GIVE HER A KISS.
IT'S JUST THAT, UH...
MAYBE YOU NEED ANOTHER WIFE?

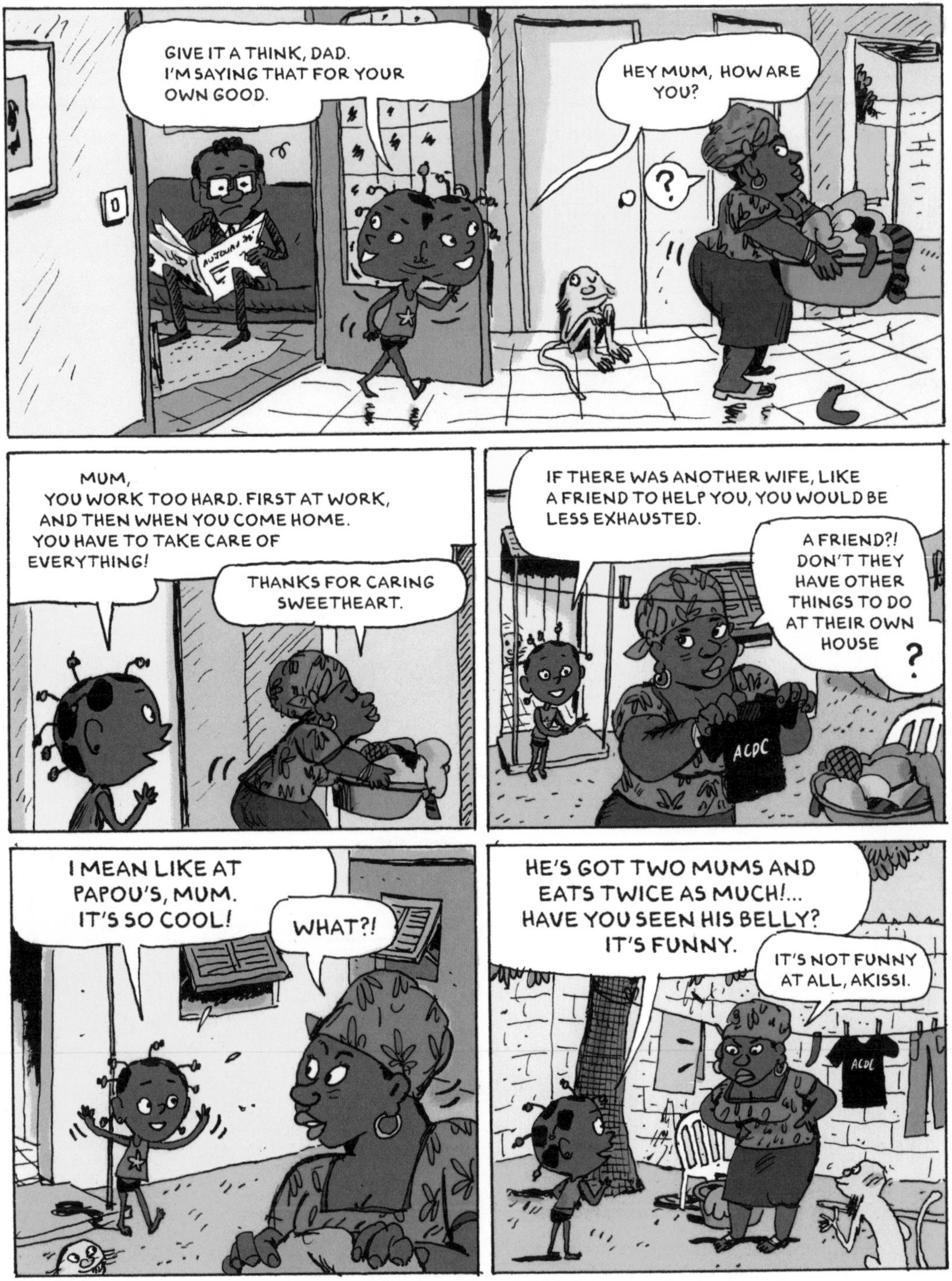
GIVE IT A THINK, DAD. I'M SAYING THAT FOR YOUR OWN GOOD.
AUJOURD'HUI
HEY MUM, HOW ARE YOU?
?
MUM, YOU WORK TOO HARD. FIRST AT WORK, AND THEN WHEN YOU COME HOME. YOU HAVE TO TAKE CARE OF EVERYTHING!
THANKS FOR CARING SWEETHEART.
IF THERE WAS ANOTHER WIFE, LIKE A FRIEND TO HELP YOU, YOU WOULD BE LESS EXHAUSTED.
A FRIEND?! DON'T THEY HAVE OTHER THINGS TO DO AT THEIR OWN HOUSE ?
ACDC
I MEAN LIKE AT PAPOU'S, MUM. IT'S SO COOL!
WHAT?!
HE'S GOT TWO MUMS AND EATS TWICE AS MUCH!... HAVE YOU SEEN HIS BELLY? IT'S FUNNY.
IT'S NOT FUNNY AT ALL, AKISSI.
ACDC

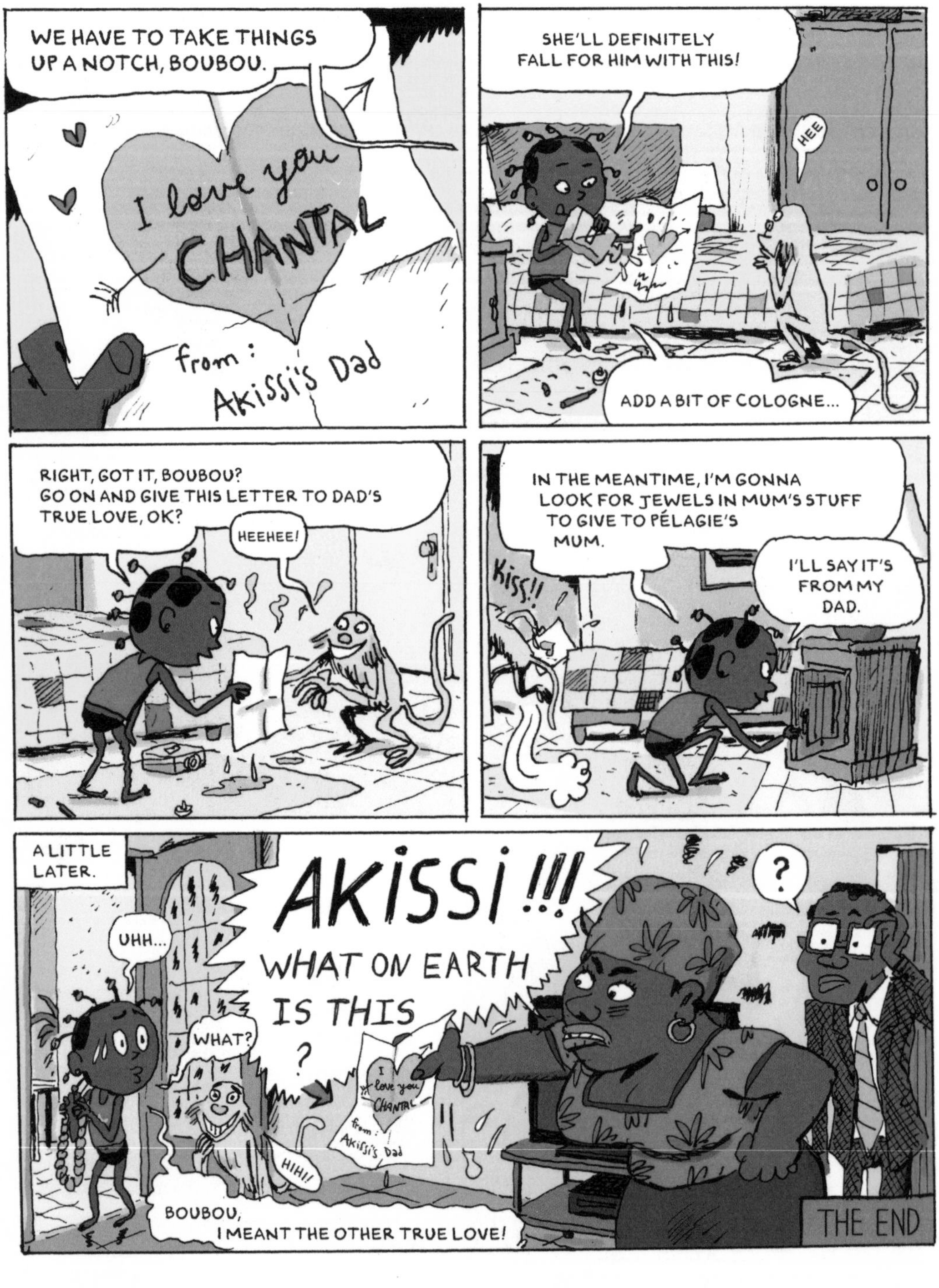
WE HAVE TO TAKE THINGS UP A NOTCH, BOUBOU.
I love you CHANTAL
from : Akissi's Dad
SHE'LL DEFINITELY FALL FOR HIM WITH THIS!
HEE
ADD A BIT OF COLOGNE...
RIGHT, GOT IT, BOUBOU? GO ON AND GIVE THIS LETTER TO DAD'S TRUE LOVE, OK?
HEEHEE!
IN THE MEANTIME, I'M GONNA LOOK FOR JEWELS IN MUM'S STUFF TO GIVE TO PÉLAGIE'S MUM.
Kiss!!
I'LL SAY IT'S FROM MY DAD.
A LITTLE LATER.
AKISSI !!!
WHAT ON EARTH IS THIS ?
?
UHH...
WHAT?
I love you CHANTAL
from : Akissi's Dad
HIHI!
BOUBOU, I MEANT THE OTHER TRUE LOVE!
THE END

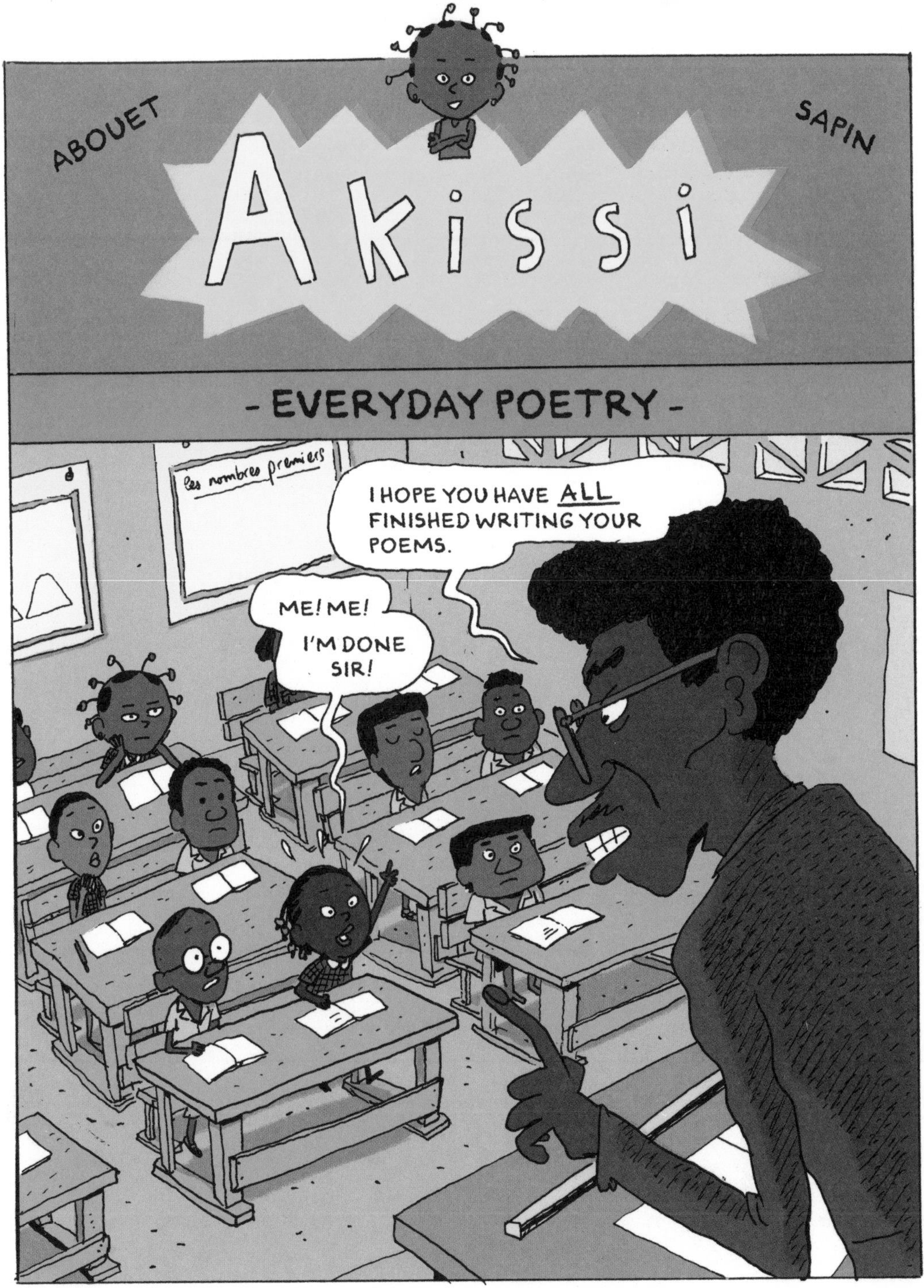
ABOUET
SAPIN
Akissi
- EVERYDAY POETRY -
les nombres premiers
I HOPE YOU HAVE ALL FINISHED WRITING YOUR POEMS.
ME! ME! I'M DONE SIR!

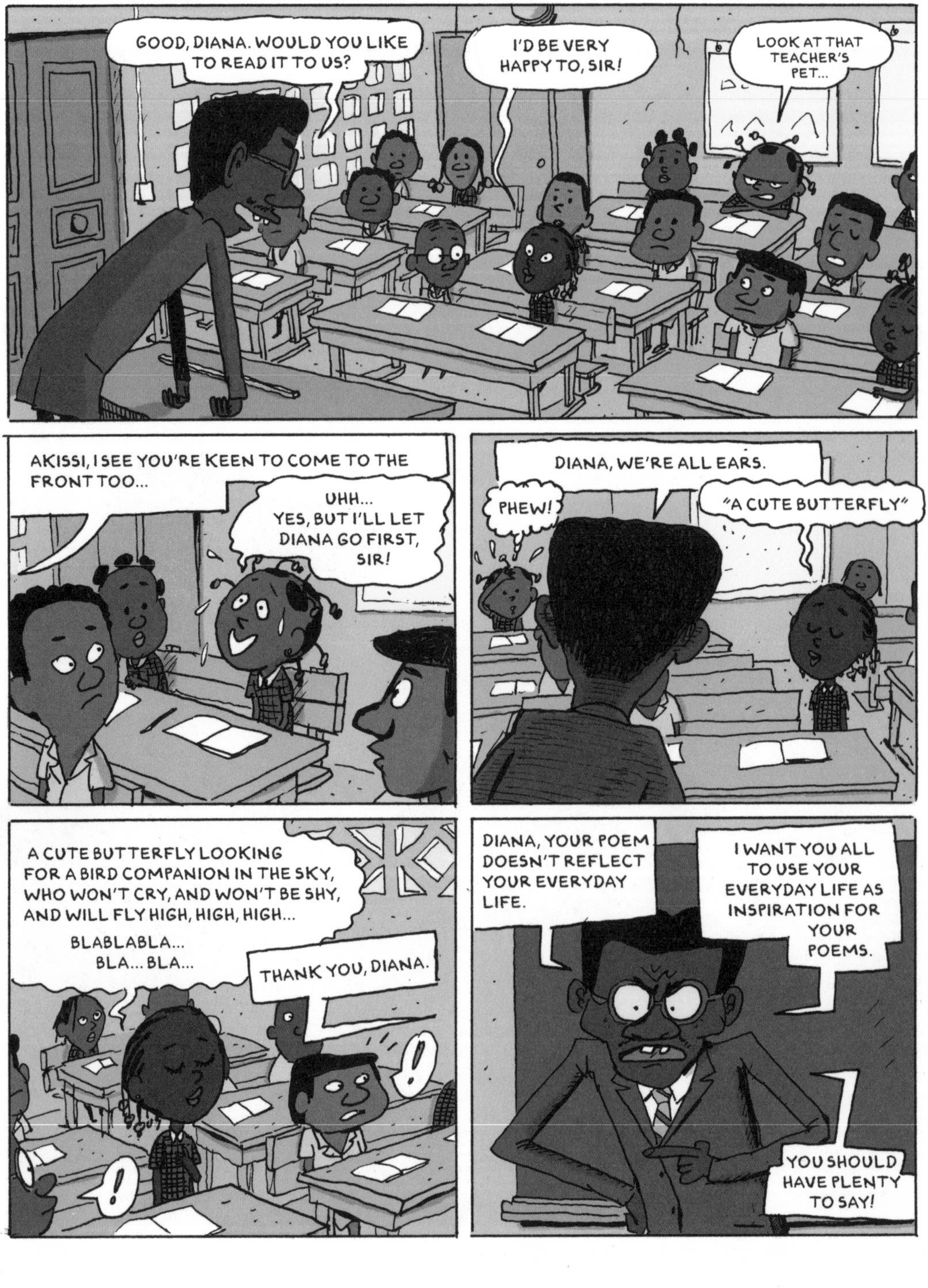
GOOD, DIANA. WOULD YOU LIKE TO READ IT TO US?
I'D BE VERY HAPPY TO, SIR!
LOOK AT THAT TEACHER'S PET...
AKISSI, I SEE YOU'RE KEEN TO COME TO THE FRONT TOO...
UHH... YES, BUT I'LL LET DIANA GO FIRST, SIR!
DIANA, WE'RE ALL EARS.
PHEW!
"A CUTE BUTTERFLY"
A CUTE BUTTERFLY LOOKING FOR A BIRD COMPANION IN THE SKY, WHO WON'T CRY, AND WON'T BE SHY, AND WILL FLY HIGH, HIGH, HIGH...
BLABLABLA... BLA... BLA...
THANK YOU, DIANA.
!
!
DIANA, YOUR POEM DOESN'T REFLECT YOUR EVERYDAY LIFE.
I WANT YOU ALL TO USE YOUR EVERYDAY LIFE AS INSPIRATION FOR YOUR POEMS.
YOU SHOULD HAVE PLENTY TO SAY!

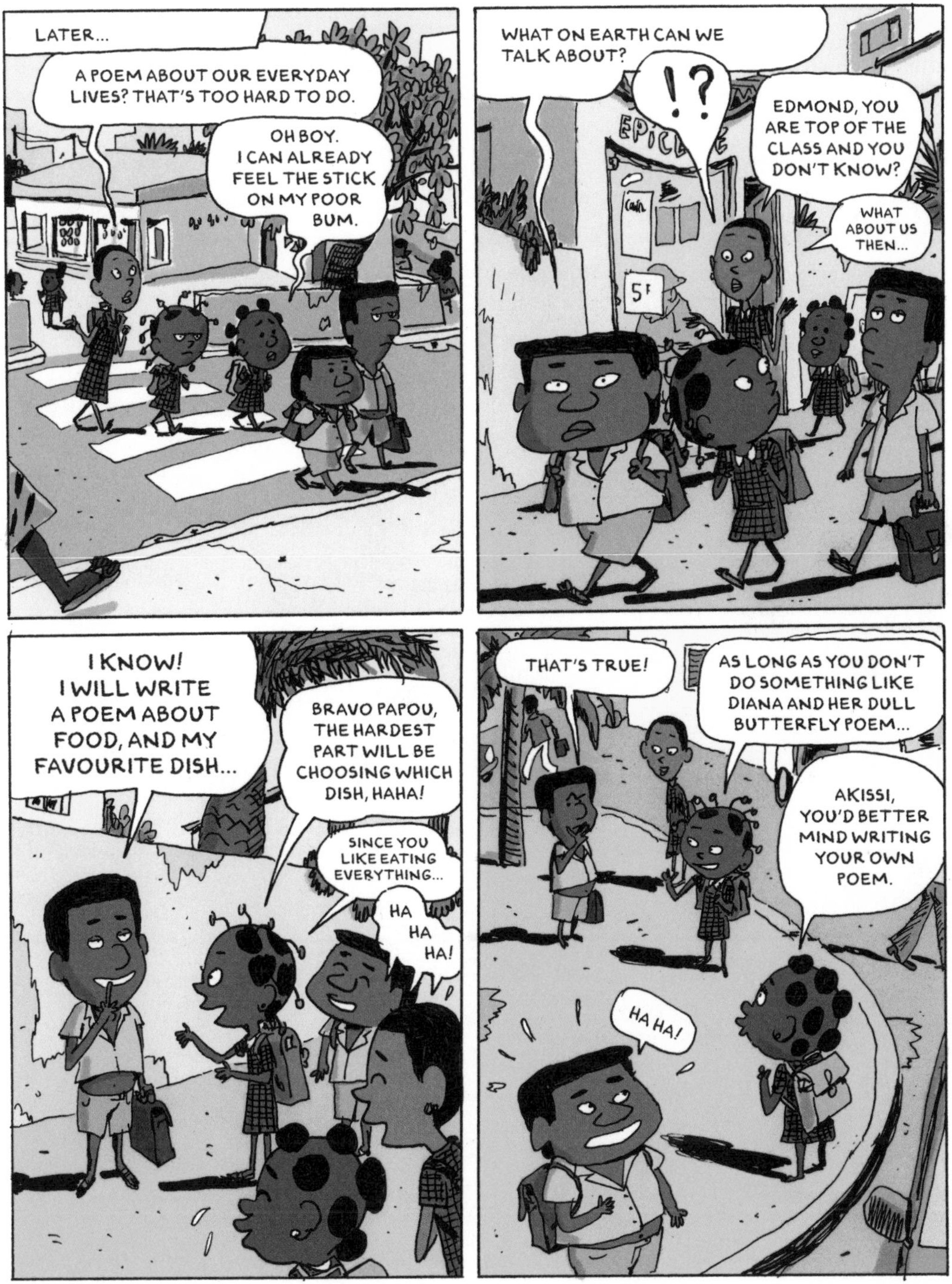
LATER...
A POEM ABOUT OUR EVERYDAY LIVES? THAT'S TOO HARD TO DO.
OH BOY. I CAN ALREADY FEEL THE STICK ON MY POOR BUM.
WHAT ON EARTH CAN WE TALK ABOUT?
!?
EPICERIE
EDMOND, YOU ARE TOP OF THE CLASS AND YOU DON'T KNOW?
WHAT ABOUT US THEN...
I KNOW! I WILL WRITE A POEM ABOUT FOOD, AND MY FAVOURITE DISH...
BRAVO PAPOU, THE HARDEST PART WILL BE CHOOSING WHICH DISH, HAHA!
SINCE YOU LIKE EATING EVERYTHING...
HA HA HA!
THAT'S TRUE!
AS LONG AS YOU DON'T DO SOMETHING LIKE DIANA AND HER DULL BUTTERFLY POEM...
AKISSI, YOU'D BETTER MIND WRITING YOUR OWN POEM.
HA HA!

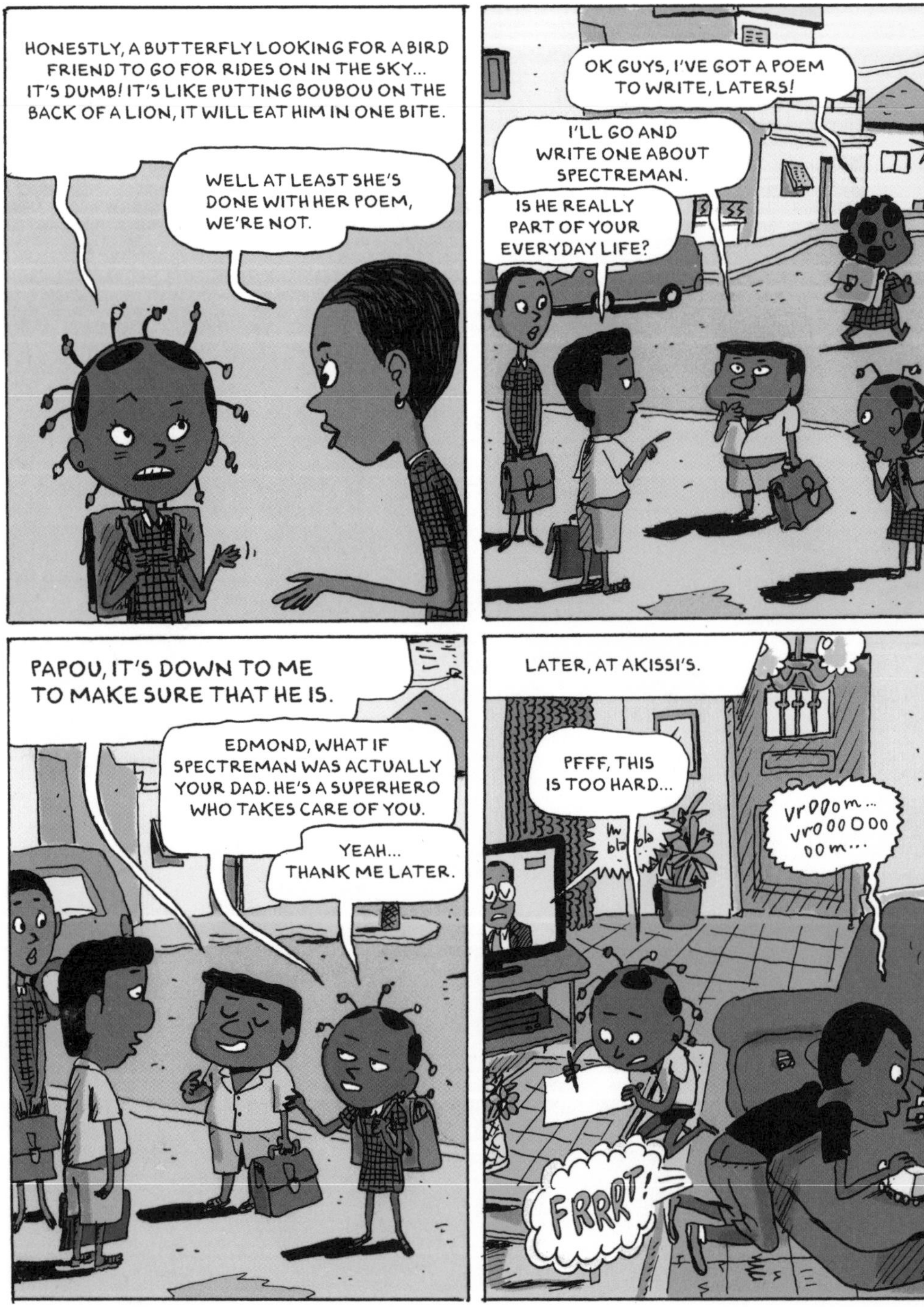
HONESTLY, A BUTTERFLY LOOKING FOR A BIRD FRIEND TO GO FOR RIDES ON IN THE SKY... IT'S DUMB! IT'S LIKE PUTTING BOUBOU ON THE BACK OF A LION, IT WILL EAT HIM IN ONE BITE.
WELL AT LEAST SHE'S DONE WITH HER POEM, WE'RE NOT.
OK GUYS, I'VE GOT A POEM TO WRITE, LATERS!
I'LL GO AND WRITE ONE ABOUT SPECTREMAN.
IS HE REALLY PART OF YOUR EVERYDAY LIFE?
PAPOU, IT'S DOWN TO ME TO MAKE SURE THAT HE IS.
EDMOND, WHAT IF SPECTREMAN WAS ACTUALLY YOUR DAD. HE'S A SUPERHERO WHO TAKES CARE OF YOU.
YEAH... THANK ME LATER.
LATER, AT AKISSI'S.
PFFF, THIS IS TOO HARD...
bla bla
vrooom... vrooooooo oom...
FRRRT!

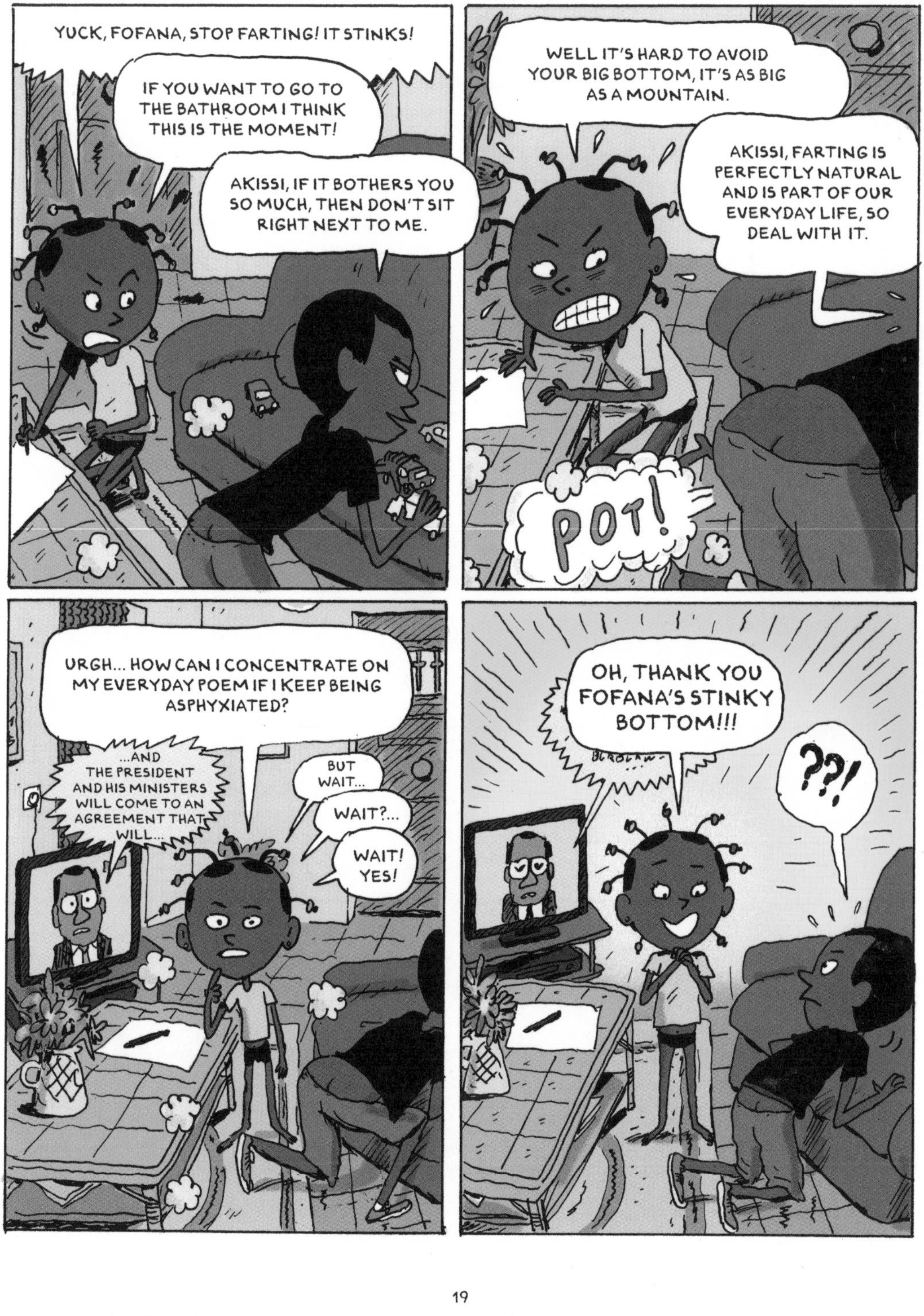
YUCK, FOFANA, STOP FARTING! IT STINKS!
IF YOU WANT TO GO TO THE BATHROOM I THINK THIS IS THE MOMENT!
AKISSI, IF IT BOTHERS YOU SO MUCH, THEN DON'T SIT RIGHT NEXT TO ME.
WELL IT'S HARD TO AVOID YOUR BIG BOTTOM, IT'S AS BIG AS A MOUNTAIN.
AKISSI, FARTING IS PERFECTLY NATURAL AND IS PART OF OUR EVERYDAY LIFE, SO DEAL WITH IT.
POT!
URGH... HOW CAN I CONCENTRATE ON MY EVERYDAY POEM IF I KEEP BEING ASPHYXIATED?
...AND THE PRESIDENT AND HIS MINISTERS WILL COME TO AN AGREEMENT THAT WILL...
BUT WAIT...
WAIT?...
WAIT! YES!
OH, THANK YOU FOFANA'S STINKY BOTTOM!!!
??!

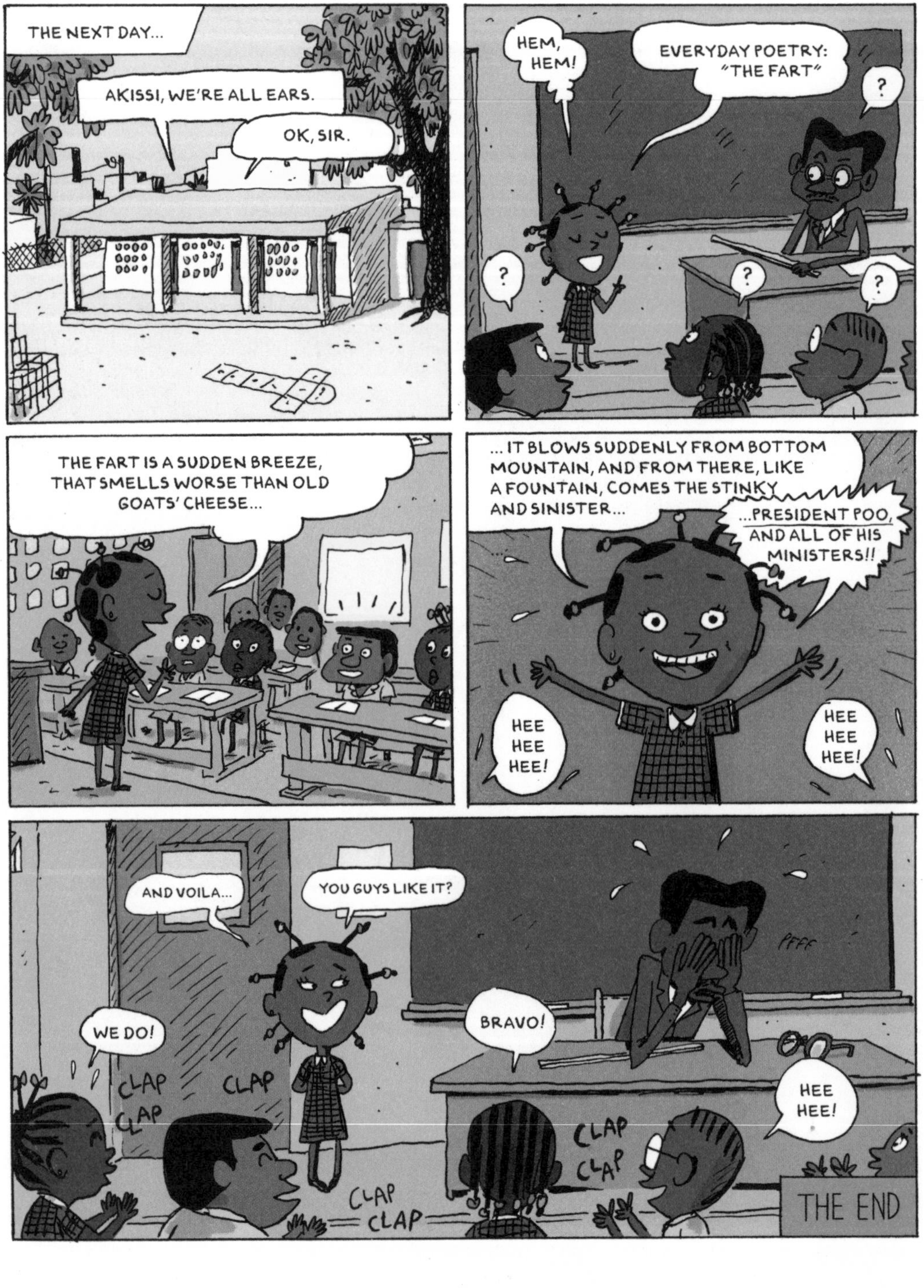

THE NEXT DAY...
AKISSI, WE'RE ALL EARS.
OK, SIR.
HEM, HEM!
EVERYDAY POETRY: "THE FART"
?
?
?
?
THE FART IS A SUDDEN BREEZE, THAT SMELLS WORSE THAN OLD GOATS' CHEESE...
... IT BLOWS SUDDENLY FROM BOTTOM MOUNTAIN, AND FROM THERE, LIKE A FOUNTAIN, COMES THE STINKY AND SINISTER...
...PRESIDENT POO, AND ALL OF HIS MINISTERS!!
HEE HEE HEE!
HEE HEE HEE!
AND VOILA...
YOU GUYS LIKE IT?
PFFF
WE DO!
BRAVO!
HEE HEE!
CLAP CLAP CLAP
CLAP CLAP
CLAP CLAP
THE END

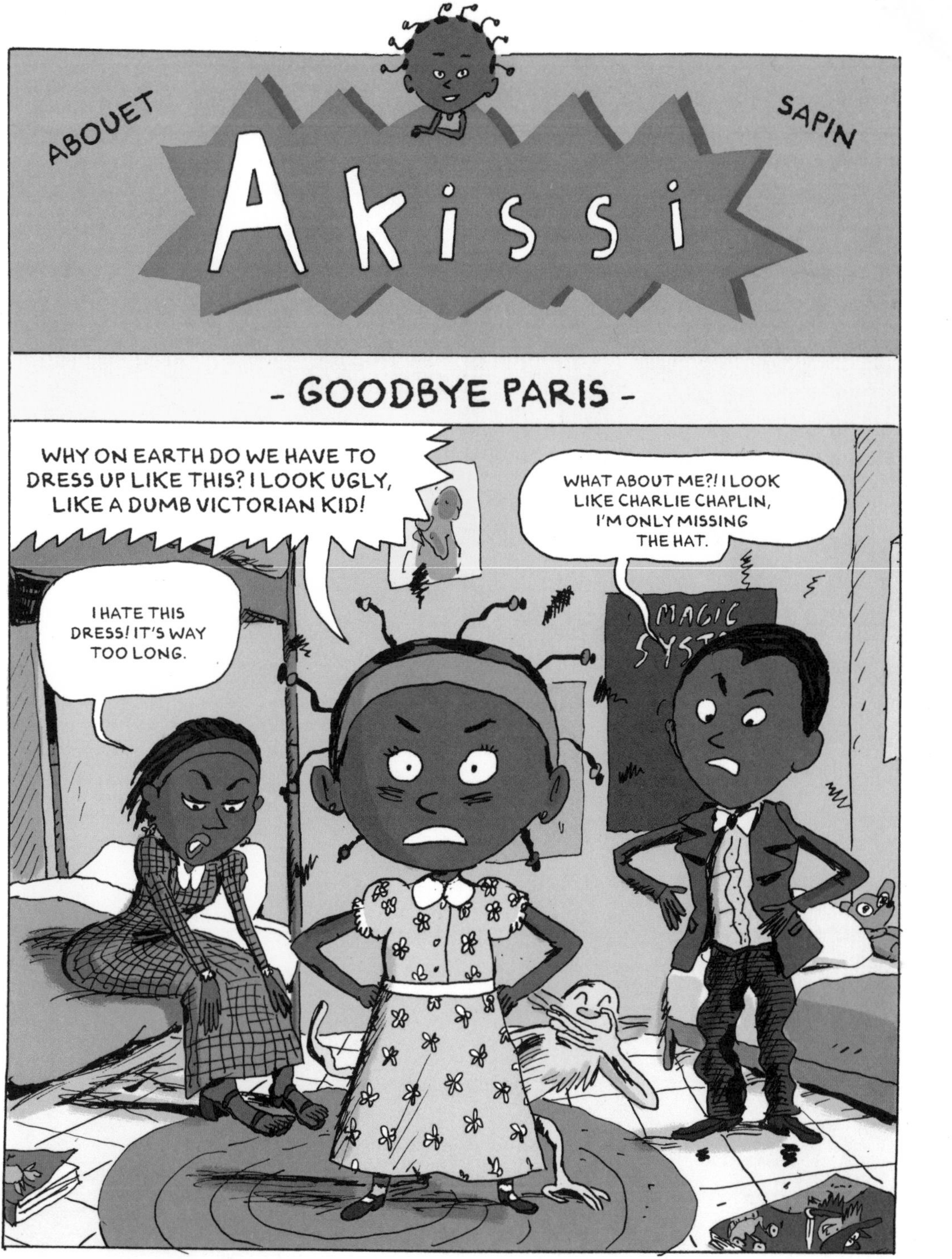
ABOUET
Akissi
SAPIN
- GOODBYE PARIS -
WHY ON EARTH DO WE HAVE TO DRESS UP LIKE THIS? I LOOK UGLY, LIKE A DUMB VICTORIAN KID!
WHAT ABOUT ME?! I LOOK LIKE CHARLIE CHAPLIN, I'M ONLY MISSING THE HAT.
I HATE THIS DRESS! IT'S WAY TOO LONG.

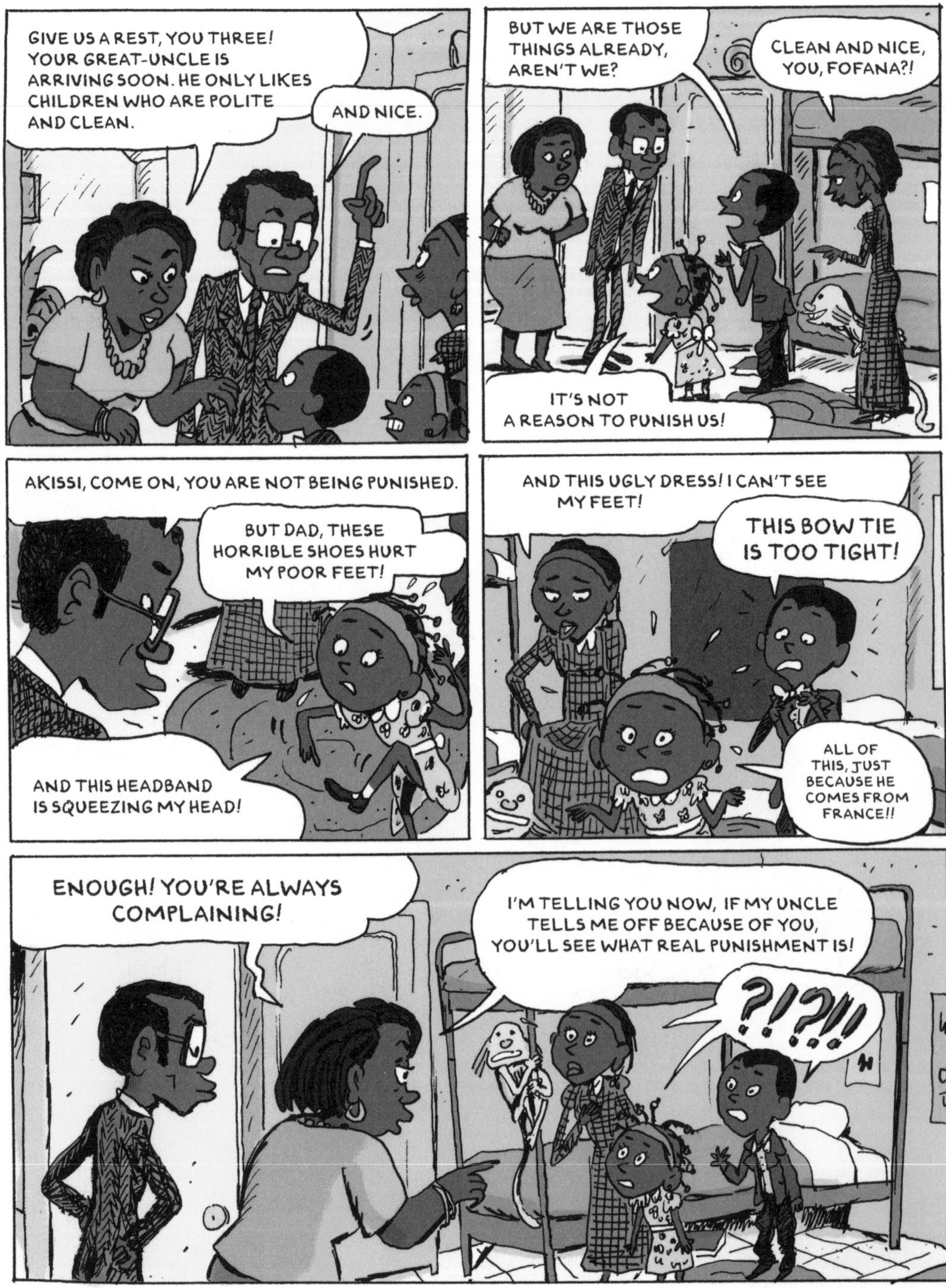

GIVE US A REST, YOU THREE! YOUR GREAT-UNCLE IS ARRIVING SOON. HE ONLY LIKES CHILDREN WHO ARE POLITE AND CLEAN.
AND NICE.
BUT WE ARE THOSE THINGS ALREADY, AREN'T WE?
CLEAN AND NICE, YOU, FOFANA?!
IT'S NOT A REASON TO PUNISH US!
AKISSI, COME ON, YOU ARE NOT BEING PUNISHED.
BUT DAD, THESE HORRIBLE SHOES HURT MY POOR FEET!
AND THIS HEADBAND IS SQUEEZING MY HEAD!
AND THIS UGLY DRESS! I CAN'T SEE MY FEET!
THIS BOW TIE IS TOO TIGHT!
ALL OF THIS, JUST BECAUSE HE COMES FROM FRANCE!!
ENOUGH! YOU'RE ALWAYS COMPLAINING!
I'M TELLING YOU NOW, IF MY UNCLE TELLS ME OFF BECAUSE OF YOU, YOU'LL SEE WHAT REAL PUNISHMENT IS!
?!?!!

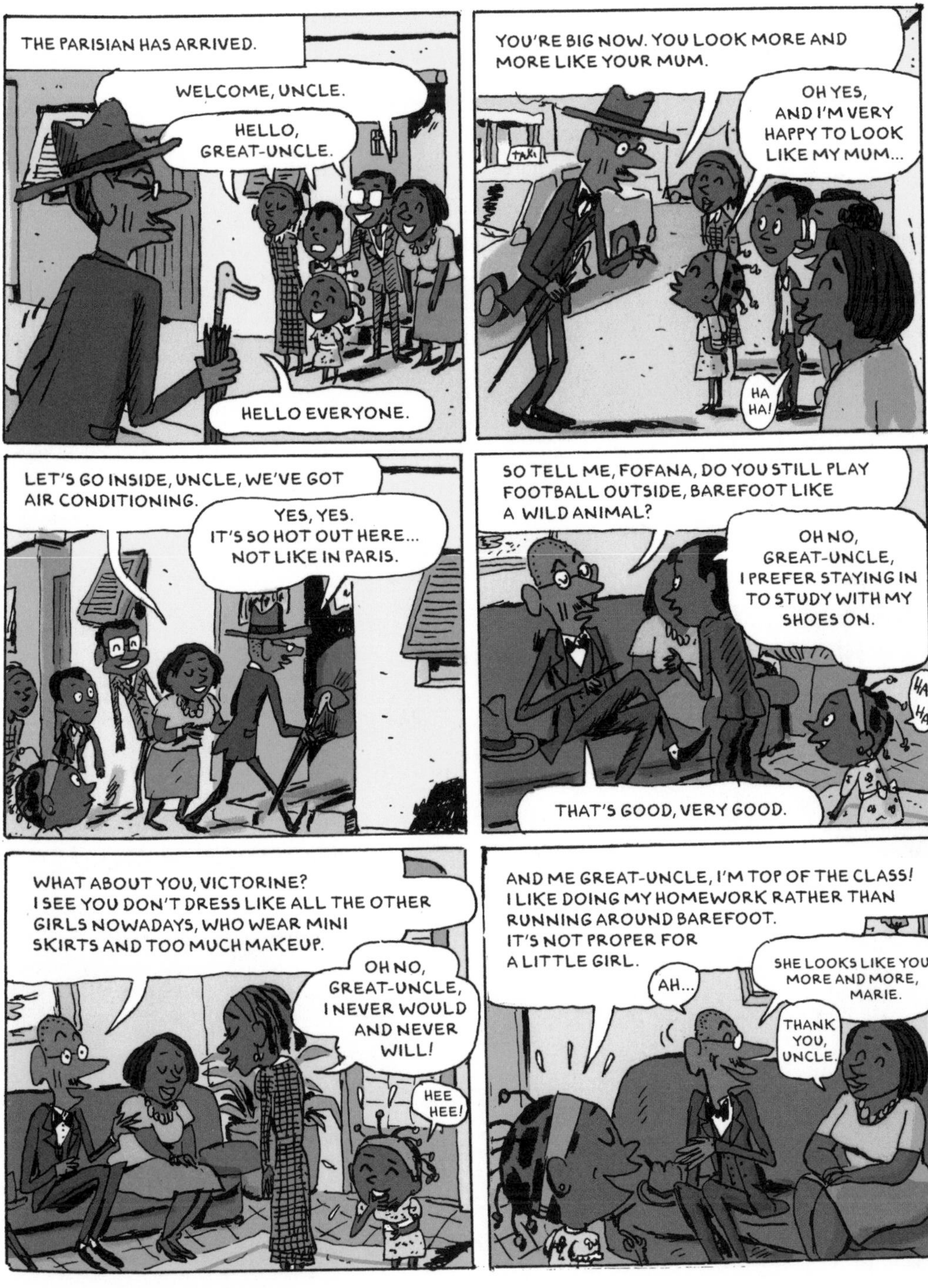
THE PARISIAN HAS ARRIVED.
WELCOME, UNCLE.
HELLO, GREAT-UNCLE.
HELLO EVERYONE.
YOU'RE BIG NOW. YOU LOOK MORE AND MORE LIKE YOUR MUM.
OH YES, AND I'M VERY HAPPY TO LOOK LIKE MY MUM...
HA HA!
LET'S GO INSIDE, UNCLE, WE'VE GOT AIR CONDITIONING.
YES, YES. IT'S SO HOT OUT HERE... NOT LIKE IN PARIS.
SO TELL ME, FOFANA, DO YOU STILL PLAY FOOTBALL OUTSIDE, BAREFOOT LIKE A WILD ANIMAL?
OH NO, GREAT-UNCLE, I PREFER STAYING IN TO STUDY WITH MY SHOES ON.
HA HA
THAT'S GOOD, VERY GOOD.
WHAT ABOUT YOU, VICTORINE? I SEE YOU DON'T DRESS LIKE ALL THE OTHER GIRLS NOWADAYS, WHO WEAR MINI SKIRTS AND TOO MUCH MAKEUP.
OH NO, GREAT-UNCLE, I NEVER WOULD AND NEVER WILL!
HEE HEE!
AND ME GREAT-UNCLE, I'M TOP OF THE CLASS! I LIKE DOING MY HOMEWORK RATHER THAN RUNNING AROUND BAREFOOT. IT'S NOT PROPER FOR A LITTLE GIRL.
AH...
SHE LOOKS LIKE YOU MORE AND MORE, MARIE.
THANK YOU, UNCLE.

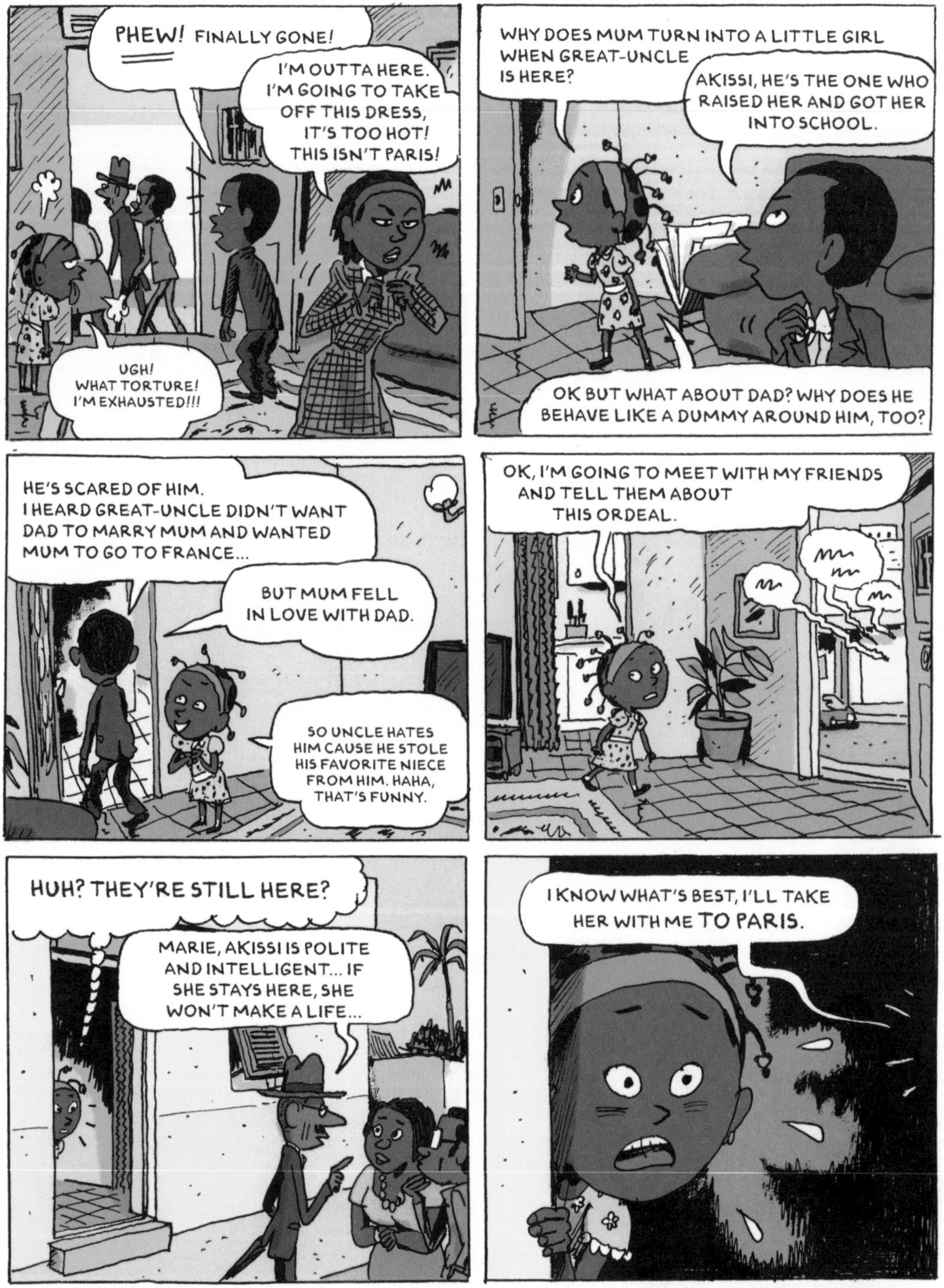
PHEW! FINALLY GONE!
I'M OUTTA HERE. I'M GOING TO TAKE OFF THIS DRESS, IT'S TOO HOT! THIS ISN'T PARIS!
UGH! WHAT TORTURE! I'M EXHAUSTED!!!
WHY DOES MUM TURN INTO A LITTLE GIRL WHEN GREAT-UNCLE IS HERE?
AKISSI, HE'S THE ONE WHO RAISED HER AND GOT HER INTO SCHOOL.
OK BUT WHAT ABOUT DAD? WHY DOES HE BEHAVE LIKE A DUMMY AROUND HIM, TOO?
HE'S SCARED OF HIM. I HEARD GREAT-UNCLE DIDN'T WANT DAD TO MARRY MUM AND WANTED MUM TO GO TO FRANCE...
BUT MUM FELL IN LOVE WITH DAD.
SO UNCLE HATES HIM CAUSE HE STOLE HIS FAVORITE NIECE FROM HIM. HAHA, THAT'S FUNNY.
OK, I'M GOING TO MEET WITH MY FRIENDS AND TELL THEM ABOUT THIS ORDEAL.
HUH? THEY'RE STILL HERE?
MARIE, AKISSI IS POLITE AND INTELLIGENT... IF SHE STAYS HERE, SHE WON'T MAKE A LIFE...
I KNOW WHAT'S BEST, I'LL TAKE HER WITH ME TO PARIS.

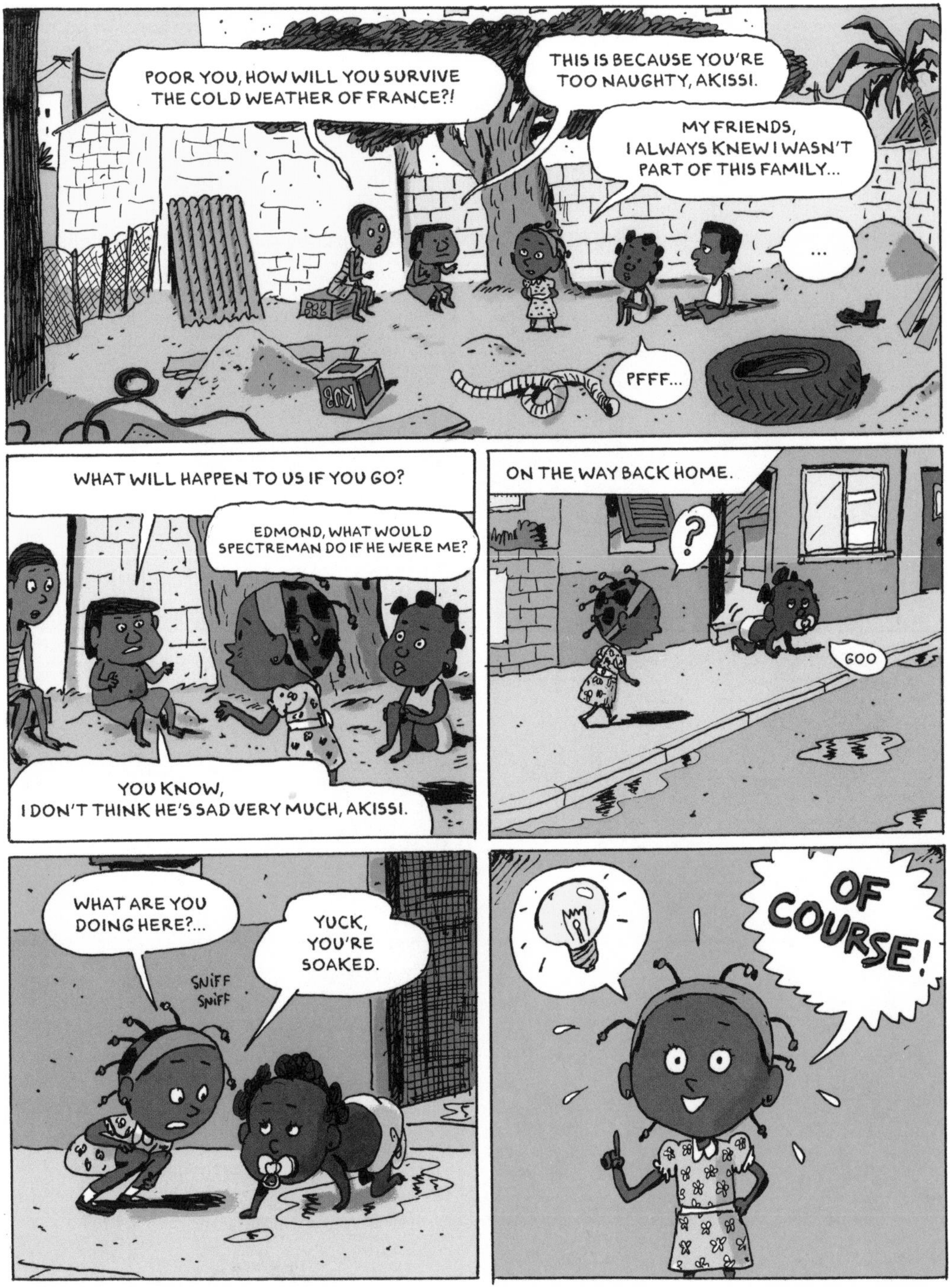
POOR YOU, HOW WILL YOU SURVIVE THE COLD WEATHER OF FRANCE?!
THIS IS BECAUSE YOU'RE TOO NAUGHTY, AKISSI.
MY FRIENDS, I ALWAYS KNEW I WASN'T PART OF THIS FAMILY...
...
KUB
PFFF...
WHAT WILL HAPPEN TO US IF YOU GO?
EDMOND, WHAT WOULD SPECTREMAN DO IF HE WERE ME?
YOU KNOW, I DON'T THINK HE'S SAD VERY MUCH, AKISSI.
ON THE WAY BACK HOME.
?
GOO
WHAT ARE YOU DOING HERE?...
YUCK, YOU'RE SOAKED.
SNIFF SNIFF
!
OF COURSE!

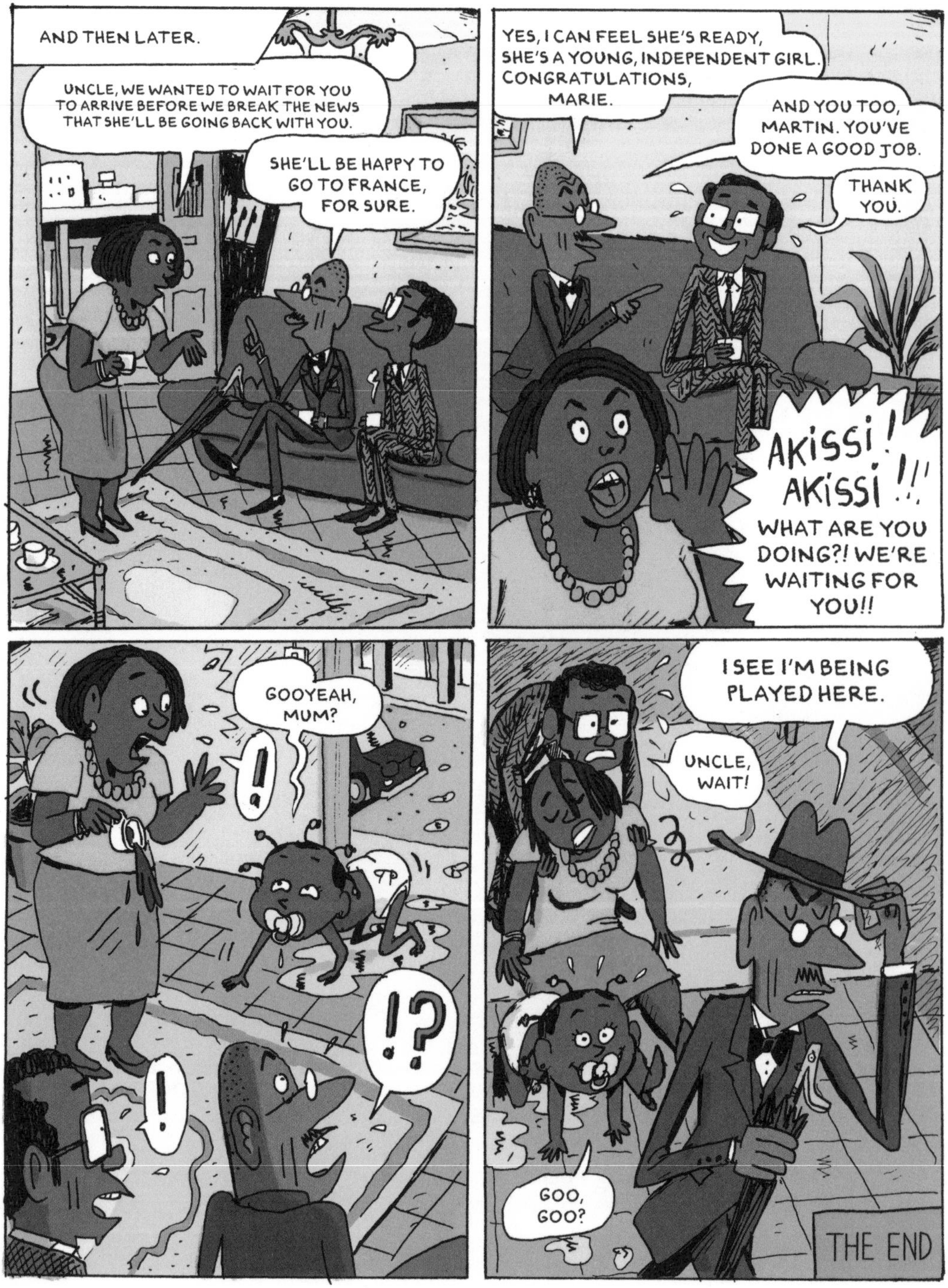
AND THEN LATER.
UNCLE, WE WANTED TO WAIT FOR YOU TO ARRIVE BEFORE WE BREAK THE NEWS THAT SHE'LL BE GOING BACK WITH YOU.
SHE'LL BE HAPPY TO GO TO FRANCE, FOR SURE.
YES, I CAN FEEL SHE'S READY, SHE'S A YOUNG, INDEPENDENT GIRL. CONGRATULATIONS, MARIE.
AND YOU TOO, MARTIN. YOU'VE DONE A GOOD JOB.
THANK YOU.
AKISSI! AKISSI!!! WHAT ARE YOU DOING?! WE'RE WAITING FOR YOU!!
GOOYEAH, MUM?
!
!?
!
I SEE I'M BEING PLAYED HERE.
UNCLE, WAIT!
GOO, GOO?
THE END

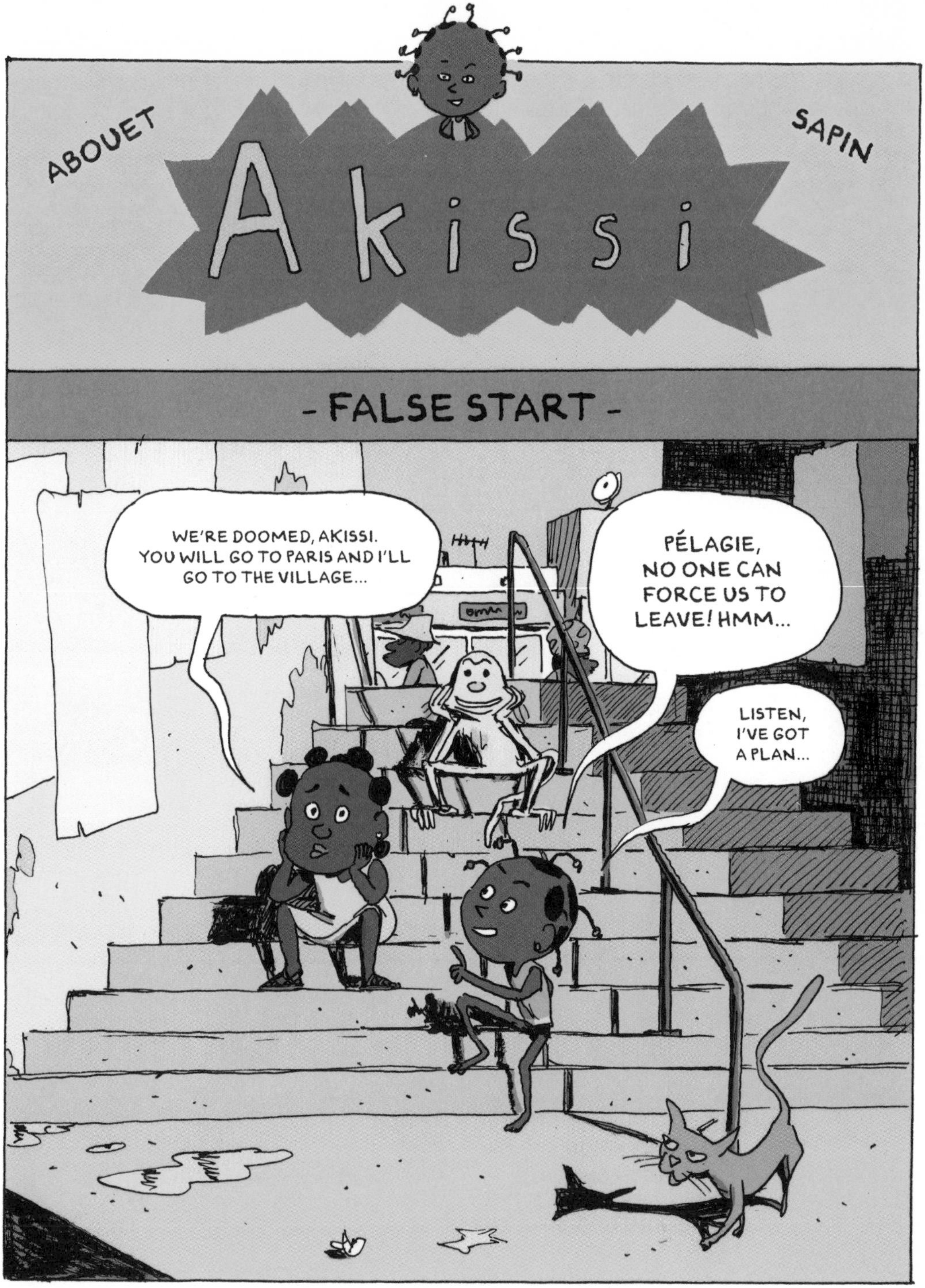
ABOUET
SAPIN
Akissi
- FALSE START -
WE'RE DOOMED, AKISSI. YOU WILL GO TO PARIS AND I'LL GO TO THE VILLAGE...
PÉLAGIE, NO ONE CAN FORCE US TO LEAVE! HMM...
LISTEN, I'VE GOT A PLAN...

A LITTLE BIT LATER...
OK, LET ME CHECK WE'VE GOT EVERYTHING.
run away list :
SAUSAGE
SWEETS
CAKE
BREAD
T-SHIRT
COAL
TV
YOU'RE SURE THIS IS A GOOD IDEA, AKISSI?
WE'RE GONNA LIVE SOMEWHERE ELSE. SOMEWHERE WE CHOOSE!
PARIS! CAN YOU IMAGINE?! WHAT WOULD I DO THERE?
FREEZE TO DEATH?
AND ME AT THE VILLAGE... NO WAY! I'M SCARED OF ANIMALS.
WE NEED TWO PAIRS OF UNDERPANTS, ONE FOR YOU, ONE FOR ME.
SAUSAGES? CHECK. SWEETS? CHECK. CAKE? CHECK. TSHIRT... I'VE ALREADY GOT ONE ON, THAT'LL DO RIGHT?
DRESSES, AKISSI!
OK THEN, DRESSES, CHECK...
COAL TO COOK FOOD, CHECK. FOOD CANS ...

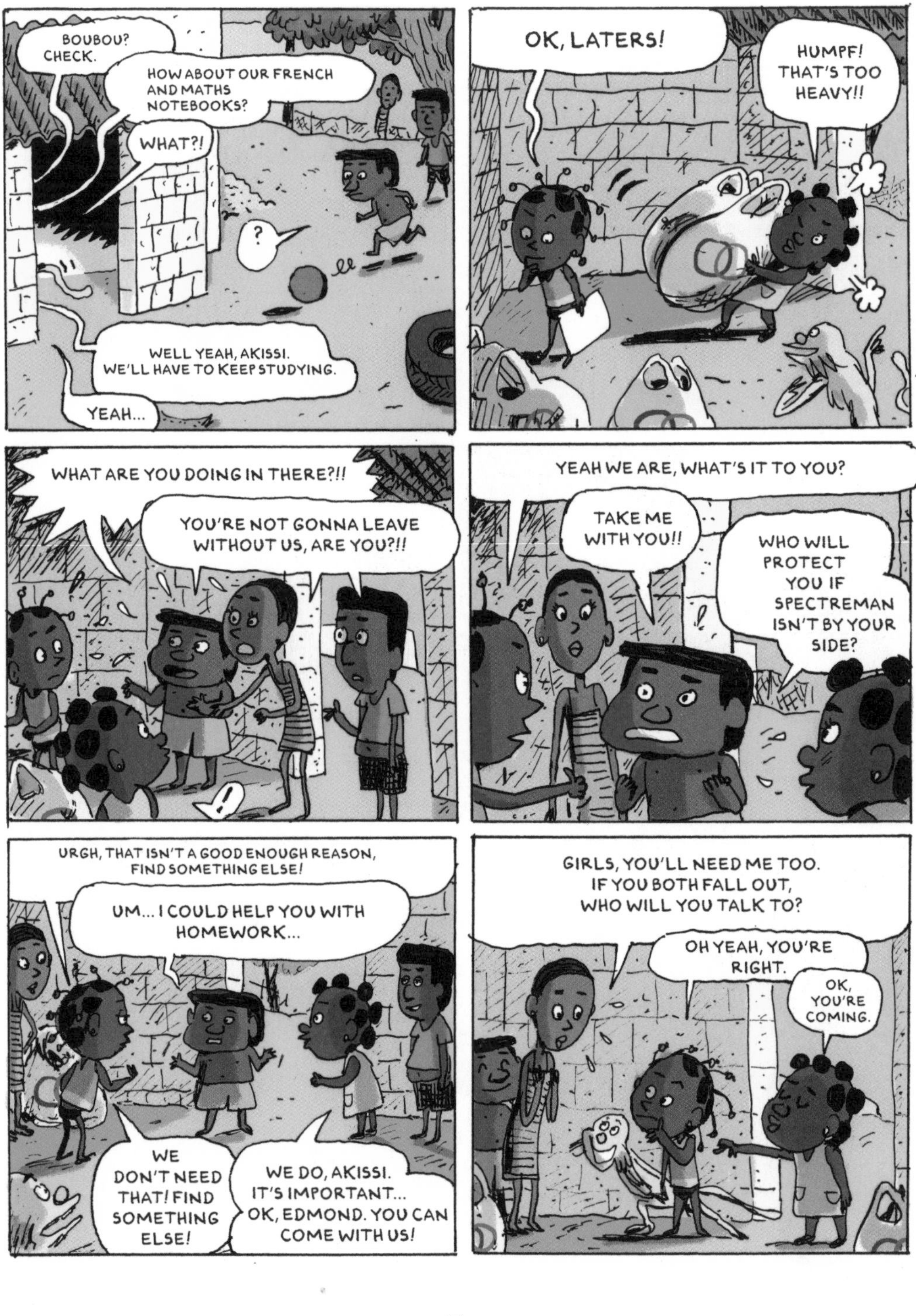
BOUBOU? CHECK.
HOW ABOUT OUR FRENCH AND MATHS NOTEBOOKS?
WHAT?!
?
WELL YEAH, AKISSI. WE'LL HAVE TO KEEP STUDYING.
YEAH...
OK, LATERS!
HUMPF! THAT'S TOO HEAVY!!
WHAT ARE YOU DOING IN THERE?!!
YOU'RE NOT GONNA LEAVE WITHOUT US, ARE YOU?!!
!
YEAH WE ARE, WHAT'S IT TO YOU?
TAKE ME WITH YOU!!
WHO WILL PROTECT YOU IF SPECTREMAN ISN'T BY YOUR SIDE?
URGH, THAT ISN'T A GOOD ENOUGH REASON, FIND SOMETHING ELSE!
UM... I COULD HELP YOU WITH HOMEWORK...
WE DON'T NEED THAT! FIND SOMETHING ELSE!
WE DO, AKISSI. IT'S IMPORTANT... OK, EDMOND. YOU CAN COME WITH US!
GIRLS, YOU'LL NEED ME TOO. IF YOU BOTH FALL OUT, WHO WILL YOU TALK TO?
OH YEAH, YOU'RE RIGHT.
OK, YOU'RE COMING.

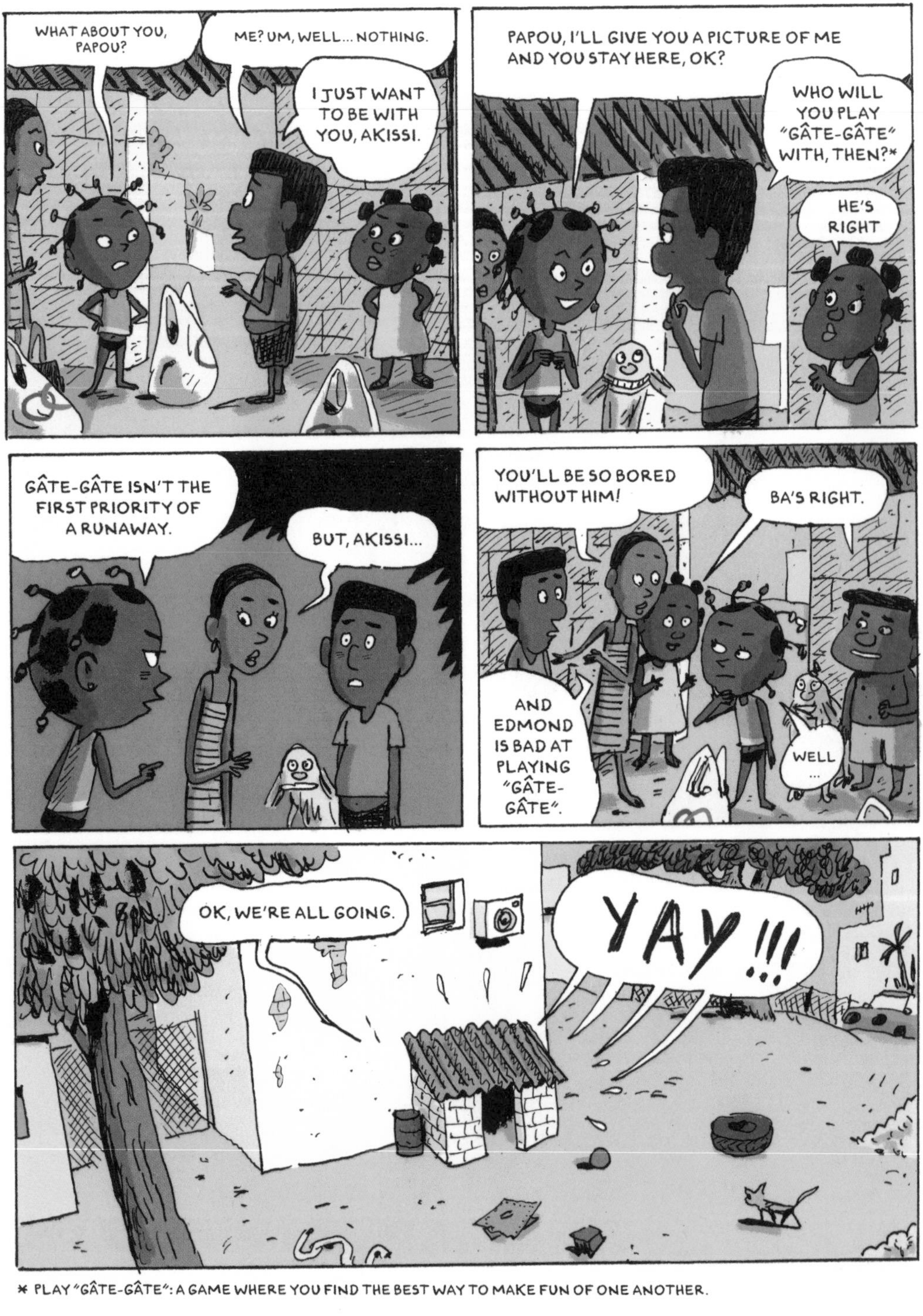
WHAT ABOUT YOU, PAPOU?
ME? UM, WELL... NOTHING.
I JUST WANT TO BE WITH YOU, AKISSI.
PAPOU, I'LL GIVE YOU A PICTURE OF ME AND YOU STAY HERE, OK?
WHO WILL YOU PLAY "GÂTE-GÂTE" WITH, THEN?*
HE'S RIGHT
GÂTE-GÂTE ISN'T THE FIRST PRIORITY OF A RUNAWAY.
BUT, AKISSI...
YOU'LL BE SO BORED WITHOUT HIM!
BA'S RIGHT.
AND EDMOND IS BAD AT PLAYING "GÂTE-GÂTE".
WELL ...
OK, WE'RE ALL GOING.
YAY!!!

* PLAY "GÂTE-GÂTE": A GAME WHERE YOU FIND THE BEST WAY TO MAKE FUN OF ONE ANOTHER.

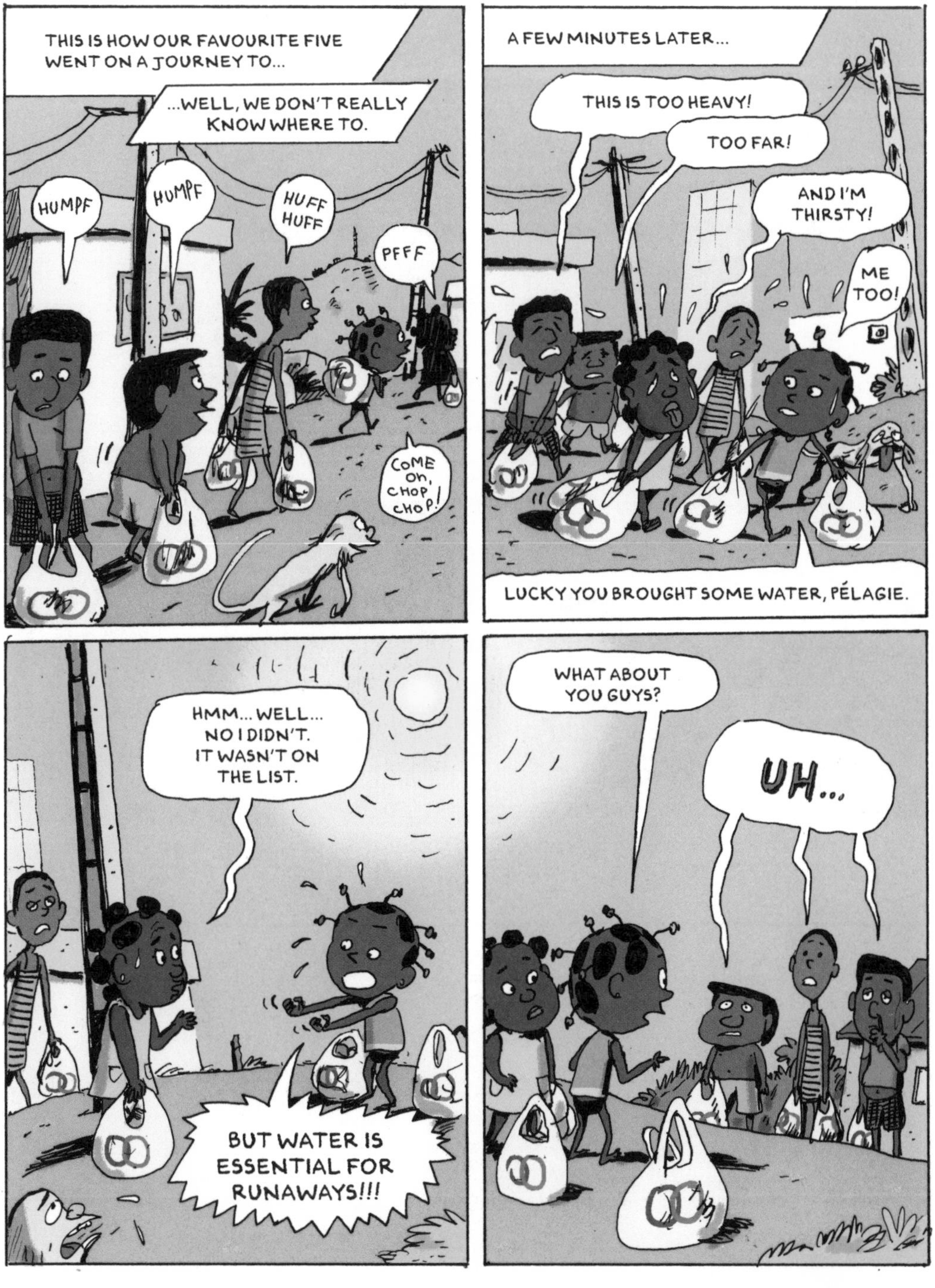
THIS IS HOW OUR FAVOURITE FIVE WENT ON A JOURNEY TO...
...WELL, WE DON'T REALLY KNOW WHERE TO.
HUMPF
HUMPF
HUFF HUFF
PFFF
COME ON, CHOP CHOP!
A FEW MINUTES LATER...
THIS IS TOO HEAVY!
TOO FAR!
AND I'M THIRSTY!
ME TOO!
LUCKY YOU BROUGHT SOME WATER, PÉLAGIE.
HMM... WELL... NO I DIDN'T. IT WASN'T ON THE LIST.
BUT WATER IS ESSENTIAL FOR RUNAWAYS!!!
WHAT ABOUT YOU GUYS?
UH...

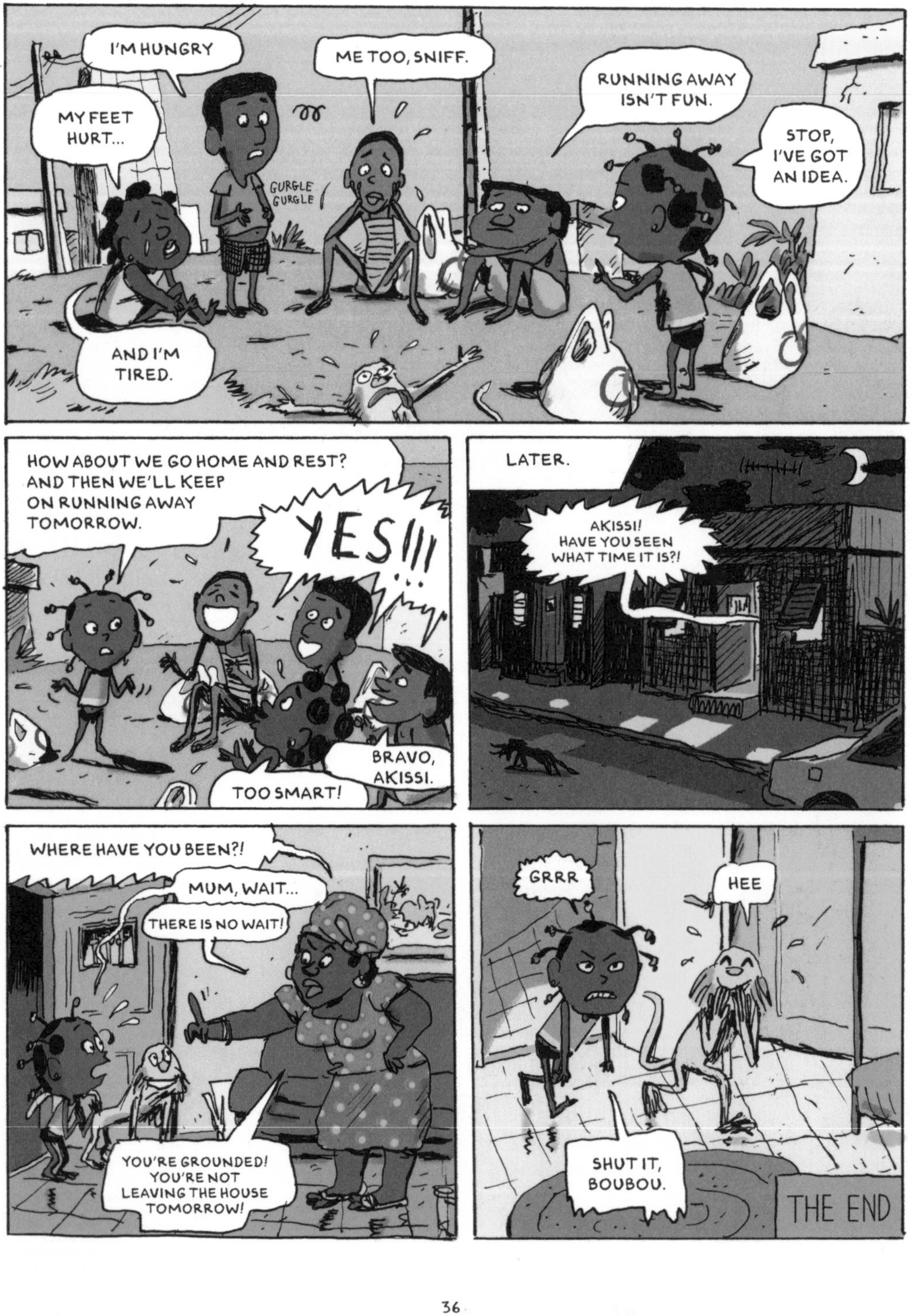
I'M HUNGRY
MY FEET HURT...
AND I'M TIRED.
GURGLE GURGLE
ME TOO, SNIFF.
RUNNING AWAY ISN'T FUN.
STOP, I'VE GOT AN IDEA.
HOW ABOUT WE GO HOME AND REST? AND THEN WE'LL KEEP ON RUNNING AWAY TOMORROW.
YES!!!
BRAVO, AKISSI.
TOO SMART!
LATER.
AKISSI! HAVE YOU SEEN WHAT TIME IT IS?!
WHERE HAVE YOU BEEN?!
MUM, WAIT...
THERE IS NO WAIT!
YOU'RE GROUNDED! YOU'RE NOT LEAVING THE HOUSE TOMORROW!
GRRR
HEE
SHUT IT, BOUBOU.
THE END

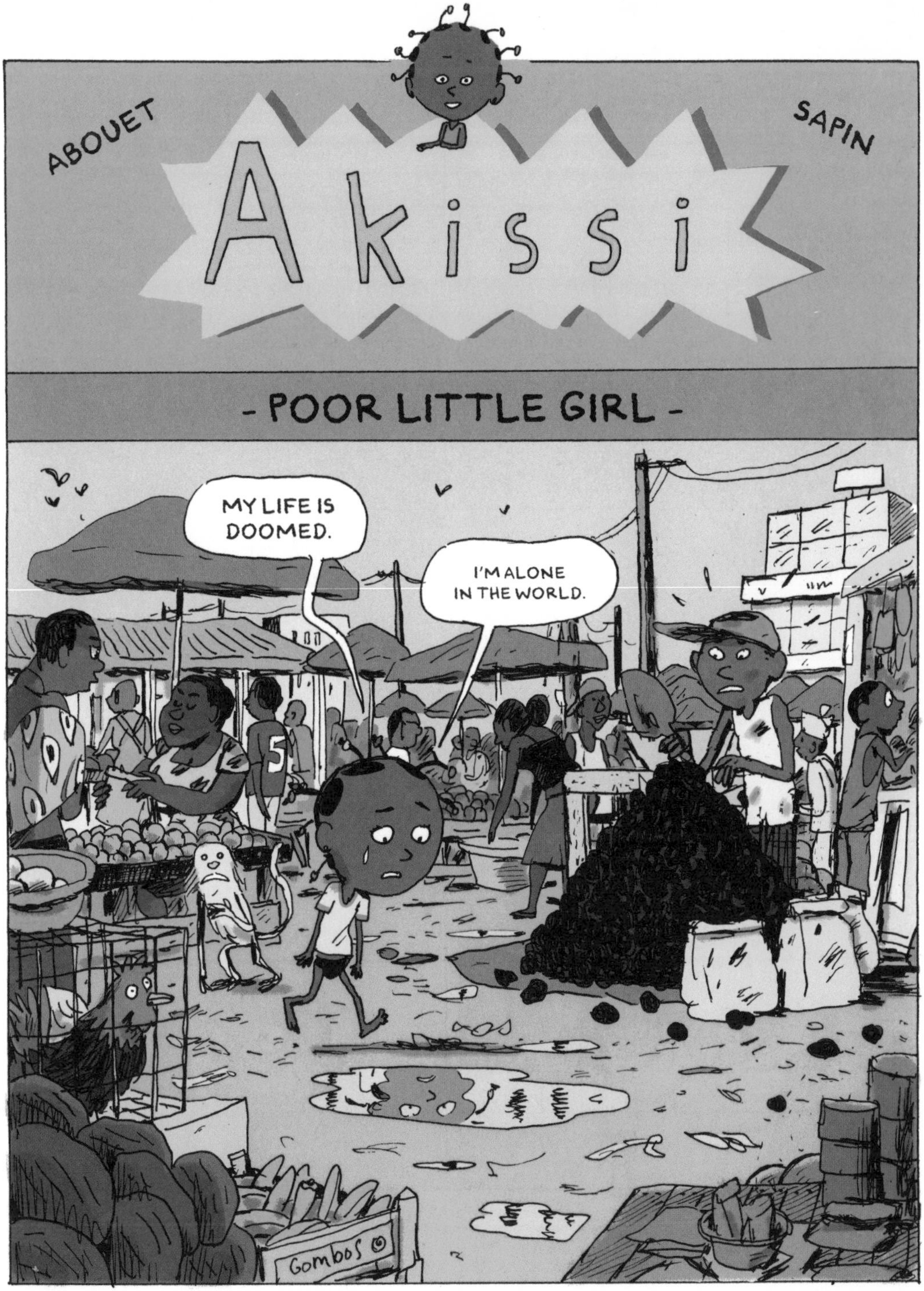
ABOUET
Akissi
SAPIN
- POOR LITTLE GIRL -
MY LIFE IS DOOMED.
I'M ALONE IN THE WORLD.
Gombos

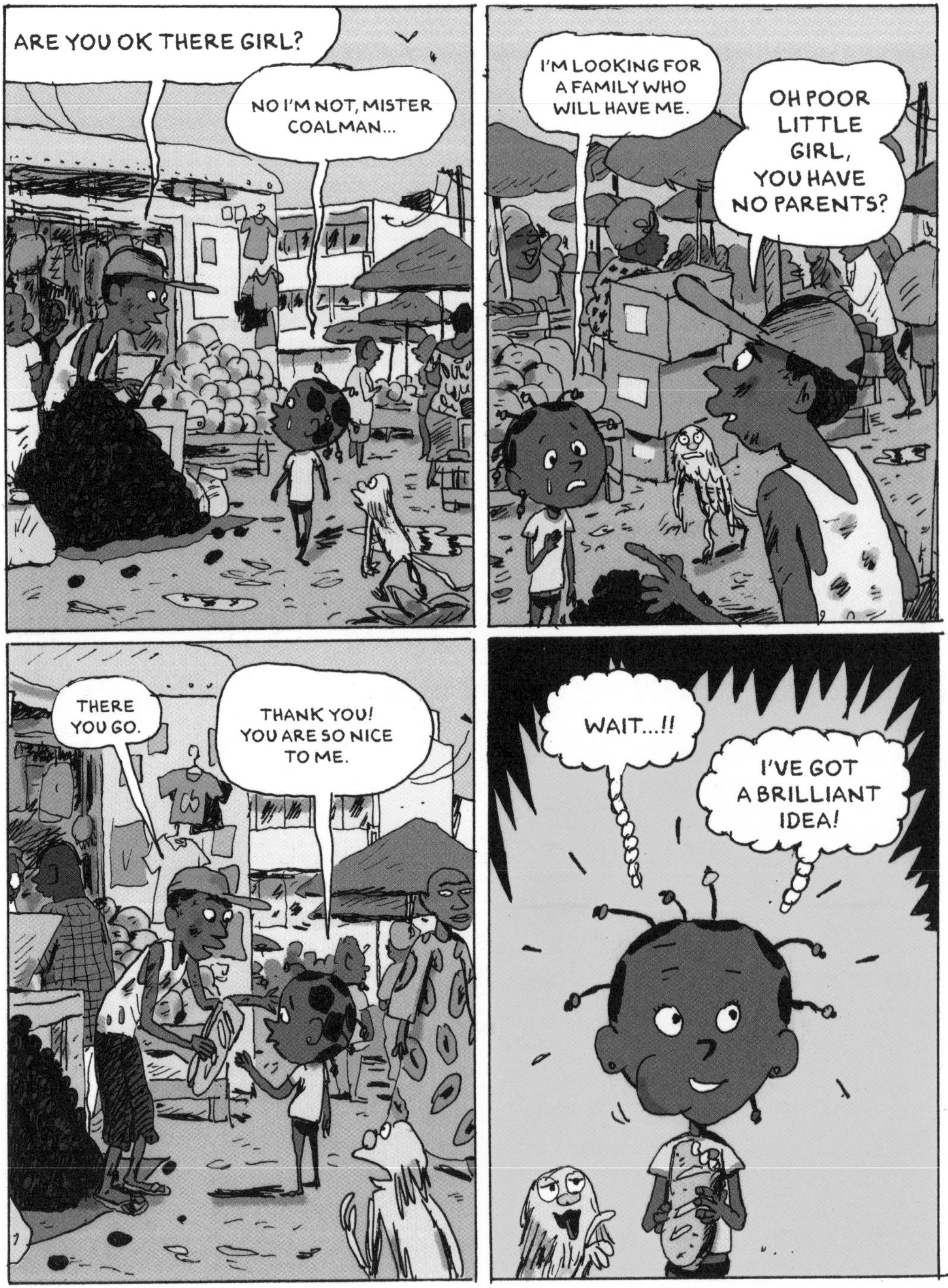
ARE YOU OK THERE GIRL?
NO I'M NOT, MISTER COALMAN...
I'M LOOKING FOR A FAMILY WHO WILL HAVE ME.
OH POOR LITTLE GIRL, YOU HAVE NO PARENTS?
THERE YOU GO.
THANK YOU! YOU ARE SO NICE TO ME.
WAIT...!!
I'VE GOT A BRILLIANT IDEA!

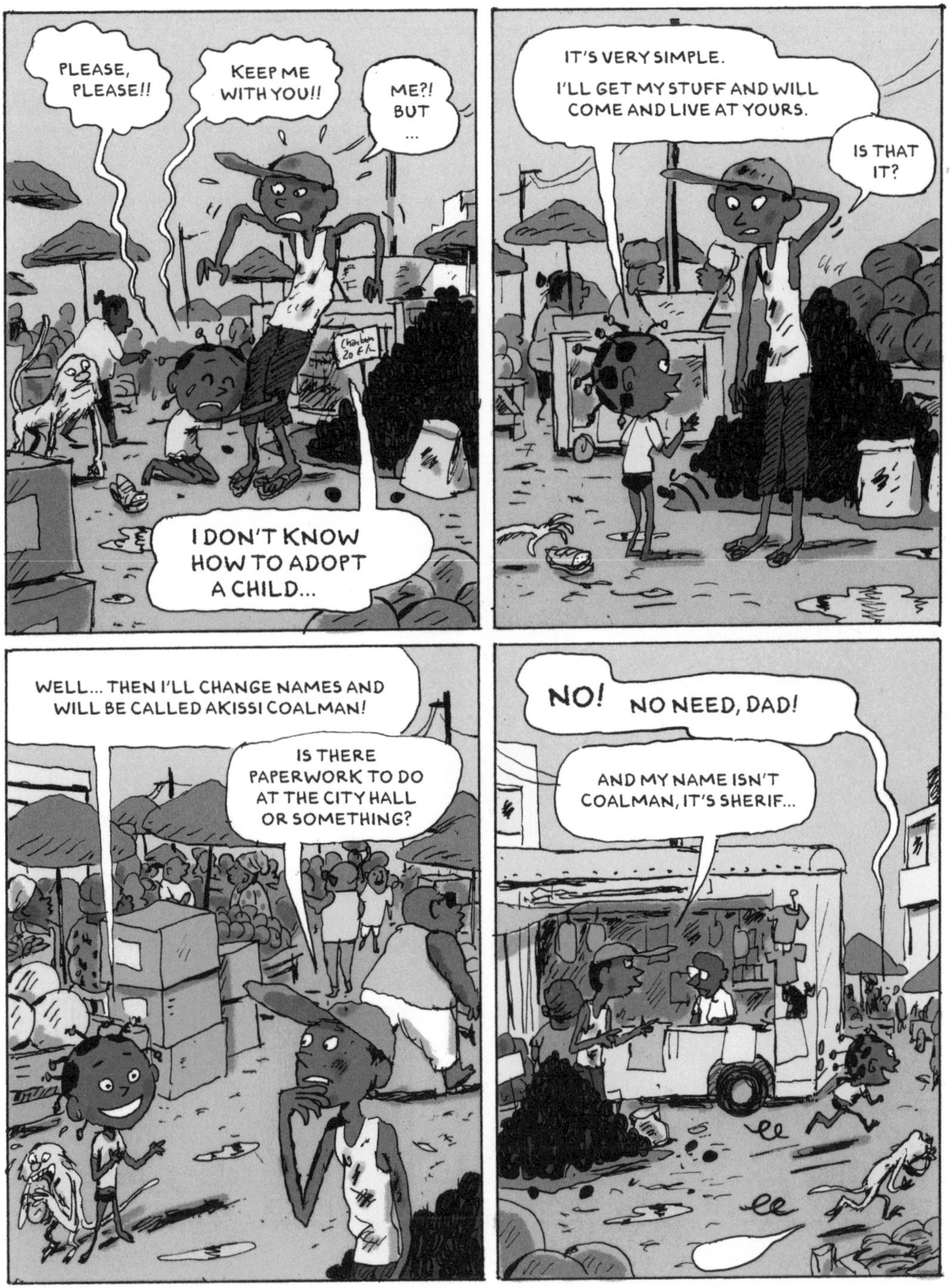
PLEASE, PLEASE!!
KEEP ME WITH YOU!!
ME?! BUT ...
Charbon 20 F/L
I DON'T KNOW HOW TO ADOPT A CHILD...
IT'S VERY SIMPLE.
I'LL GET MY STUFF AND WILL COME AND LIVE AT YOURS.
IS THAT IT?
WELL... THEN I'LL CHANGE NAMES AND WILL BE CALLED AKISSI COALMAN!
IS THERE PAPERWORK TO DO AT THE CITY HALL OR SOMETHING?
NO!
NO NEED, DAD!
AND MY NAME ISN'T COALMAN, IT'S SHERIF...

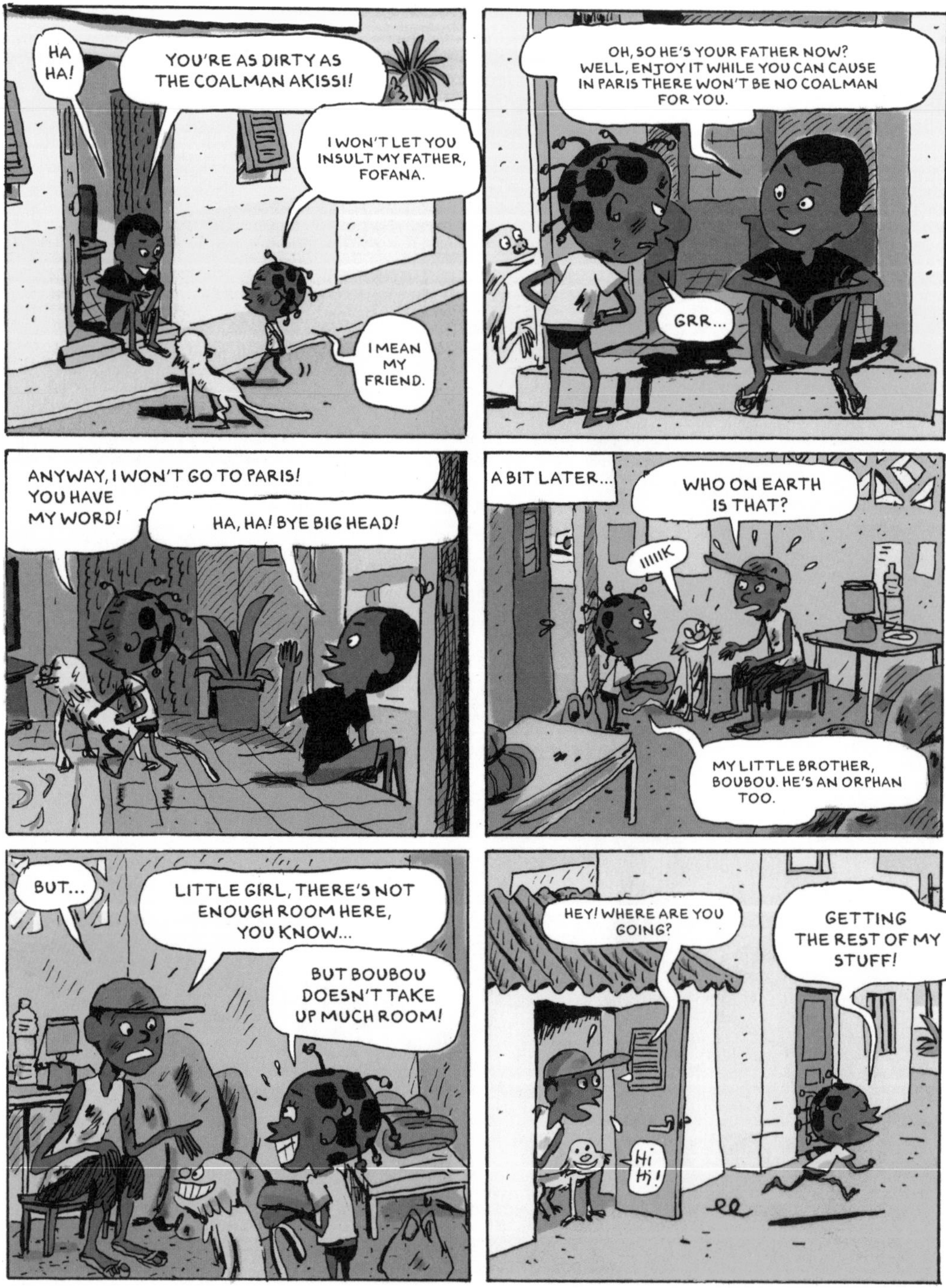
HA HA!
YOU'RE AS DIRTY AS THE COALMAN AKISSI!
I WON'T LET YOU INSULT MY FATHER, FOFANA.
I MEAN MY FRIEND.
OH, SO HE'S YOUR FATHER NOW? WELL, ENJOY IT WHILE YOU CAN CAUSE IN PARIS THERE WON'T BE NO COALMAN FOR YOU.
GRR...
ANYWAY, I WON'T GO TO PARIS! YOU HAVE MY WORD!
HA, HA! BYE BIG HEAD!
A BIT LATER...
WHO ON EARTH IS THAT?
IIIIIK
MY LITTLE BROTHER, BOUBOU. HE'S AN ORPHAN TOO.
BUT...
LITTLE GIRL, THERE'S NOT ENOUGH ROOM HERE, YOU KNOW...
BUT BOUBOU DOESN'T TAKE UP MUCH ROOM!
HEY! WHERE ARE YOU GOING?
GETTING THE REST OF MY STUFF!
Hi Hi!

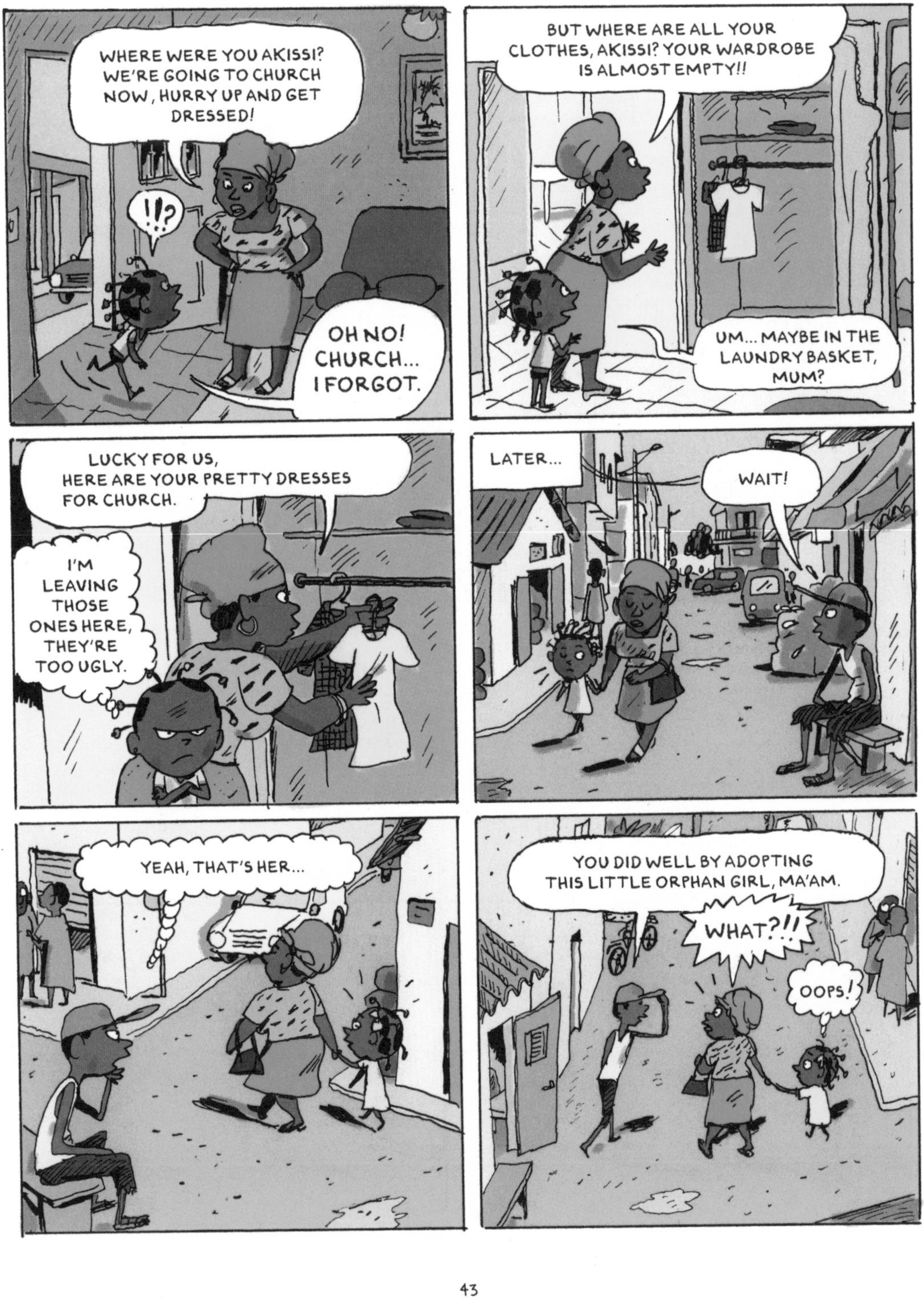
WHERE WERE YOU AKISSI? WE'RE GOING TO CHURCH NOW, HURRY UP AND GET DRESSED!
!!?
OH NO! CHURCH... I FORGOT.
BUT WHERE ARE ALL YOUR CLOTHES, AKISSI? YOUR WARDROBE IS ALMOST EMPTY!!
UM... MAYBE IN THE LAUNDRY BASKET, MUM?
LUCKY FOR US, HERE ARE YOUR PRETTY DRESSES FOR CHURCH.
I'M LEAVING THOSE ONES HERE, THEY'RE TOO UGLY.
LATER...
WAIT!
YEAH, THAT'S HER...
YOU DID WELL BY ADOPTING THIS LITTLE ORPHAN GIRL, MA'AM.
WHAT?!!
OOPS!

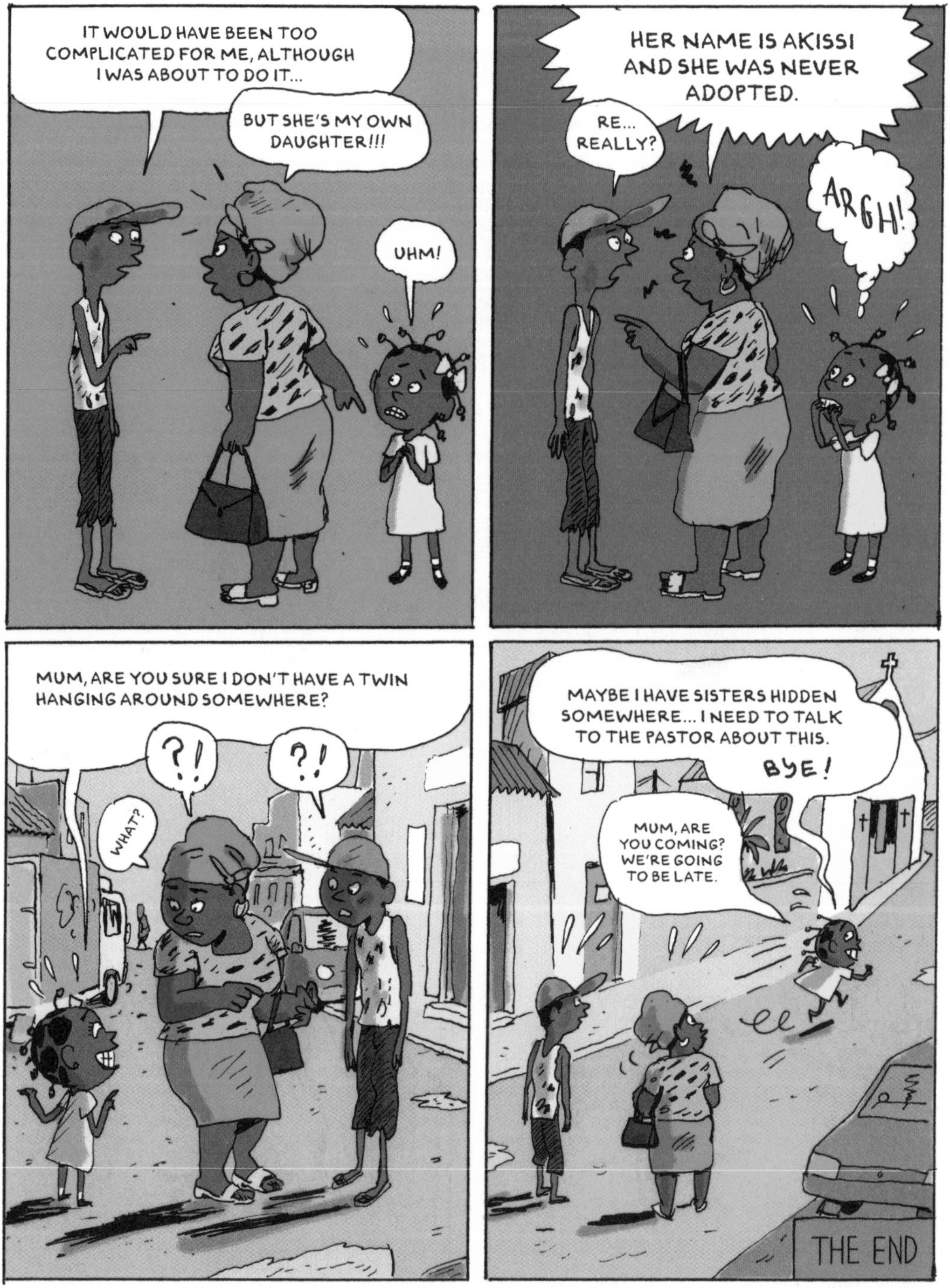
IT WOULD HAVE BEEN TOO COMPLICATED FOR ME, ALTHOUGH I WAS ABOUT TO DO IT...
BUT SHE'S MY OWN DAUGHTER!!!
UHM!
HER NAME IS AKISSI AND SHE WAS NEVER ADOPTED.
RE... REALLY?
ARGH!
MUM, ARE YOU SURE I DON'T HAVE A TWIN HANGING AROUND SOMEWHERE?
WHAT?
?!
?!
MAYBE I HAVE SISTERS HIDDEN SOMEWHERE... I NEED TO TALK TO THE PASTOR ABOUT THIS.
BYE!
MUM, ARE YOU COMING? WE'RE GOING TO BE LATE.
THE END

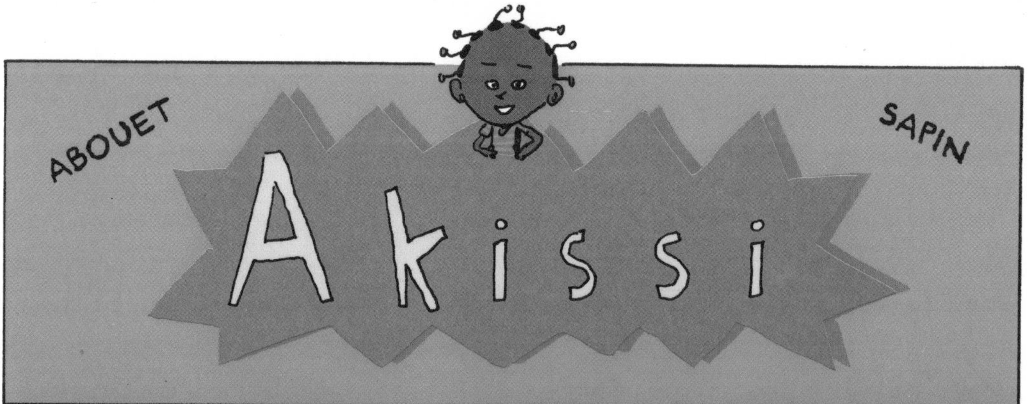
ABOUET
SAPIN
Akissi

- END OF THE STRIKE -

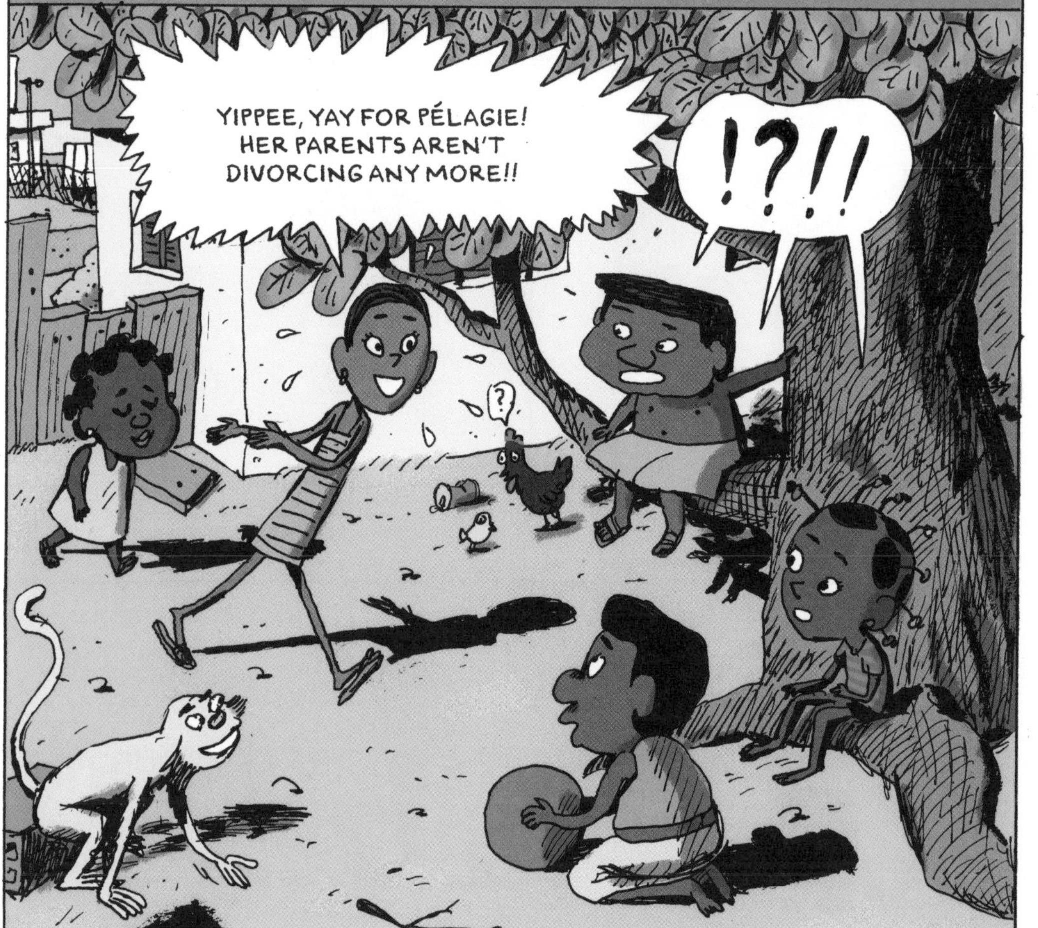
YIPPEE, YAY FOR PÉLAGIE! HER PARENTS AREN'T DIVORCING ANY MORE!!
!?!!
?

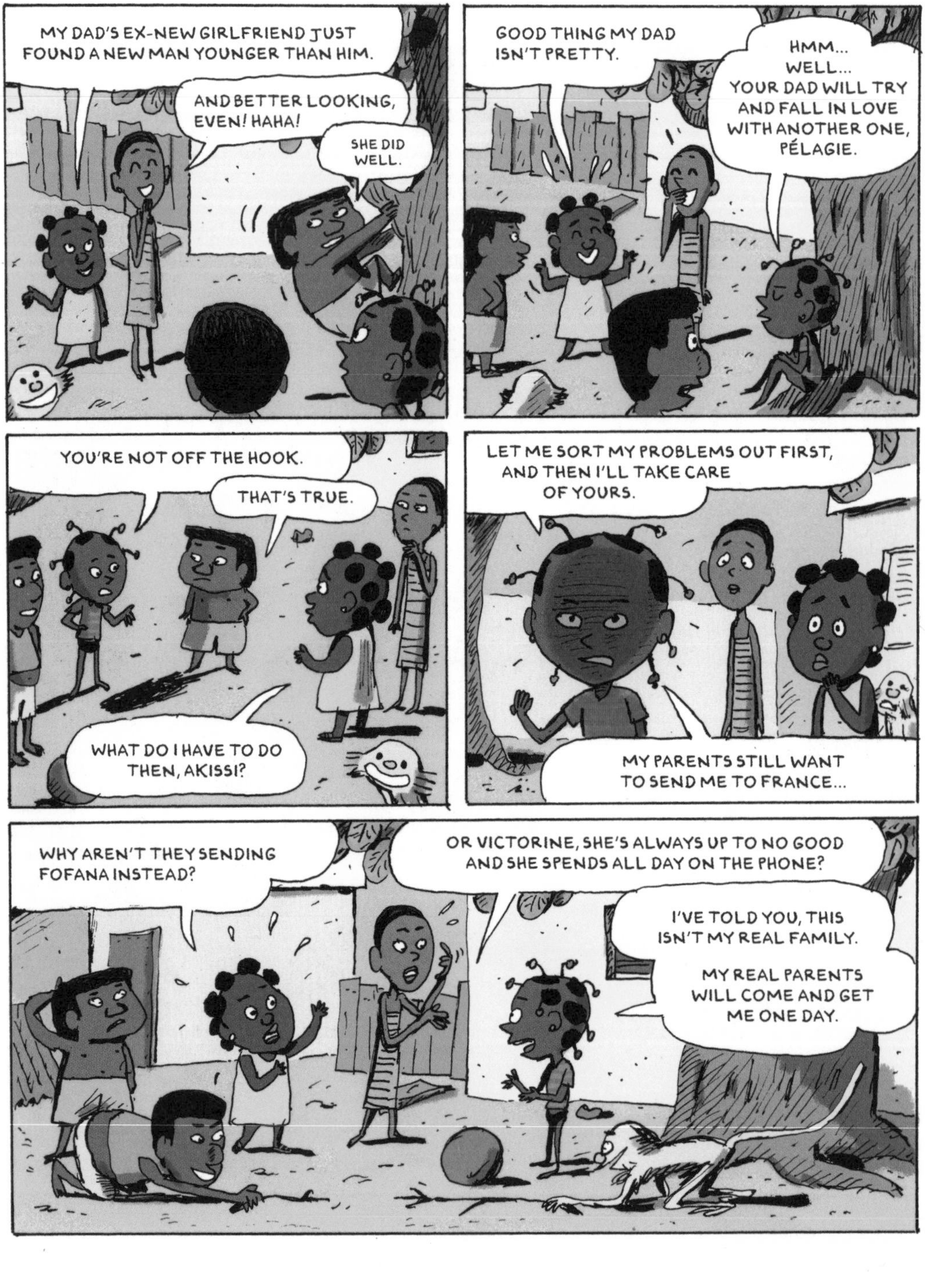
MY DAD'S EX-NEW GIRLFRIEND JUST FOUND A NEW MAN YOUNGER THAN HIM.
AND BETTER LOOKING, EVEN! HAHA!
SHE DID WELL.
GOOD THING MY DAD ISN'T PRETTY.
HMM... WELL... YOUR DAD WILL TRY AND FALL IN LOVE WITH ANOTHER ONE, PÉLAGIE.
YOU'RE NOT OFF THE HOOK.
THAT'S TRUE.
WHAT DO I HAVE TO DO THEN, AKISSI?
LET ME SORT MY PROBLEMS OUT FIRST, AND THEN I'LL TAKE CARE OF YOURS.
MY PARENTS STILL WANT TO SEND ME TO FRANCE...
WHY AREN'T THEY SENDING FOFANA INSTEAD?
OR VICTORINE, SHE'S ALWAYS UP TO NO GOOD AND SHE SPENDS ALL DAY ON THE PHONE?
I'VE TOLD YOU, THIS ISN'T MY REAL FAMILY.
MY REAL PARENTS WILL COME AND GET ME ONE DAY.

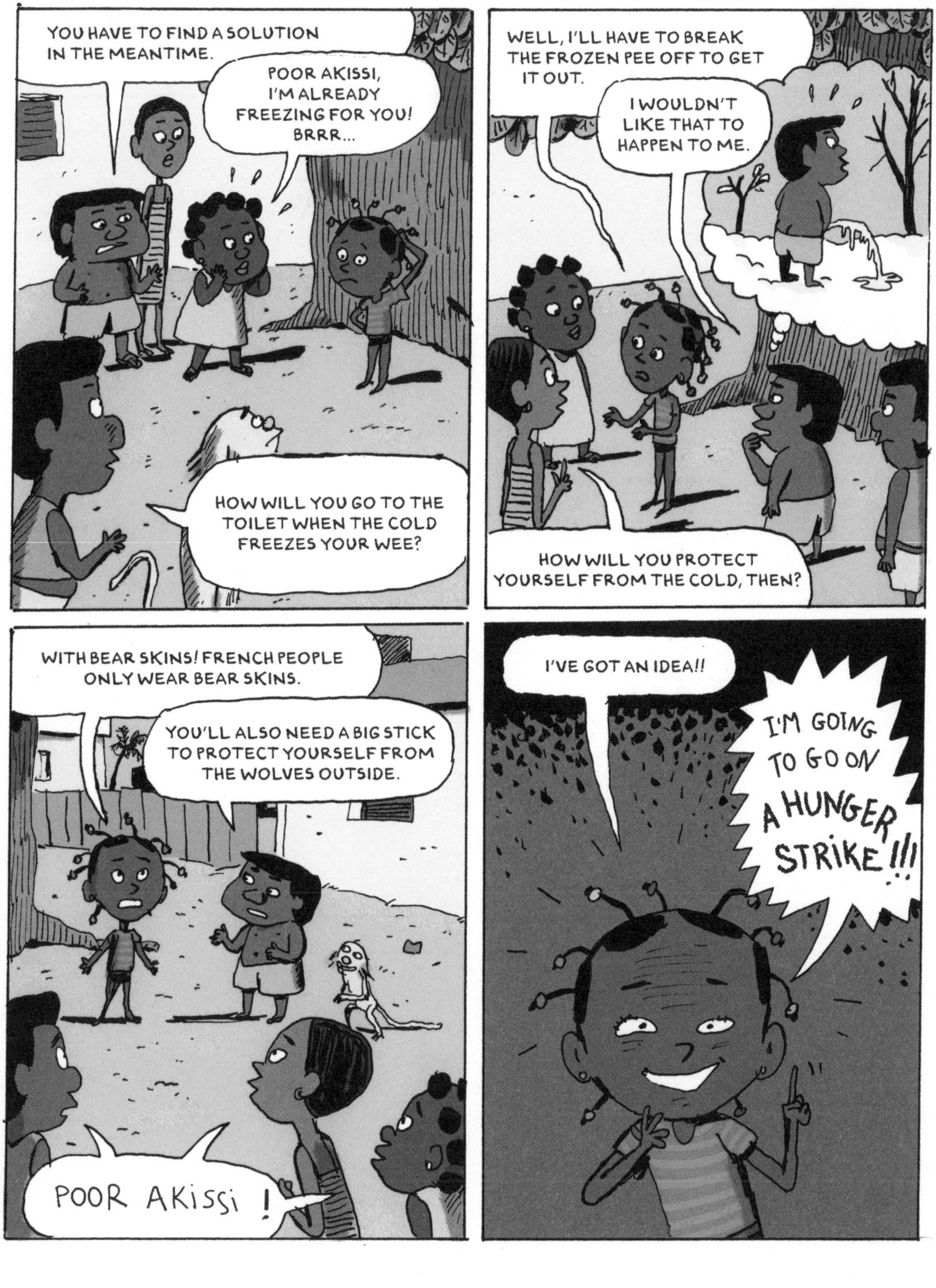
YOU HAVE TO FIND A SOLUTION IN THE MEANTIME.
POOR AKISSI, I'M ALREADY FREEZING FOR YOU! BRRR...
HOW WILL YOU GO TO THE TOILET WHEN THE COLD FREEZES YOUR WEE?
WELL, I'LL HAVE TO BREAK THE FROZEN PEE OFF TO GET IT OUT.
I WOULDN'T LIKE THAT TO HAPPEN TO ME.
HOW WILL YOU PROTECT YOURSELF FROM THE COLD, THEN?
WITH BEAR SKINS! FRENCH PEOPLE ONLY WEAR BEAR SKINS.
YOU'LL ALSO NEED A BIG STICK TO PROTECT YOURSELF FROM THE WOLVES OUTSIDE.
POOR AKISSI !
I'VE GOT AN IDEA!!
I'M GOING TO GO ON A HUNGER STRIKE !!!

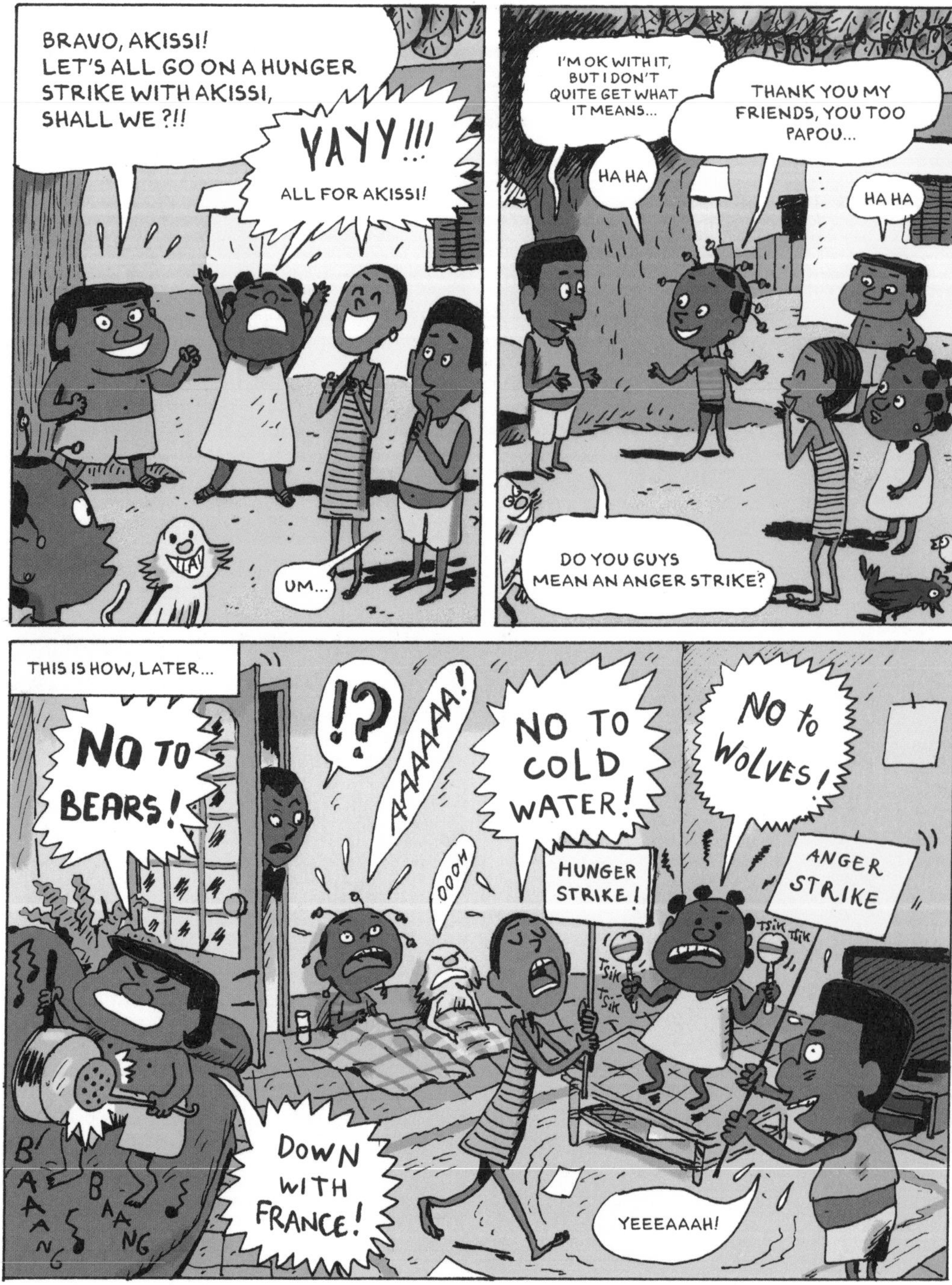
BRAVO, AKISSI!
LET'S ALL GO ON A HUNGER STRIKE WITH AKISSI, SHALL WE ?!!
YAYY!!!
ALL FOR AKISSI!
UM...
I'M OK WITH IT, BUT I DON'T QUITE GET WHAT IT MEANS...
HA HA
THANK YOU MY FRIENDS, YOU TOO PAPOU...
HA HA
DO YOU GUYS MEAN AN ANGER STRIKE?
THIS IS HOW, LATER...
NO TO BEARS!
!?
AAAAAA!
OOOH
NO TO COLD WATER!
NO to WOLVES!
HUNGER STRIKE!
ANGER STRIKE
TSIK TSIK
TSIK TSIK
DOWN WITH FRANCE!
YEEEAAAH!
BAAANG
BAANG

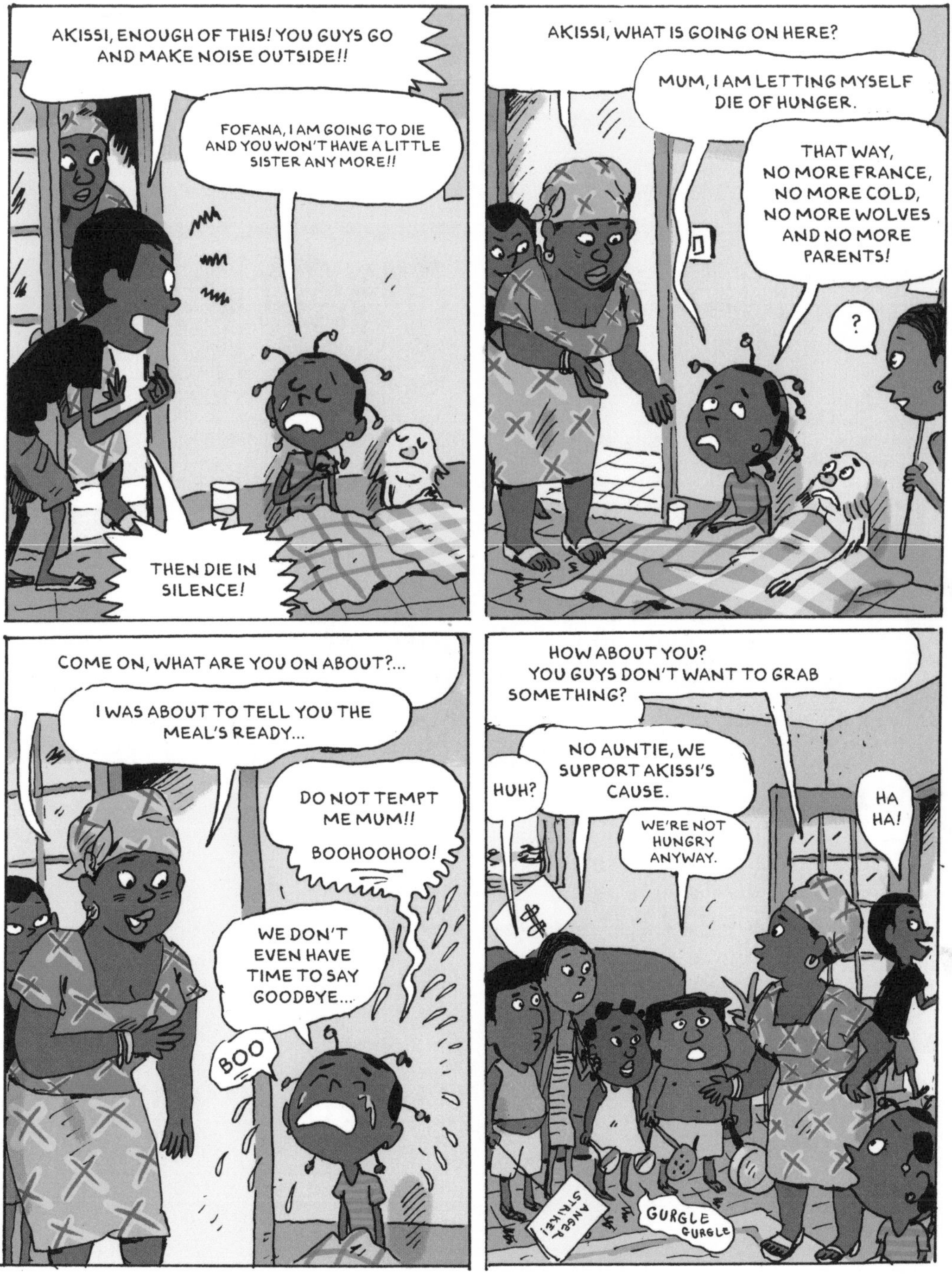
AKISSI, ENOUGH OF THIS! YOU GUYS GO AND MAKE NOISE OUTSIDE!!
FOFANA, I AM GOING TO DIE AND YOU WON'T HAVE A LITTLE SISTER ANY MORE!!
THEN DIE IN SILENCE!
AKISSI, WHAT IS GOING ON HERE?
MUM, I AM LETTING MYSELF DIE OF HUNGER.
THAT WAY, NO MORE FRANCE, NO MORE COLD, NO MORE WOLVES AND NO MORE PARENTS!
?
COME ON, WHAT ARE YOU ON ABOUT?...
I WAS ABOUT TO TELL YOU THE MEAL'S READY...
DO NOT TEMPT ME MUM!!
BOOHOOHOO!
WE DON'T EVEN HAVE TIME TO SAY GOODBYE...
BOO
HOW ABOUT YOU? YOU GUYS DON'T WANT TO GRAB SOMETHING?
HUH?
NO AUNTIE, WE SUPPORT AKISSI'S CAUSE.
WE'RE NOT HUNGRY ANYWAY.
HA HA!
ANGER STRIKE!
GURGLE
GURGLE

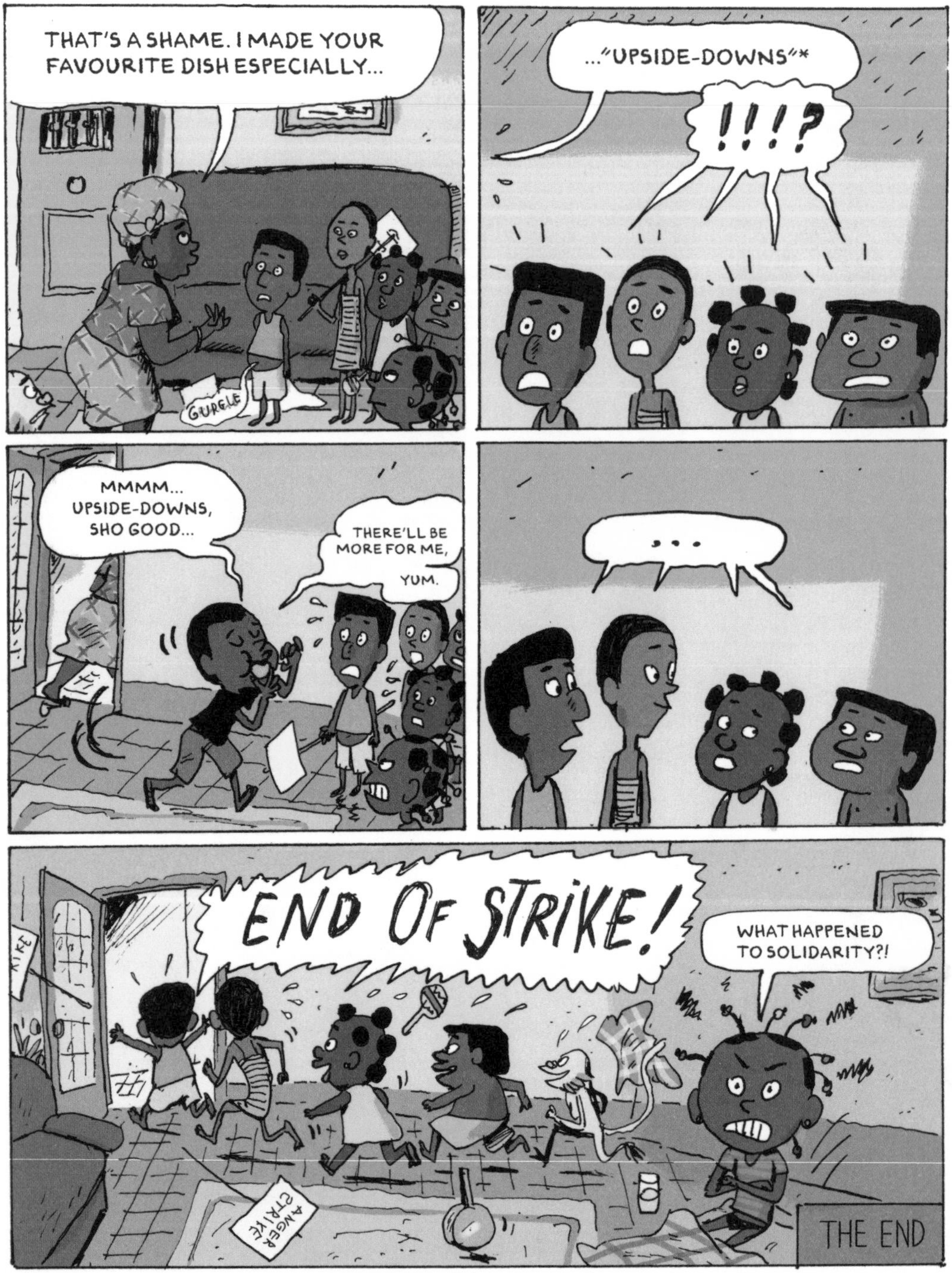

THAT'S A SHAME. I MADE YOUR FAVOURITE DISH ESPECIALLY...
GURGLE
..."UPSIDE-DOWNS"*
!!!?
MMMM... UPSIDE-DOWNS, SHO GOOD...
THERE'LL BE MORE FOR ME,
YUM.
...
END OF STRIKE!
WHAT HAPPENED TO SOLIDARITY?!
THE END

* UPSIDE-DOWNS: MEAT DOUGHNUTS FROM THE IVORY COAST.

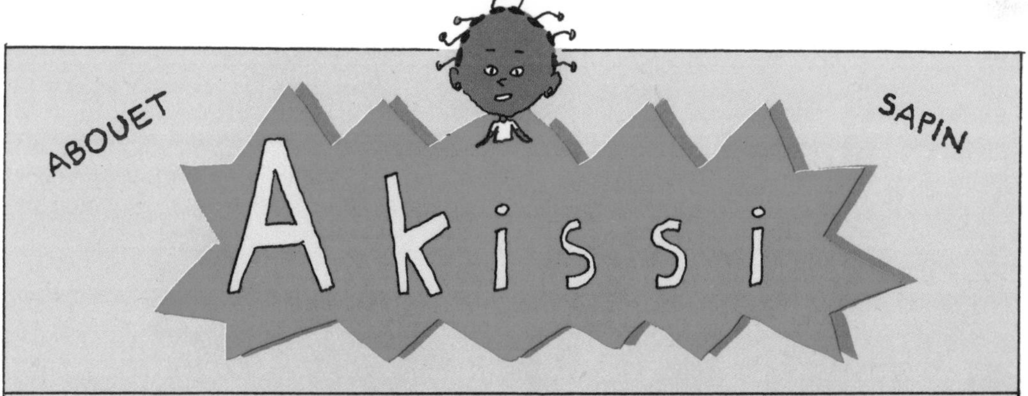
ABOUET
Akissi
SAPIN

- WISE DECISION -

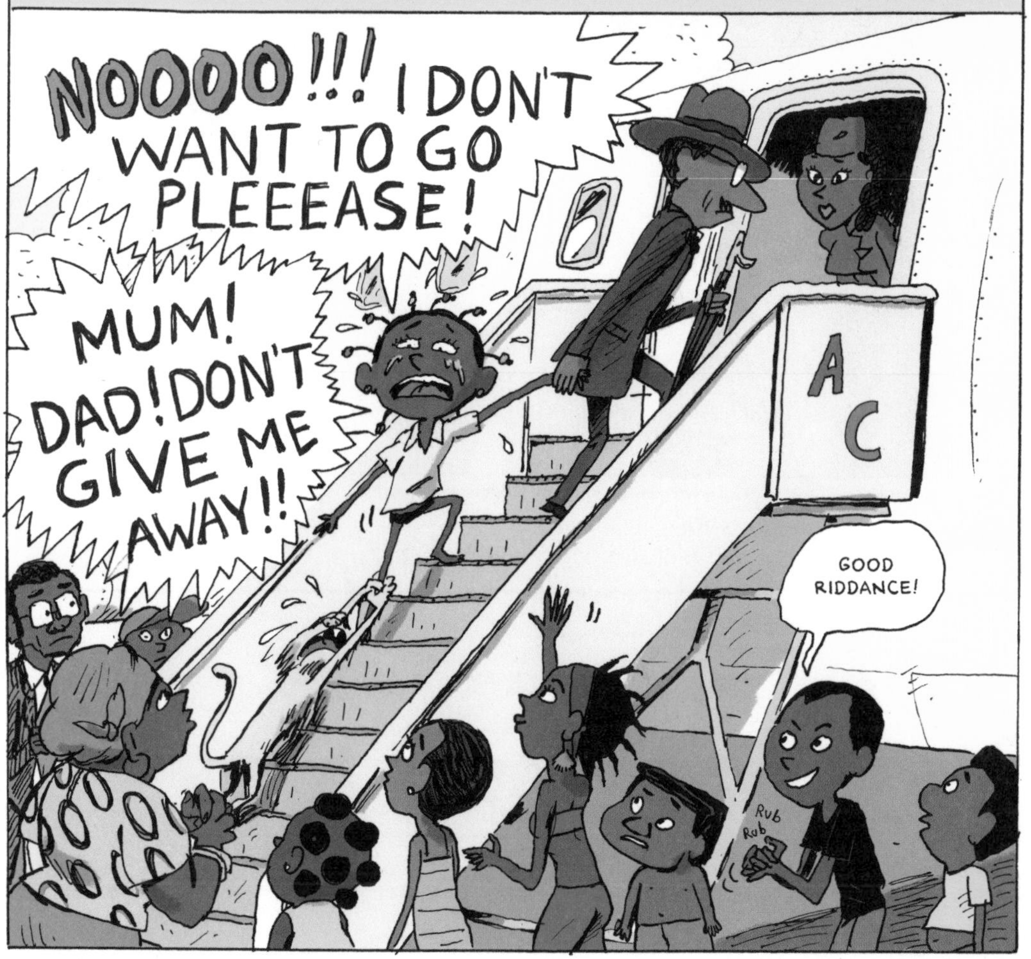
NOOOO!!! I DON'T WANT TO GO PLEEEASE!
MUM! DAD! DON'T GIVE ME AWAY!!
A
C
GOOD RIDDANCE!
Rub Rub

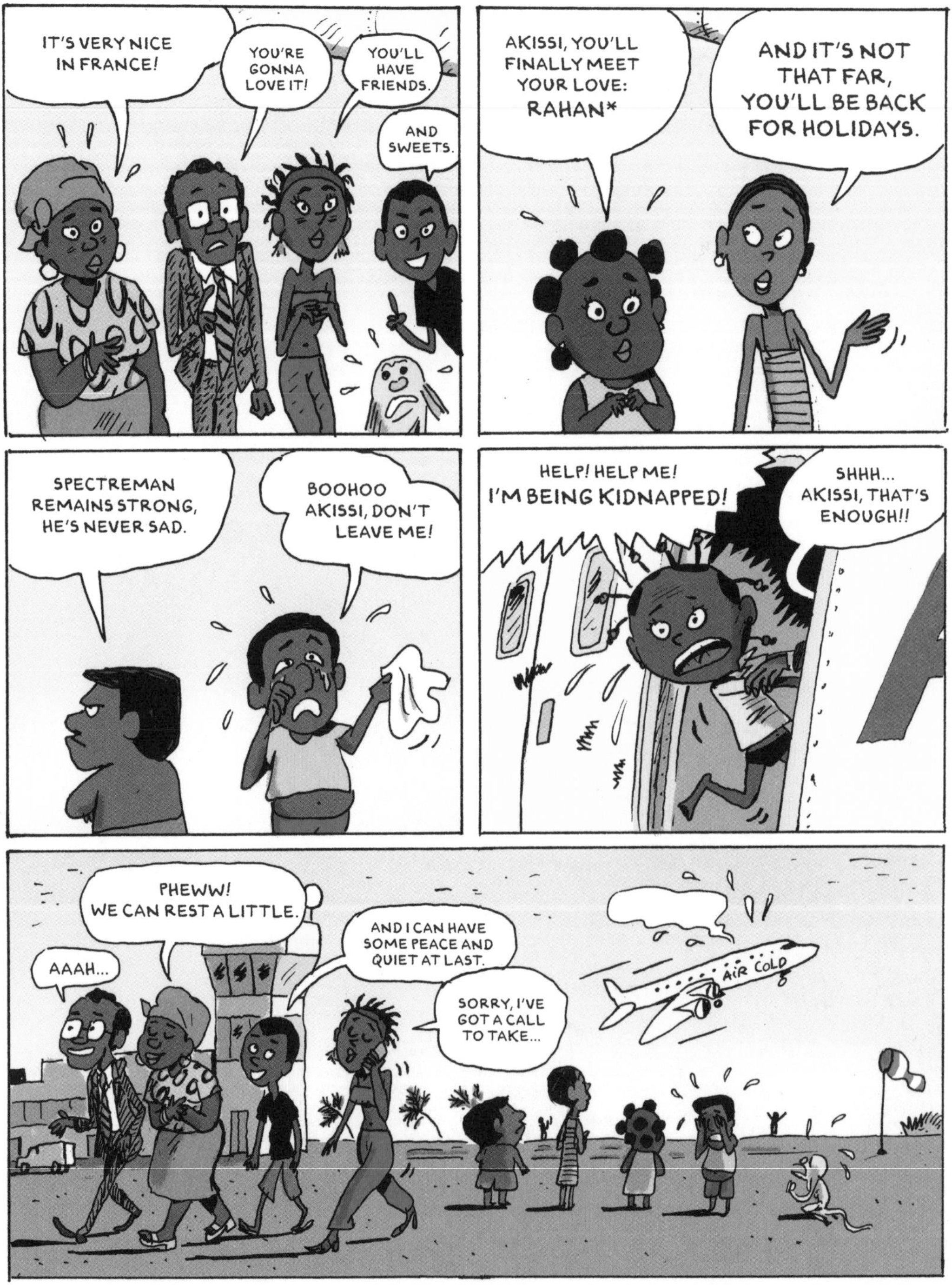
IT'S VERY NICE IN FRANCE!
YOU'RE GONNA LOVE IT!
YOU'LL HAVE FRIENDS.
AND SWEETS.
AKISSI, YOU'LL FINALLY MEET YOUR LOVE: RAHAN*
AND IT'S NOT THAT FAR, YOU'LL BE BACK FOR HOLIDAYS.
SPECTREMAN REMAINS STRONG, HE'S NEVER SAD.
BOOHOO AKISSI, DON'T LEAVE ME!
HELP! HELP ME! I'M BEING KIDNAPPED!
SHHH... AKISSI, THAT'S ENOUGH!!
PHEWW! WE CAN REST A LITTLE.
AAAH...
AND I CAN HAVE SOME PEACE AND QUIET AT LAST.
SORRY, I'VE GOT A CALL TO TAKE...
AIR COLD

* RAHAN: A FAMOUS HERO OF THE PREHISTORIC TIMES AND ALSO THE ICONIC LEAD OF A POPULAR FRENCH COMIC.

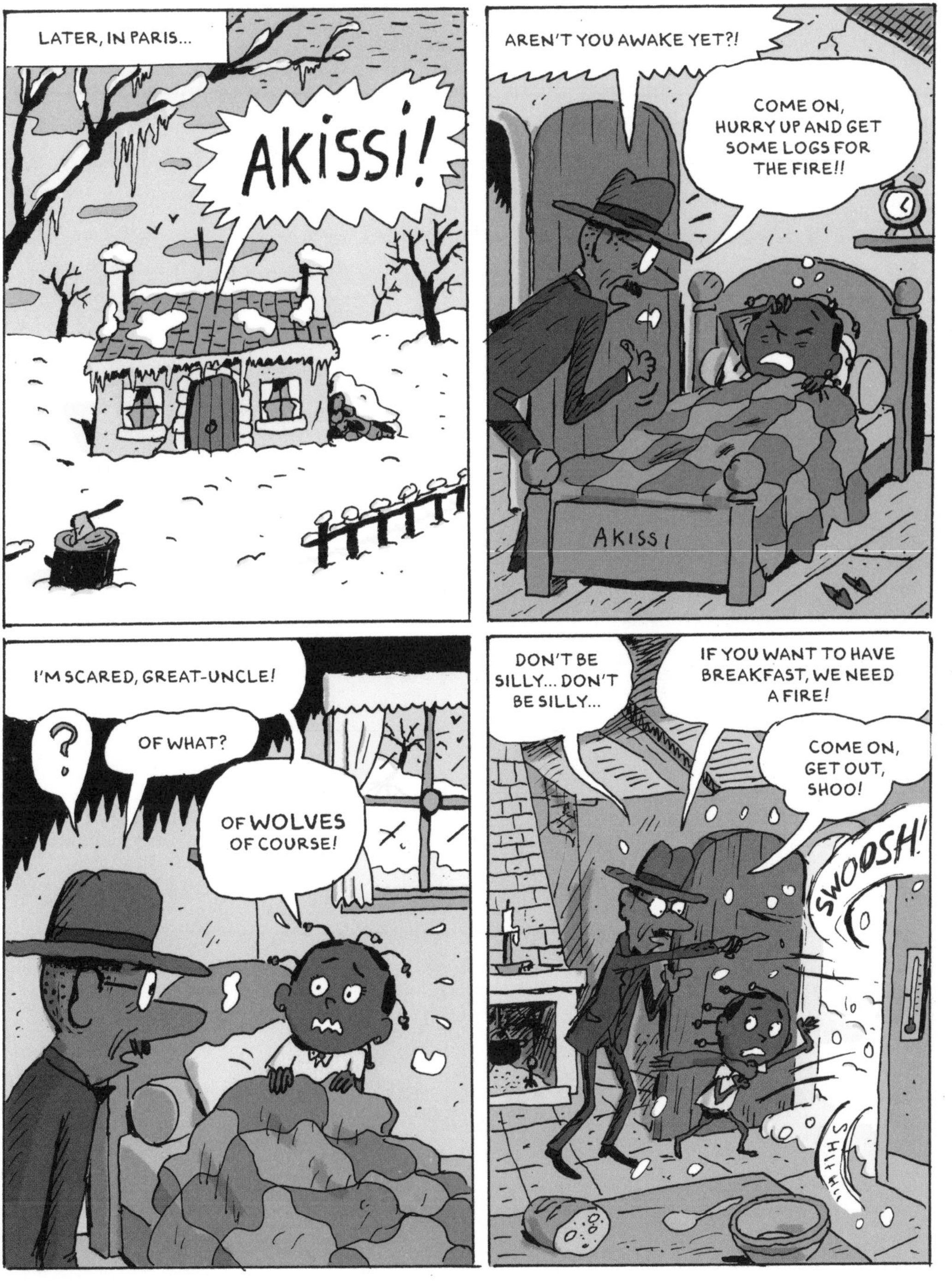
LATER, IN PARIS...
AKISSI!
AREN'T YOU AWAKE YET?!
COME ON, HURRY UP AND GET SOME LOGS FOR THE FIRE!!
AKISSI
I'M SCARED, GREAT-UNCLE!
?
OF WHAT?
OF WOLVES OF COURSE!
DON'T BE SILLY... DON'T BE SILLY...
IF YOU WANT TO HAVE BREAKFAST, WE NEED A FIRE!
COME ON, GET OUT, SHOO!
SWOOSH!

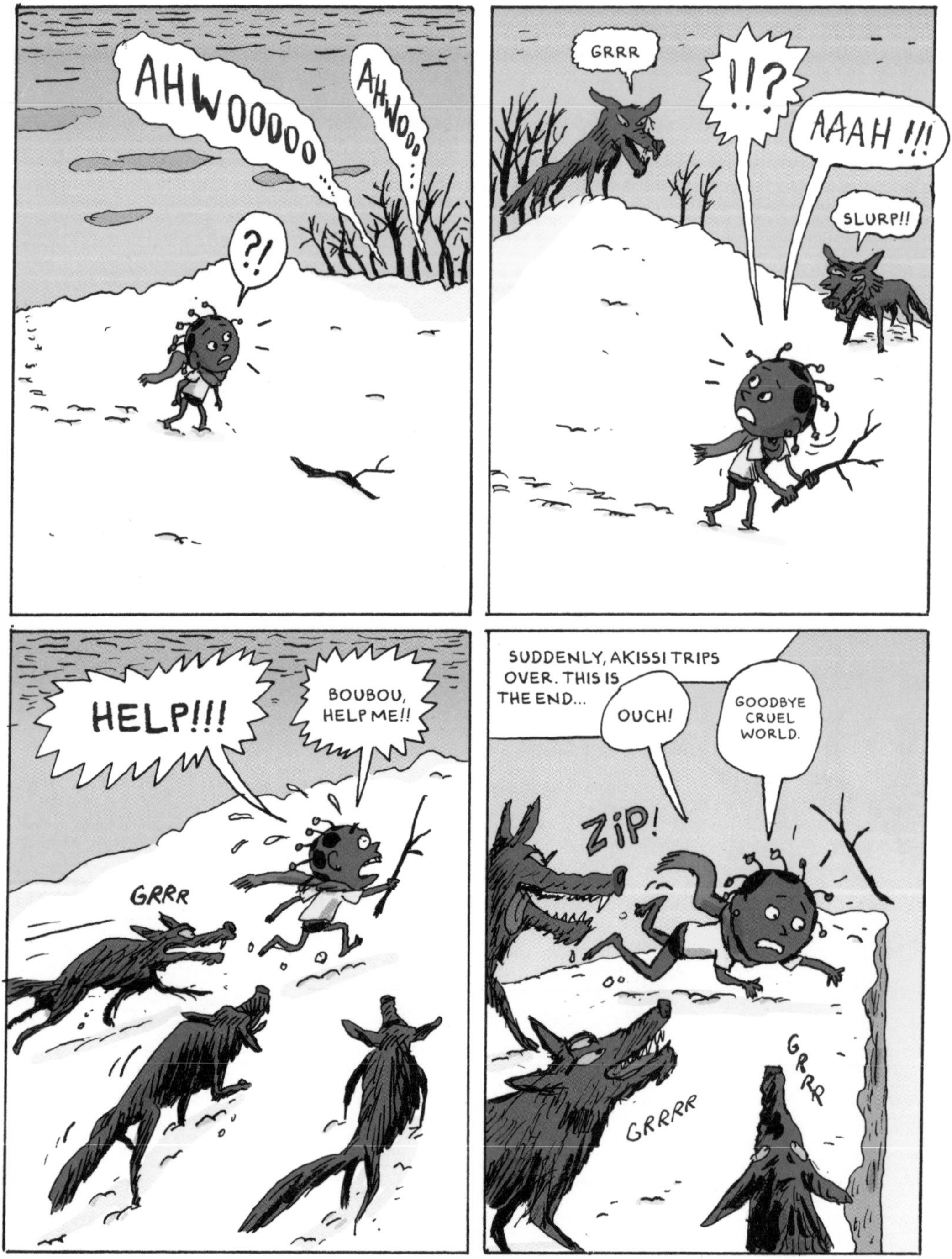
AHWOOOOOO...
AHWOOO...
?!
GRRR
!!?
AAAH!!!
SLURP!!
HELP!!!
BOUBOU, HELP ME!!
GRRR
SUDDENLY, AKISSI TRIPS OVER. THIS IS THE END...
OUCH!
GOODBYE CRUEL WORLD.
ZIP!
GRRRR
GRRR

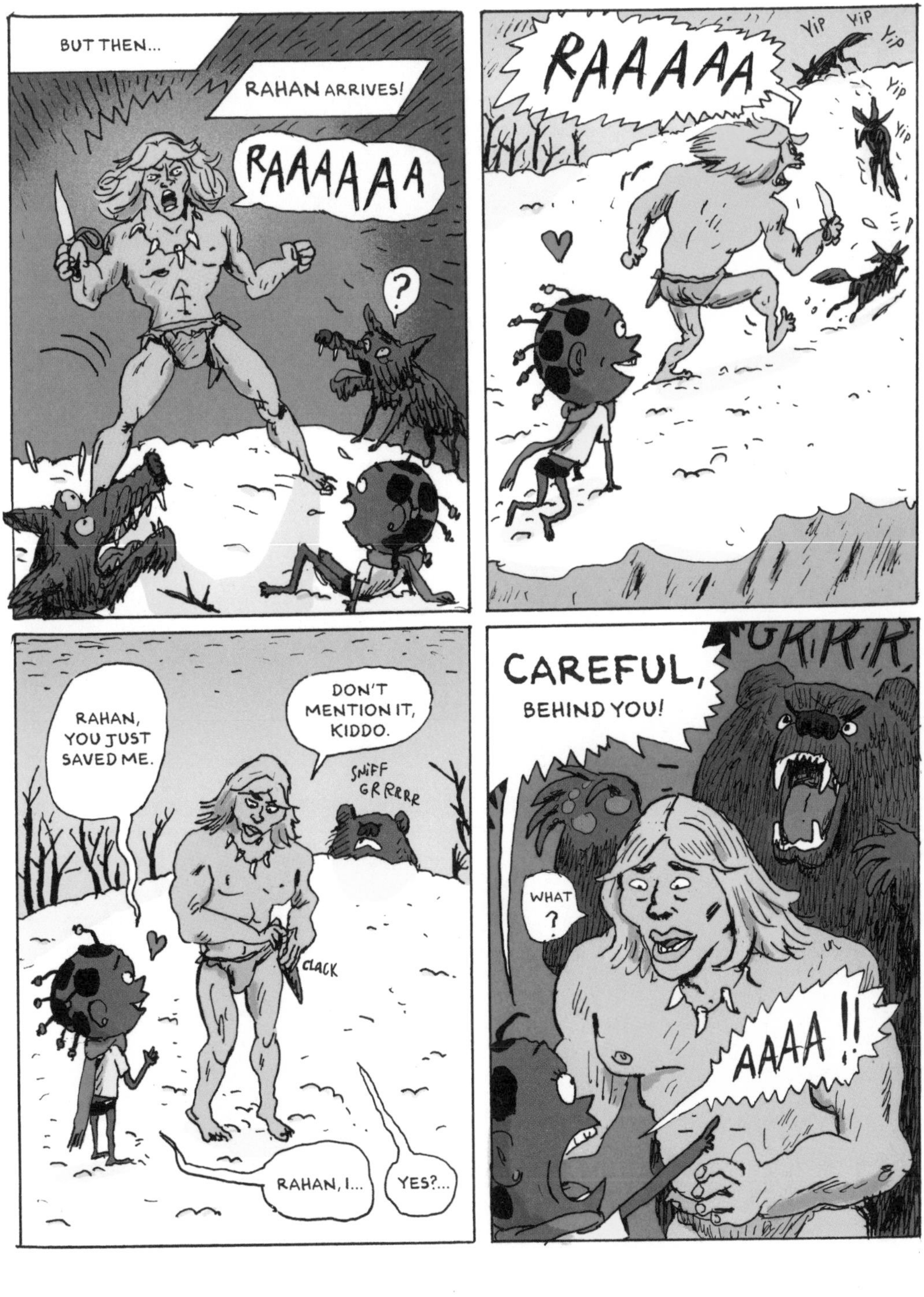
BUT THEN...
RAHAN ARRIVES!
RAAAAAA
?
RAAAAA
YIP YIP YIP
YIP
YIP
RAHAN, YOU JUST SAVED ME.
DON'T MENTION IT, KIDDO.
SNIFF GRRRRR
CLACK
RAHAN, I...
YES?...
GRRR
CAREFUL, BEHIND YOU!
WHAT ?
AAAA !!

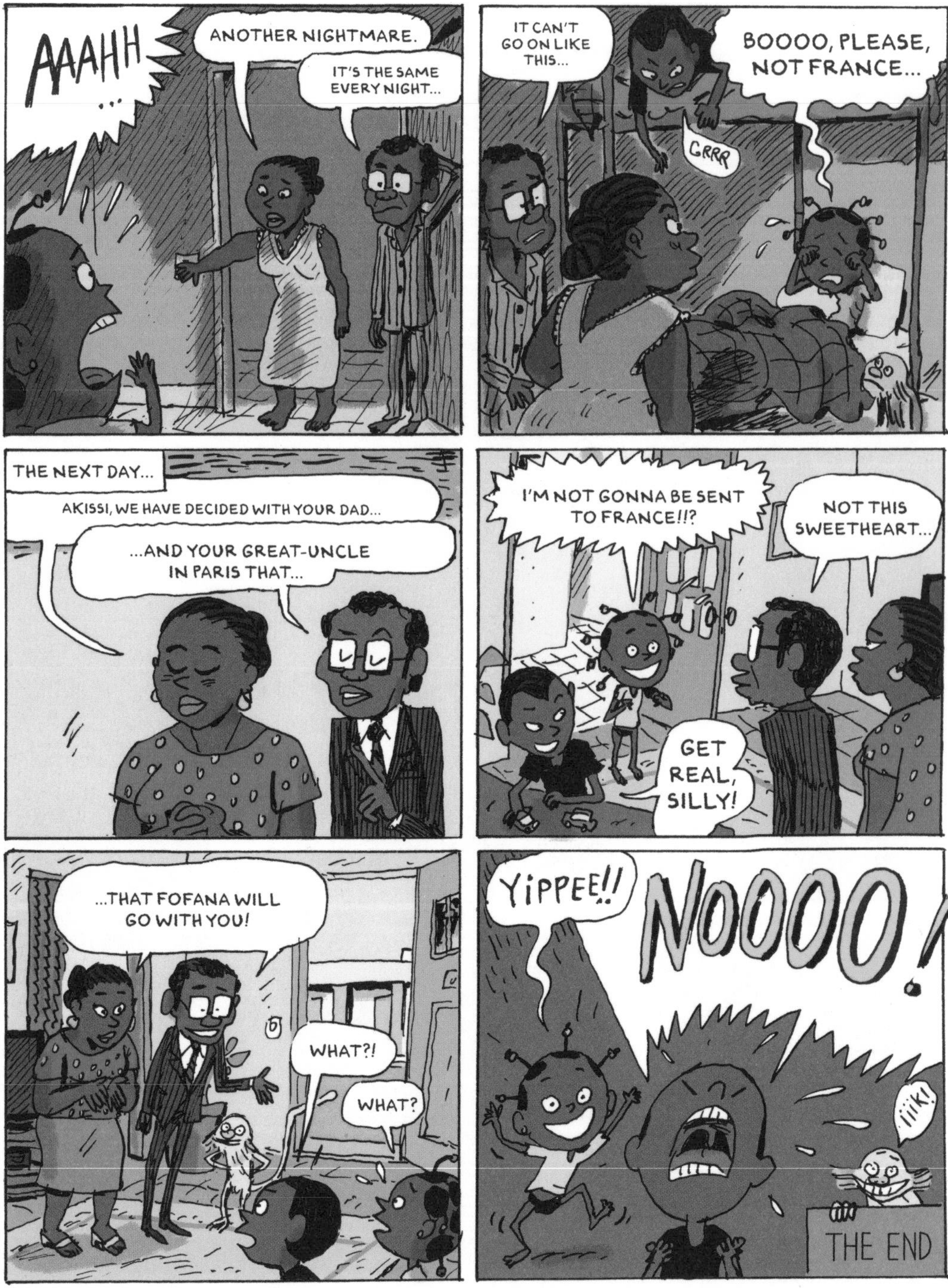
AAAHH ...
ANOTHER NIGHTMARE.
IT'S THE SAME EVERY NIGHT...
IT CAN'T GO ON LIKE THIS...
BOOOO, PLEASE, NOT FRANCE...
GRRR
THE NEXT DAY...
AKISSI, WE HAVE DECIDED WITH YOUR DAD...
...AND YOUR GREAT-UNCLE IN PARIS THAT...
I'M NOT GONNA BE SENT TO FRANCE!!?
NOT THIS SWEETHEART...
GET REAL, SILLY!
...THAT FOFANA WILL GO WITH YOU!
WHAT?!
WHAT?
YIPPEE!!
NOOOO!
iiiik!
THE END

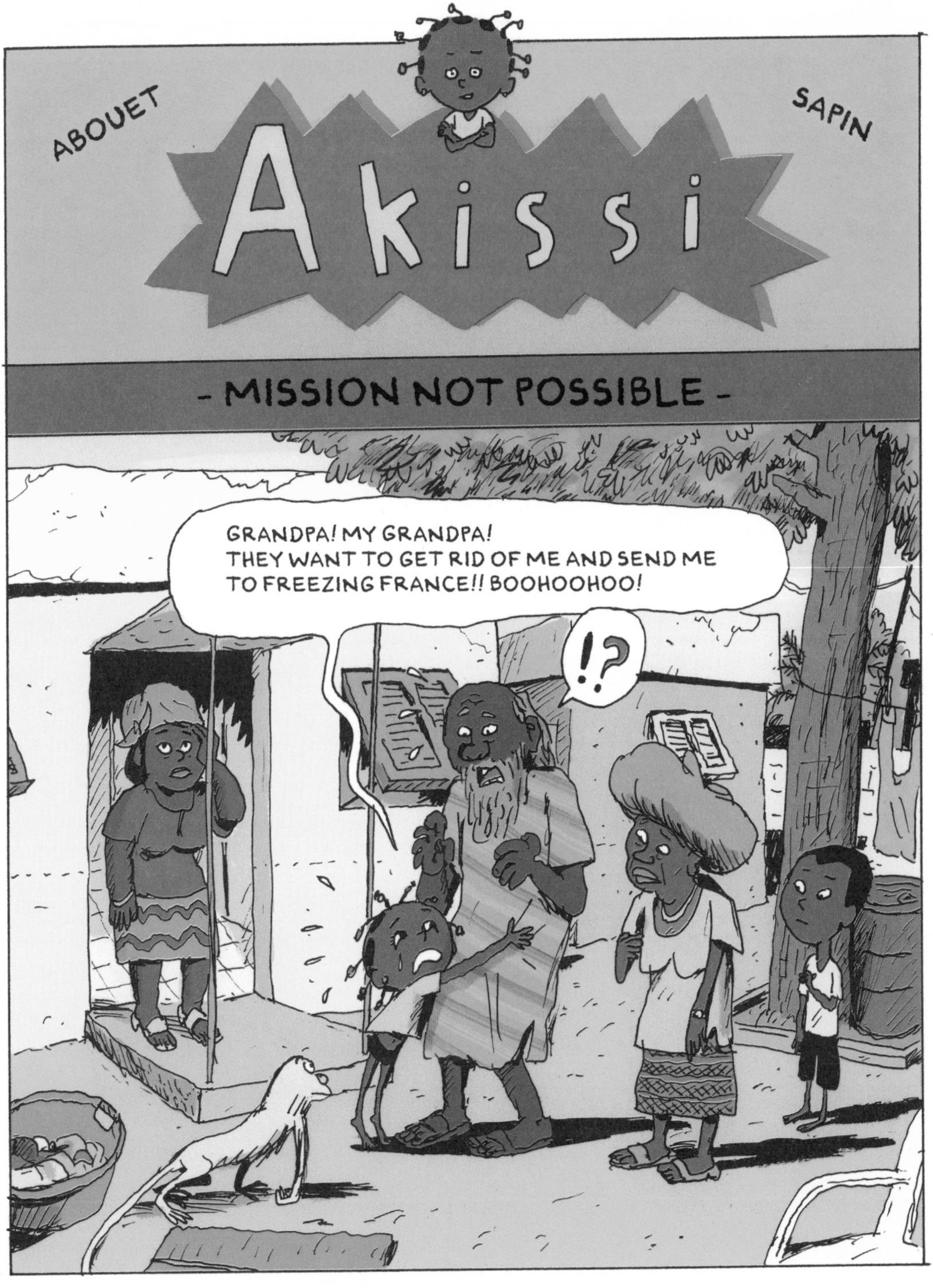
ABOUET
SAPIN
Akissi
- MISSION NOT POSSIBLE -
GRANDPA! MY GRANDPA!
THEY WANT TO GET RID OF ME AND SEND ME
TO FREEZING FRANCE!! BOOHOOHOO!
!?

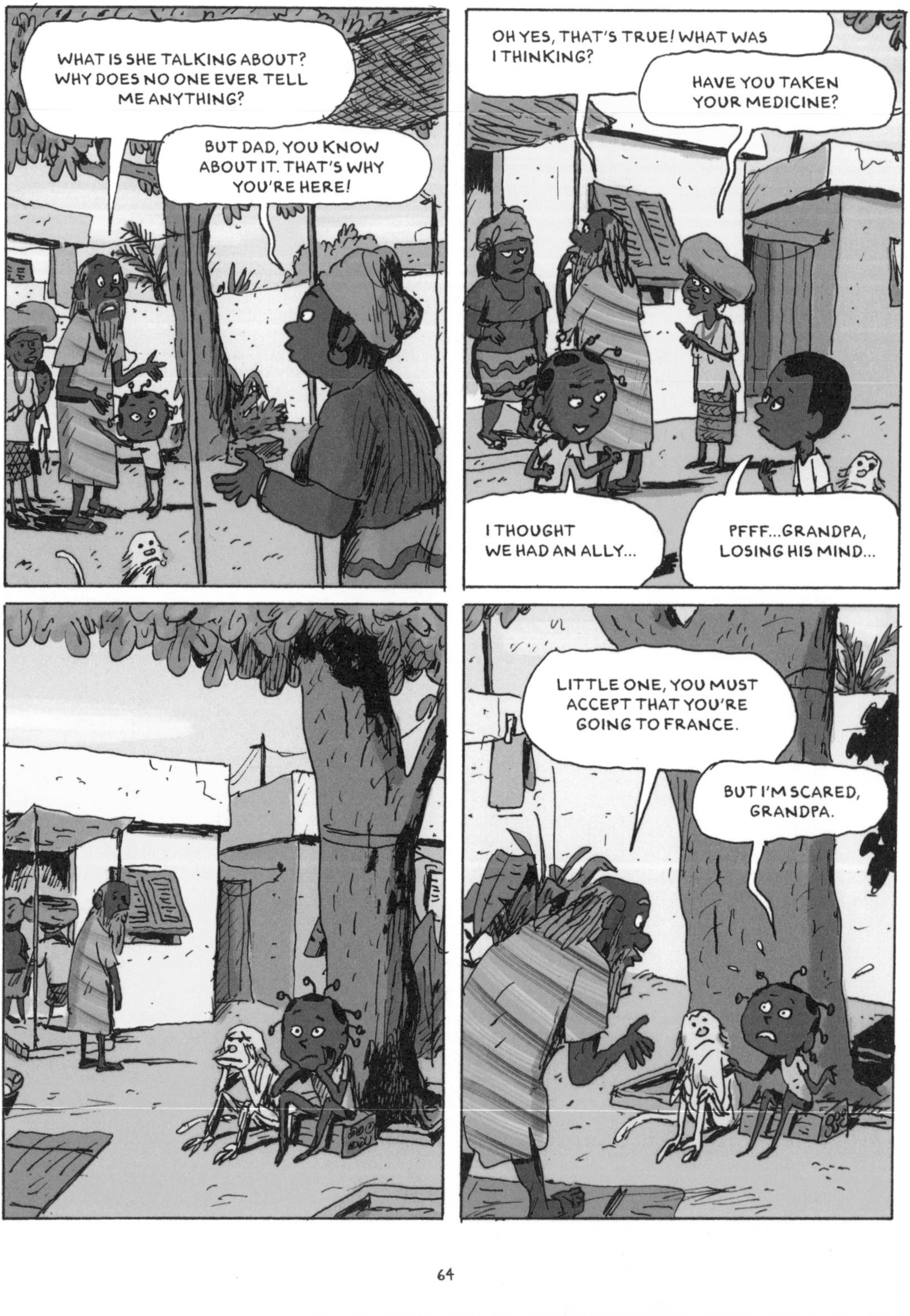
WHAT IS SHE TALKING ABOUT? WHY DOES NO ONE EVER TELL ME ANYTHING?
BUT DAD, YOU KNOW ABOUT IT. THAT'S WHY YOU'RE HERE!
OH YES, THAT'S TRUE! WHAT WAS I THINKING?
HAVE YOU TAKEN YOUR MEDICINE?
I THOUGHT WE HAD AN ALLY...
PFFF...GRANDPA, LOSING HIS MIND...
LITTLE ONE, YOU MUST ACCEPT THAT YOU'RE GOING TO FRANCE.
BUT I'M SCARED, GRANDPA.

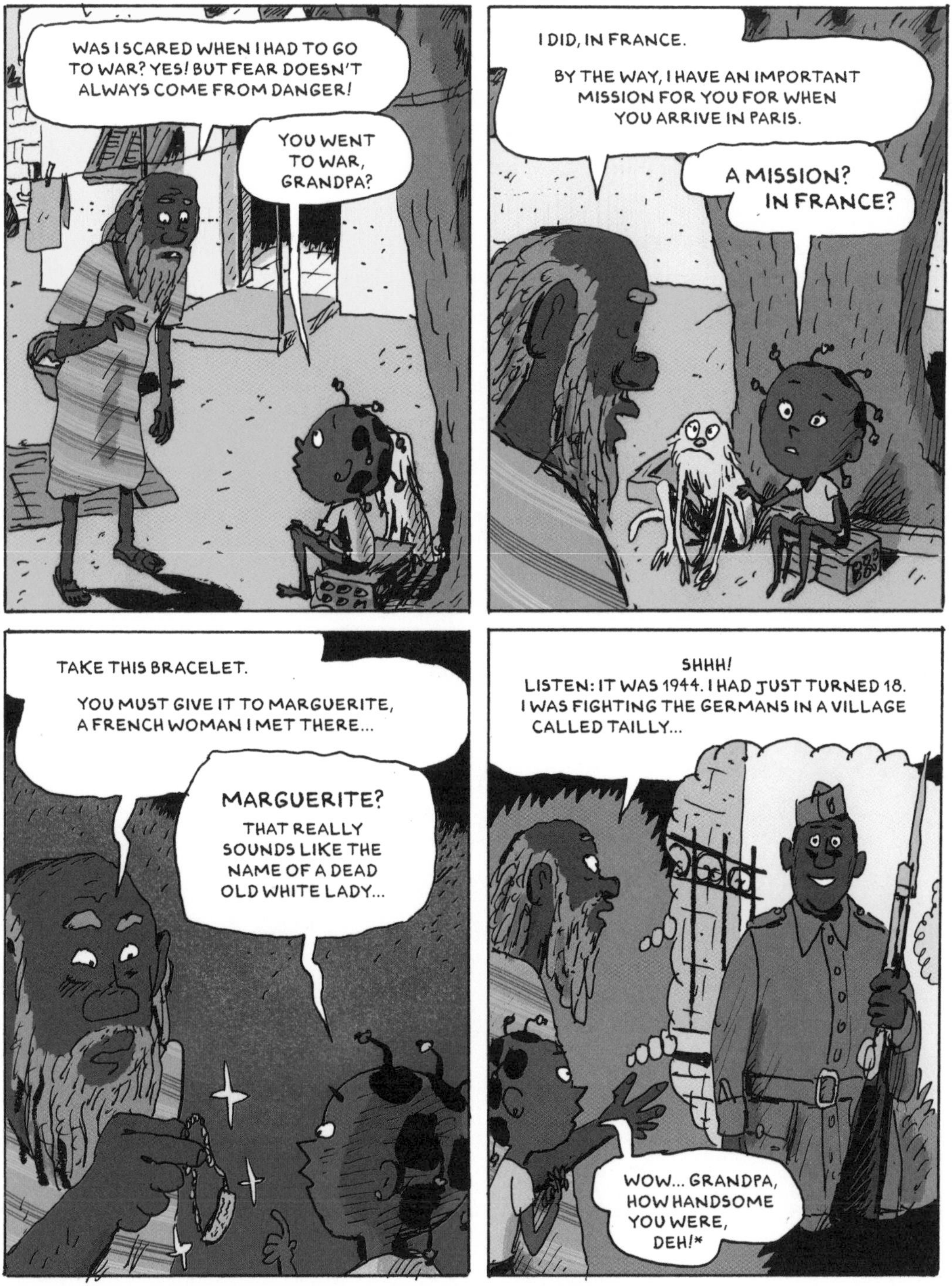
WAS I SCARED WHEN I HAD TO GO TO WAR? YES! BUT FEAR DOESN'T ALWAYS COME FROM DANGER!
YOU WENT TO WAR, GRANDPA?
I DID, IN FRANCE.
BY THE WAY, I HAVE AN IMPORTANT MISSION FOR YOU FOR WHEN YOU ARRIVE IN PARIS.
A MISSION? IN FRANCE?
TAKE THIS BRACELET.
YOU MUST GIVE IT TO MARGUERITE, A FRENCH WOMAN I MET THERE...
MARGUERITE? THAT REALLY SOUNDS LIKE THE NAME OF A DEAD OLD WHITE LADY...
SHHH!
LISTEN: IT WAS 1944. I HAD JUST TURNED 18. I WAS FIGHTING THE GERMANS IN A VILLAGE CALLED TAILLY...
WOW... GRANDPA, HOW HANDSOME YOU WERE, DEH!*

* DEH OR DEY IS AN IVORIAN WORD USED AT THE END OF SENTENCES, IN THIS CASE IT EXPRESSES ADMIRATION.

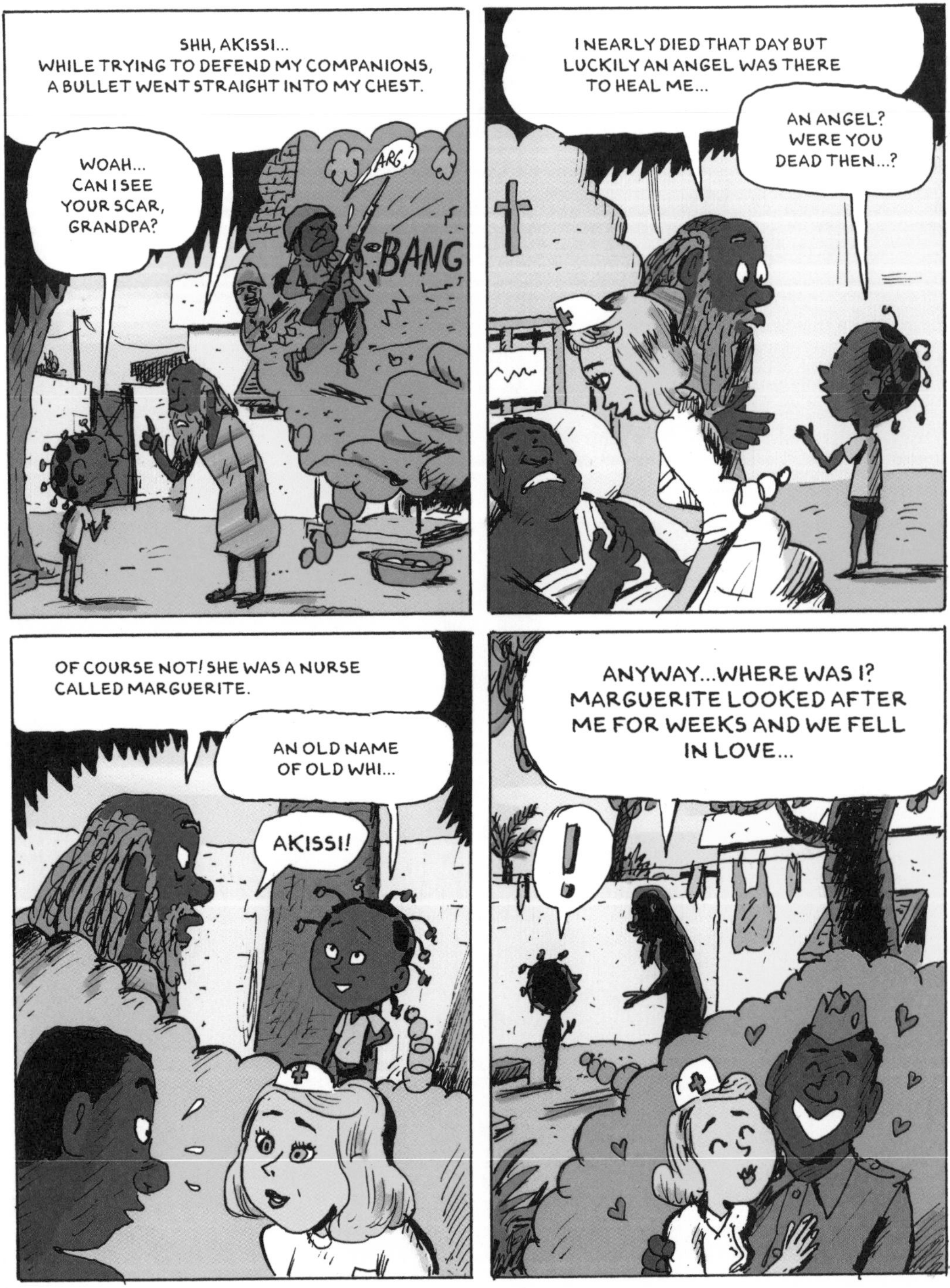
SHH, AKISSI...
WHILE TRYING TO DEFEND MY COMPANIONS, A BULLET WENT STRAIGHT INTO MY CHEST.
ARG!
BANG
WOAH... CAN I SEE YOUR SCAR, GRANDPA?
I NEARLY DIED THAT DAY BUT LUCKILY AN ANGEL WAS THERE TO HEAL ME...
AN ANGEL? WERE YOU DEAD THEN...?
OF COURSE NOT! SHE WAS A NURSE CALLED MARGUERITE.
AN OLD NAME OF OLD WHI...
AKISSI!
ANYWAY...WHERE WAS I? MARGUERITE LOOKED AFTER ME FOR WEEKS AND WE FELL IN LOVE...
!

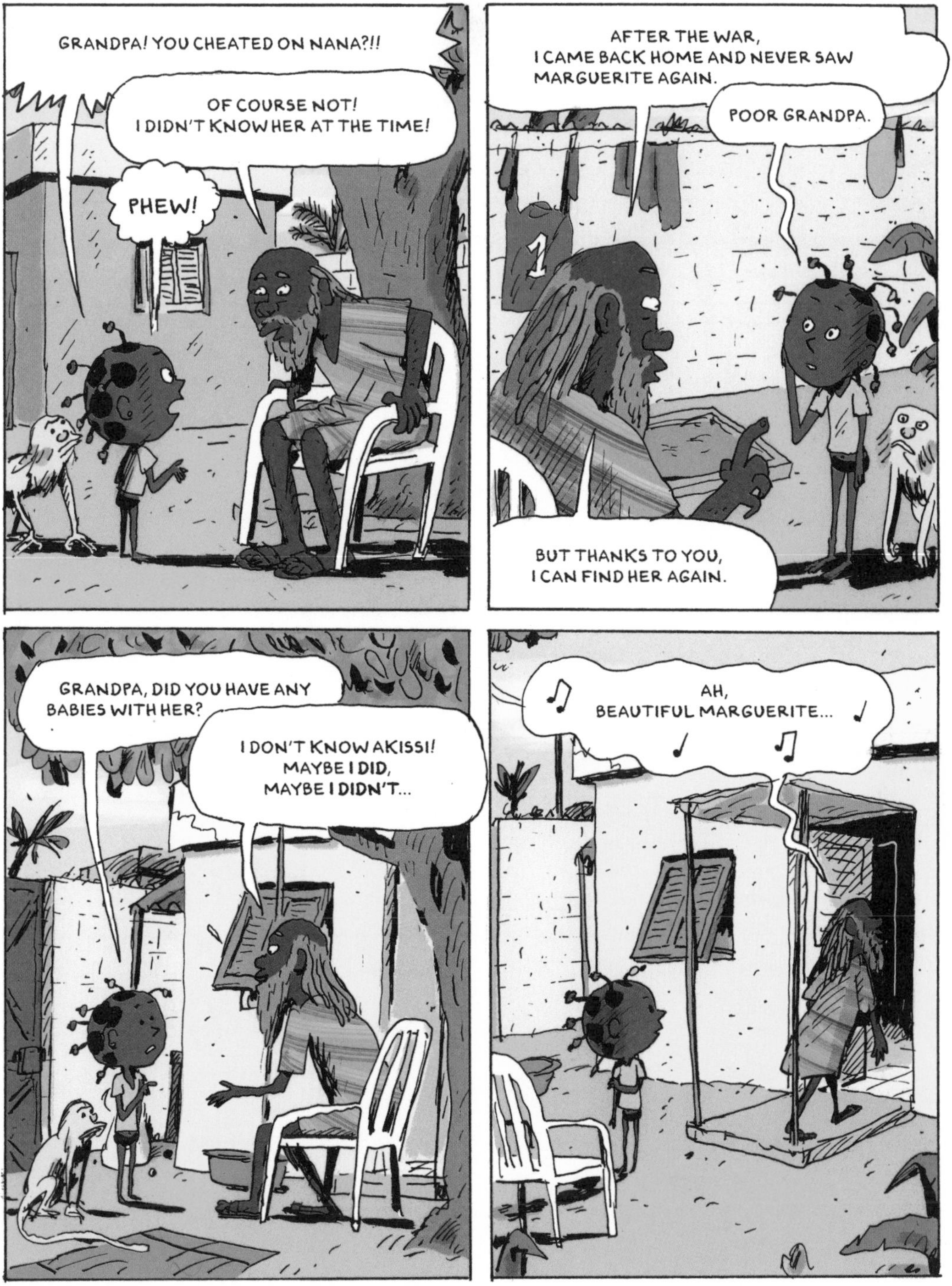
GRANDPA! YOU CHEATED ON NANA?!!
OF COURSE NOT! I DIDN'T KNOW HER AT THE TIME!
PHEW!
AFTER THE WAR, I CAME BACK HOME AND NEVER SAW MARGUERITE AGAIN.
POOR GRANDPA.
BUT THANKS TO YOU, I CAN FIND HER AGAIN.
GRANDPA, DID YOU HAVE ANY BABIES WITH HER?
I DON'T KNOW AKISSI! MAYBE I DID, MAYBE I DIDN'T...
AH, BEAUTIFUL MARGUERITE...

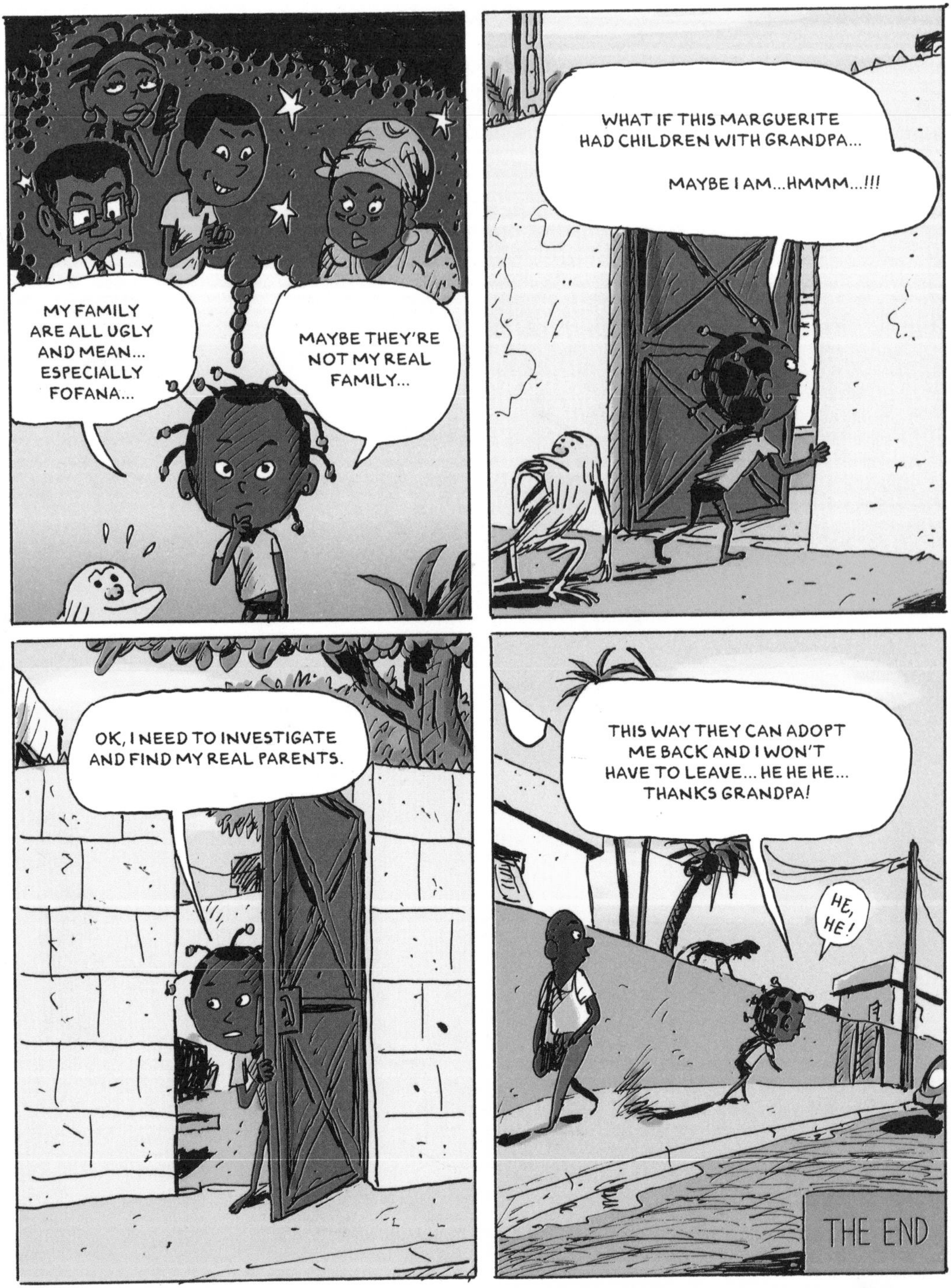
MY FAMILY ARE ALL UGLY AND MEAN... ESPECIALLY FOFANA...
MAYBE THEY'RE NOT MY REAL FAMILY...
WHAT IF THIS MARGUERITE HAD CHILDREN WITH GRANDPA...
MAYBE I AM...HMMM...!!!
OK, I NEED TO INVESTIGATE AND FIND MY REAL PARENTS.
THIS WAY THEY CAN ADOPT ME BACK AND I WON'T HAVE TO LEAVE... HE HE HE... THANKS GRANDPA!
HE, HE!
THE END

ABOUET
Akissi
SAPIN
- PATERNITY INVESTIGATION -
HEY BUDDIES,
NOW I KNOW MY PARENTS
AREN'T MY REAL PARENTS!!!
I'M GONNA HAVE TO SOLVE
THIS MYSTERY!!
BRAVO,
AKISSI!!!

WHAT WILL YOU START WITH?
WITH THE START, PAPOU!
OH YEAH, FAIR ENOUGH.
OK, ON TO SERIOUS BUSINESS NOW!
MY INVESTIGATION CALLS!
AKISSI, LISTEN!...
I THINK YOU WILL NEED SPECTREMAN'S STRENGTH!
WILL I?
POISSONS
HMM...FINE, EDMOND. IT COULD BE DANGEROUS. I'LL BE THE CAPTAIN, YOU WILL BE MY DEPUTY.
LET'S WORM THE INFORMATION OUT OF THE NEIGHBOURS!
YUCK, THAT'S DISGUSTING! NO, BEFORE WE GET TO TORTURE THEM WITH WORMS, I NEED TO TALK TO MY MUM.
YOU'RE RIGHT! THE FIRST SUSPECT!

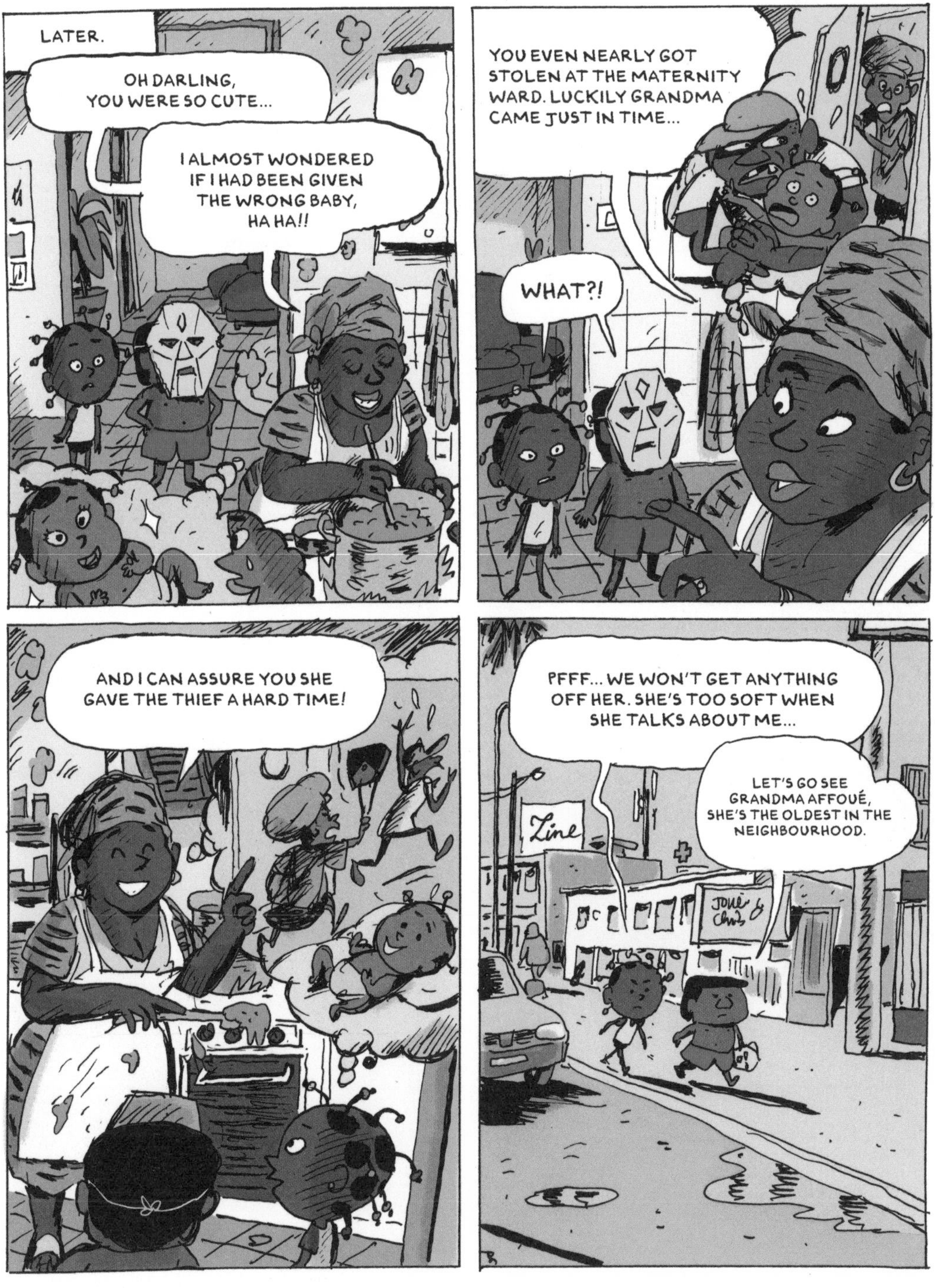
LATER.
OH DARLING, YOU WERE SO CUTE...
I ALMOST WONDERED IF I HAD BEEN GIVEN THE WRONG BABY, HA HA!!
YOU EVEN NEARLY GOT STOLEN AT THE MATERNITY WARD. LUCKILY GRANDMA CAME JUST IN TIME...
WHAT?!
AND I CAN ASSURE YOU SHE GAVE THE THIEF A HARD TIME!
PFFF... WE WON'T GET ANYTHING OFF HER. SHE'S TOO SOFT WHEN SHE TALKS ABOUT ME...
LET'S GO SEE GRANDMA AFFOUÉ, SHE'S THE OLDEST IN THE NEIGHBOURHOOD.

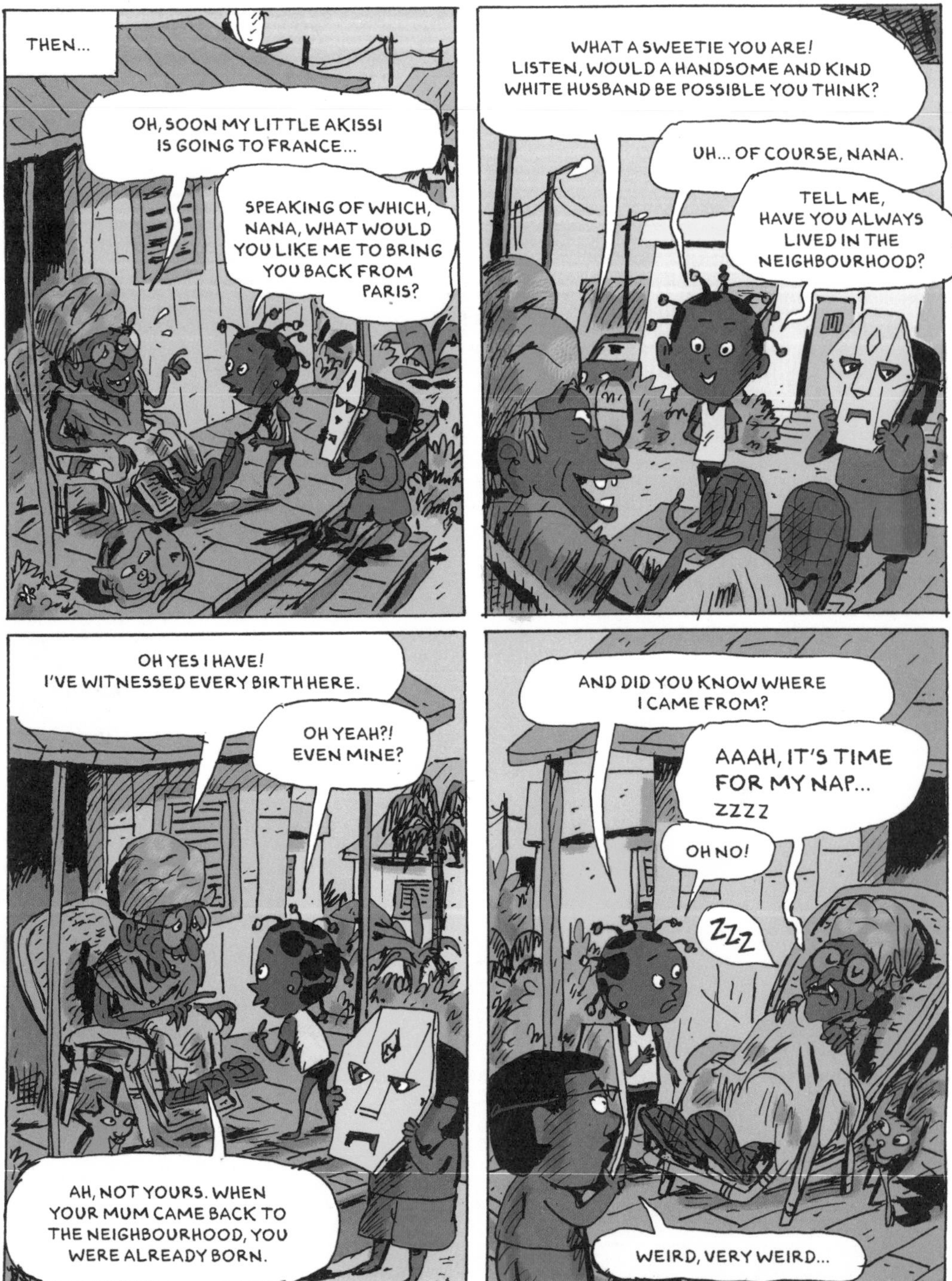
THEN...
OH, SOON MY LITTLE AKISSI IS GOING TO FRANCE...
SPEAKING OF WHICH, NANA, WHAT WOULD YOU LIKE ME TO BRING YOU BACK FROM PARIS?
WHAT A SWEETIE YOU ARE! LISTEN, WOULD A HANDSOME AND KIND WHITE HUSBAND BE POSSIBLE YOU THINK?
UH... OF COURSE, NANA.
TELL ME, HAVE YOU ALWAYS LIVED IN THE NEIGHBOURHOOD?
OH YES I HAVE! I'VE WITNESSED EVERY BIRTH HERE.
OH YEAH?! EVEN MINE?
AH, NOT YOURS. WHEN YOUR MUM CAME BACK TO THE NEIGHBOURHOOD, YOU WERE ALREADY BORN.
AND DID YOU KNOW WHERE I CAME FROM?
AAAH, IT'S TIME FOR MY NAP... ZZZZ
OH NO!
ZZZ
WEIRD, VERY WEIRD...

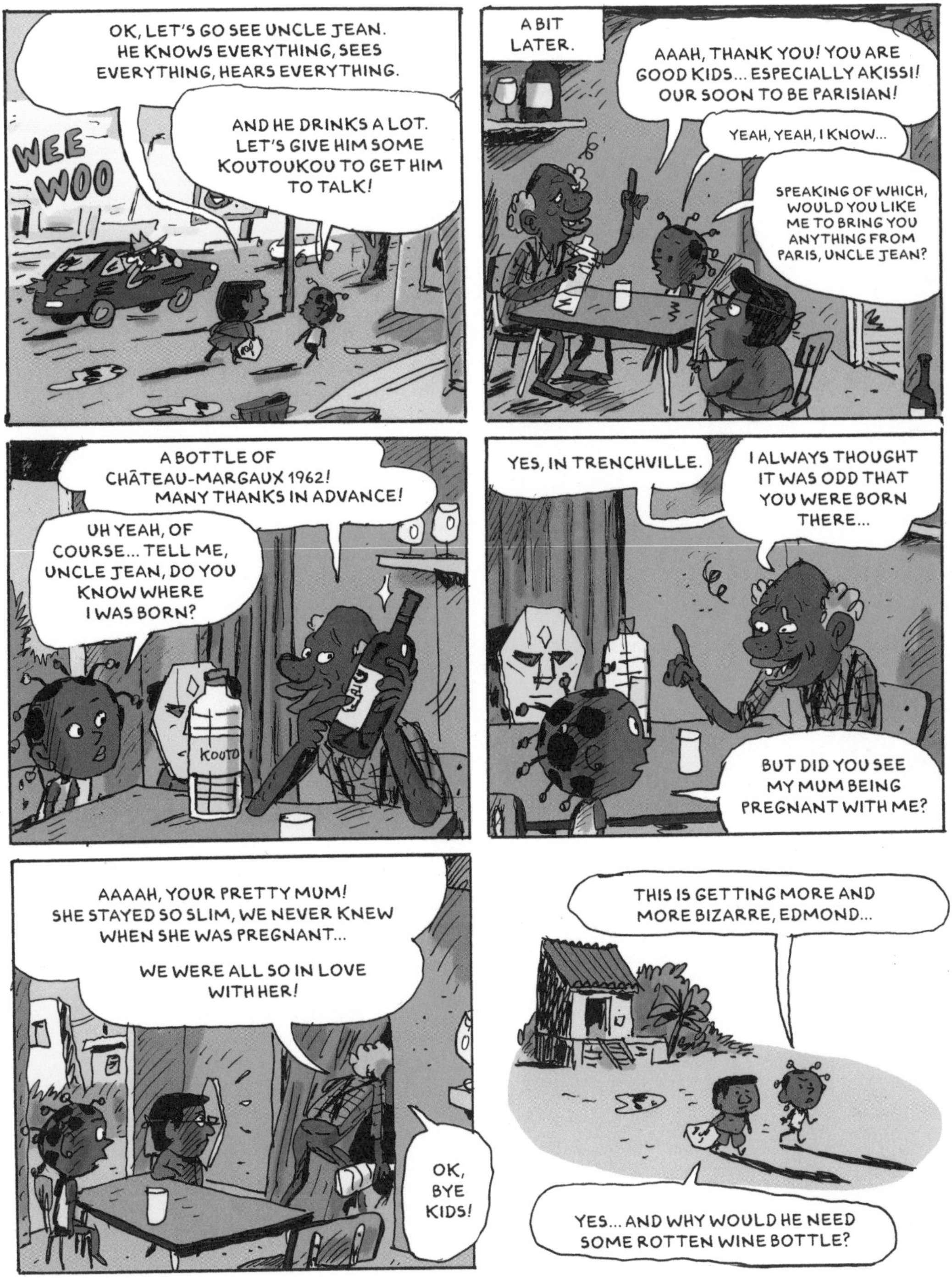
OK, LET'S GO SEE UNCLE JEAN. HE KNOWS EVERYTHING, SEES EVERYTHING, HEARS EVERYTHING.
AND HE DRINKS A LOT. LET'S GIVE HIM SOME KOUTOUKOU TO GET HIM TO TALK!
WEE WOO
A BIT LATER.
AAAH, THANK YOU! YOU ARE GOOD KIDS... ESPECIALLY AKISSI! OUR SOON TO BE PARISIAN!
YEAH, YEAH, I KNOW...
SPEAKING OF WHICH, WOULD YOU LIKE ME TO BRING YOU ANYTHING FROM PARIS, UNCLE JEAN?
A BOTTLE OF CHÂTEAU-MARGAUX 1962! MANY THANKS IN ADVANCE!
UH YEAH, OF COURSE... TELL ME, UNCLE JEAN, DO YOU KNOW WHERE I WAS BORN?
KOUTO
YES, IN TRENCHVILLE.
I ALWAYS THOUGHT IT WAS ODD THAT YOU WERE BORN THERE...
BUT DID YOU SEE MY MUM BEING PREGNANT WITH ME?
AAAAH, YOUR PRETTY MUM! SHE STAYED SO SLIM, WE NEVER KNEW WHEN SHE WAS PREGNANT...
WE WERE ALL SO IN LOVE WITH HER!
OK, BYE KIDS!
THIS IS GETTING MORE AND MORE BIZARRE, EDMOND...
YES... AND WHY WOULD HE NEED SOME ROTTEN WINE BOTTLE?

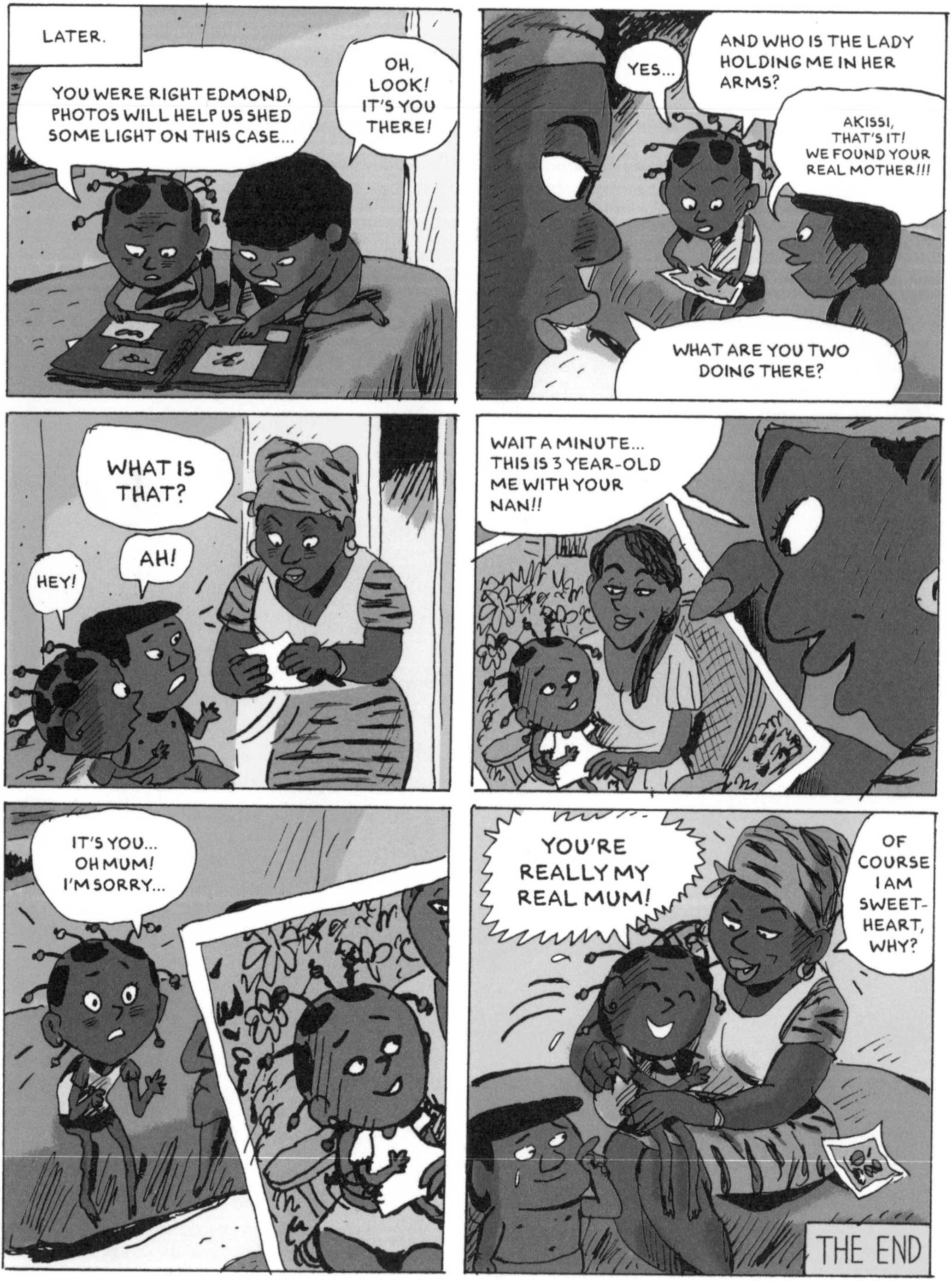
LATER.
YOU WERE RIGHT EDMOND, PHOTOS WILL HELP US SHED SOME LIGHT ON THIS CASE...
OH, LOOK! IT'S YOU THERE!
YES...
AND WHO IS THE LADY HOLDING ME IN HER ARMS?
AKISSI, THAT'S IT! WE FOUND YOUR REAL MOTHER!!!
WHAT ARE YOU TWO DOING THERE?
WHAT IS THAT?
AH!
HEY!
WAIT A MINUTE... THIS IS 3 YEAR-OLD ME WITH YOUR NAN!!
IT'S YOU... OH MUM! I'M SORRY...
YOU'RE REALLY MY REAL MUM!
OF COURSE I AM SWEET-HEART, WHY?
THE END

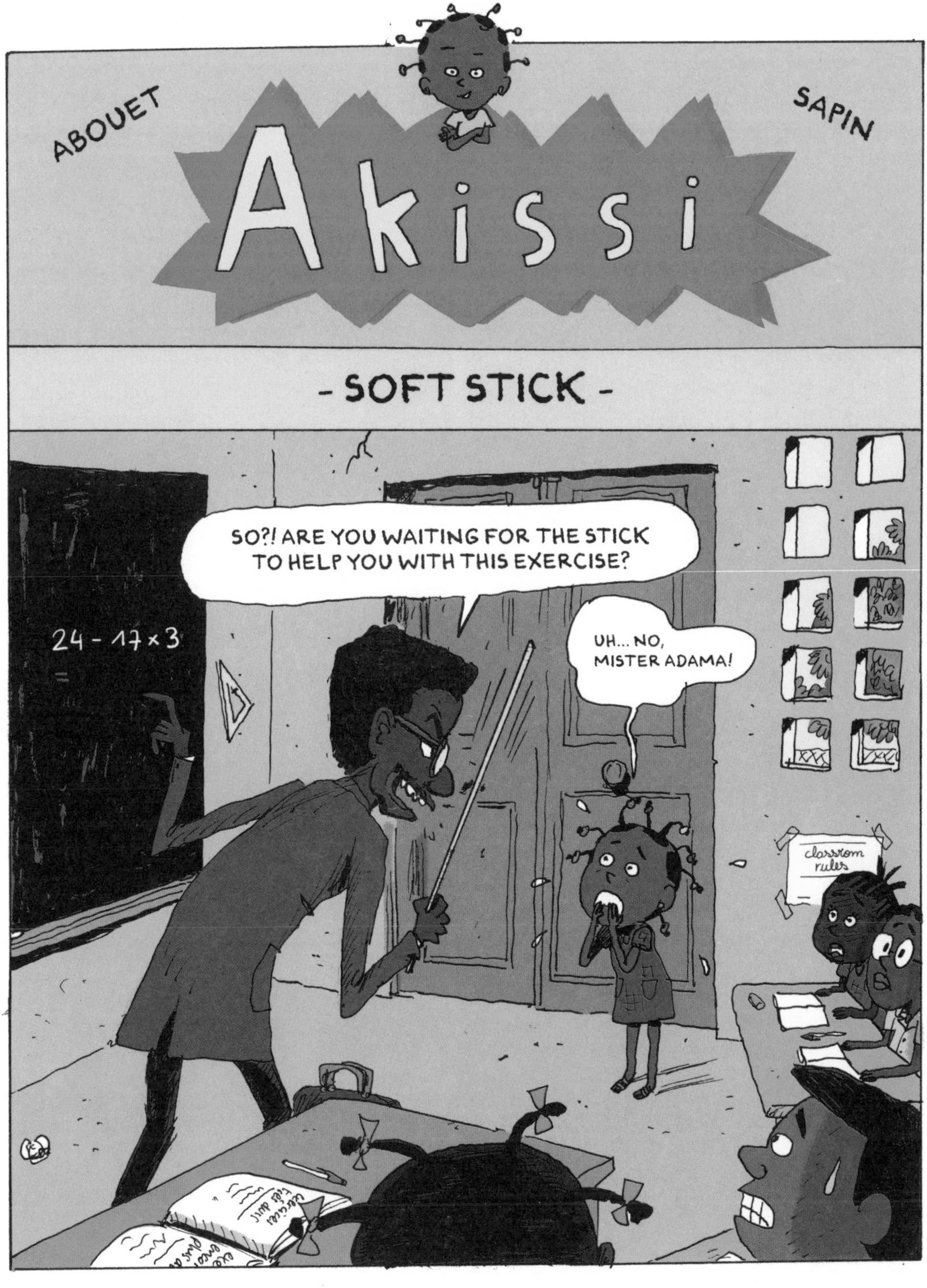
ABOUET
Akissi
SAPIN
- SOFT STICK -
SO?! ARE YOU WAITING FOR THE STICK TO HELP YOU WITH THIS EXERCISE?
24 - 17 × 3
UH... NO, MISTER ADAMA!
classroom rules

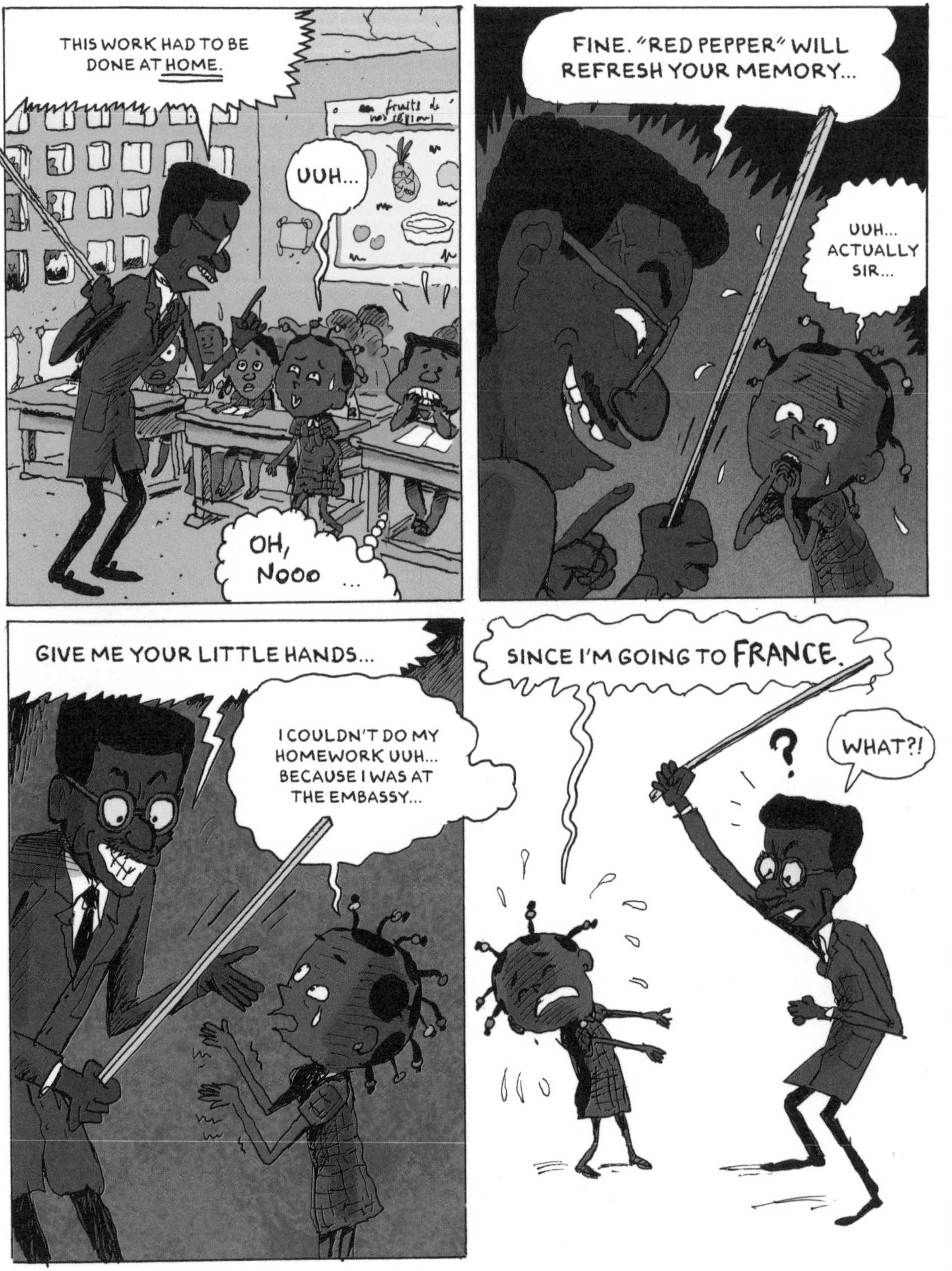
THIS WORK HAD TO BE DONE AT HOME.
UUH...
OH, NOOO ...
FINE. "RED PEPPER" WILL REFRESH YOUR MEMORY...
UUH... ACTUALLY SIR...
GIVE ME YOUR LITTLE HANDS...
I COULDN'T DO MY HOMEWORK UUH... BECAUSE I WAS AT THE EMBASSY...
SINCE I'M GOING TO FRANCE.
?
WHAT?!

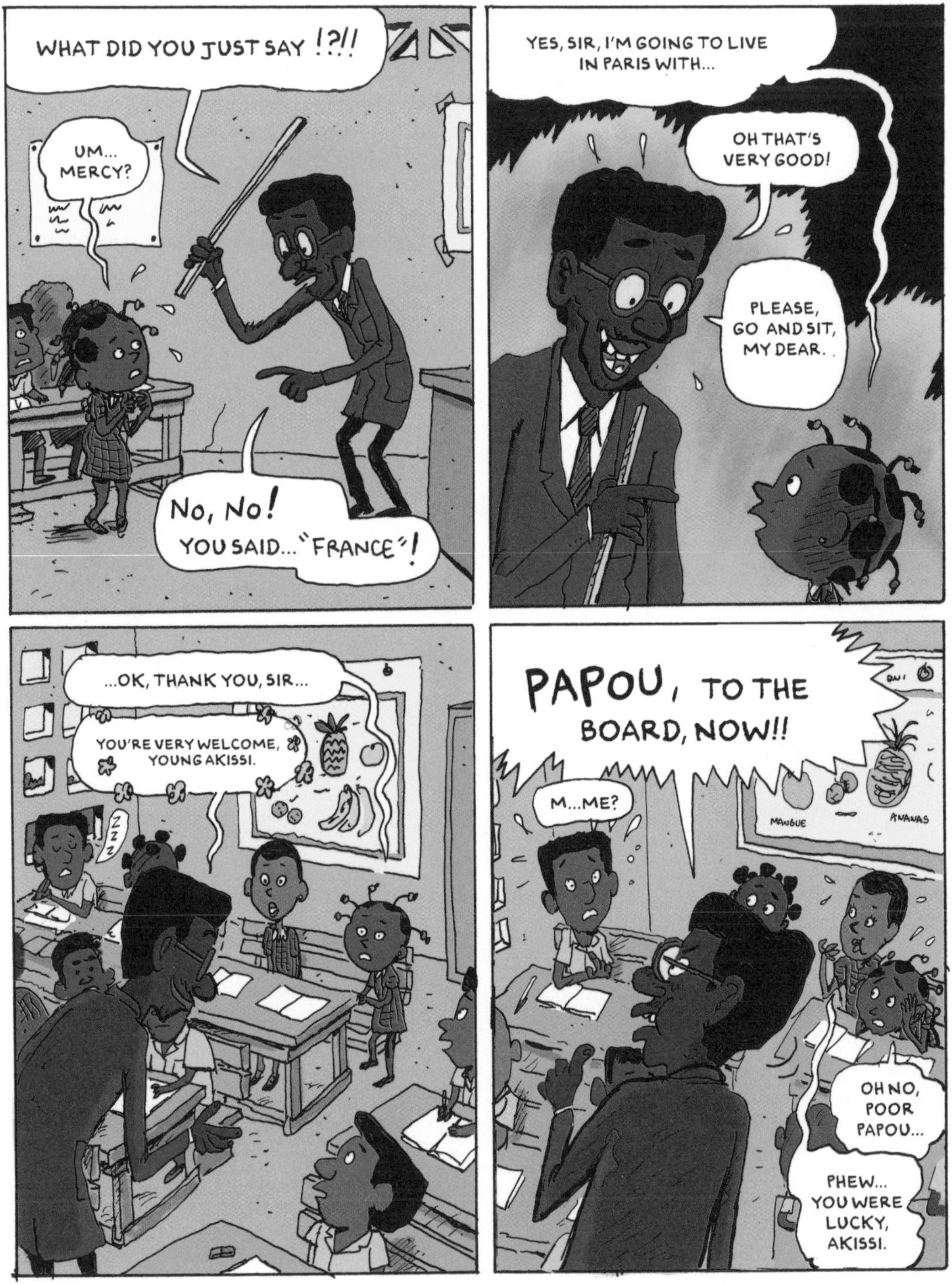
WHAT DID YOU JUST SAY !?!!
UM... MERCY?
No, No! YOU SAID... "FRANCE"!
YES, SIR, I'M GOING TO LIVE IN PARIS WITH...
OH THAT'S VERY GOOD!
PLEASE, GO AND SIT, MY DEAR.
...OK, THANK YOU, SIR...
YOU'RE VERY WELCOME, YOUNG AKISSI.
ZZZ
PAPOU, TO THE BOARD, NOW!!
M...ME?
MANGUE
ANANAS
OH NO, POOR PAPOU...
PHEW... YOU WERE LUCKY, AKISSI.

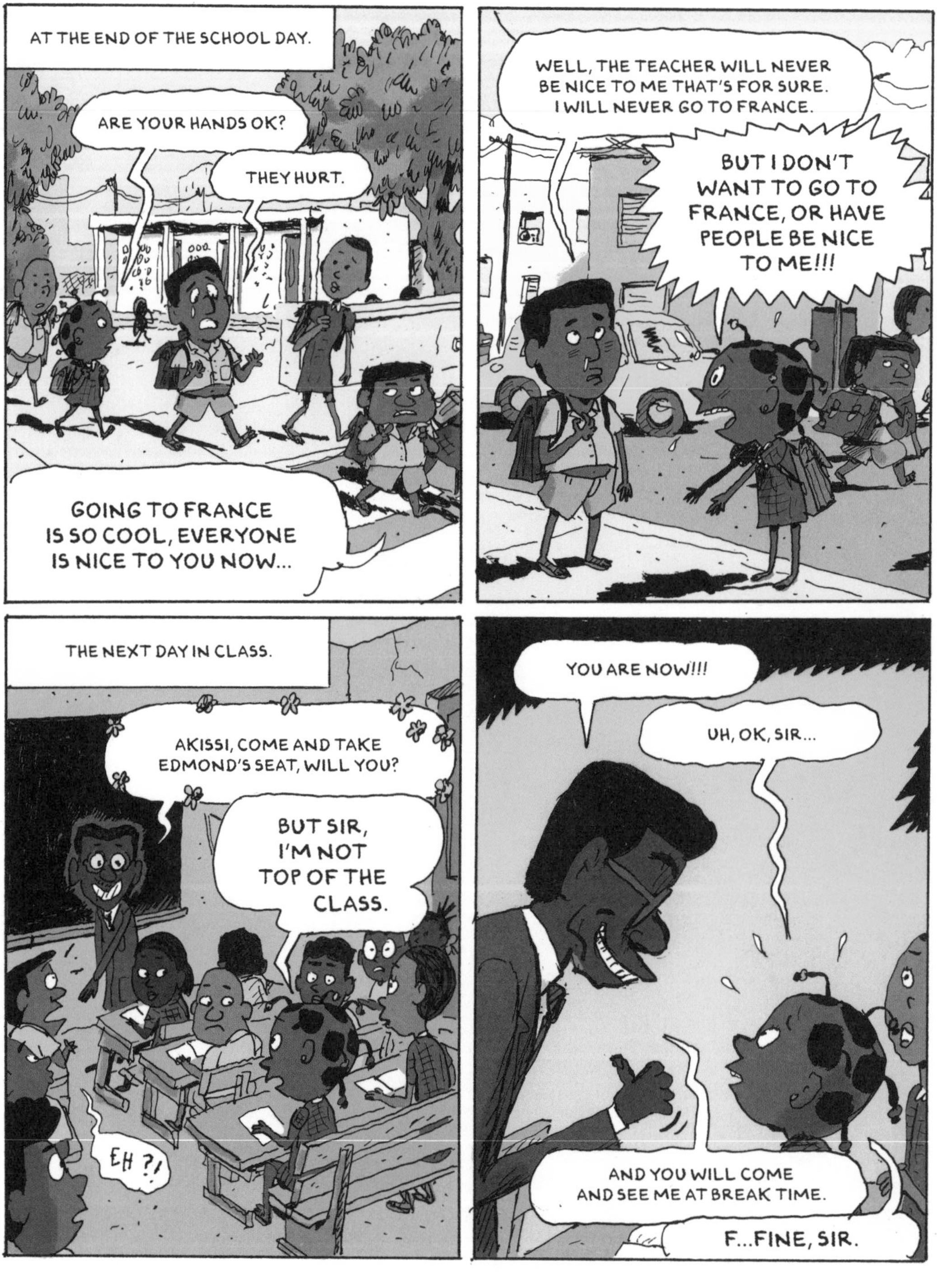
AT THE END OF THE SCHOOL DAY.
ARE YOUR HANDS OK?
THEY HURT.
GOING TO FRANCE IS SO COOL, EVERYONE IS NICE TO YOU NOW...
WELL, THE TEACHER WILL NEVER BE NICE TO ME THAT'S FOR SURE. I WILL NEVER GO TO FRANCE.
BUT I DON'T WANT TO GO TO FRANCE, OR HAVE PEOPLE BE NICE TO ME!!!
THE NEXT DAY IN CLASS.
AKISSI, COME AND TAKE EDMOND'S SEAT, WILL YOU?
BUT SIR, I'M NOT TOP OF THE CLASS.
EH ?!
YOU ARE NOW!!!
UH, OK, SIR...
AND YOU WILL COME AND SEE ME AT BREAK TIME.
F...FINE, SIR.

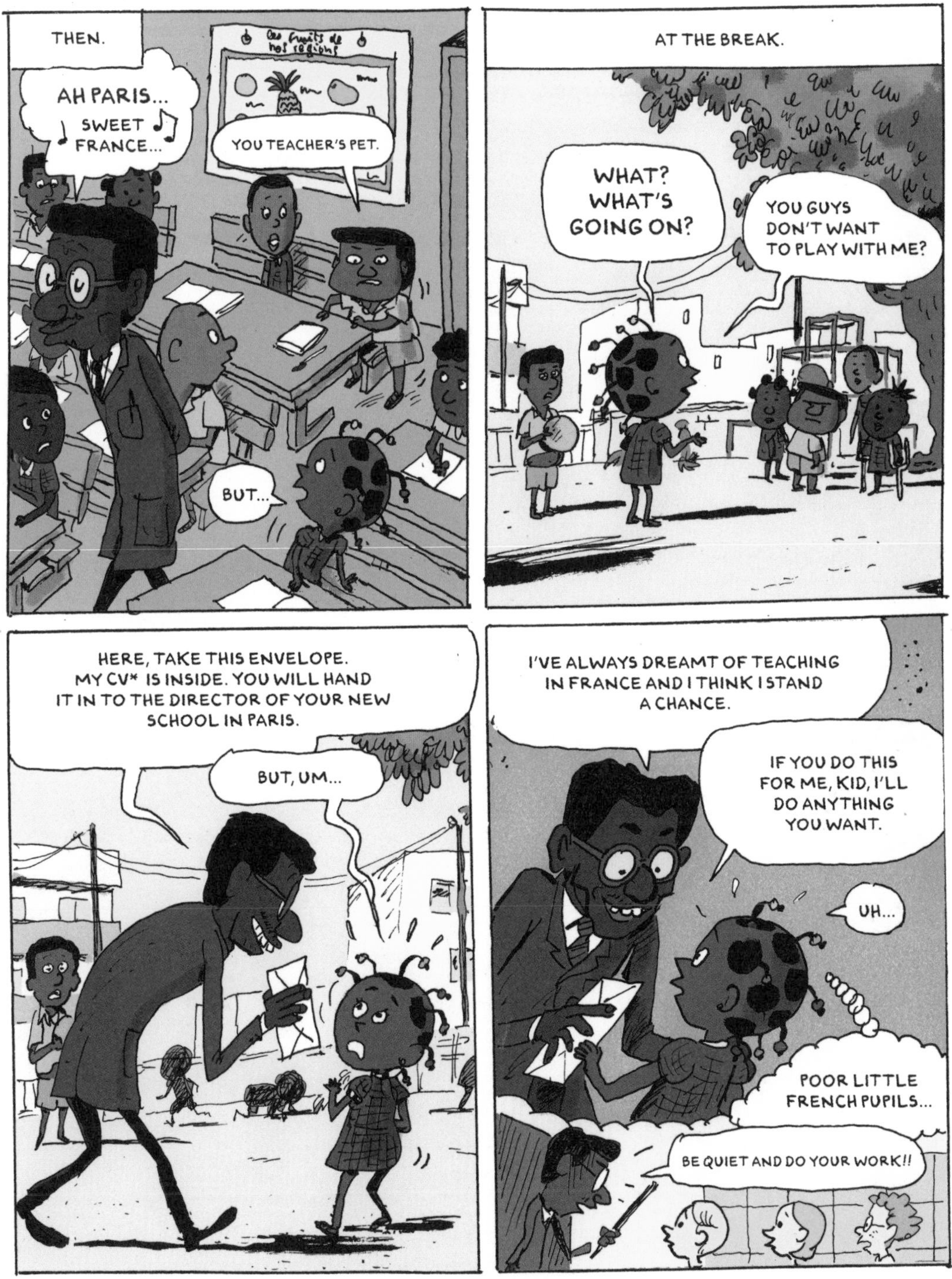
THEN.
AH PARIS... SWEET FRANCE...
YOU TEACHER'S PET.
BUT...
AT THE BREAK.
WHAT? WHAT'S GOING ON?
YOU GUYS DON'T WANT TO PLAY WITH ME?
HERE, TAKE THIS ENVELOPE. MY CV* IS INSIDE. YOU WILL HAND IT IN TO THE DIRECTOR OF YOUR NEW SCHOOL IN PARIS.
BUT, UM...
I'VE ALWAYS DREAMT OF TEACHING IN FRANCE AND I THINK I STAND A CHANCE.
IF YOU DO THIS FOR ME, KID, I'LL DO ANYTHING YOU WANT.
UH...
POOR LITTLE FRENCH PUPILS...
BE QUIET AND DO YOUR WORK!!

* CV/CURRICULUM VITAE: A SUMMARY OF SOMEONE'S PREVIOUS JOBS AND EDUCATION WHICH HELPS THEM GET A NEW JOB.

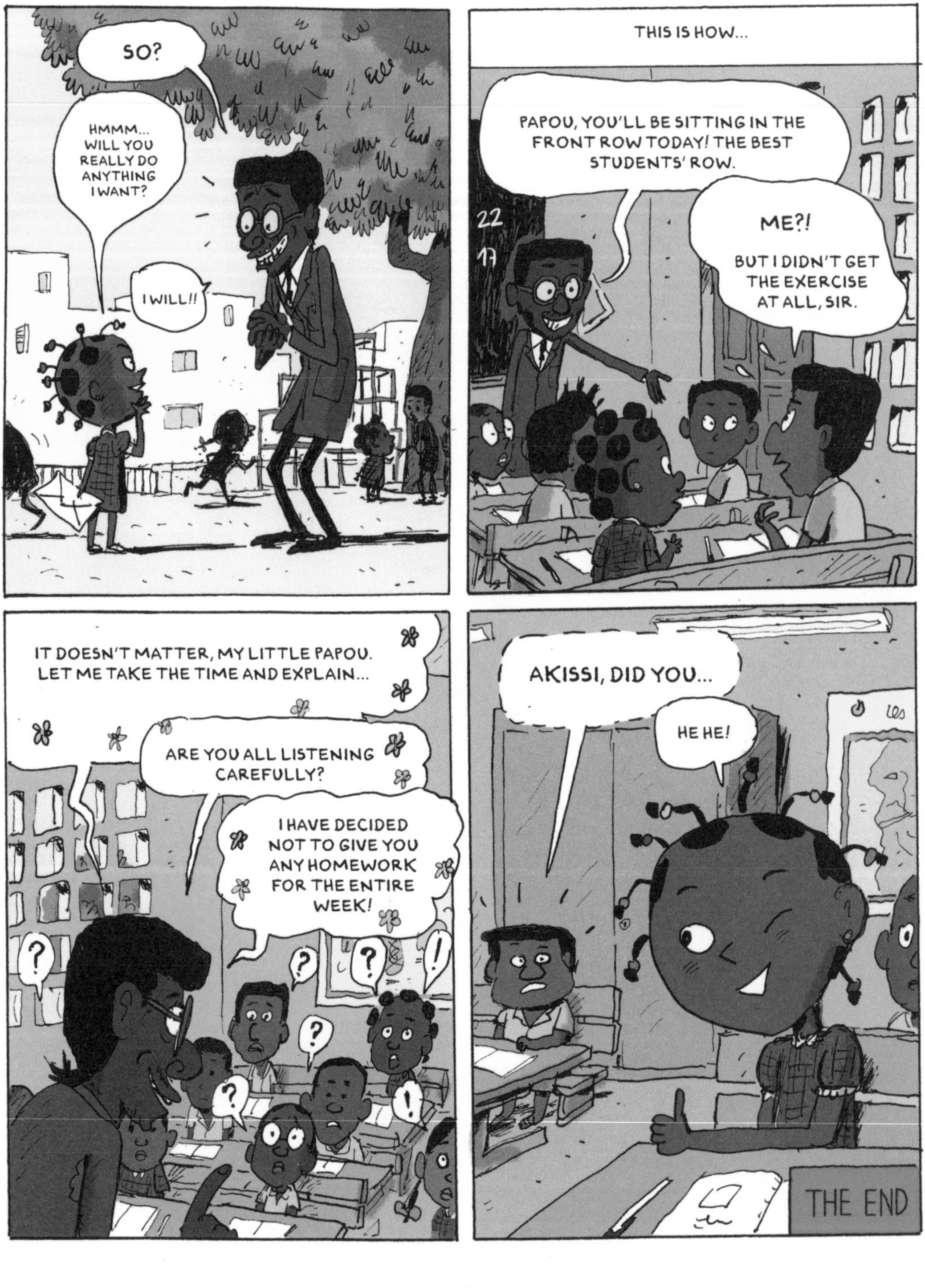
SO?
HMMM... WILL YOU REALLY DO ANYTHING I WANT?
I WILL!!
THIS IS HOW...
PAPOU, YOU'LL BE SITTING IN THE FRONT ROW TODAY! THE BEST STUDENTS' ROW.
22
17
ME?!
BUT I DIDN'T GET THE EXERCISE AT ALL, SIR.
IT DOESN'T MATTER, MY LITTLE PAPOU. LET ME TAKE THE TIME AND EXPLAIN...
ARE YOU ALL LISTENING CAREFULLY?
I HAVE DECIDED NOT TO GIVE YOU ANY HOMEWORK FOR THE ENTIRE WEEK!
AKISSI, DID YOU...
HE HE!
THE END

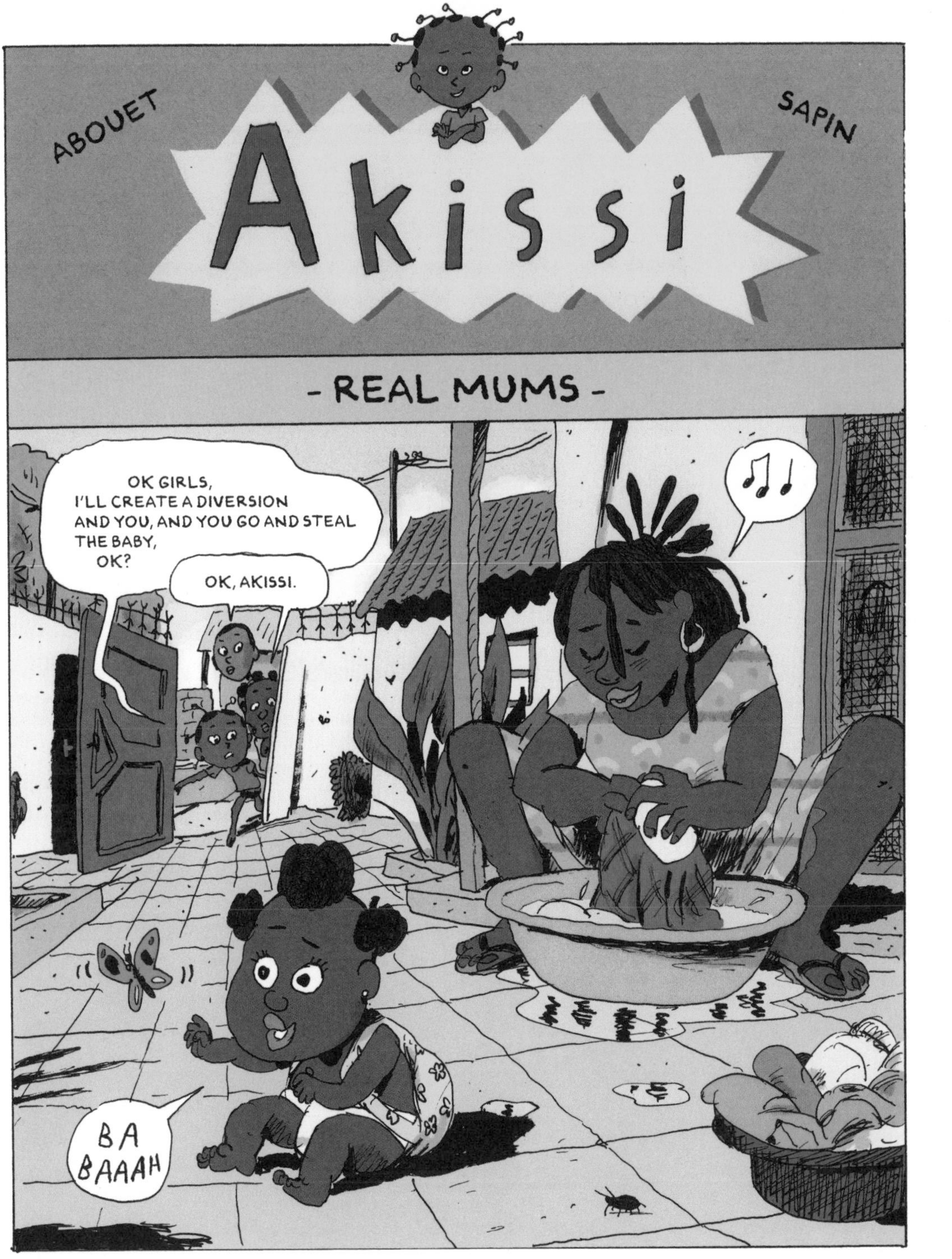
ABOUET
SAPIN
Akissi
- REAL MUMS -
OK GIRLS, I'LL CREATE A DIVERSION AND YOU, AND YOU GO AND STEAL THE BABY, OK?
OK, AKISSI.
♫♩
BA BAAAH

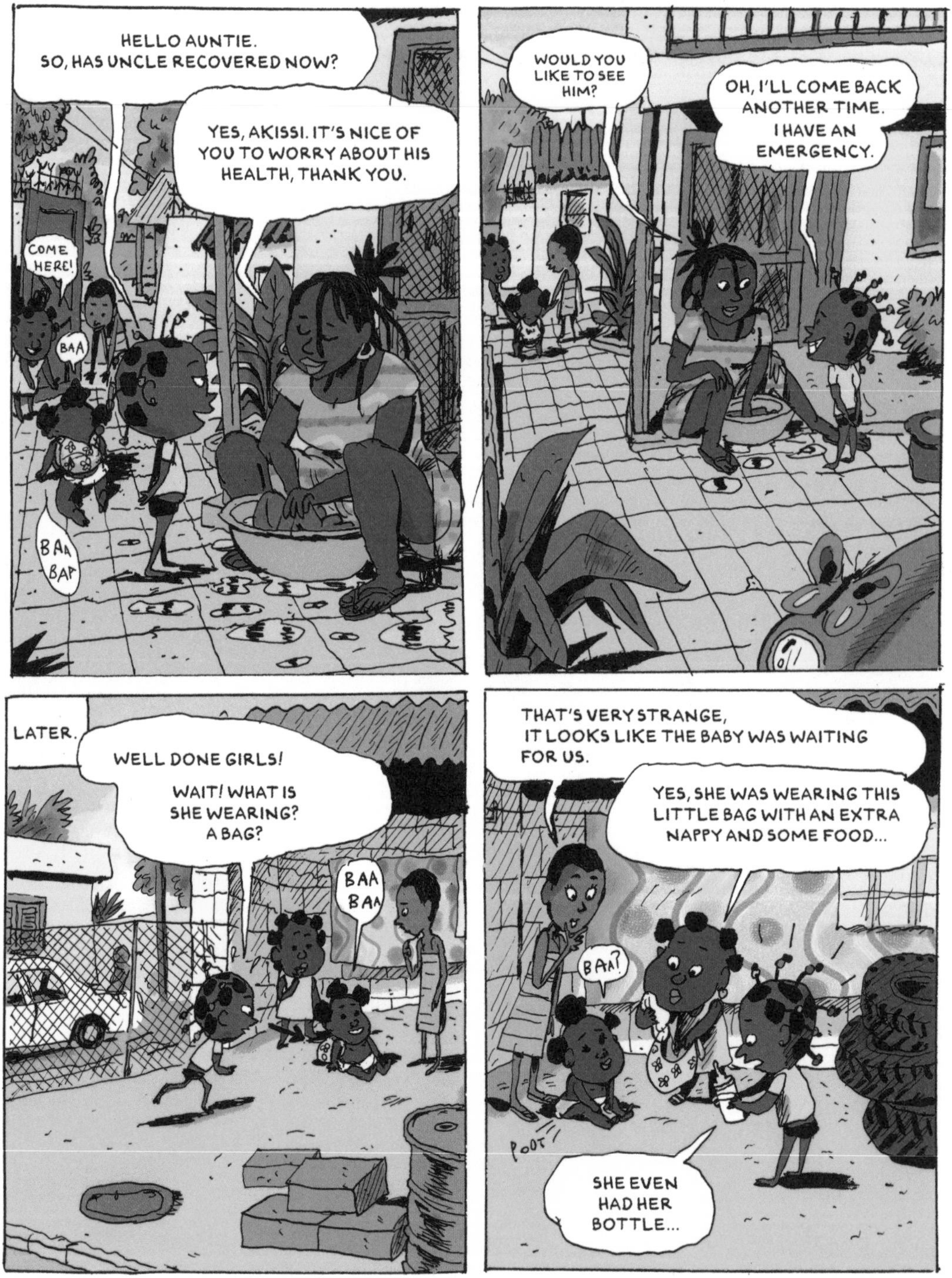
HELLO AUNTIE.
SO, HAS UNCLE RECOVERED NOW?
YES, AKISSI. IT'S NICE OF YOU TO WORRY ABOUT HIS HEALTH, THANK YOU.
COME HERE!
BAA
BAA BAP
WOULD YOU LIKE TO SEE HIM?
OH, I'LL COME BACK ANOTHER TIME. I HAVE AN EMERGENCY.
LATER.
WELL DONE GIRLS!
WAIT! WHAT IS SHE WEARING? A BAG?
BAA BAA
THAT'S VERY STRANGE, IT LOOKS LIKE THE BABY WAS WAITING FOR US.
YES, SHE WAS WEARING THIS LITTLE BAG WITH AN EXTRA NAPPY AND SOME FOOD...
BAA?
POOT
SHE EVEN HAD HER BOTTLE...

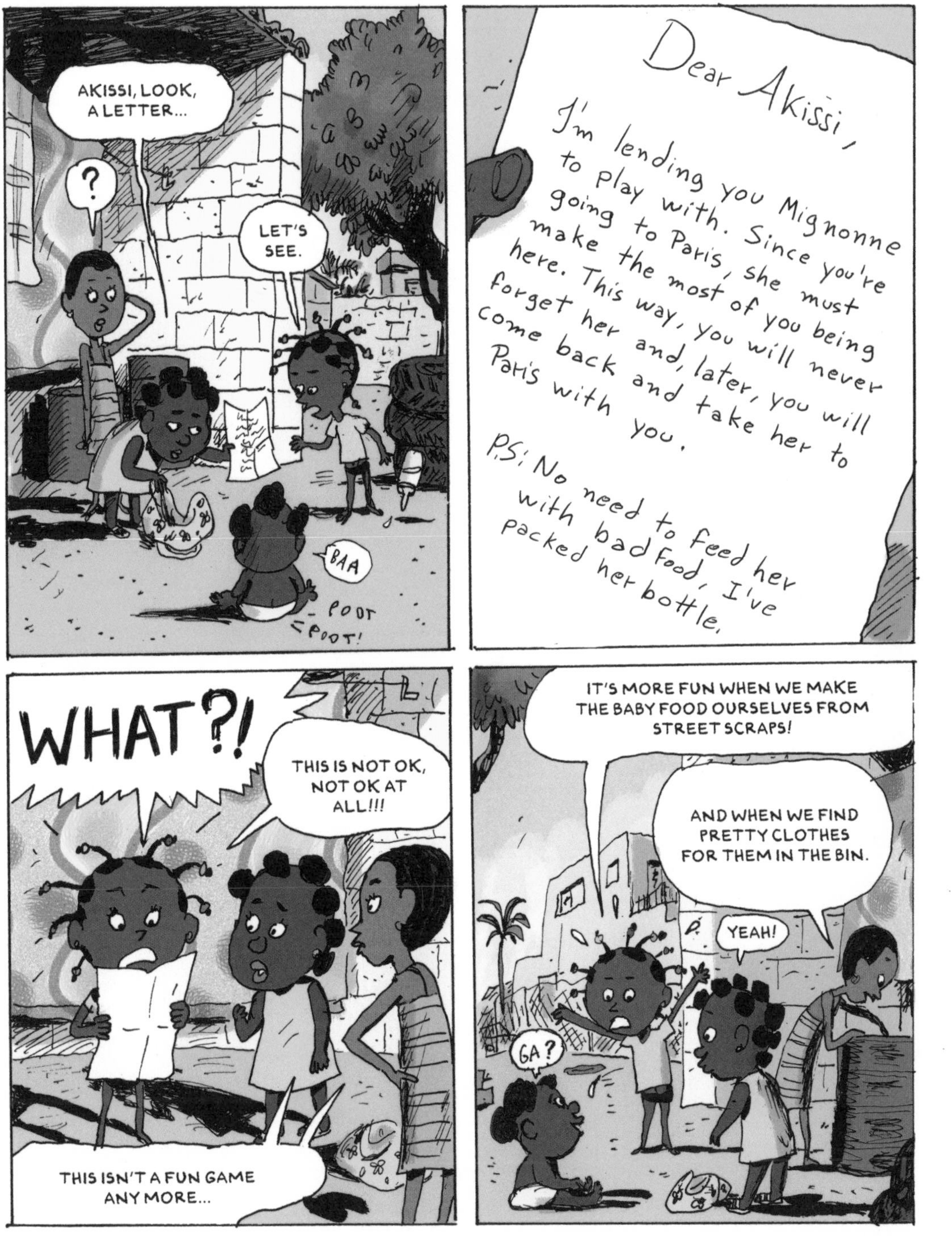
AKISSI, LOOK, A LETTER...
?
LET'S SEE.
BAA
POOT POOT!
Dear Akissi,
I'm lending you Mignonne to play with. Since you're going to Paris, she must make the most of you being here. This way, you will never forget her and, later, you will come back and take her to Paris with you.
P.S: No need to feed her with bad food, I've packed her bottle.
WHAT?!
THIS IS NOT OK, NOT OK AT ALL!!!
THIS ISN'T A FUN GAME ANYMORE...
IT'S MORE FUN WHEN WE MAKE THE BABY FOOD OURSELVES FROM STREET SCRAPS!
AND WHEN WE FIND PRETTY CLOTHES FOR THEM IN THE BIN.
YEAH!
GA?

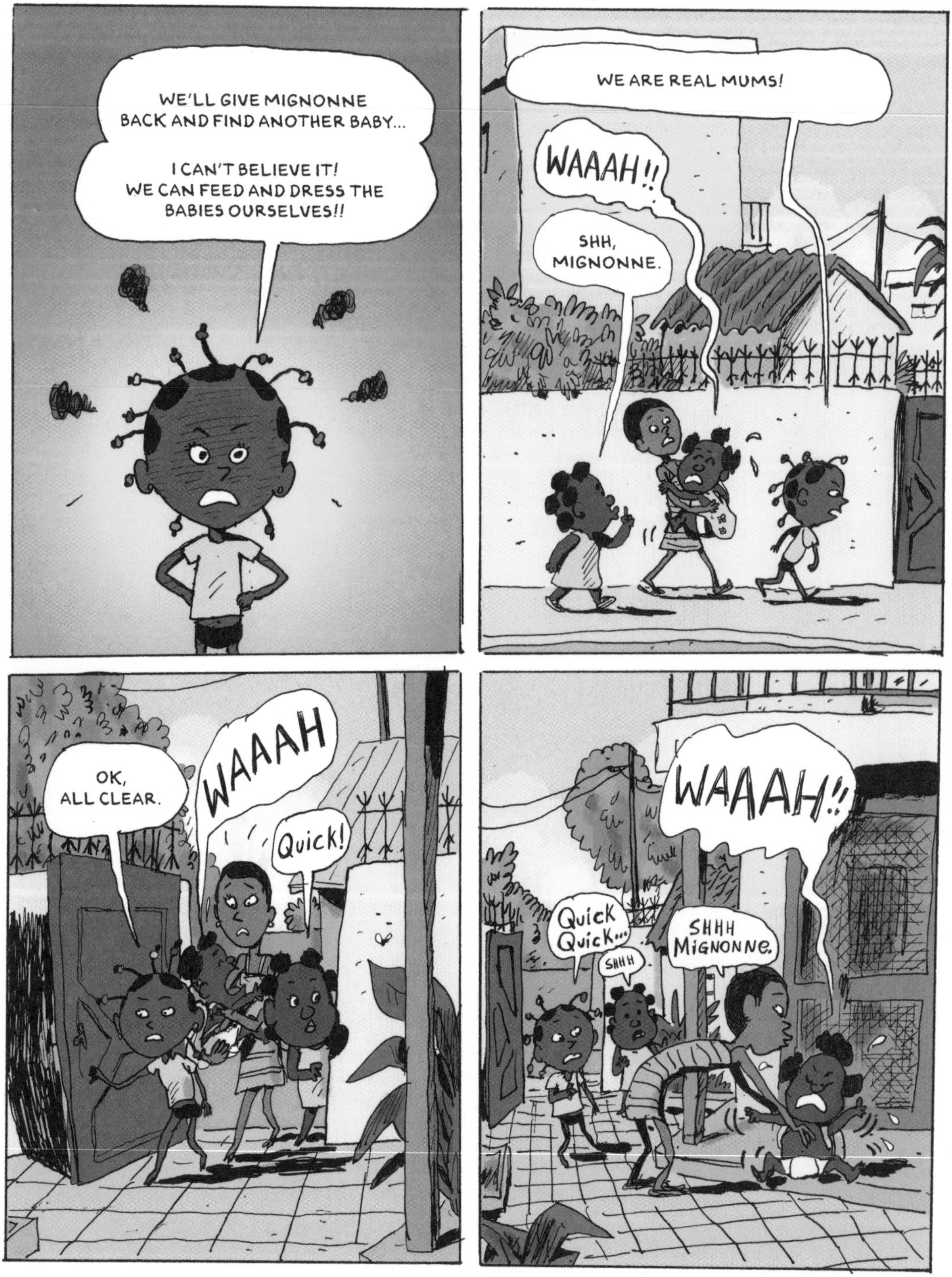
WE'LL GIVE MIGNONNE BACK AND FIND ANOTHER BABY...
I CAN'T BELIEVE IT! WE CAN FEED AND DRESS THE BABIES OURSELVES!!
WE ARE REAL MUMS!
WAAAH!!
SHH, MIGNONNE.
OK, ALL CLEAR.
WAAAH
Quick!
WAAAH!!
Quick Quick...
SHHH
SHHH Mignonne.

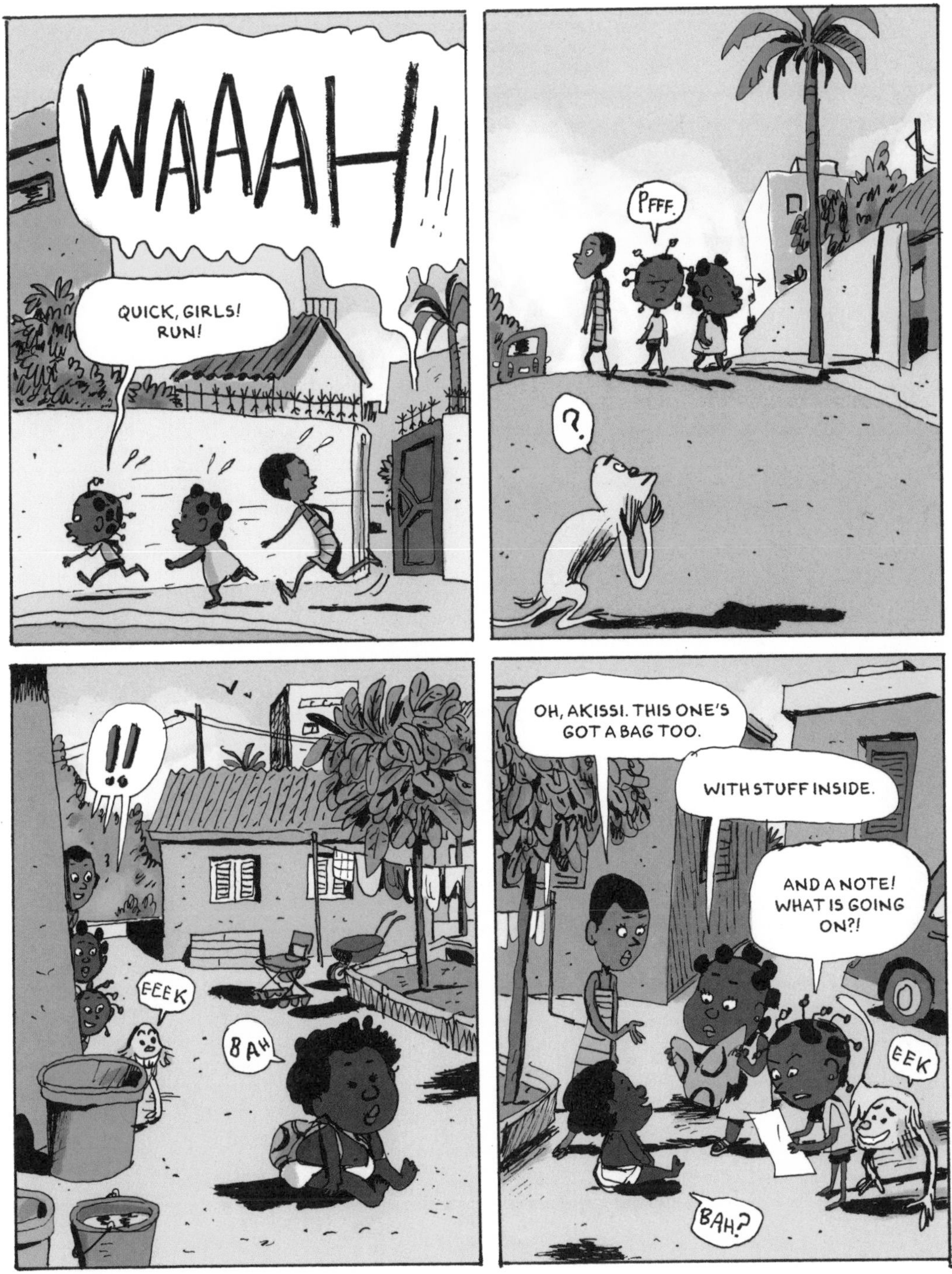
WAAAH
QUICK, GIRLS! RUN!
PFFF.
?
!!
EEEK
BAH
OH, AKISSI. THIS ONE'S GOT A BAG TOO.
WITH STUFF INSIDE.
AND A NOTE! WHAT IS GOING ON?!
EEK
BAH?

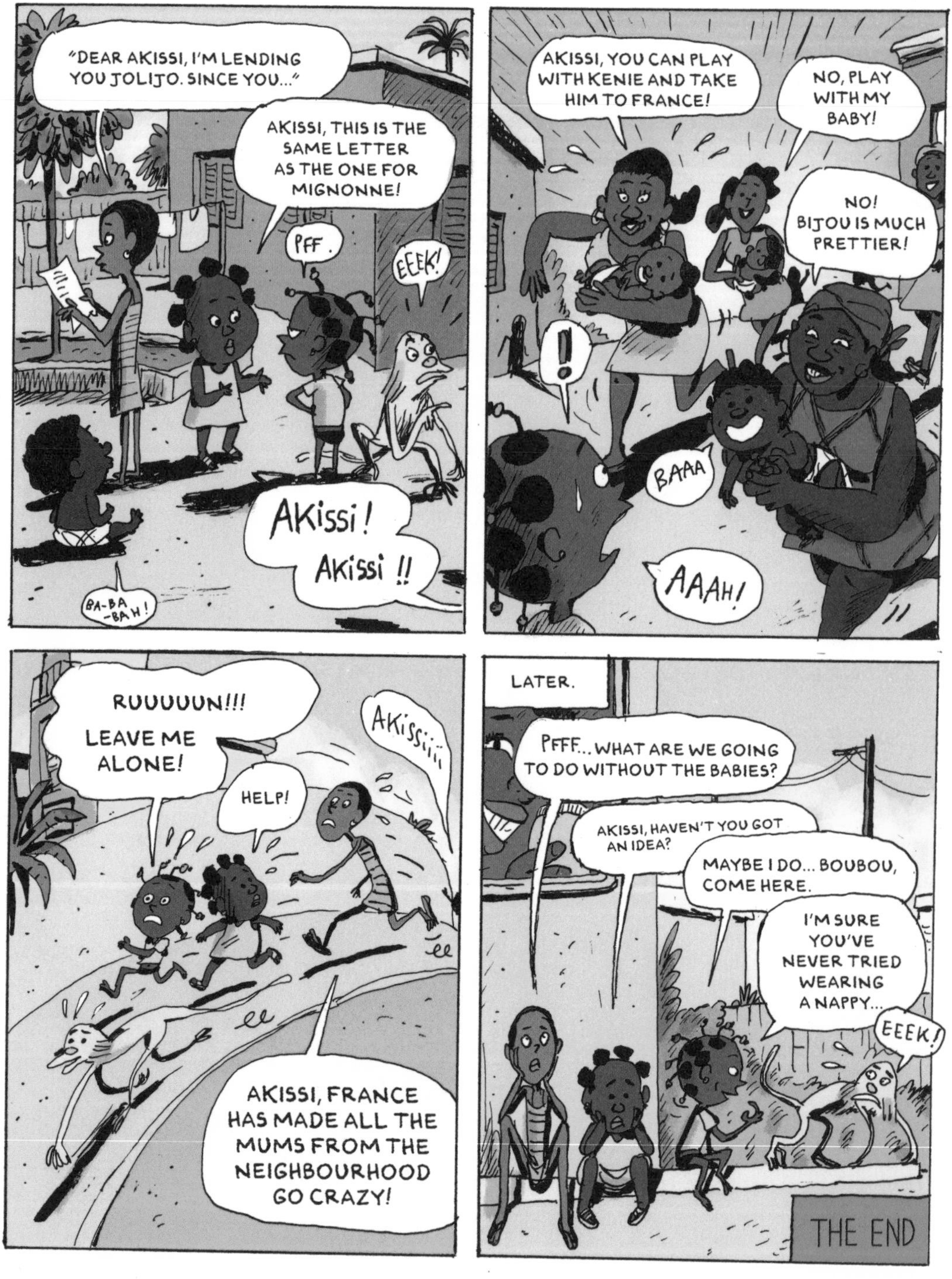
"DEAR AKISSI, I'M LENDING YOU JOLIJO. SINCE YOU..."
AKISSI, THIS IS THE SAME LETTER AS THE ONE FOR MIGNONNE!
PFF.
EEEK!
AKissi! Akissi !!
BA-BA-BAH!
AKISSI, YOU CAN PLAY WITH KENIE AND TAKE HIM TO FRANCE!
NO, PLAY WITH MY BABY!
NO! BIJOU IS MUCH PRETTIER!
!
BAAA
AAAH!
RUUUUUN!!!
LEAVE ME ALONE!
HELP!
AKissi!!!
AKISSI, FRANCE HAS MADE ALL THE MUMS FROM THE NEIGHBOURHOOD GO CRAZY!
LATER.
PFFF... WHAT ARE WE GOING TO DO WITHOUT THE BABIES?
AKISSI, HAVEN'T YOU GOT AN IDEA?
MAYBE I DO... BOUBOU, COME HERE.
I'M SURE YOU'VE NEVER TRIED WEARING A NAPPY...
EEEK!
THE END

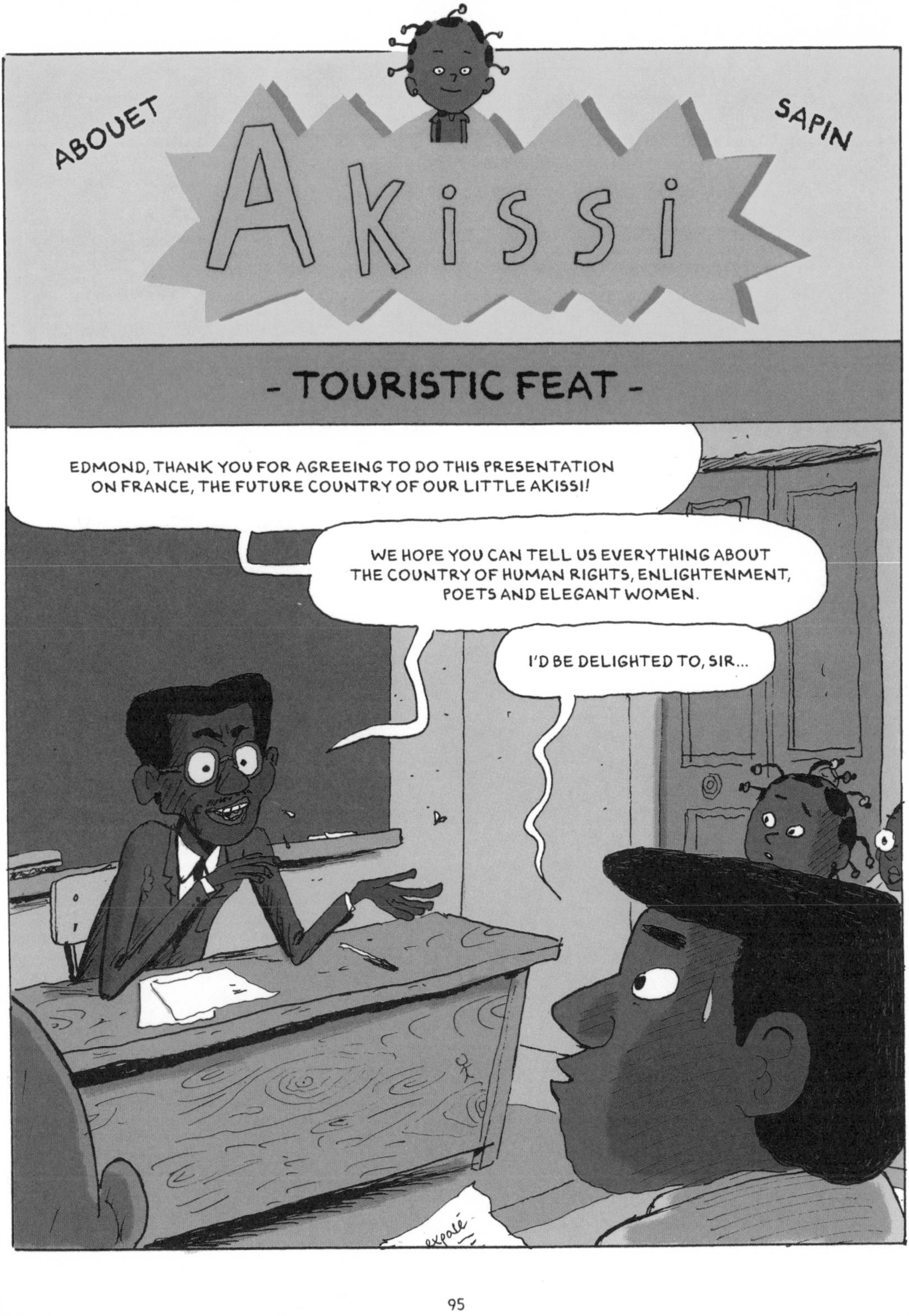
ABOUET
Akissi
SAPIN
- TOURISTIC FEAT -
EDMOND, THANK YOU FOR AGREEING TO DO THIS PRESENTATION ON FRANCE, THE FUTURE COUNTRY OF OUR LITTLE AKISSI!
WE HOPE YOU CAN TELL US EVERYTHING ABOUT THE COUNTRY OF HUMAN RIGHTS, ENLIGHTENMENT, POETS AND ELEGANT WOMEN.
I'D BE DELIGHTED TO, SIR...

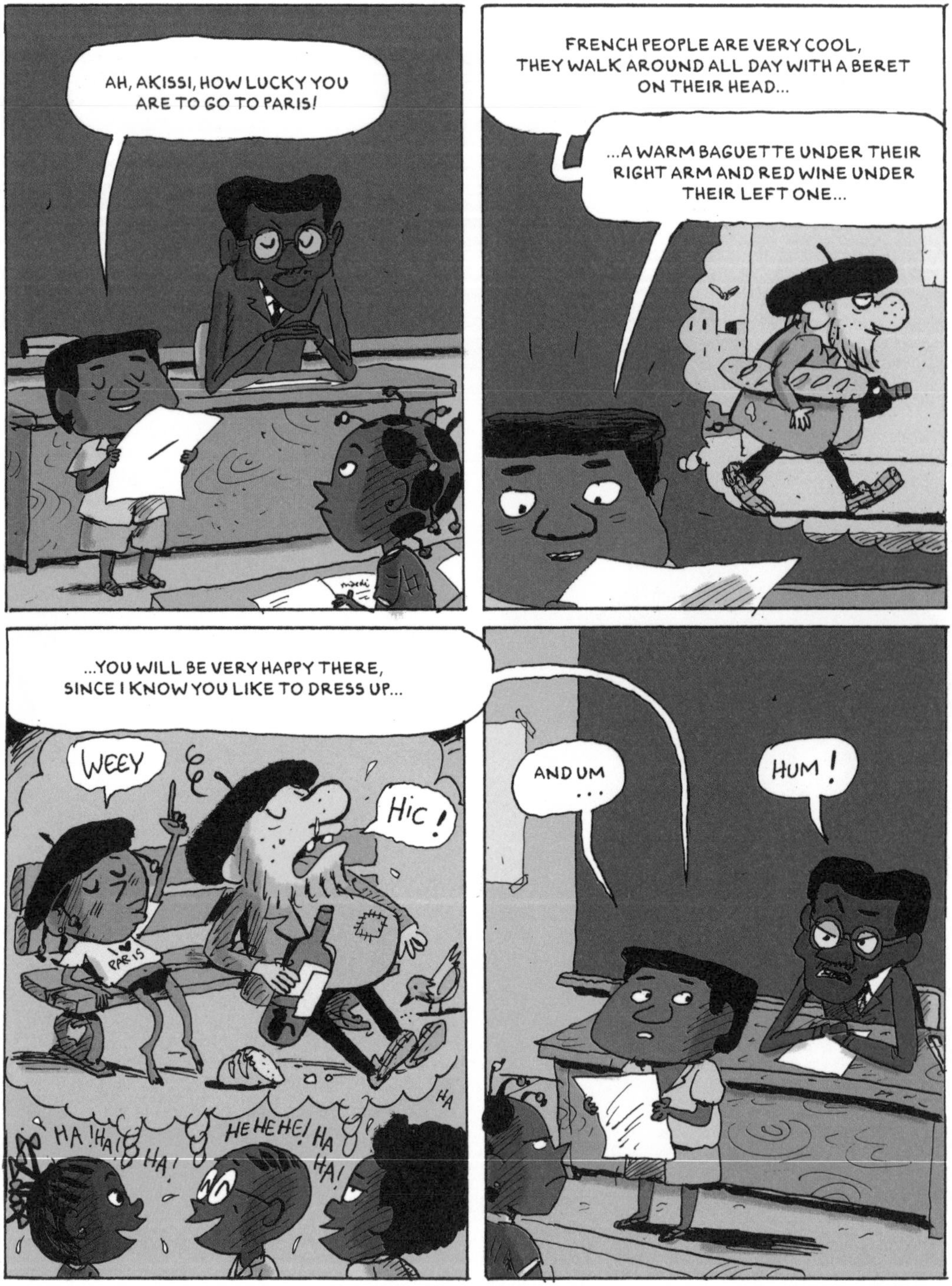
AH, AKISSI, HOW LUCKY YOU ARE TO GO TO PARIS!
FRENCH PEOPLE ARE VERY COOL, THEY WALK AROUND ALL DAY WITH A BERET ON THEIR HEAD...
...A WARM BAGUETTE UNDER THEIR RIGHT ARM AND RED WINE UNDER THEIR LEFT ONE...
...YOU WILL BE VERY HAPPY THERE, SINCE I KNOW YOU LIKE TO DRESS UP...
WEEY
Hic!
I ♥ PARIS
HA!HA! HA! HA!
HEHEHE! HA HA!
HA
AND UM ...
HUM!

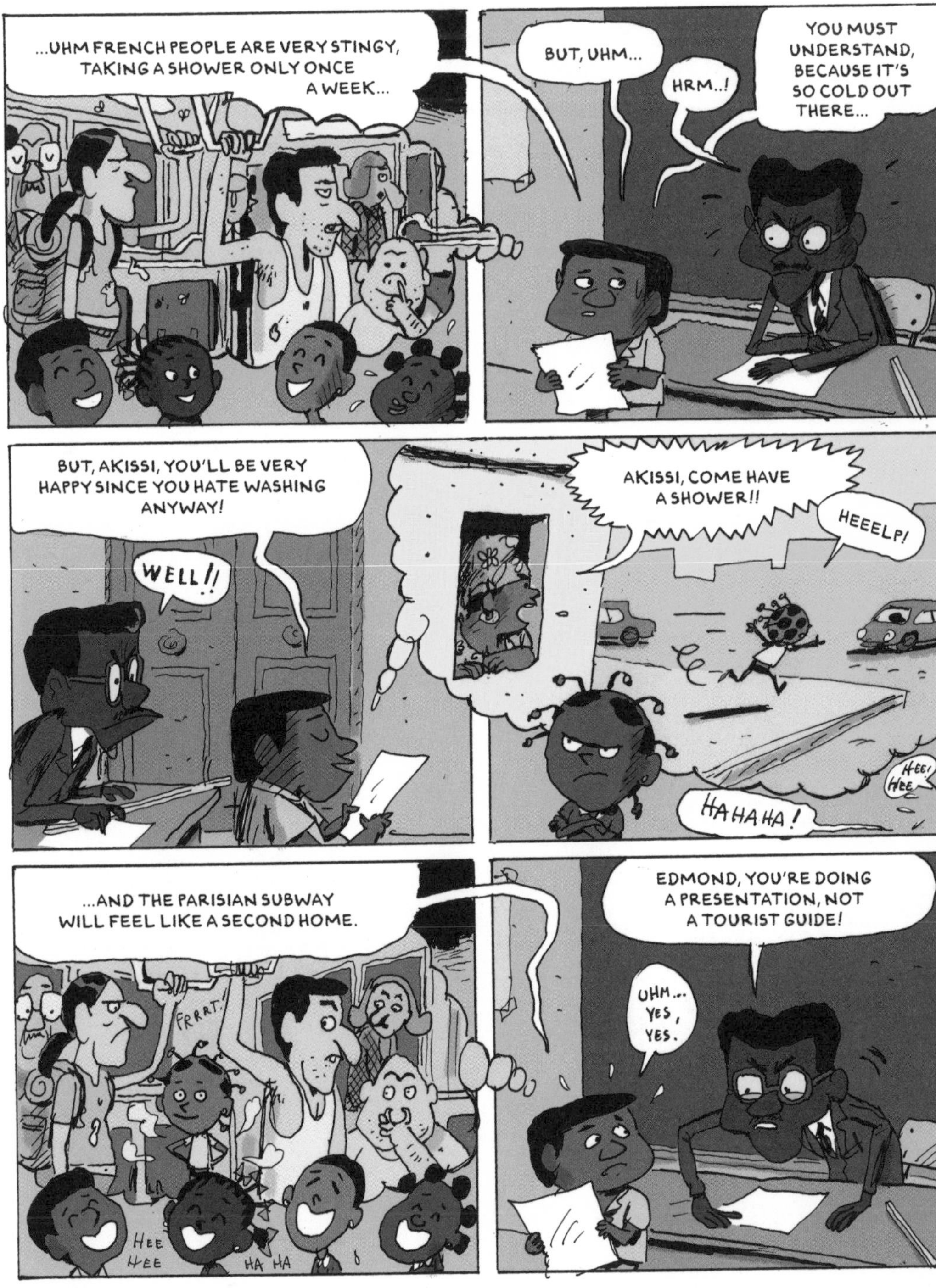
...UHM FRENCH PEOPLE ARE VERY STINGY, TAKING A SHOWER ONLY ONCE A WEEK...
BUT, UHM...
HRM..!
YOU MUST UNDERSTAND, BECAUSE IT'S SO COLD OUT THERE...
BUT, AKISSI, YOU'LL BE VERY HAPPY SINCE YOU HATE WASHING ANYWAY!
WELL!!
AKISSI, COME HAVE A SHOWER!!
HEEELP!
HEE! HEE
HAHAHA!
...AND THE PARISIAN SUBWAY WILL FEEL LIKE A SECOND HOME.
FRRRT!
HEE HEE
HA HA
EDMOND, YOU'RE DOING A PRESENTATION, NOT A TOURIST GUIDE!
UHM... YES, YES.

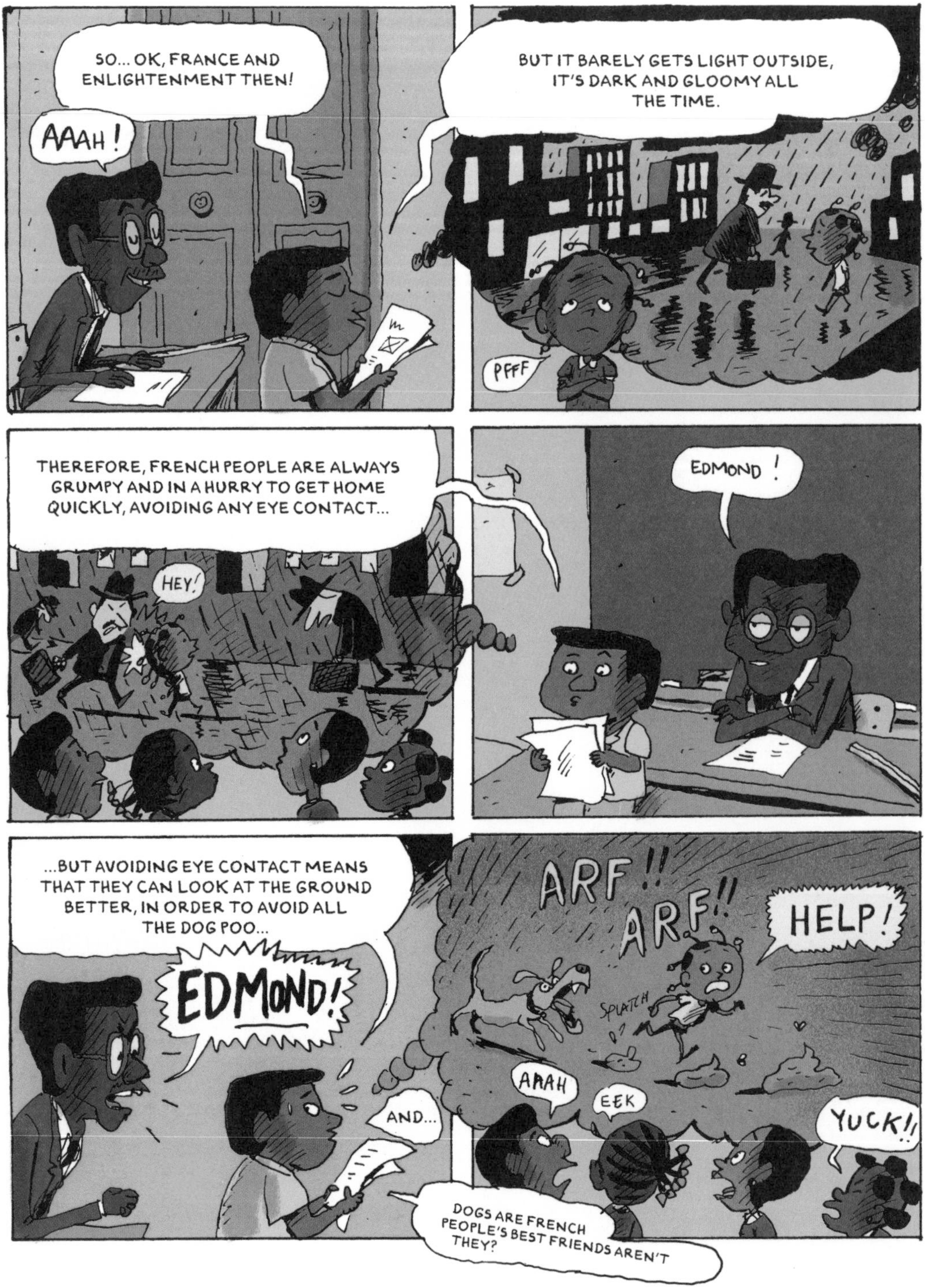

SO... OK, FRANCE AND ENLIGHTENMENT THEN!
AAAH!
BUT IT BARELY GETS LIGHT OUTSIDE, IT'S DARK AND GLOOMY ALL THE TIME.
PFFF
THEREFORE, FRENCH PEOPLE ARE ALWAYS GRUMPY AND IN A HURRY TO GET HOME QUICKLY, AVOIDING ANY EYE CONTACT...
HEY!
EDMOND!
...BUT AVOIDING EYE CONTACT MEANS THAT THEY CAN LOOK AT THE GROUND BETTER, IN ORDER TO AVOID ALL THE DOG POO...
EDMOND!
ARF!!
ARF!!
HELP!
SPLATCH
AAAH
EEK
AND...
YUCK!!
DOGS ARE FRENCH PEOPLE'S BEST FRIENDS AREN'T THEY?

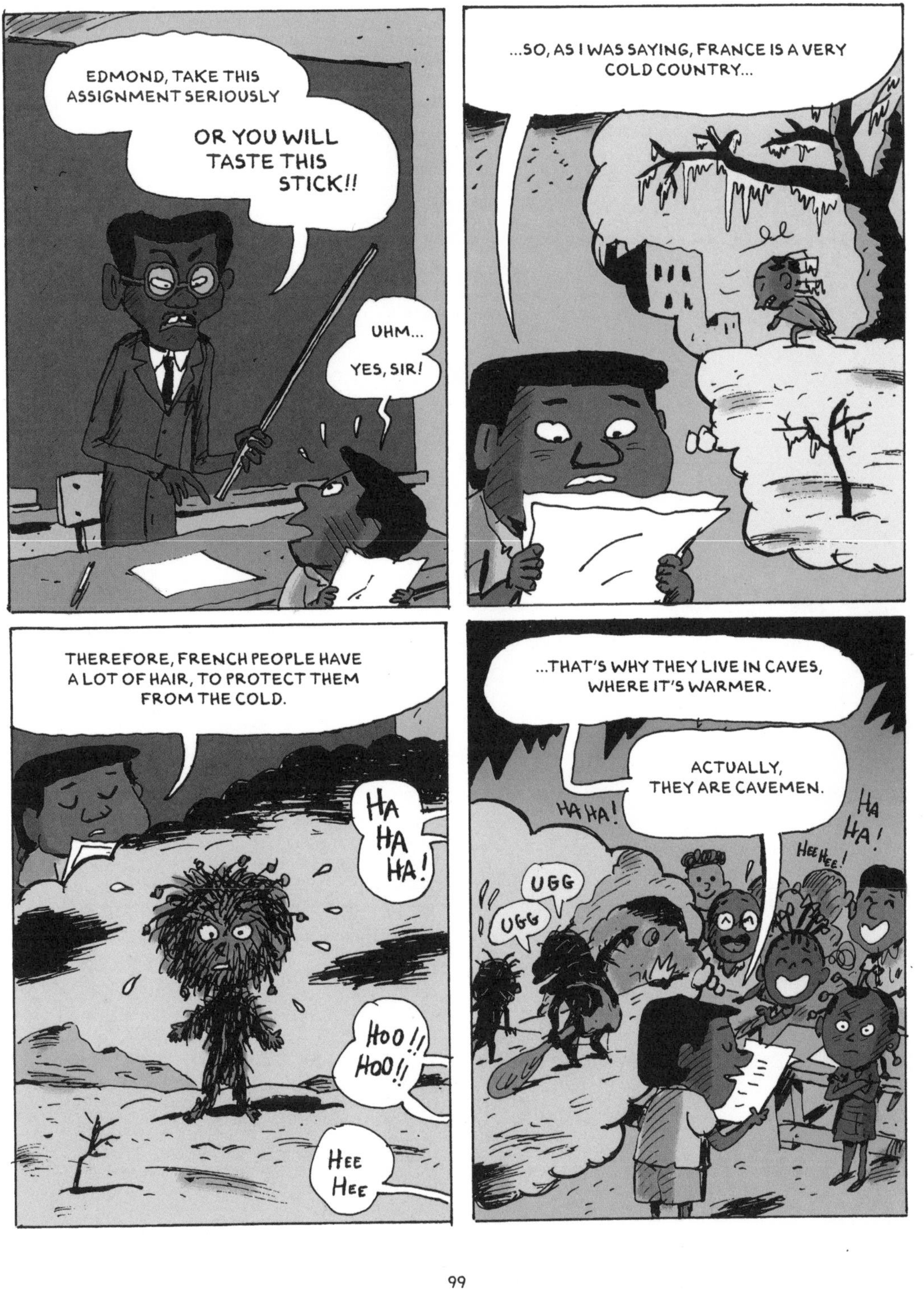
EDMOND, TAKE THIS ASSIGNMENT SERIOUSLY
OR YOU WILL TASTE THIS STICK!!
UHM...
YES, SIR!
...SO, AS I WAS SAYING, FRANCE IS A VERY COLD COUNTRY...
THEREFORE, FRENCH PEOPLE HAVE A LOT OF HAIR, TO PROTECT THEM FROM THE COLD.
HA HA HA!
HOO!! HOO!!
HEE HEE
...THAT'S WHY THEY LIVE IN CAVES, WHERE IT'S WARMER.
ACTUALLY, THEY ARE CAVEMEN.
HA HA!
HA HA!
HEE HEE!
UGG
UGG

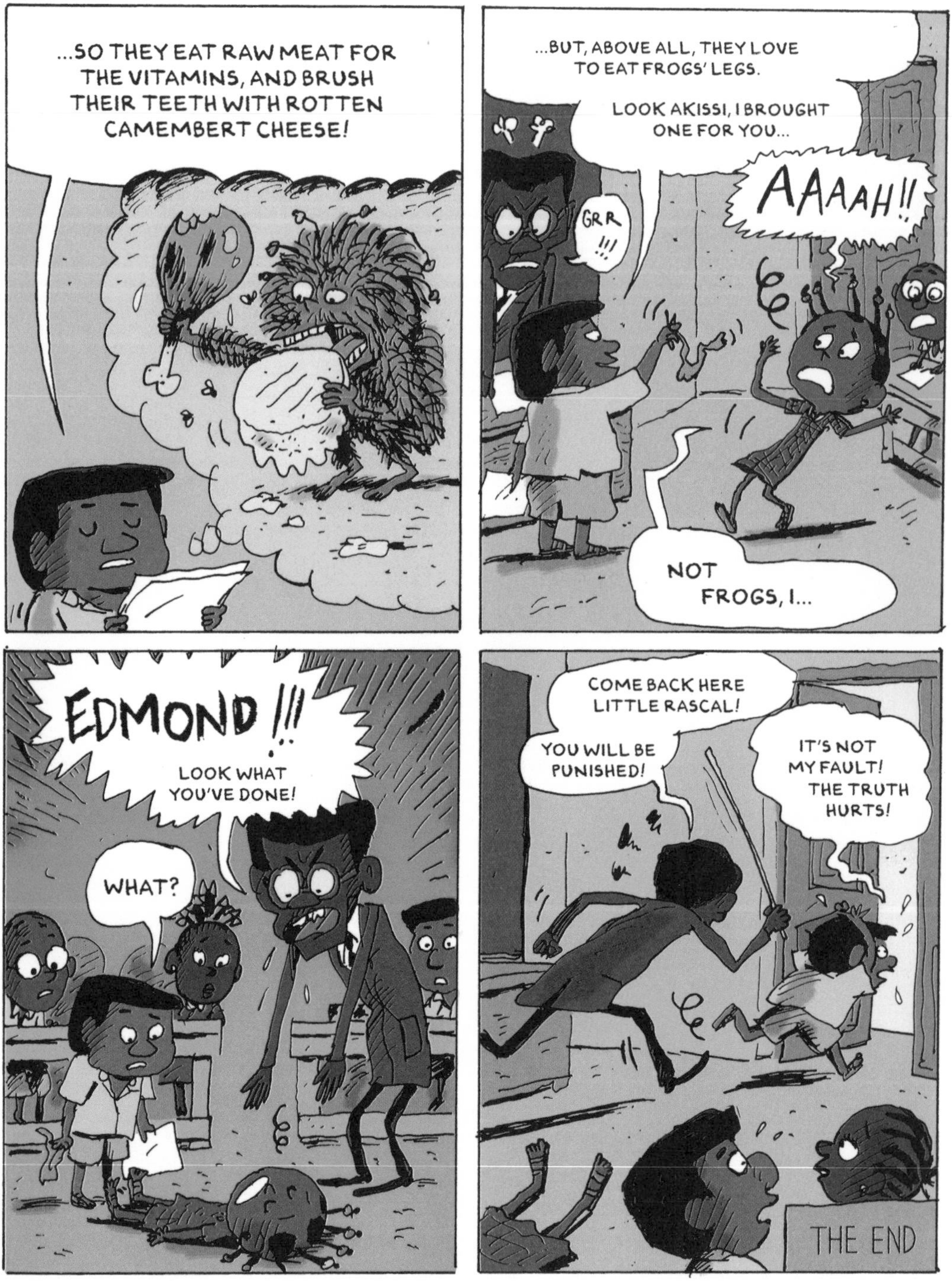

...SO THEY EAT RAW MEAT FOR THE VITAMINS, AND BRUSH THEIR TEETH WITH ROTTEN CAMEMBERT CHEESE!
...BUT, ABOVE ALL, THEY LOVE TO EAT FROGS' LEGS.
LOOK AKISSI, I BROUGHT ONE FOR YOU...
GRR !!!
AAAAH!!
NOT FROGS, I...
EDMOND!!!
LOOK WHAT YOU'VE DONE!
WHAT?
COME BACK HERE LITTLE RASCAL!
YOU WILL BE PUNISHED!
IT'S NOT MY FAULT! THE TRUTH HURTS!
THE END

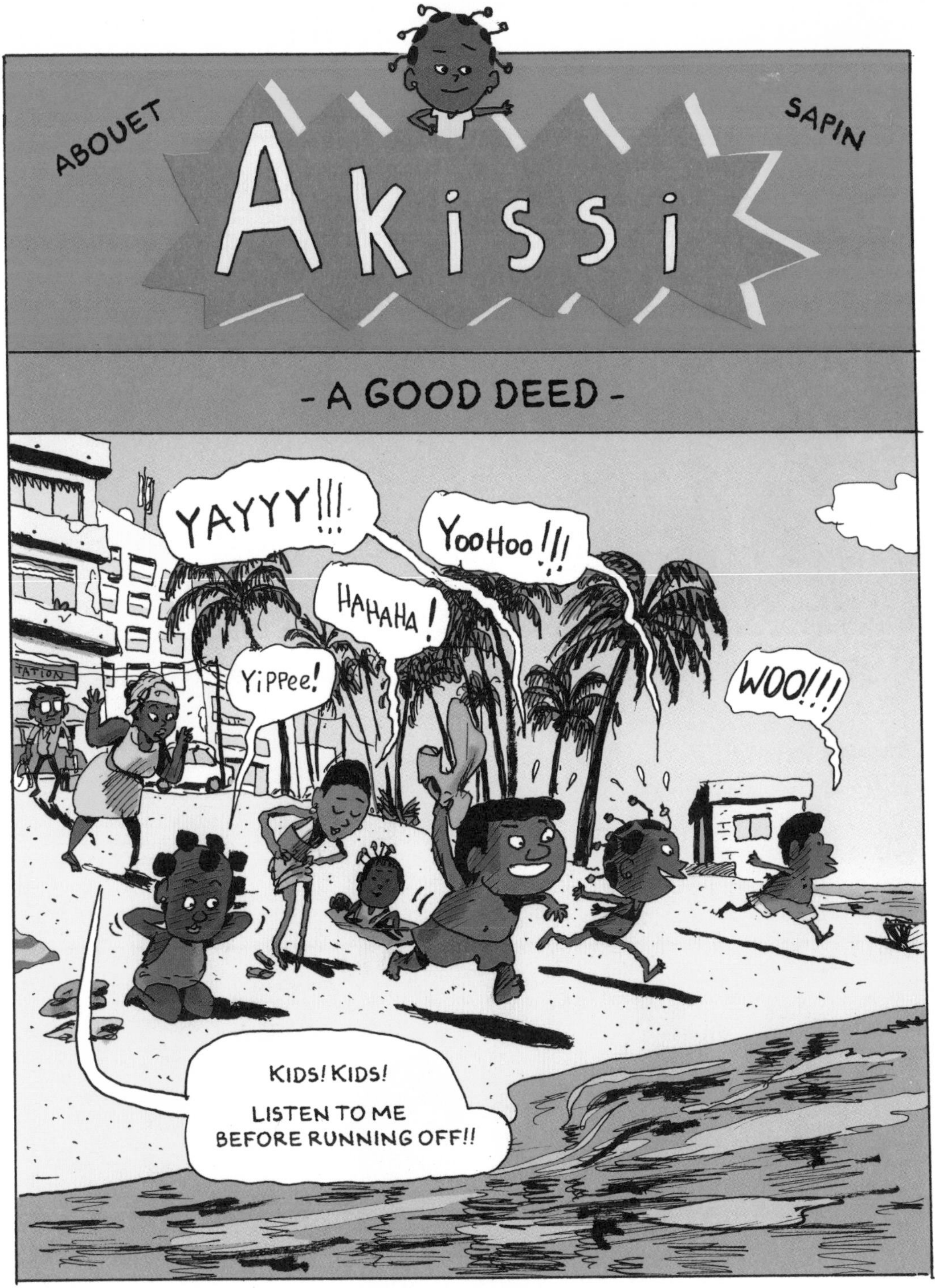
ABOUET
Akissi
SAPIN
- A GOOD DEED -
YAYYY!!!
YooHoo!!!
HAHAHA!
Yippee!
WOO!!!
TATION
KIDS! KIDS!
LISTEN TO ME BEFORE RUNNING OFF!!

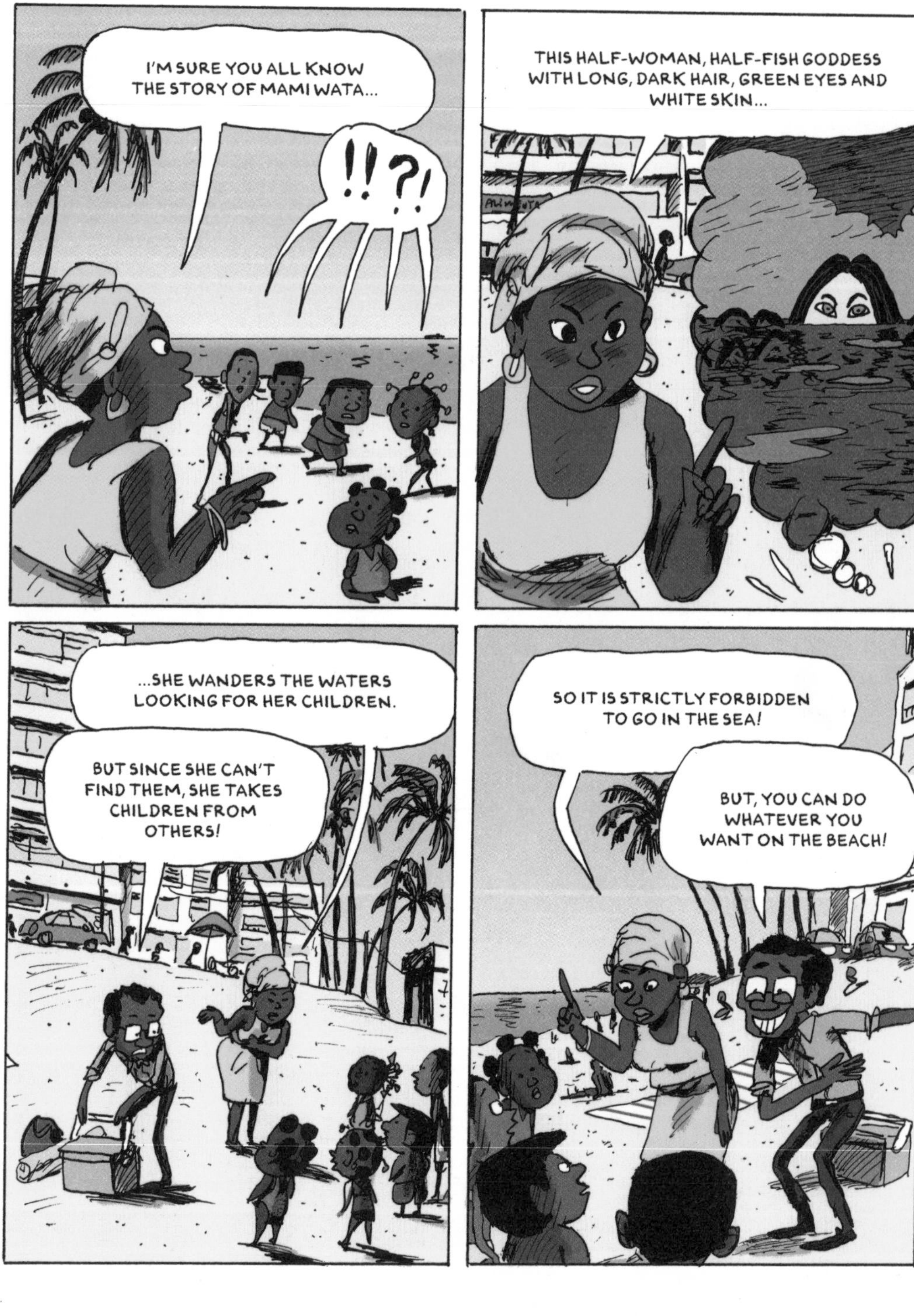
I'M SURE YOU ALL KNOW THE STORY OF MAMI WATA...
!!?!
THIS HALF-WOMAN, HALF-FISH GODDESS WITH LONG, DARK HAIR, GREEN EYES AND WHITE SKIN...
...SHE WANDERS THE WATERS LOOKING FOR HER CHILDREN.
BUT SINCE SHE CAN'T FIND THEM, SHE TAKES CHILDREN FROM OTHERS!
SO IT IS STRICTLY FORBIDDEN TO GO IN THE SEA!
BUT, YOU CAN DO WHATEVER YOU WANT ON THE BEACH!

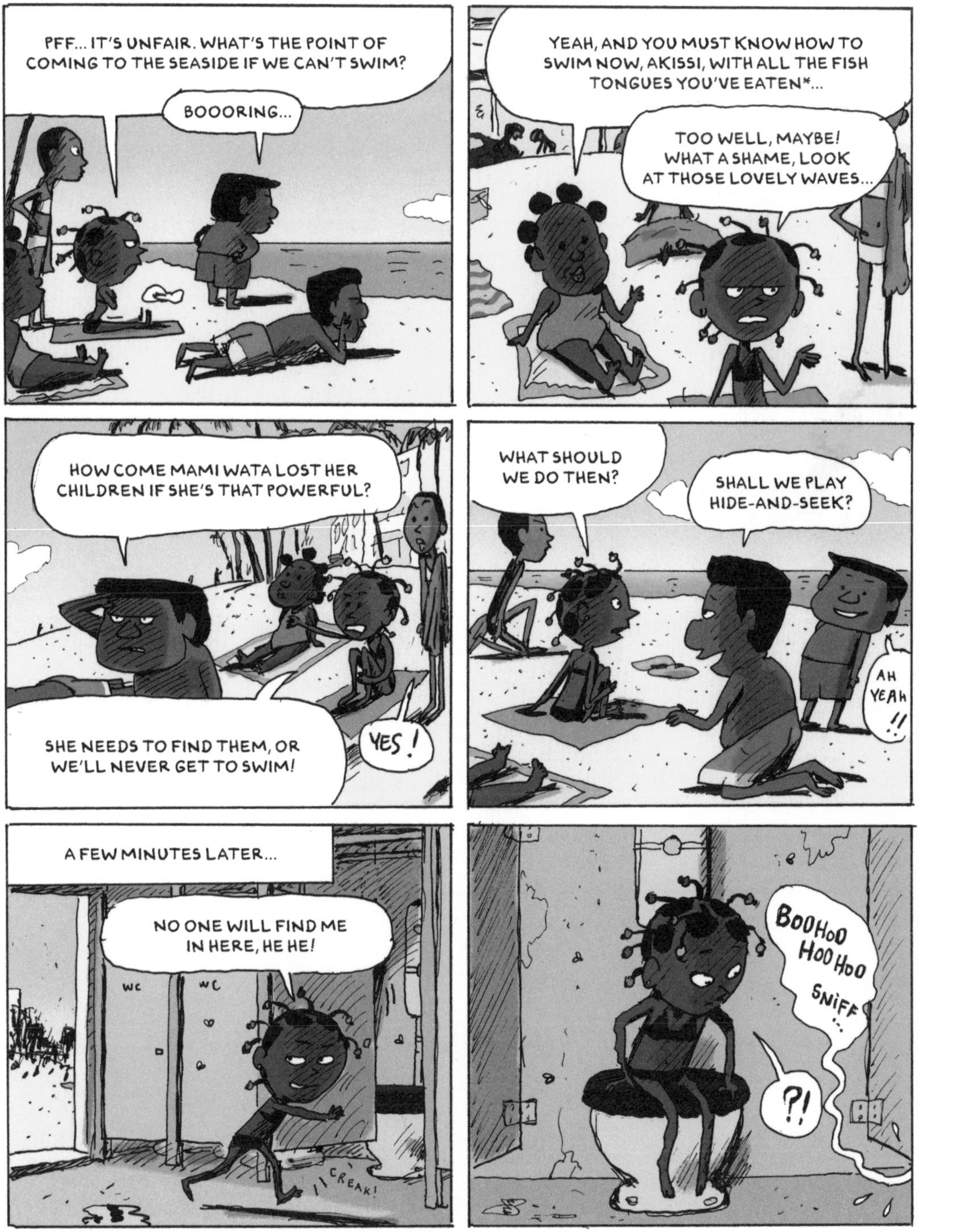
PFF... IT'S UNFAIR. WHAT'S THE POINT OF COMING TO THE SEASIDE IF WE CAN'T SWIM?
BOOORING...
YEAH, AND YOU MUST KNOW HOW TO SWIM NOW, AKISSI, WITH ALL THE FISH TONGUES YOU'VE EATEN*...
TOO WELL, MAYBE! WHAT A SHAME, LOOK AT THOSE LOVELY WAVES...
HOW COME MAMI WATA LOST HER CHILDREN IF SHE'S THAT POWERFUL?
SHE NEEDS TO FIND THEM, OR WE'LL NEVER GET TO SWIM!
YES!
WHAT SHOULD WE DO THEN?
SHALL WE PLAY HIDE-AND-SEEK?
AH YEAH !!
A FEW MINUTES LATER...
NO ONE WILL FIND ME IN HERE, HE HE!
WC
WC
CREAK!
BOOHOO HOOHOO
SNIFF...
?!

* SEE THE FISH TONGUE STORY IN *AKISSI: TALES OF MISCHIEF.*

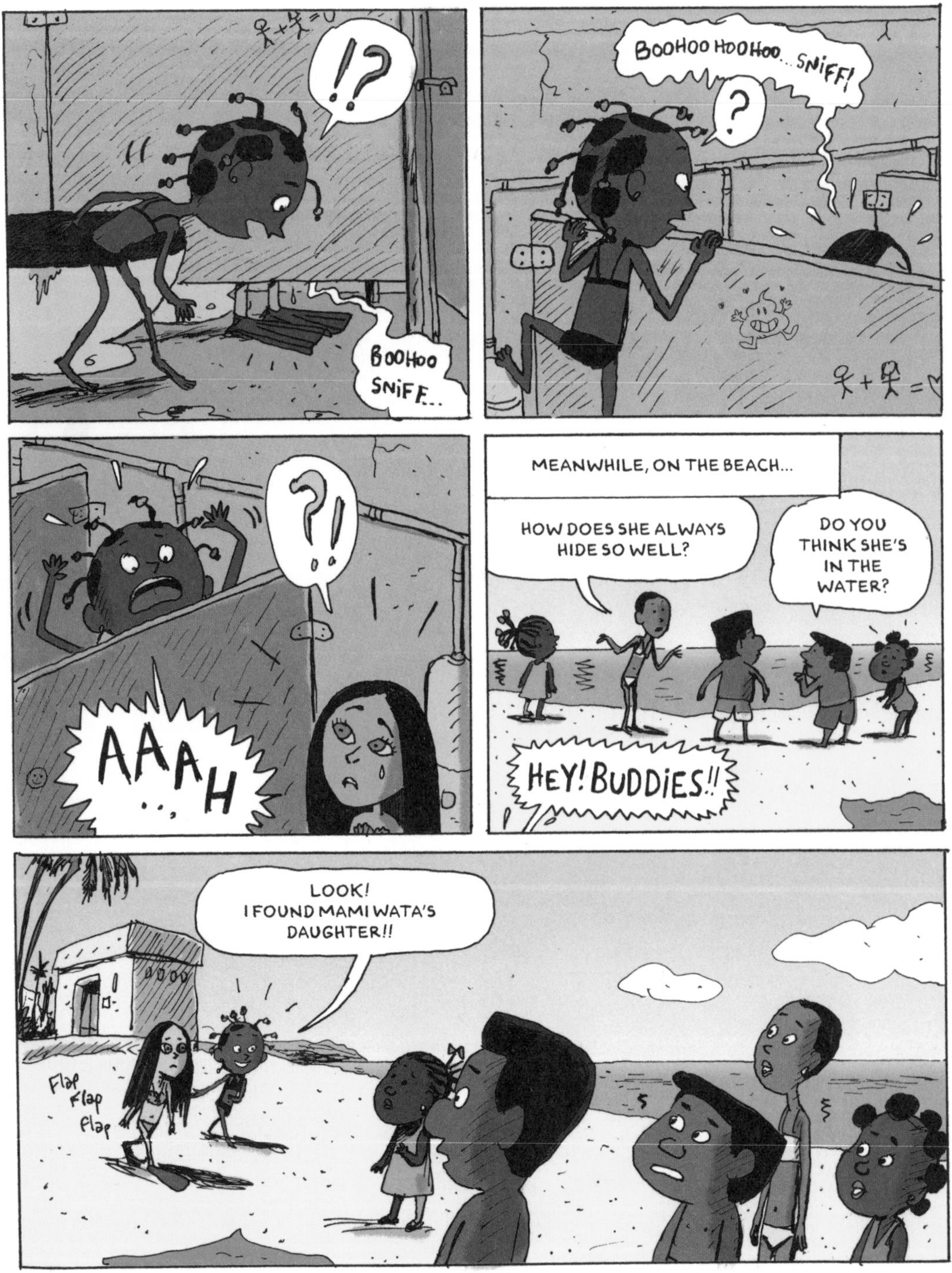

!?
BOOHOO SNIFF...
BOOHOO HOOHOO... SNIFF!
?
?!
AAAH...
MEANWHILE, ON THE BEACH...
HOW DOES SHE ALWAYS HIDE SO WELL?
DO YOU THINK SHE'S IN THE WATER?
HEY! BUDDIES!!
LOOK! I FOUND MAMI WATA'S DAUGHTER!!
Flap Flap Flap

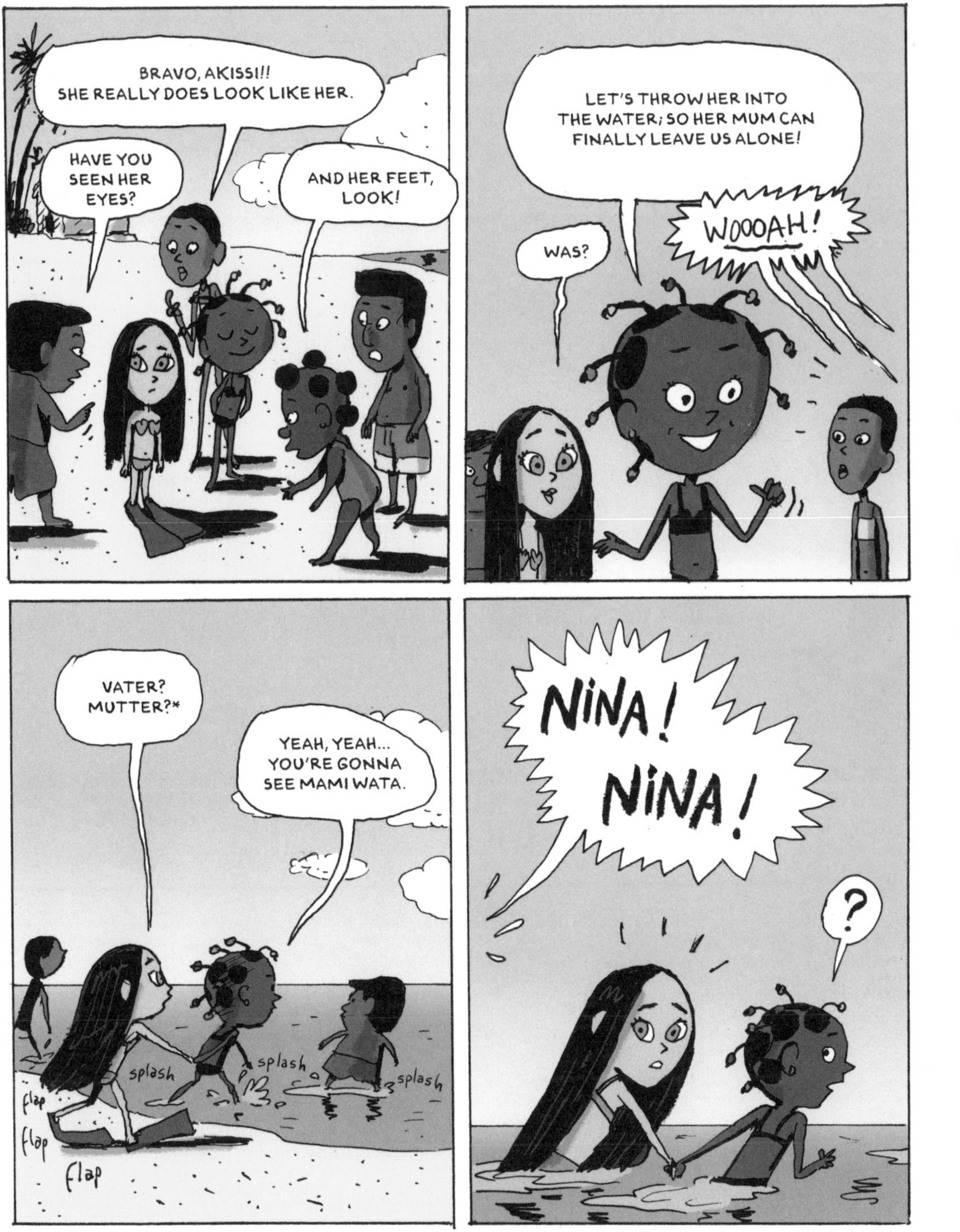
BRAVO, AKISSI!! SHE REALLY DOES LOOK LIKE HER.
HAVE YOU SEEN HER EYES?
AND HER FEET, LOOK!
LET'S THROW HER INTO THE WATER; SO HER MUM CAN FINALLY LEAVE US ALONE!
WAS?
WOOOAH!
VATER? MUTTER?*
YEAH, YEAH... YOU'RE GONNA SEE MAMI WATA.
splash
splash
splash
flap
flap
flap
NINA! NINA!
?

* VATER – FATHER IN GERMAN, MUTTER – MOTHER IN GERMAN.

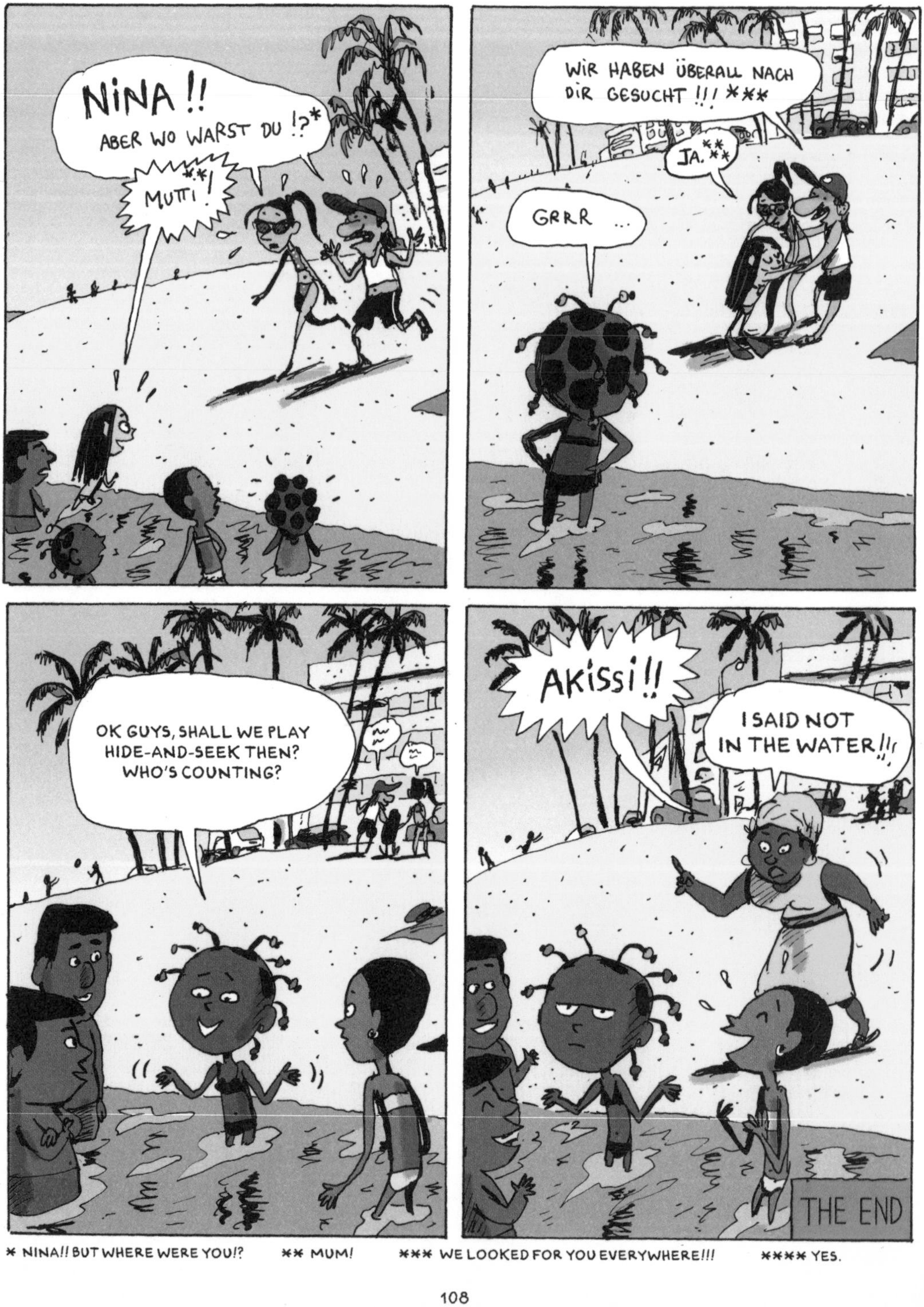
NINA!!
ABER WO WARST DU !?*
MUTTI!**
WIR HABEN ÜBERALL NACH DIR GESUCHT!!! ***
JA.****
GRRR ...
OK GUYS, SHALL WE PLAY HIDE-AND-SEEK THEN? WHO'S COUNTING?
AKISSI!!
I SAID NOT IN THE WATER!!!
THE END

* NINA!! BUT WHERE WERE YOU!? ** MUM! *** WE LOOKED FOR YOU EVERYWHERE!!! **** YES.

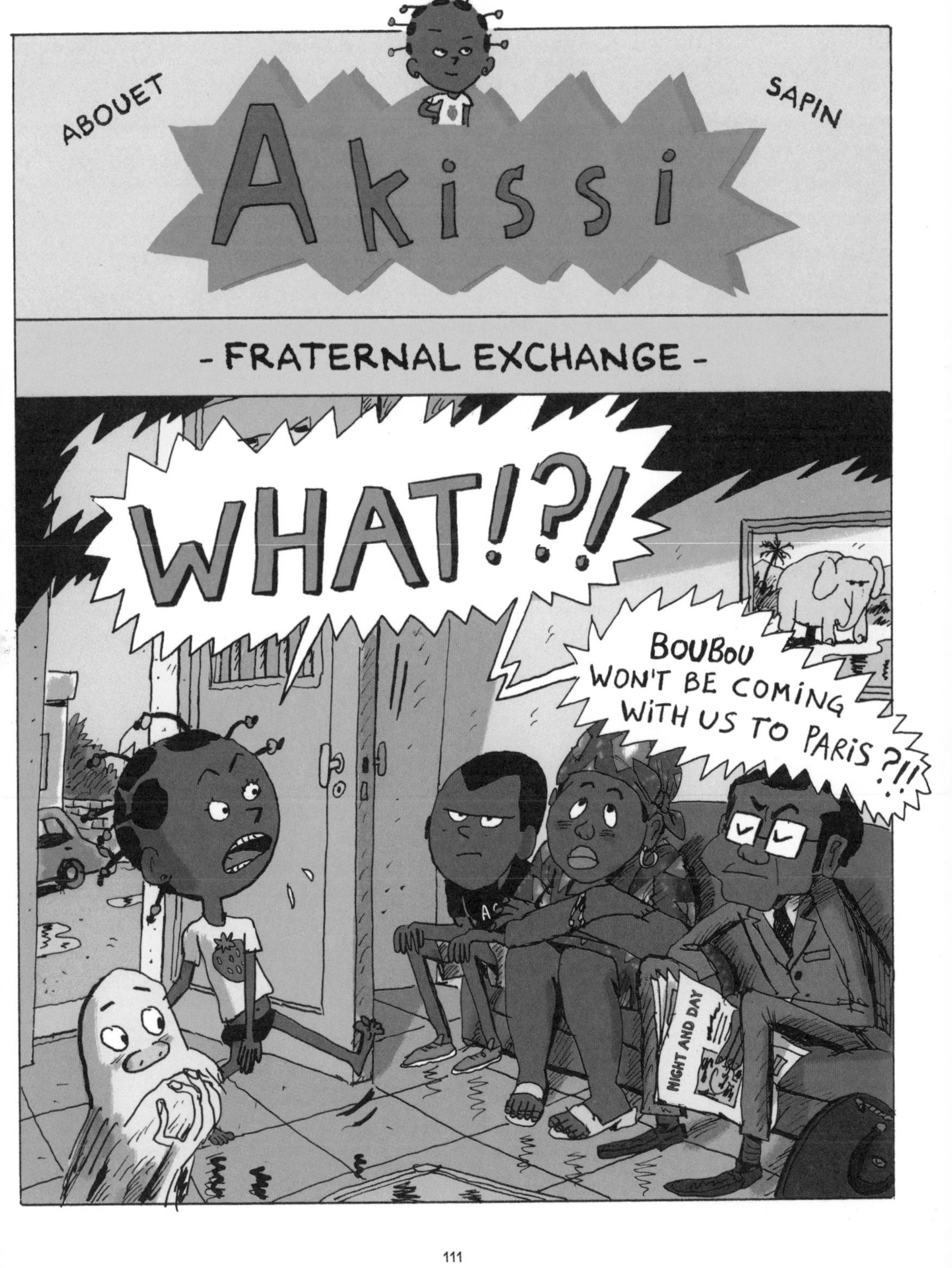
ABOUET
Akissi
SAPIN
- FRATERNAL EXCHANGE -
WHAT!?!
BOUBOU WON'T BE COMING WITH US TO PARIS ?!!
NIGHT AND DAY

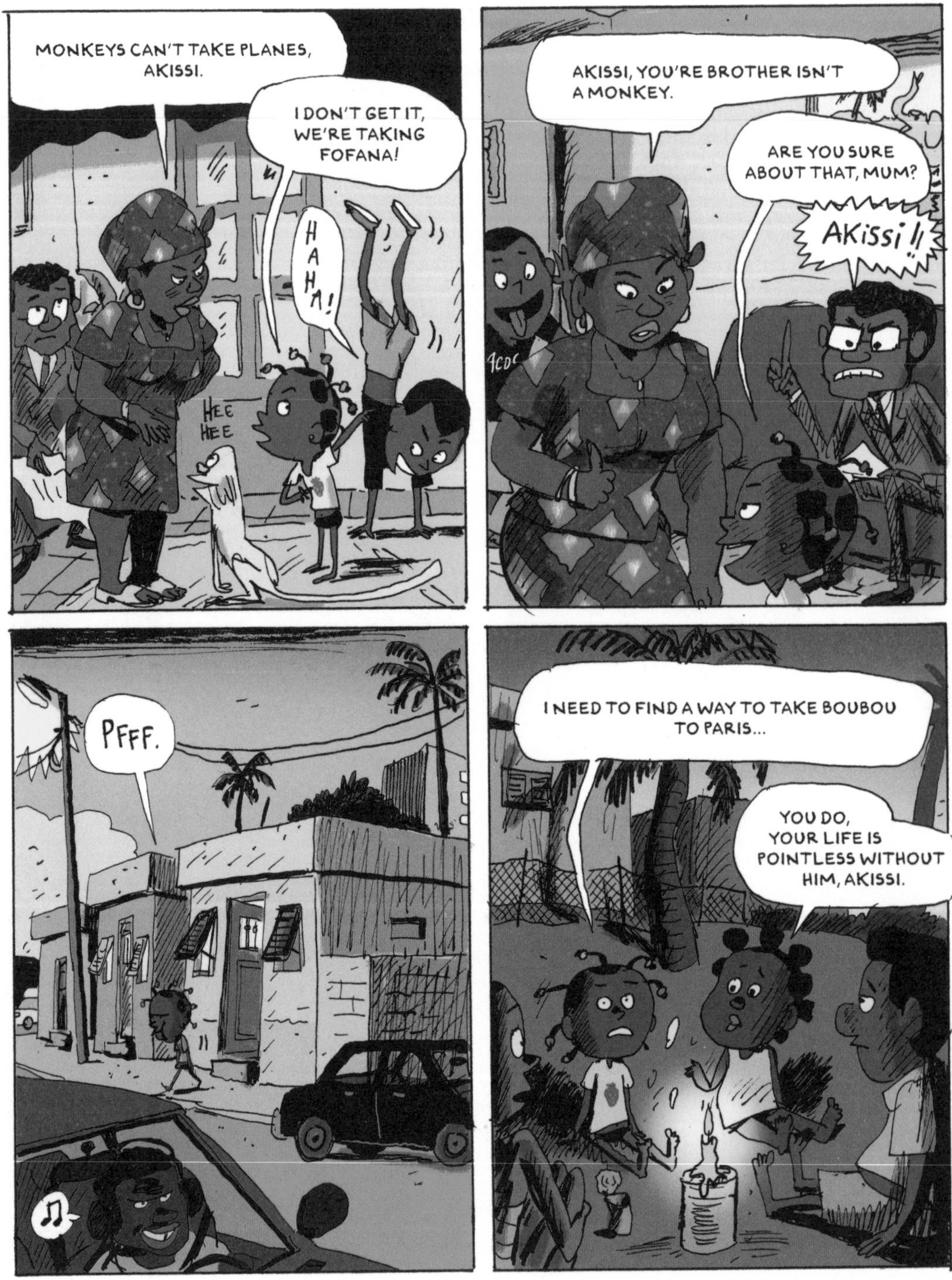
MONKEYS CAN'T TAKE PLANES, AKISSI.
I DON'T GET IT, WE'RE TAKING FOFANA!
HAHA!
HEE HEE
AKISSI, YOU'RE BROTHER ISN'T A MONKEY.
ARE YOU SURE ABOUT THAT, MUM?
AKISSI!!
PFFF.
I NEED TO FIND A WAY TO TAKE BOUBOU TO PARIS...
YOU DO, YOUR LIFE IS POINTLESS WITHOUT HIM, AKISSI.

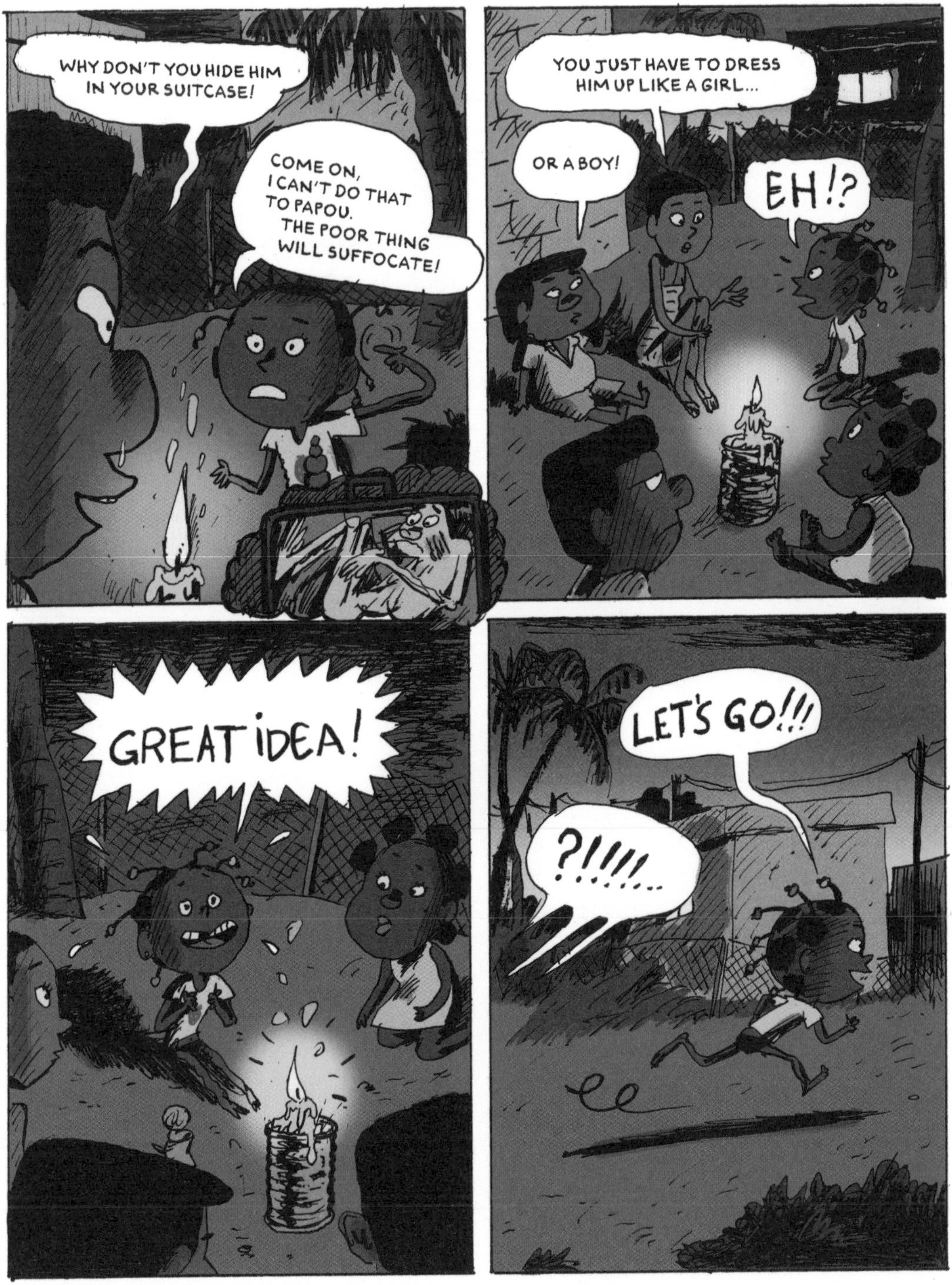
WHY DON'T YOU HIDE HIM IN YOUR SUITCASE!
COME ON, I CAN'T DO THAT TO PAPOU. THE POOR THING WILL SUFFOCATE!
YOU JUST HAVE TO DRESS HIM UP LIKE A GIRL...
OR A BOY!
EH!?
GREAT iDEA!
LET'S GO!!!
?!!!!...

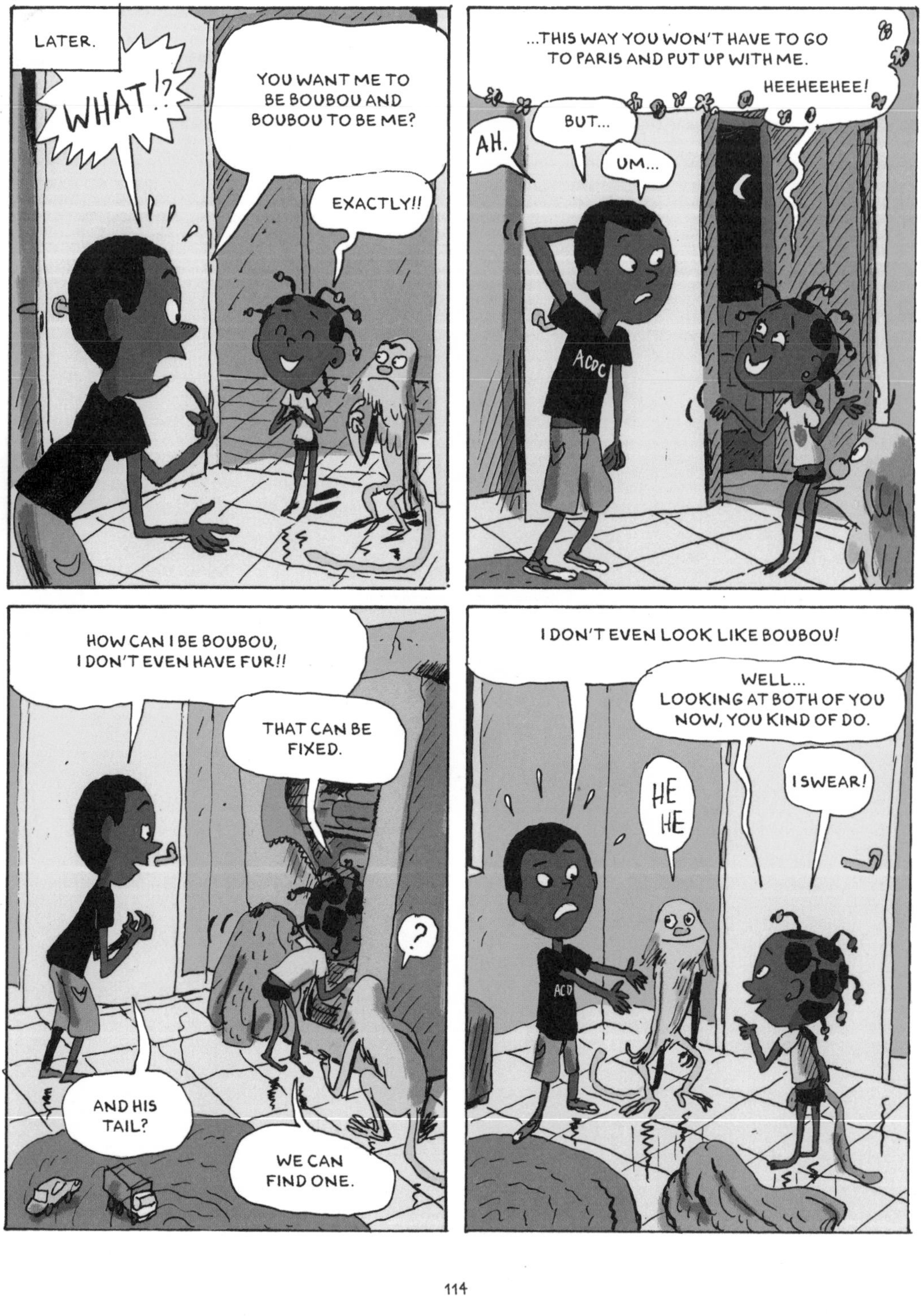
LATER.
WHAT!?
YOU WANT ME TO BE BOUBOU AND BOUBOU TO BE ME?
EXACTLY!!
...THIS WAY YOU WON'T HAVE TO GO TO PARIS AND PUT UP WITH ME.
HEEHEEHEE!
AH.
BUT...
UM...
HOW CAN I BE BOUBOU, I DON'T EVEN HAVE FUR!!
THAT CAN BE FIXED.
?
AND HIS TAIL?
WE CAN FIND ONE.
I DON'T EVEN LOOK LIKE BOUBOU!
WELL... LOOKING AT BOTH OF YOU NOW, YOU KIND OF DO.
HE HE
I SWEAR!

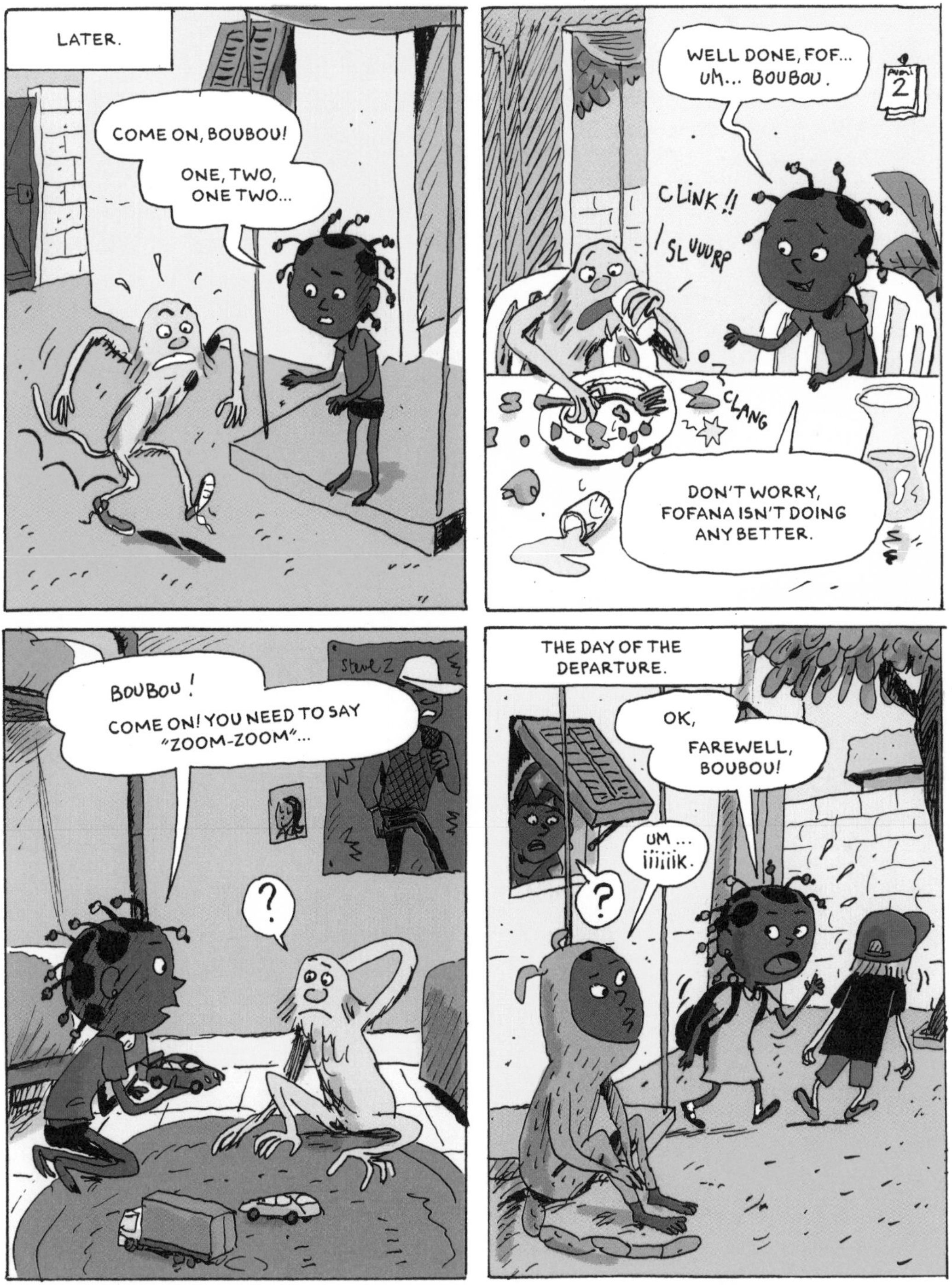
LATER.
COME ON, BOUBOU! ONE, TWO, ONE TWO...
WELL DONE, FOF... UM... BOUBOU.
CLINK!!
SLUUURP
CLANG
DON'T WORRY, FOFANA ISN'T DOING ANY BETTER.
BOUBOU! COME ON! YOU NEED TO SAY "ZOOM-ZOOM"...
?
THE DAY OF THE DEPARTURE.
OK, FAREWELL, BOUBOU!
?
UM ... iiiiiik.

HMM... THAT'S ODD, AKISSI IS TALLER THAN FOFANA.
AND FOFANA IS VERY THIN, DON'T YOU THINK?
AND THEY'RE HOLDING EACH OTHER'S HAND, THAT'S EVEN WEIRDER...
IT IS.
AND WHAT'S THAT THING COMING OUT OF FOFANA'S SHORTS?!!
FOFANA ?!!
!?
HiiiK
UM ...
AKiSSiii !!!
BOUBOU, QUICK, THERE'S STILL TIME TO RUN AWAY!
iiiK
THE END

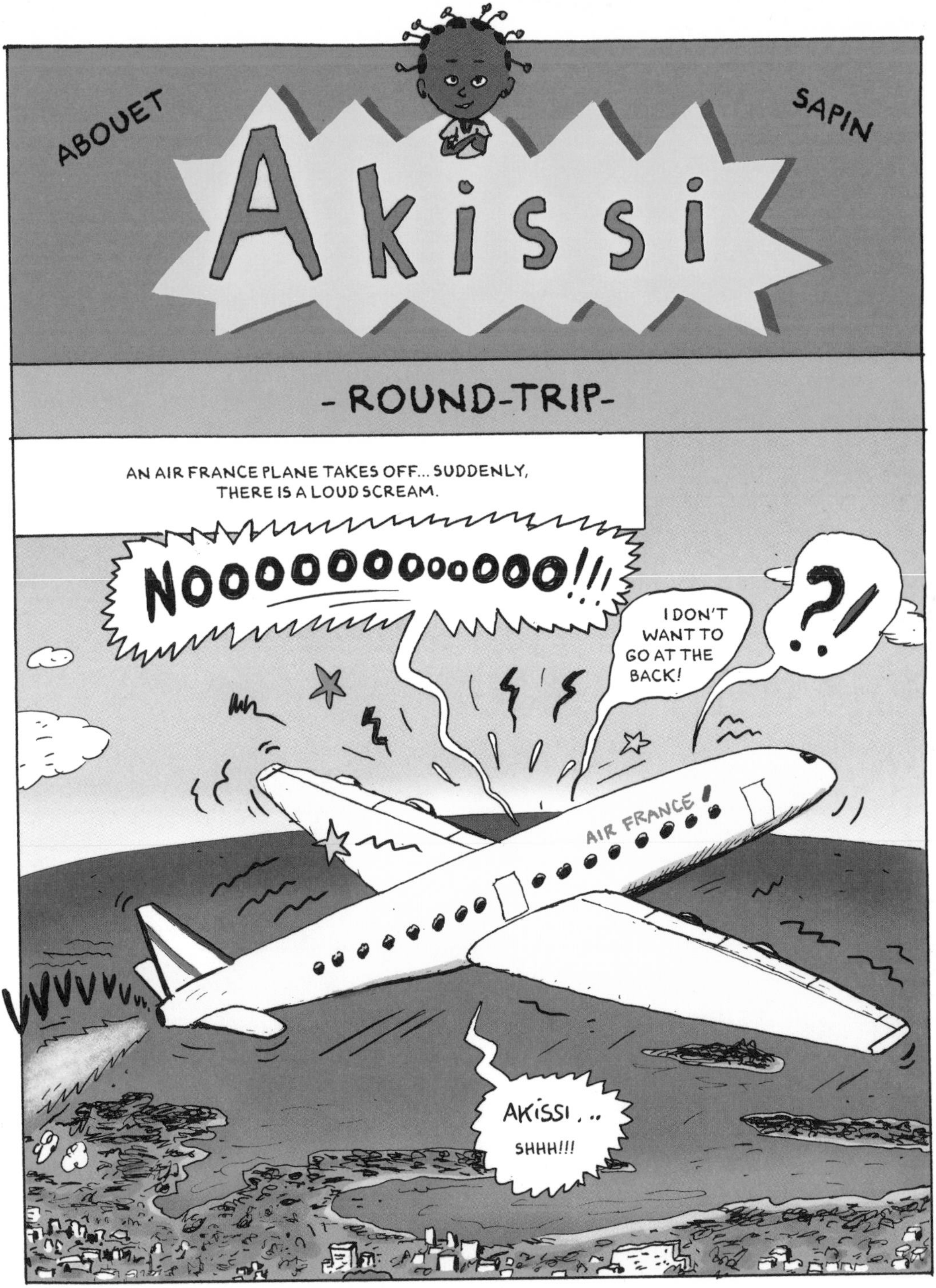
ABOUET
SAPIN
Akissi
- ROUND-TRIP -
AN AIR FRANCE PLANE TAKES OFF... SUDDENLY, THERE IS A LOUD SCREAM.
NOOOOOOOooOOO!!!
I DON'T WANT TO GO AT THE BACK!
?!
AIR FRANCE
AKISSI...
SHHH!!!

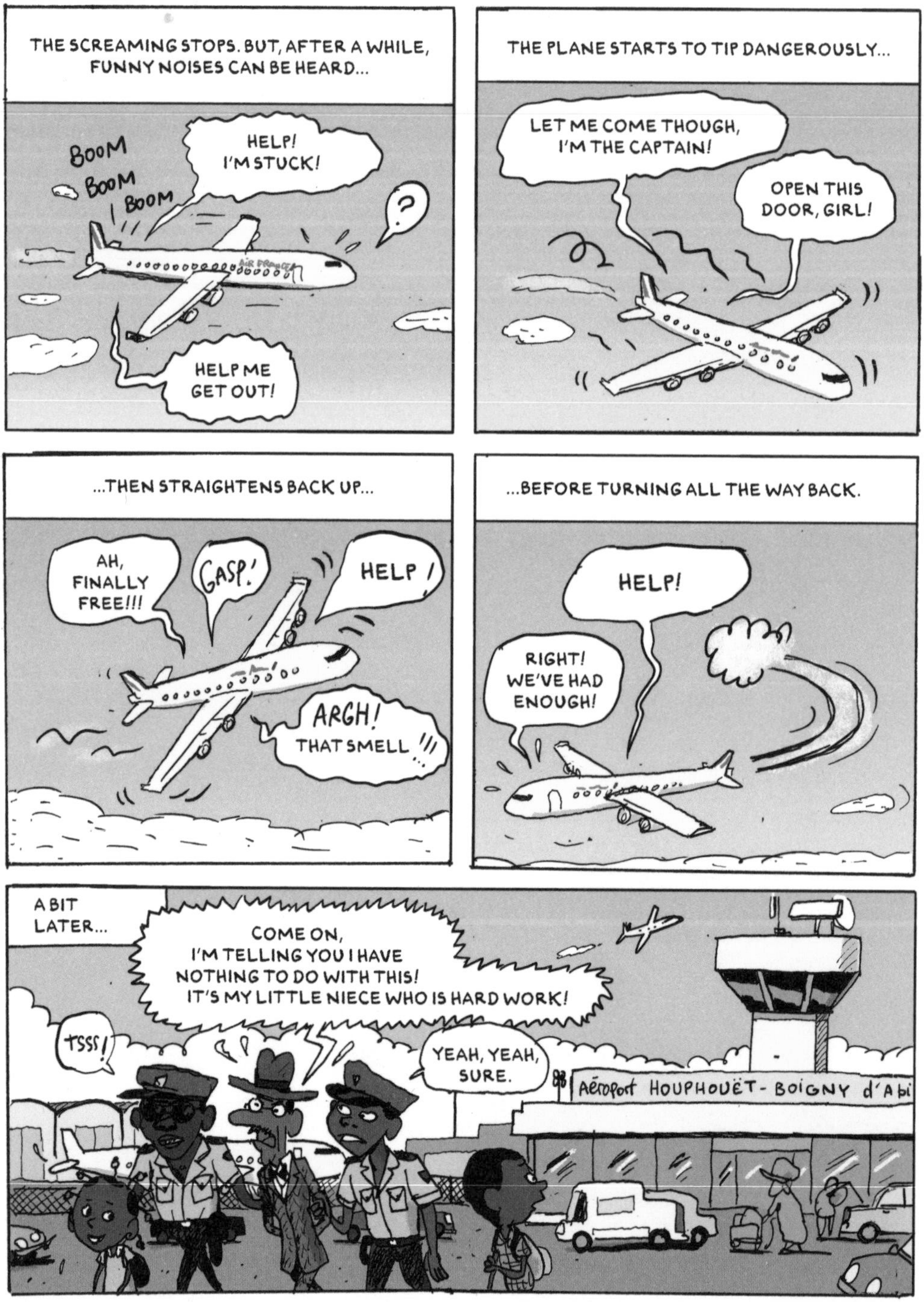
THE SCREAMING STOPS. BUT, AFTER A WHILE, FUNNY NOISES CAN BE HEARD...
BOOM BOOM BOOM
HELP! I'M STUCK!
?
HELP ME GET OUT!
THE PLANE STARTS TO TIP DANGEROUSLY...
LET ME COME THOUGH, I'M THE CAPTAIN!
OPEN THIS DOOR, GIRL!
...THEN STRAIGHTENS BACK UP...
AH, FINALLY FREE!!!
GASP!
HELP!
ARGH! THAT SMELL!!!...
...BEFORE TURNING ALL THE WAY BACK.
HELP!
RIGHT! WE'VE HAD ENOUGH!
A BIT LATER...
COME ON, I'M TELLING YOU I HAVE NOTHING TO DO WITH THIS! IT'S MY LITTLE NIECE WHO IS HARD WORK!
TSSS!
YEAH, YEAH, SURE.
Aéroport HOUPHOUËT-BOIGNY d'Abi

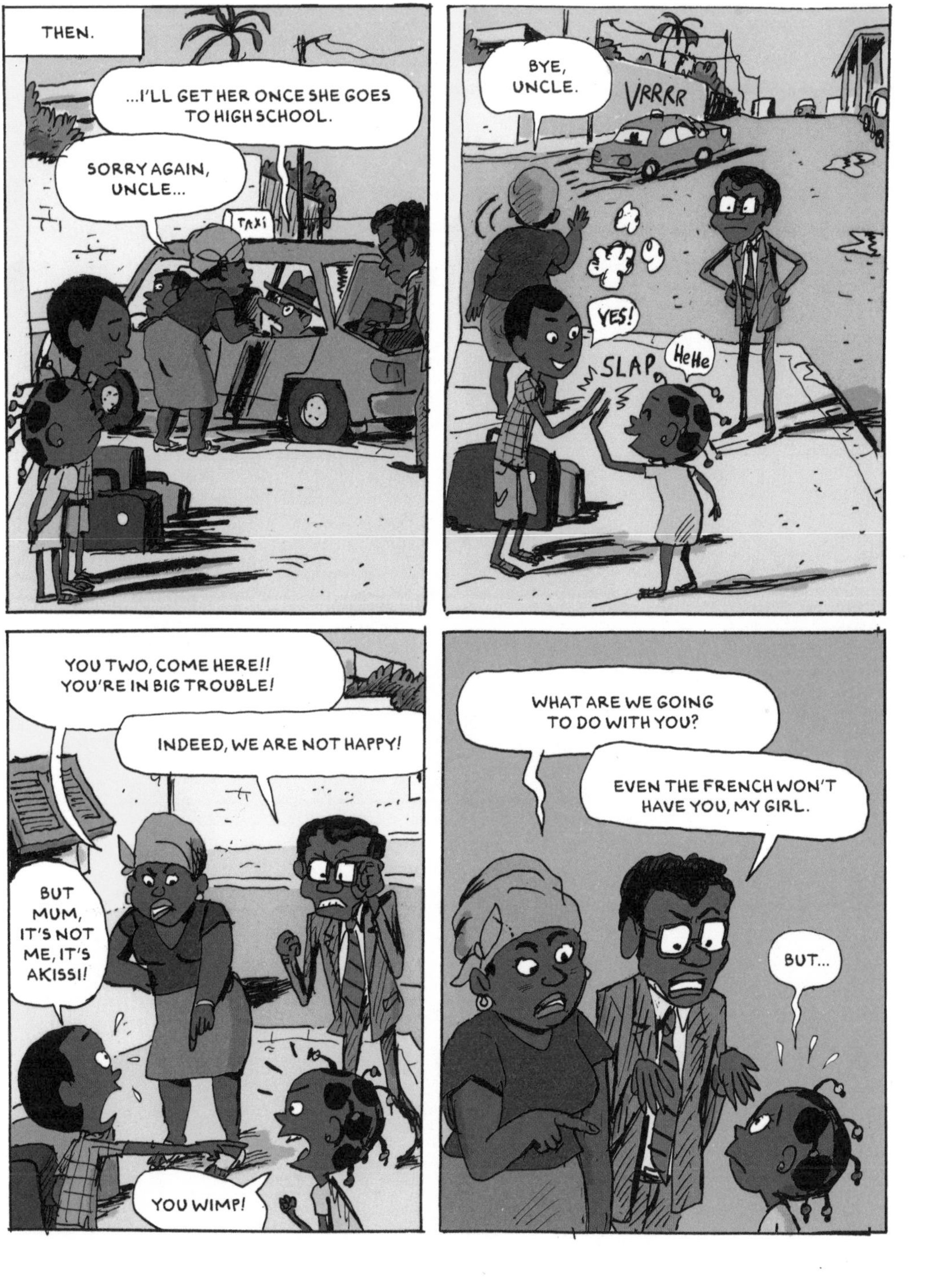

THEN.
...I'LL GET HER ONCE SHE GOES TO HIGH SCHOOL.
SORRY AGAIN, UNCLE...
TAXI
BYE, UNCLE.
VRRRR
YES!
SLAP
HeHe
YOU TWO, COME HERE!! YOU'RE IN BIG TROUBLE!
INDEED, WE ARE NOT HAPPY!
BUT MUM, IT'S NOT ME, IT'S AKISSI!
YOU WIMP!
WHAT ARE WE GOING TO DO WITH YOU?
EVEN THE FRENCH WON'T HAVE YOU, MY GIRL.
BUT...

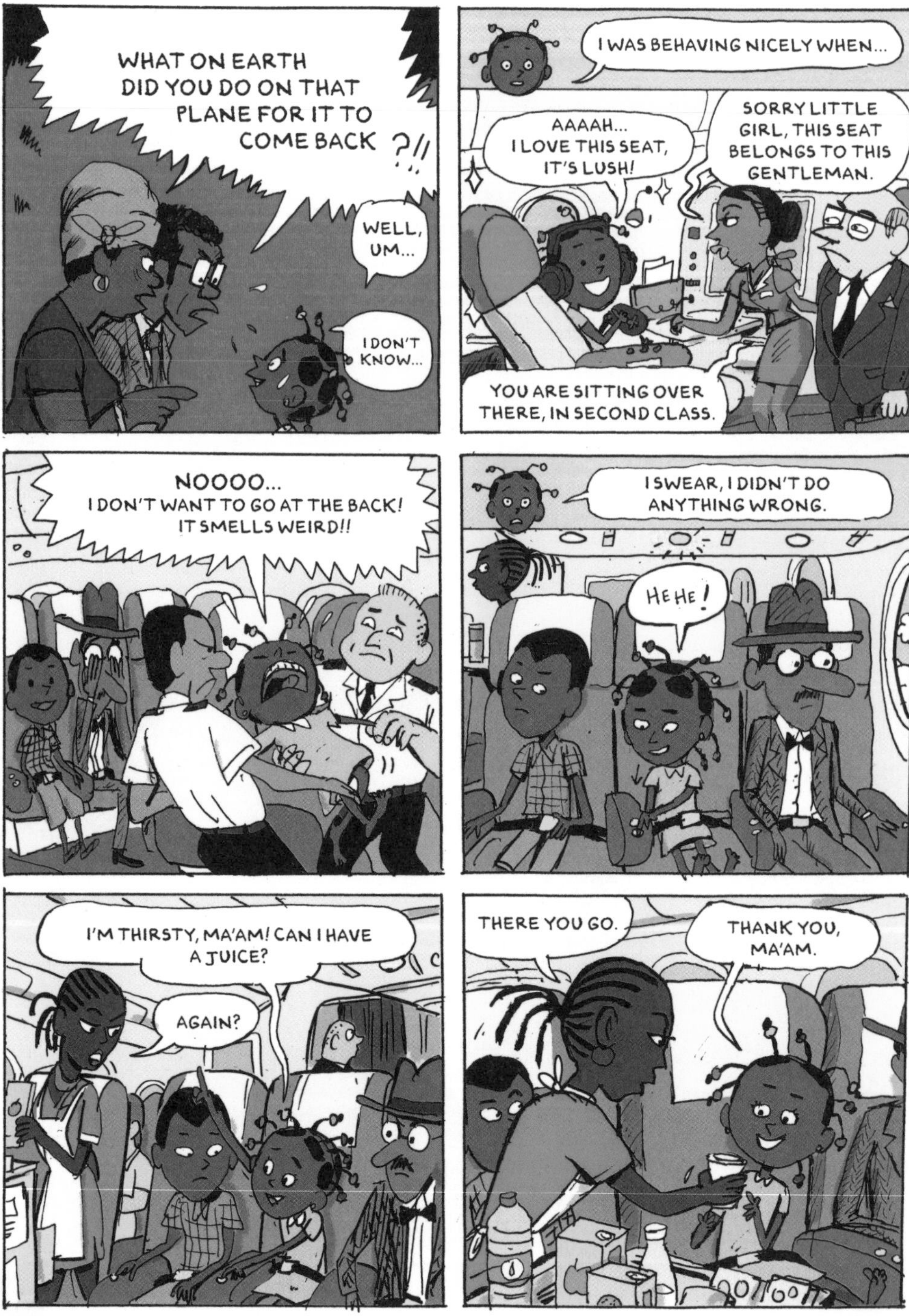
WHAT ON EARTH DID YOU DO ON THAT PLANE FOR IT TO COME BACK ?!!
WELL, UM...
I DON'T KNOW...
I WAS BEHAVING NICELY WHEN...
AAAAH... I LOVE THIS SEAT, IT'S LUSH!
SORRY LITTLE GIRL, THIS SEAT BELONGS TO THIS GENTLEMAN.
YOU ARE SITTING OVER THERE, IN SECOND CLASS.
NOOOO... I DON'T WANT TO GO AT THE BACK! IT SMELLS WEIRD!!
I SWEAR, I DIDN'T DO ANYTHING WRONG.
HE HE!
I'M THIRSTY, MA'AM! CAN I HAVE A JUICE?
AGAIN?
THERE YOU GO.
THANK YOU, MA'AM.

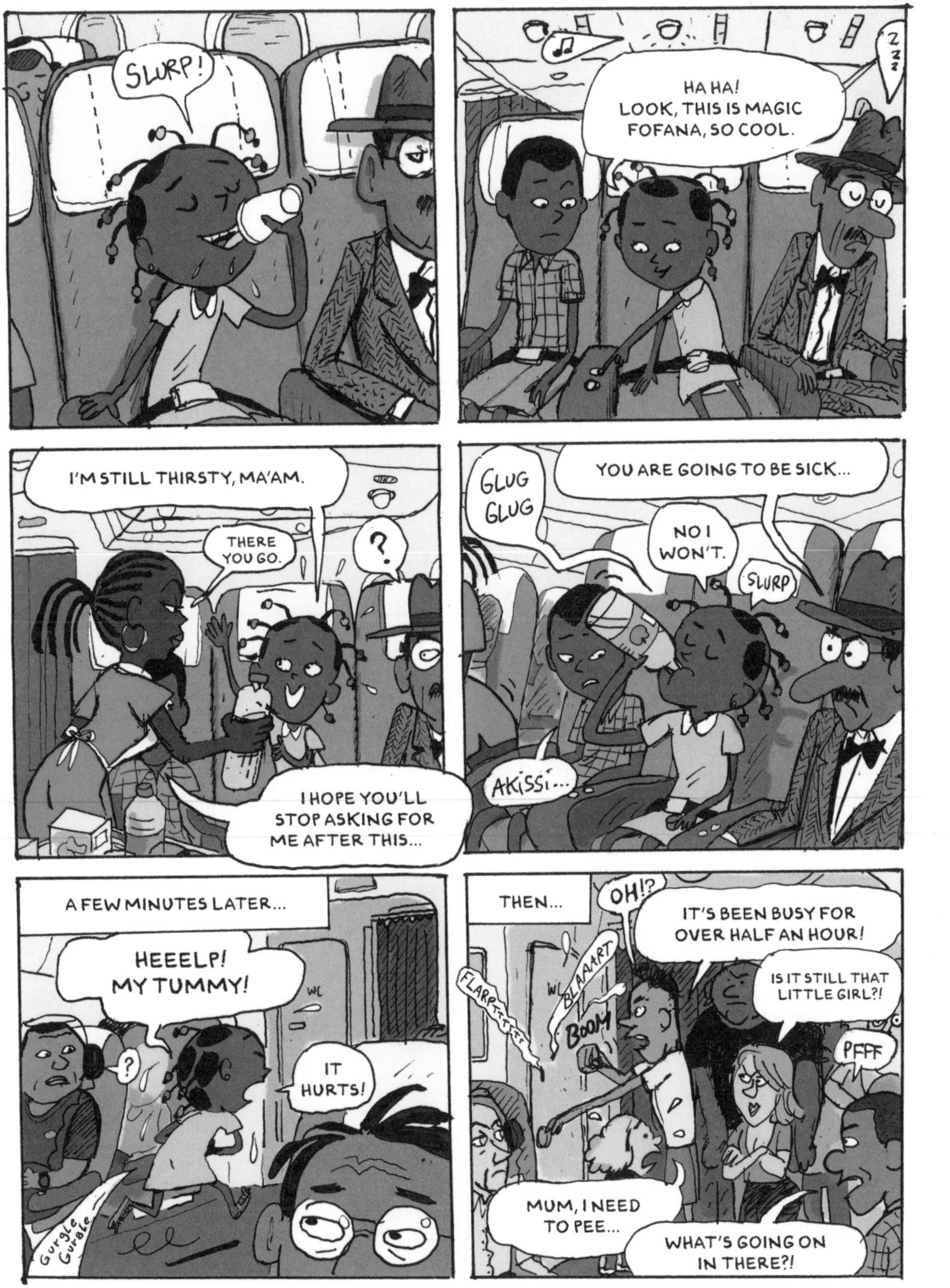
SLURP!
HA HA!
LOOK, THIS IS MAGIC
FOFANA, SO COOL.
ZZZ
I'M STILL THIRSTY, MA'AM.
THERE YOU GO.
?
I HOPE YOU'LL STOP ASKING FOR ME AFTER THIS...
GLUG GLUG
YOU ARE GOING TO BE SICK...
NO I WON'T.
SLURP
AKISSI...
A FEW MINUTES LATER...
HEEELP! MY TUMMY!
WC
?
IT HURTS!
Gurgle Gurgle
THEN...
OH!?
IT'S BEEN BUSY FOR OVER HALF AN HOUR!
IS IT STILL THAT LITTLE GIRL?!
WC
FLARP
BLAAART
BOOM
PFFF
MUM, I NEED TO PEE...
WHAT'S GOING ON IN THERE?!

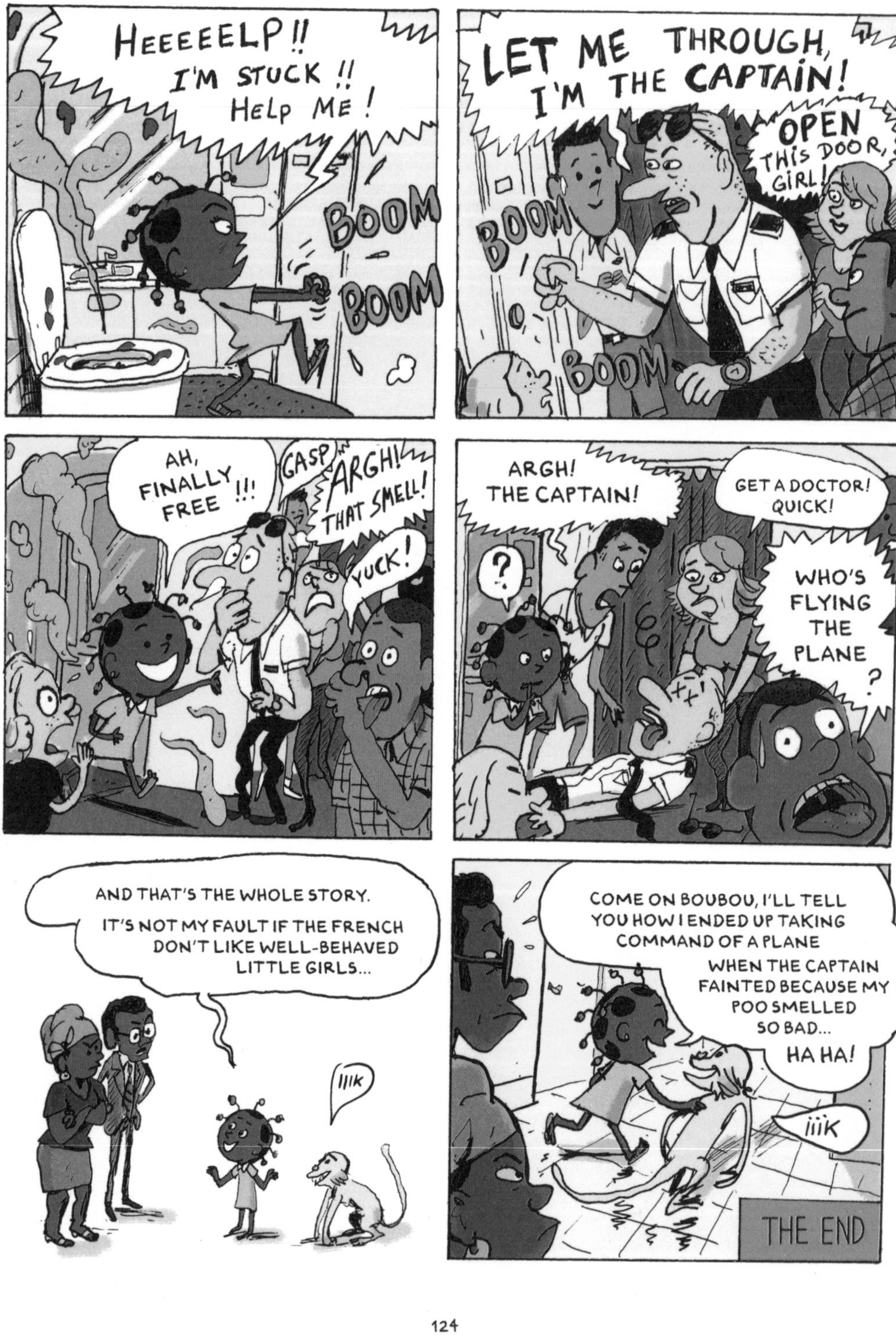
HEEEEELP!! I'M STUCK!! Help ME!
BOOM
BOOM
LET ME THROUGH, I'M THE CAPTAIN!
OPEN THIS DOOR, GIRL!
BOOM
BOOM
AH, FINALLY FREE!!!
GASP
ARGH! THAT SMELL!
YUCK!
ARGH! THE CAPTAIN!
?
GET A DOCTOR! QUICK!
WHO'S FLYING THE PLANE?
AND THAT'S THE WHOLE STORY.
IT'S NOT MY FAULT IF THE FRENCH DON'T LIKE WELL-BEHAVED LITTLE GIRLS...
IIIK
COME ON BOUBOU, I'LL TELL YOU HOW I ENDED UP TAKING COMMAND OF A PLANE
WHEN THE CAPTAIN FAINTED BECAUSE MY POO SMELLED SO BAD...
HA HA!
iiiK
THE END

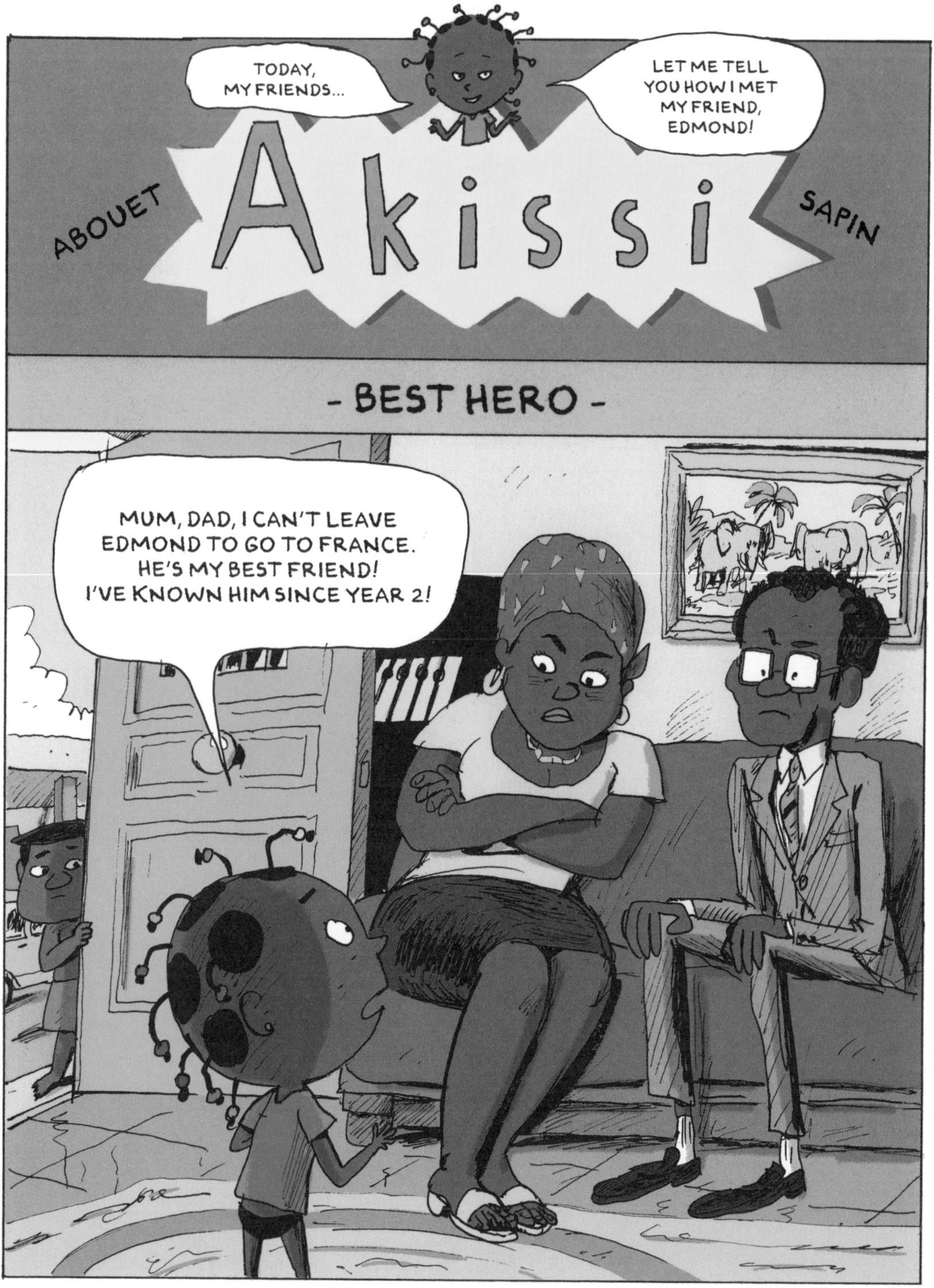
TODAY, MY FRIENDS...
LET ME TELL YOU HOW I MET MY FRIEND, EDMOND!
ABOUET
Akissi
SAPIN
- BEST HERO -
MUM, DAD, I CAN'T LEAVE EDMOND TO GO TO FRANCE. HE'S MY BEST FRIEND! I'VE KNOWN HIM SINCE YEAR 2!

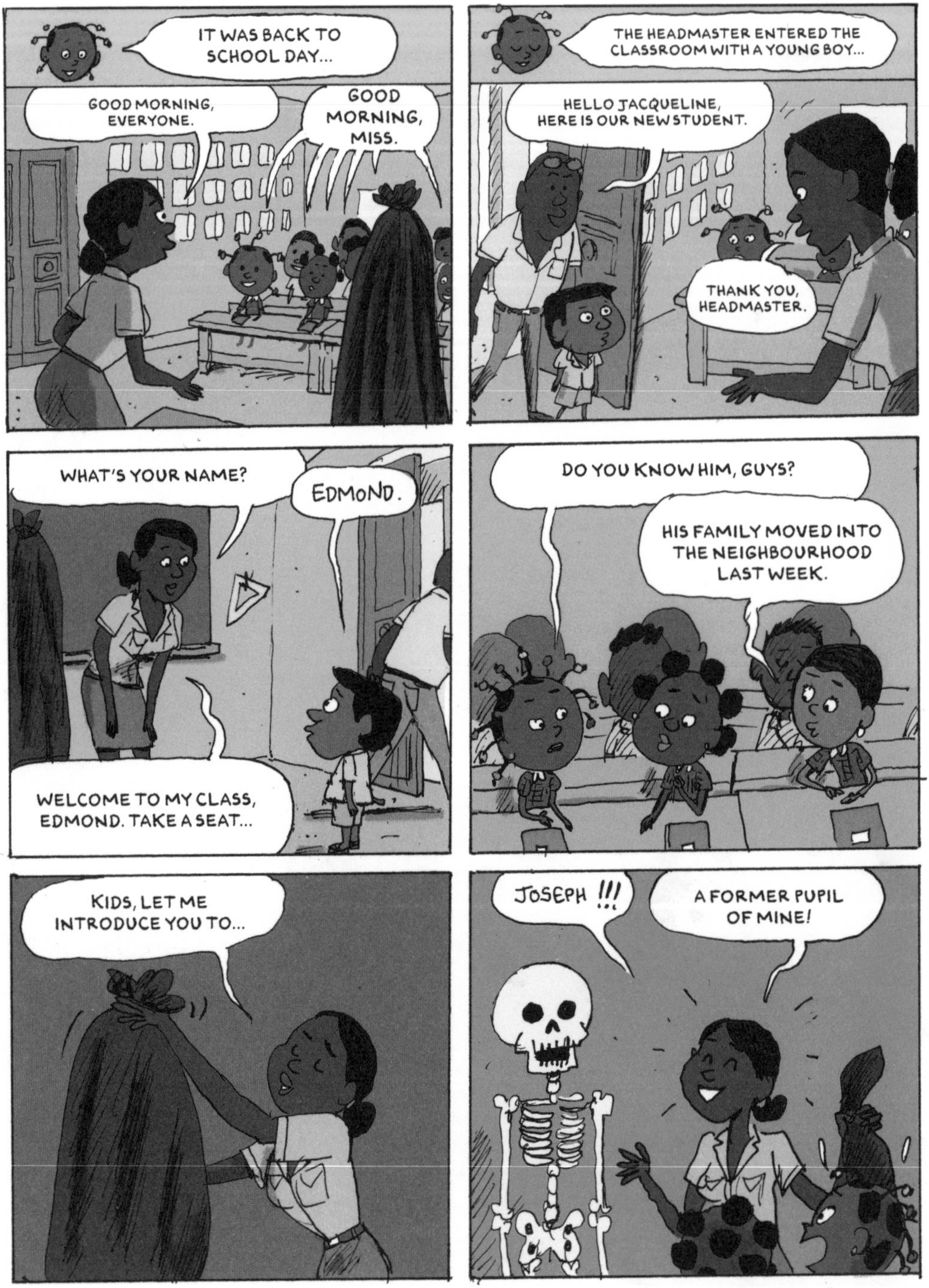
IT WAS BACK TO SCHOOL DAY...
GOOD MORNING, EVERYONE.
GOOD MORNING, MISS.
THE HEADMASTER ENTERED THE CLASSROOM WITH A YOUNG BOY...
HELLO JACQUELINE, HERE IS OUR NEW STUDENT.
THANK YOU, HEADMASTER.
WHAT'S YOUR NAME?
EDMOND.
WELCOME TO MY CLASS, EDMOND. TAKE A SEAT...
DO YOU KNOW HIM, GUYS?
HIS FAMILY MOVED INTO THE NEIGHBOURHOOD LAST WEEK.
KIDS, LET ME INTRODUCE YOU TO...
JOSEPH !!!
A FORMER PUPIL OF MINE!

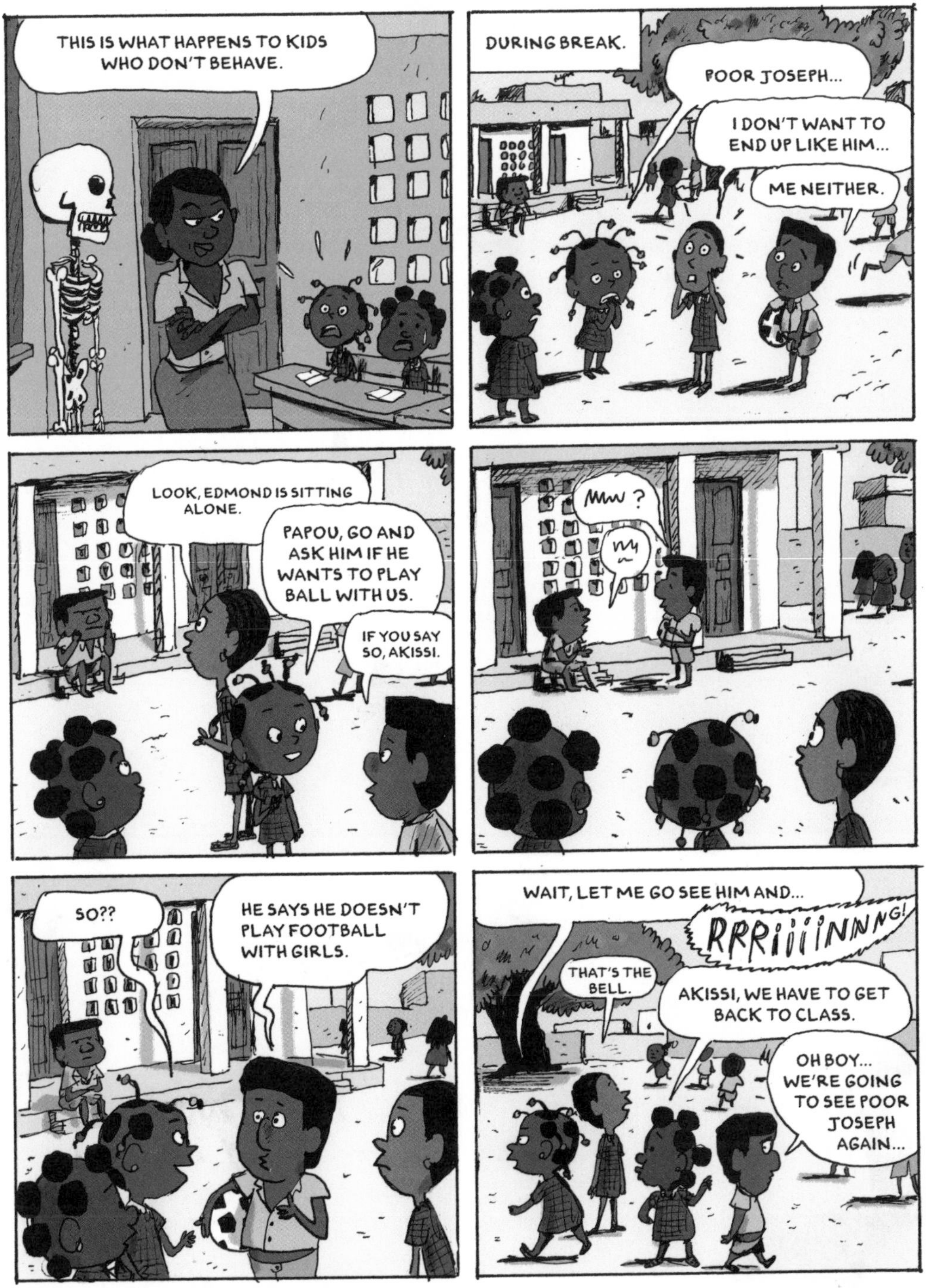
THIS IS WHAT HAPPENS TO KIDS WHO DON'T BEHAVE.
DURING BREAK.
POOR JOSEPH...
I DON'T WANT TO END UP LIKE HIM...
ME NEITHER.
LOOK, EDMOND IS SITTING ALONE.
PAPOU, GO AND ASK HIM IF HE WANTS TO PLAY BALL WITH US.
IF YOU SAY SO, AKISSI.
SO??
HE SAYS HE DOESN'T PLAY FOOTBALL WITH GIRLS.
WAIT, LET ME GO SEE HIM AND...
RRRiiiiNNNG!
THAT'S THE BELL.
AKISSI, WE HAVE TO GET BACK TO CLASS.
OH BOY... WE'RE GOING TO SEE POOR JOSEPH AGAIN...

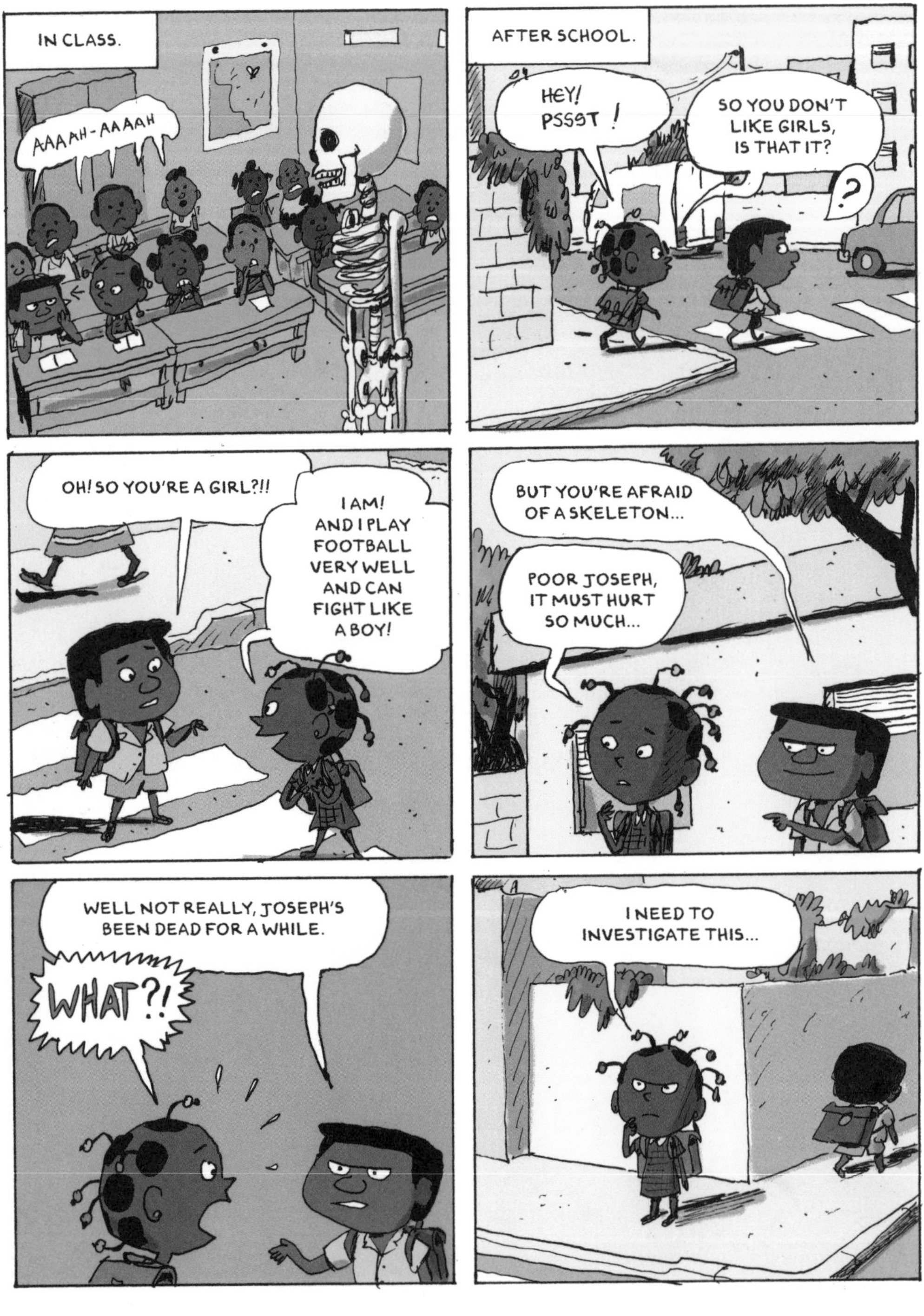
IN CLASS.
AAAAH-AAAAH
AFTER SCHOOL.
HEY! PSSST !
SO YOU DON'T LIKE GIRLS, IS THAT IT?
?
OH! SO YOU'RE A GIRL?!!
I AM! AND I PLAY FOOTBALL VERY WELL AND CAN FIGHT LIKE A BOY!
BUT YOU'RE AFRAID OF A SKELETON...
POOR JOSEPH, IT MUST HURT SO MUCH...
WELL NOT REALLY, JOSEPH'S BEEN DEAD FOR A WHILE.
WHAT?!
I NEED TO INVESTIGATE THIS...

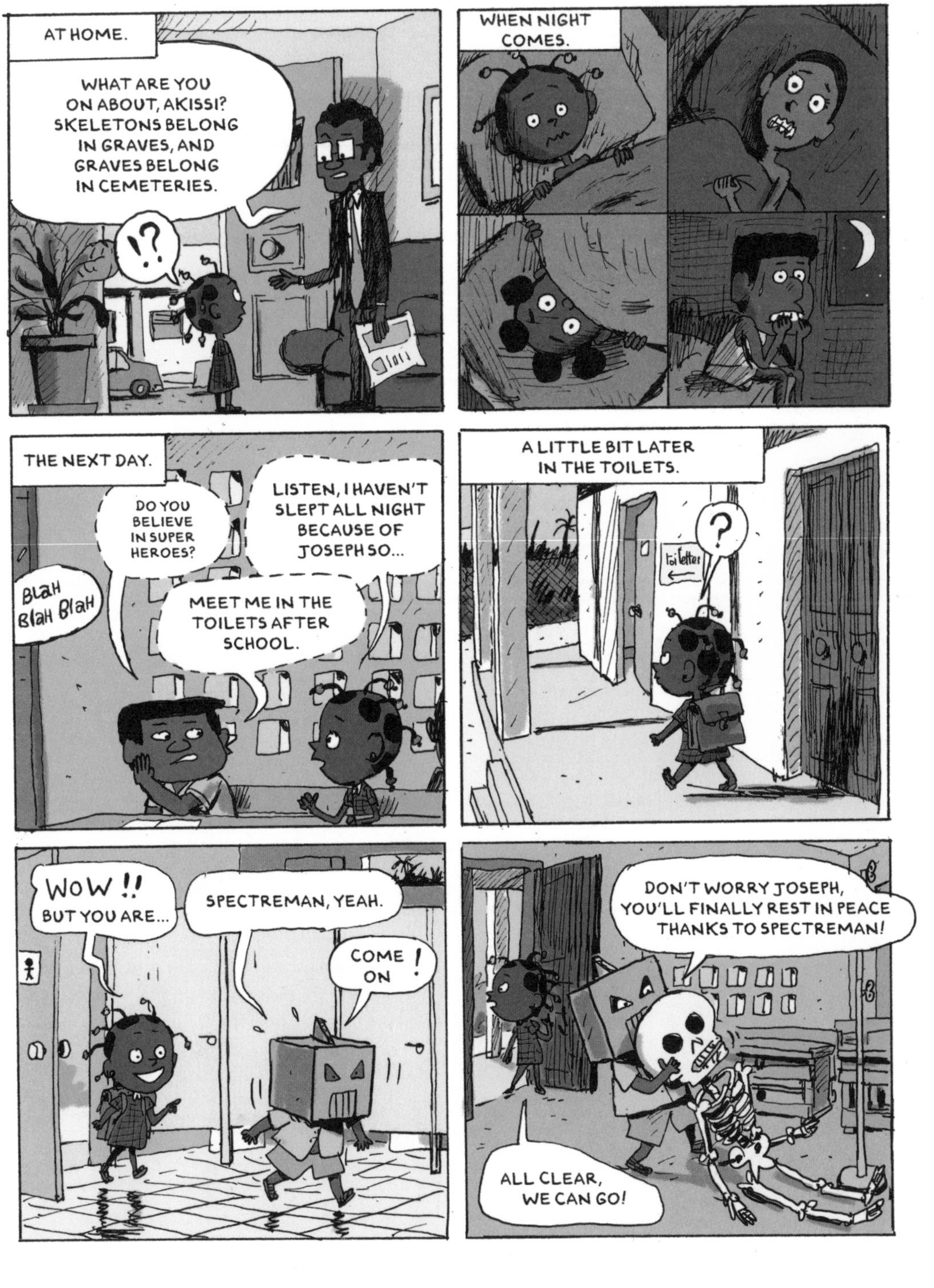
AT HOME.
WHAT ARE YOU ON ABOUT, AKISSI? SKELETONS BELONG IN GRAVES, AND GRAVES BELONG IN CEMETERIES.
!?
WHEN NIGHT COMES.
THE NEXT DAY.
DO YOU BELIEVE IN SUPER HEROES?
LISTEN, I HAVEN'T SLEPT ALL NIGHT BECAUSE OF JOSEPH SO...
MEET ME IN THE TOILETS AFTER SCHOOL.
BLAH BLAH BLAH
A LITTLE BIT LATER IN THE TOILETS.
toilettes
?
WOW !! BUT YOU ARE...
SPECTREMAN, YEAH.
COME ON !
DON'T WORRY JOSEPH, YOU'LL FINALLY REST IN PEACE THANKS TO SPECTREMAN!
ALL CLEAR, WE CAN GO!

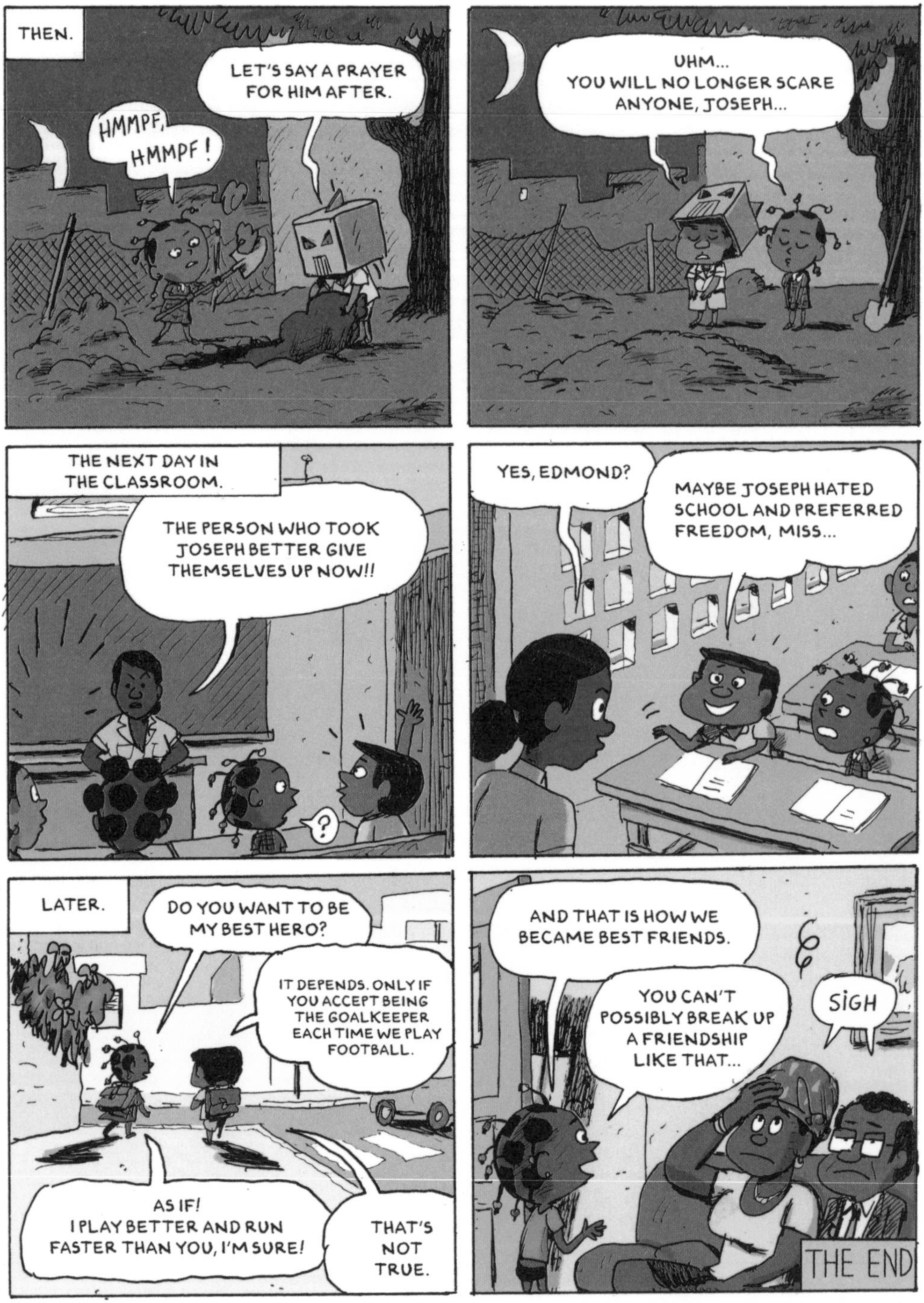
THEN.
LET'S SAY A PRAYER FOR HIM AFTER.
HMMPF, HMMPF!
UHM... YOU WILL NO LONGER SCARE ANYONE, JOSEPH...
THE NEXT DAY IN THE CLASSROOM.
THE PERSON WHO TOOK JOSEPH BETTER GIVE THEMSELVES UP NOW!!
?
YES, EDMOND?
MAYBE JOSEPH HATED SCHOOL AND PREFERRED FREEDOM, MISS...
LATER.
DO YOU WANT TO BE MY BEST HERO?
IT DEPENDS. ONLY IF YOU ACCEPT BEING THE GOALKEEPER EACH TIME WE PLAY FOOTBALL.
AS IF! I PLAY BETTER AND RUN FASTER THAN YOU, I'M SURE!
THAT'S NOT TRUE.
AND THAT IS HOW WE BECAME BEST FRIENDS.
YOU CAN'T POSSIBLY BREAK UP A FRIENDSHIP LIKE THAT...
SIGH
THE END

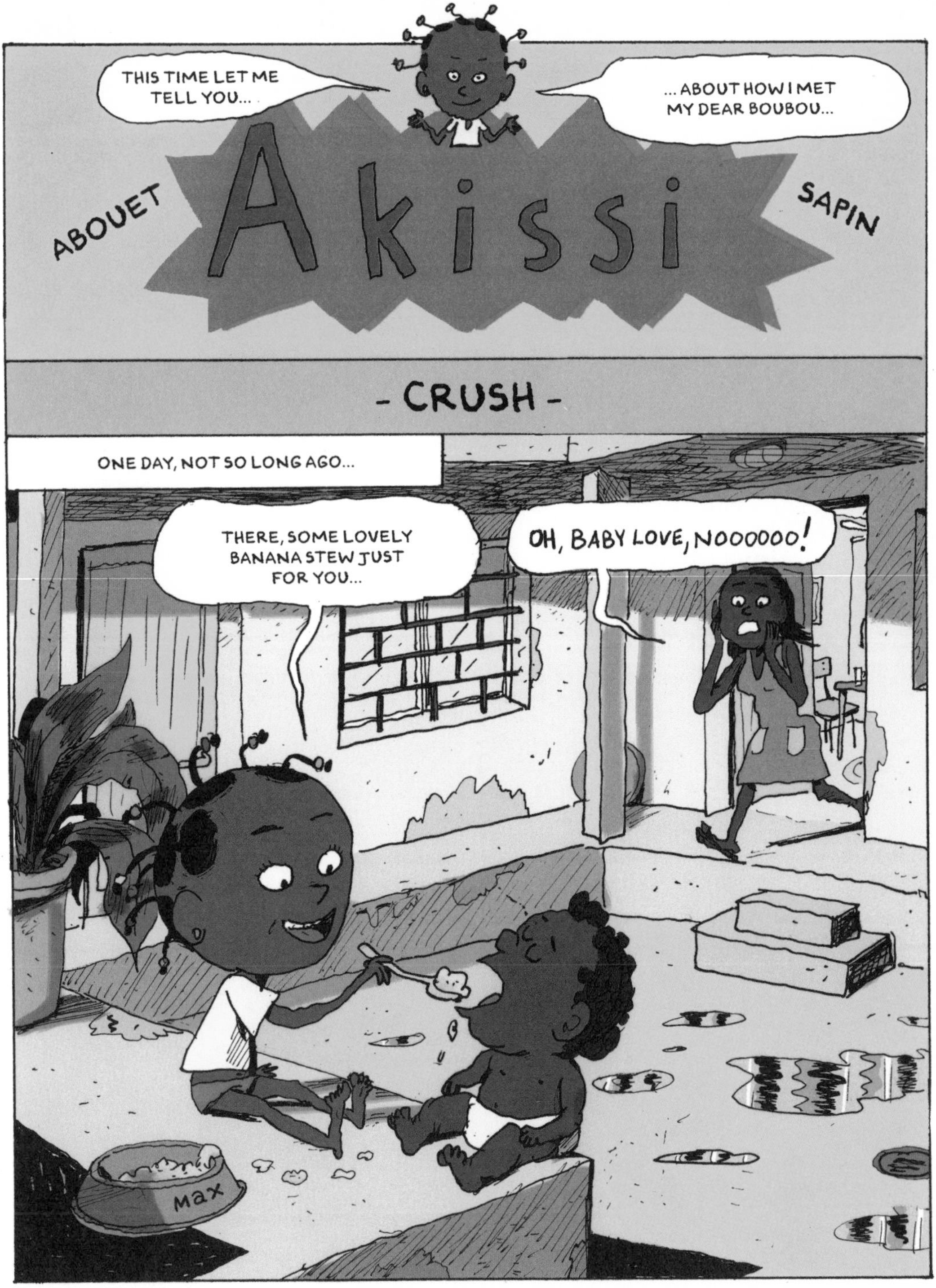
THIS TIME LET ME TELL YOU...
...ABOUT HOW I MET MY DEAR BOUBOU...
Akissi
ABOUET
SAPIN
- CRUSH -
ONE DAY, NOT SO LONG AGO...
THERE, SOME LOVELY BANANA STEW JUST FOR YOU...
OH, BABY LOVE, NOOOOOO!
MAX

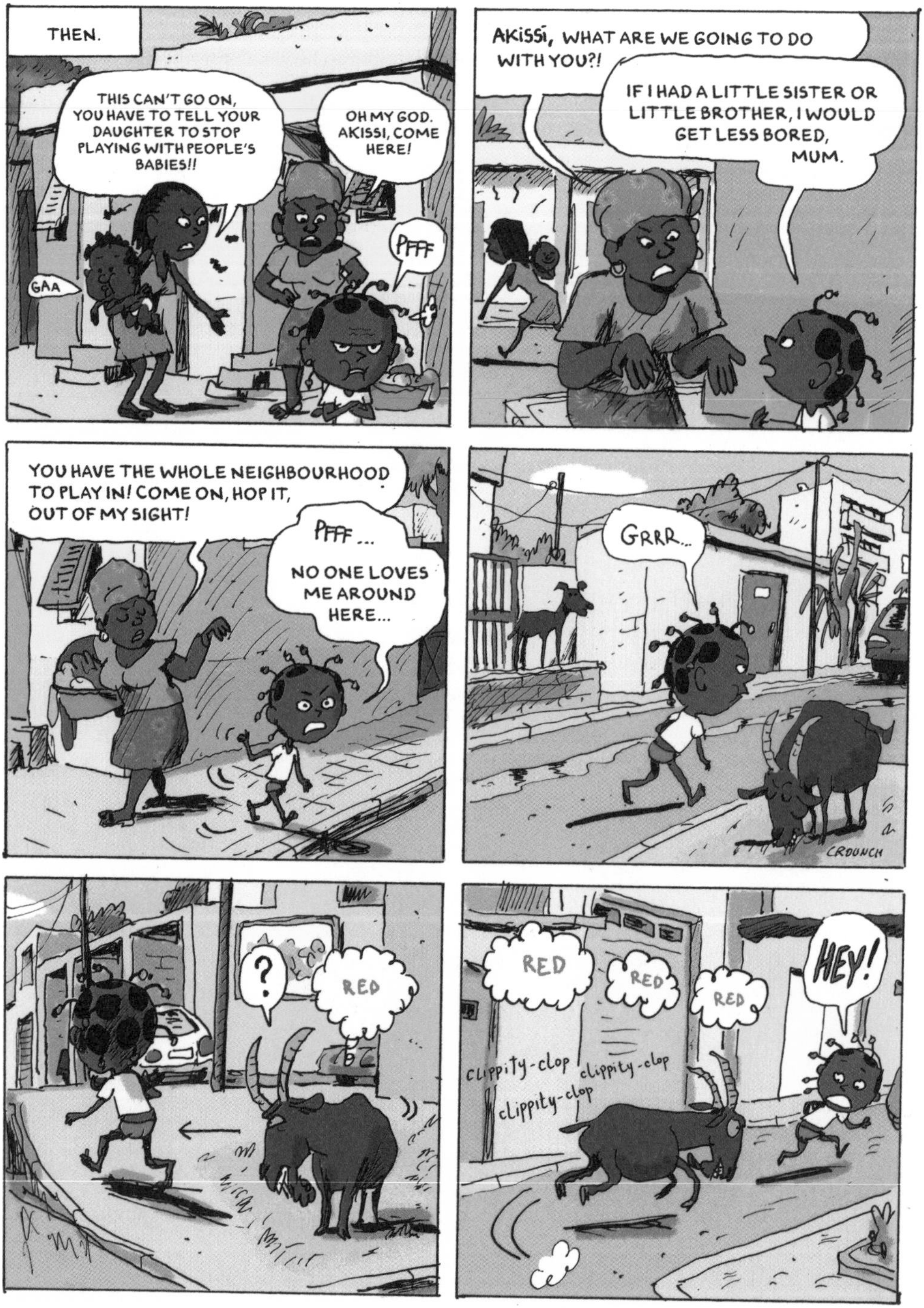
THEN.
THIS CAN'T GO ON, YOU HAVE TO TELL YOUR DAUGHTER TO STOP PLAYING WITH PEOPLE'S BABIES!!
GAA
OH MY GOD. AKISSI, COME HERE!
PFFF
AKISSI, WHAT ARE WE GOING TO DO WITH YOU?!
IF I HAD A LITTLE SISTER OR LITTLE BROTHER, I WOULD GET LESS BORED, MUM.
YOU HAVE THE WHOLE NEIGHBOURHOOD TO PLAY IN! COME ON, HOP IT, OUT OF MY SIGHT!
PFFF...
NO ONE LOVES ME AROUND HERE...
GRRR...
CROUNCH
?
RED
RED
RED
RED
HEY!
clippity-clop
clippity-clop
clippity-clop

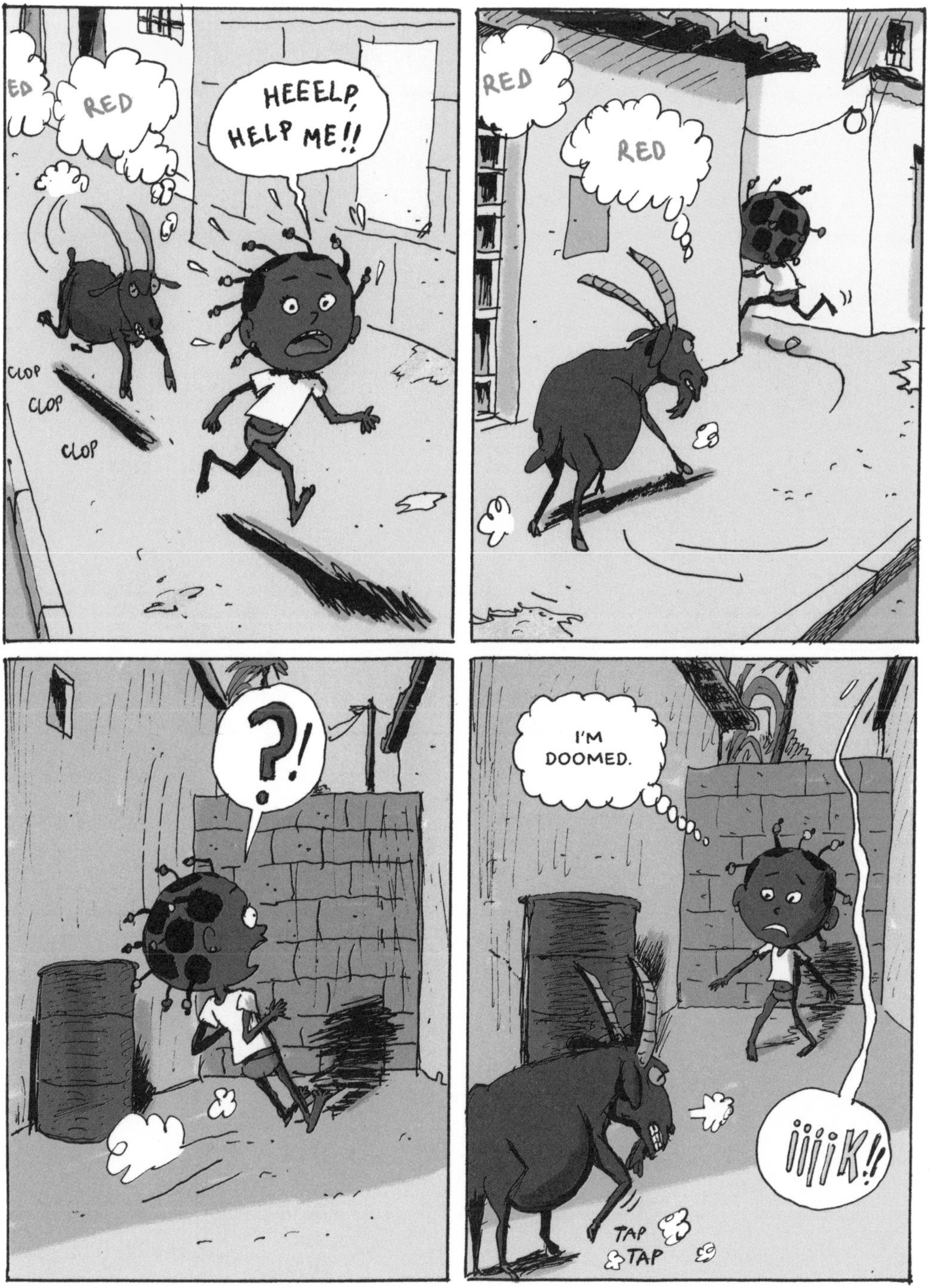
ED
RED
HEEELP, HELP ME!!
CLOP
CLOP
CLOP
RED
RED
?!
I'M DOOMED.
TAP
TAP
IIIIK!!

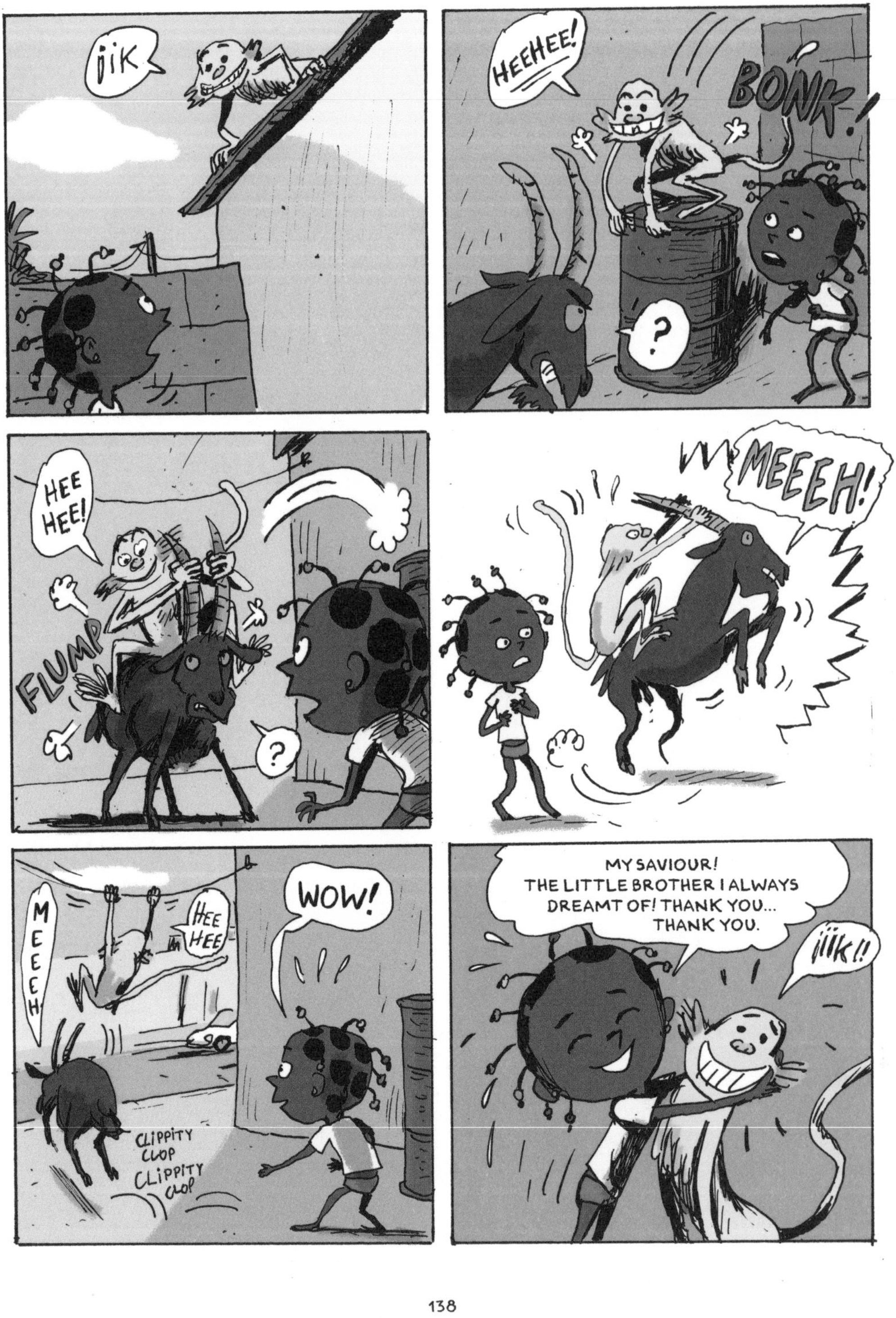
¡IK
HEEHEE!
BONK!
?
HEE HEE!
FLUMP
?
MEEEH!
MEEEEH
HEE HEE
WOW!
CLIPPITY CLOP
CLIPPITY CLOP
MY SAVIOUR! THE LITTLE BROTHER I ALWAYS DREAMT OF! THANK YOU... THANK YOU.
¡IIIK!!

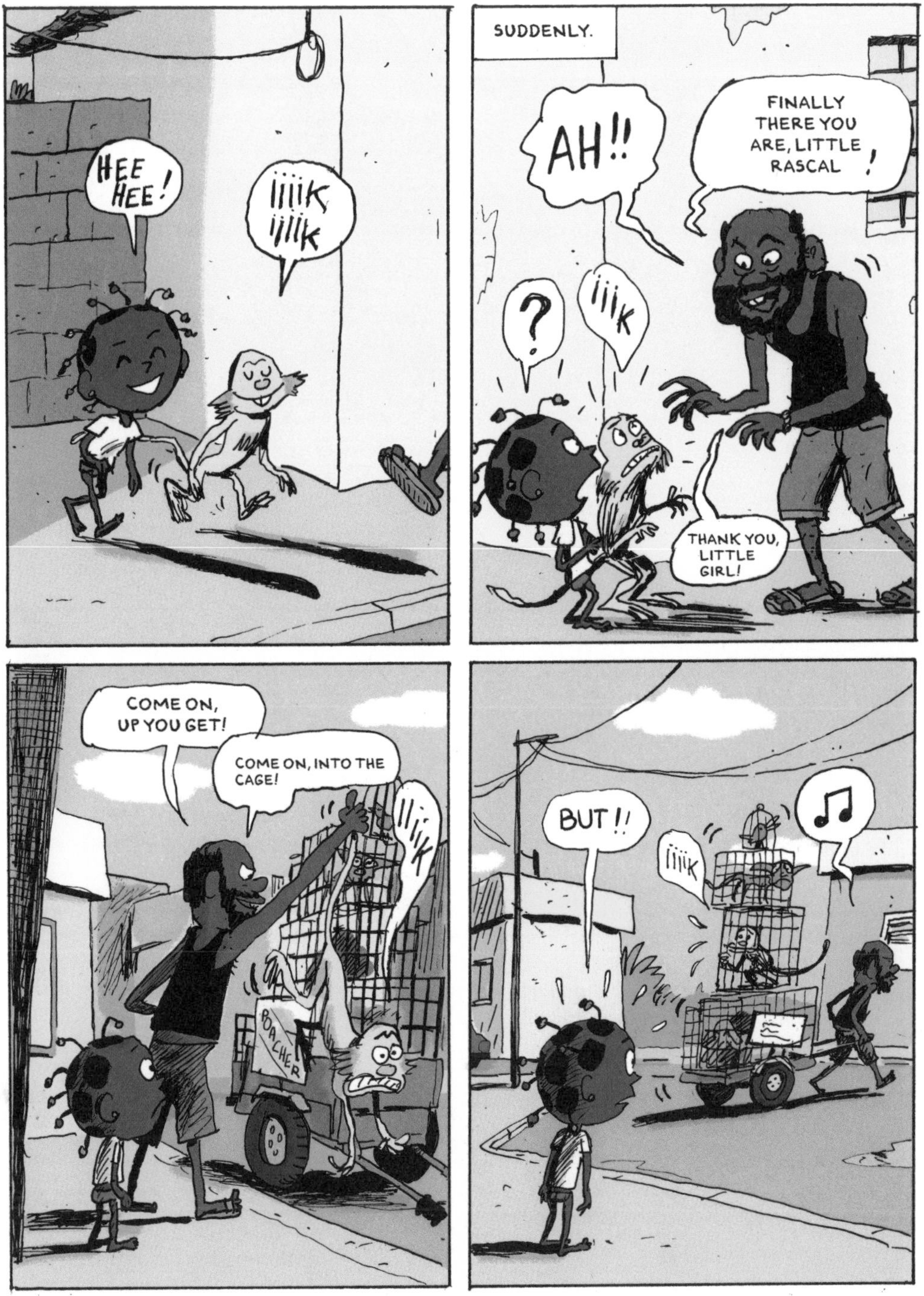
HEE HEE!
iiiik iiiik
SUDDENLY.
AH!!
FINALLY THERE YOU ARE, LITTLE RASCAL!
?
iiiik
THANK YOU, LITTLE GIRL!
COME ON, UP YOU GET!
COME ON, INTO THE CAGE!
iiiik
POACHER
BUT!!
iiiik
♫

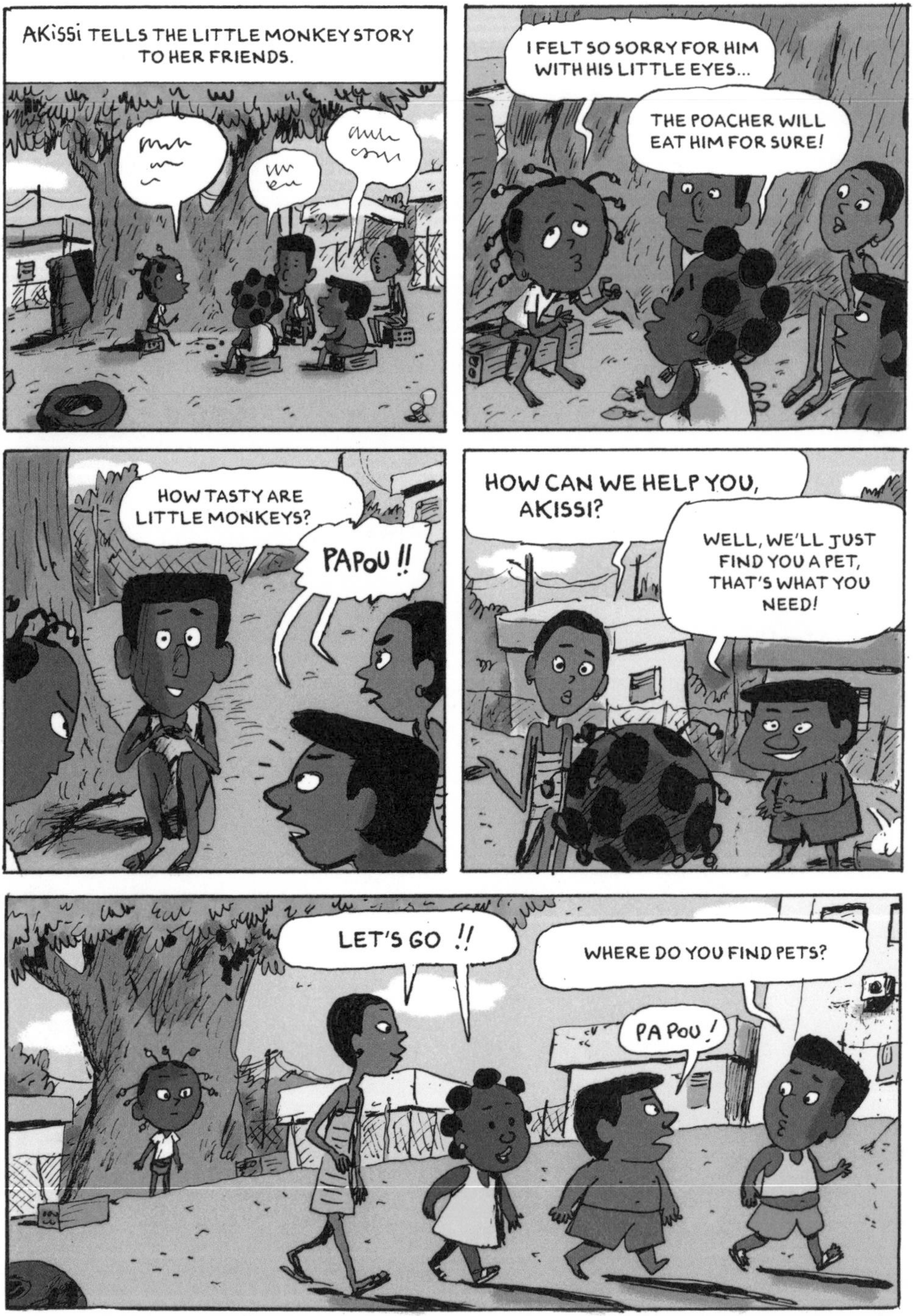
AKISSI TELLS THE LITTLE MONKEY STORY TO HER FRIENDS.
I FELT SO SORRY FOR HIM WITH HIS LITTLE EYES...
THE POACHER WILL EAT HIM FOR SURE!
HOW TASTY ARE LITTLE MONKEYS?
PAPOU !!
HOW CAN WE HELP YOU, AKISSI?
WELL, WE'LL JUST FIND YOU A PET, THAT'S WHAT YOU NEED!
LET'S GO !!
WHERE DO YOU FIND PETS?
PA POU !

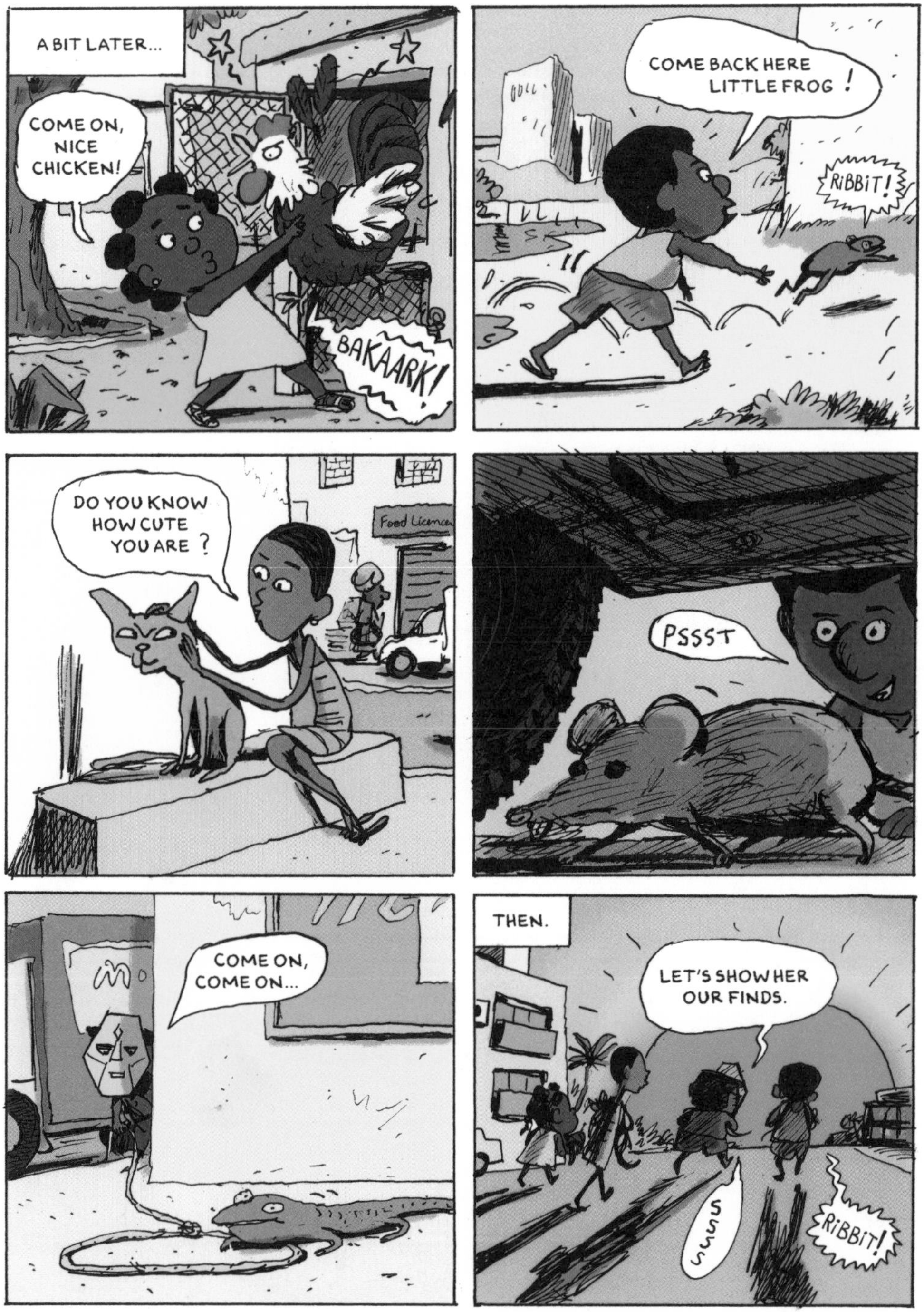
A BIT LATER...
COME ON, NICE CHICKEN!
BAKAARK!
COME BACK HERE LITTLE FROG!
RIBBIT!
DO YOU KNOW HOW CUTE YOU ARE?
Food Licence
PSSST
COME ON, COME ON...
THEN.
LET'S SHOW HER OUR FINDS.
SSSS
RIBBIT!

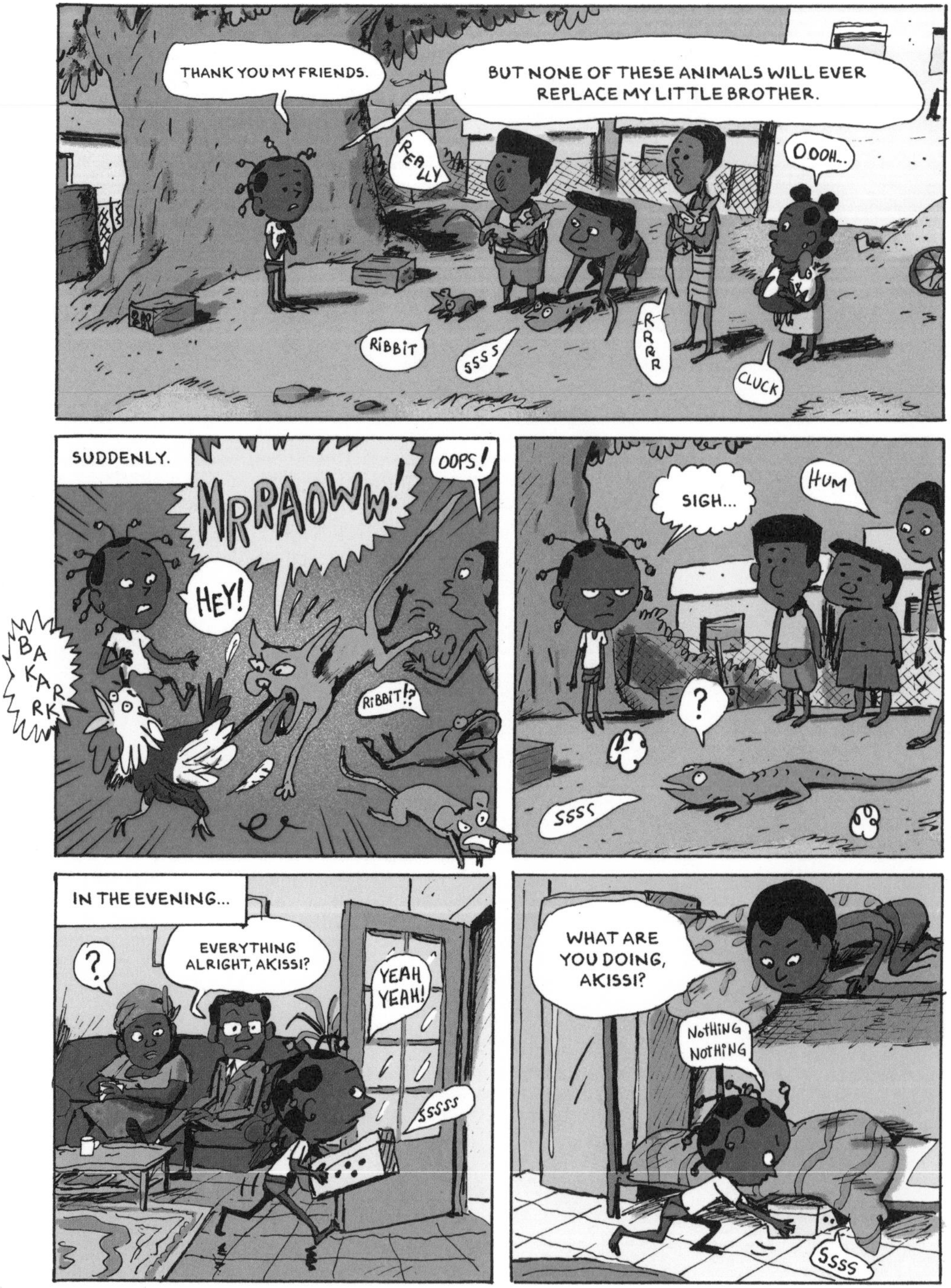
THANK YOU MY FRIENDS.
BUT NONE OF THESE ANIMALS WILL EVER REPLACE MY LITTLE BROTHER.
REALLY
OOOH...
RIBBIT
SSSS
RRRR
CLUCK
SUDDENLY.
MRRAOWW!
OOPS!
HEY!
BAKARK
RIBBIT!?
SIGH...
HUM
?
SSSS
IN THE EVENING...
?
EVERYTHING ALRIGHT, AKISSI?
YEAH YEAH!
SSSSS
WHAT ARE YOU DOING, AKISSI?
NOTHING NOTHING
SSSS

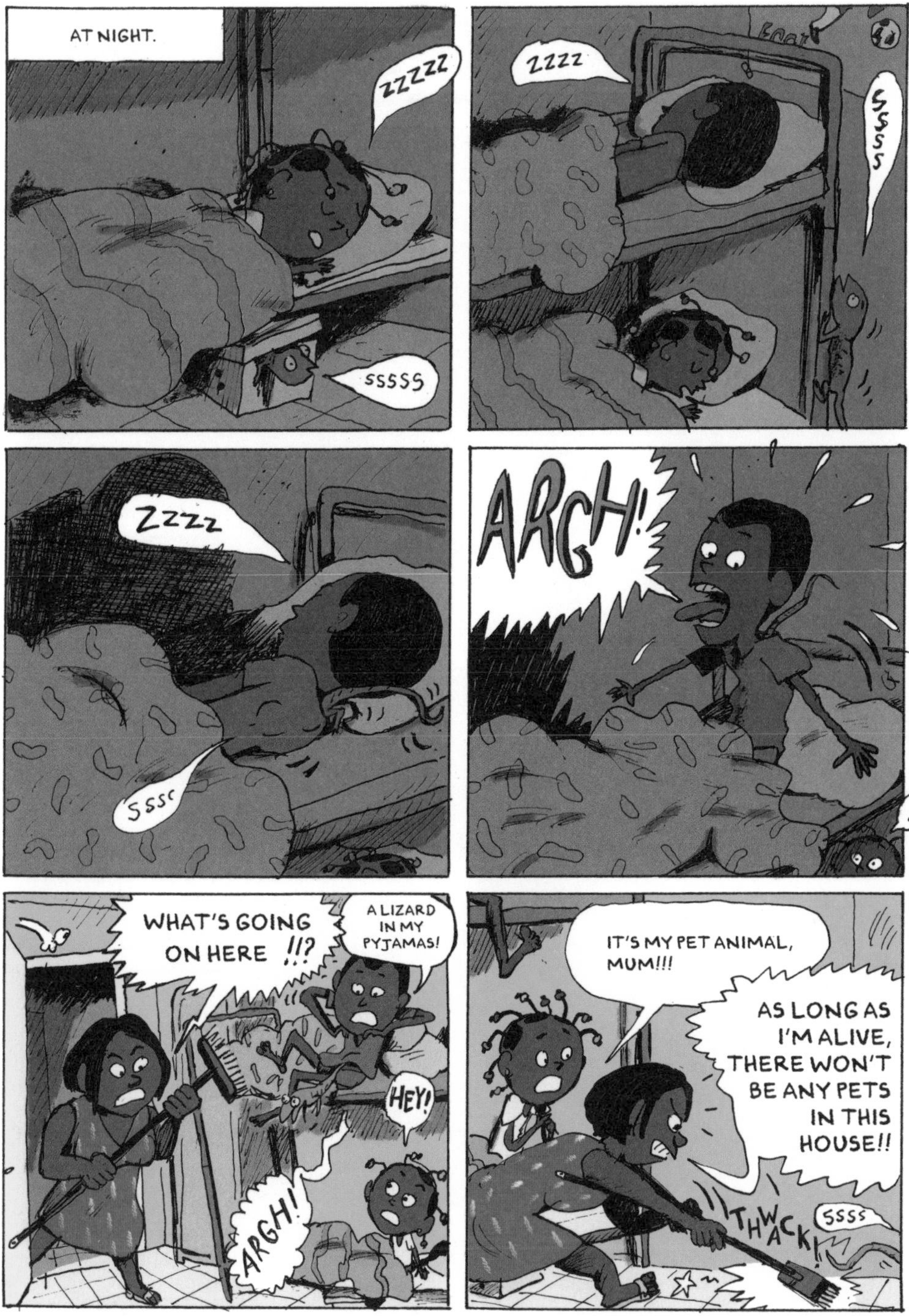
AT NIGHT.
ZZZZZ
SSSSS
ZZZZ
SSSSS
ZZZZ
SSSC
ARGH!
?
WHAT'S GOING ON HERE !!?
A LIZARD IN MY PYJAMAS!
HEY!
ARGH!
IT'S MY PET ANIMAL, MUM!!!
AS LONG AS I'M ALIVE, THERE WON'T BE ANY PETS IN THIS HOUSE!!
THWACK!
SSSS

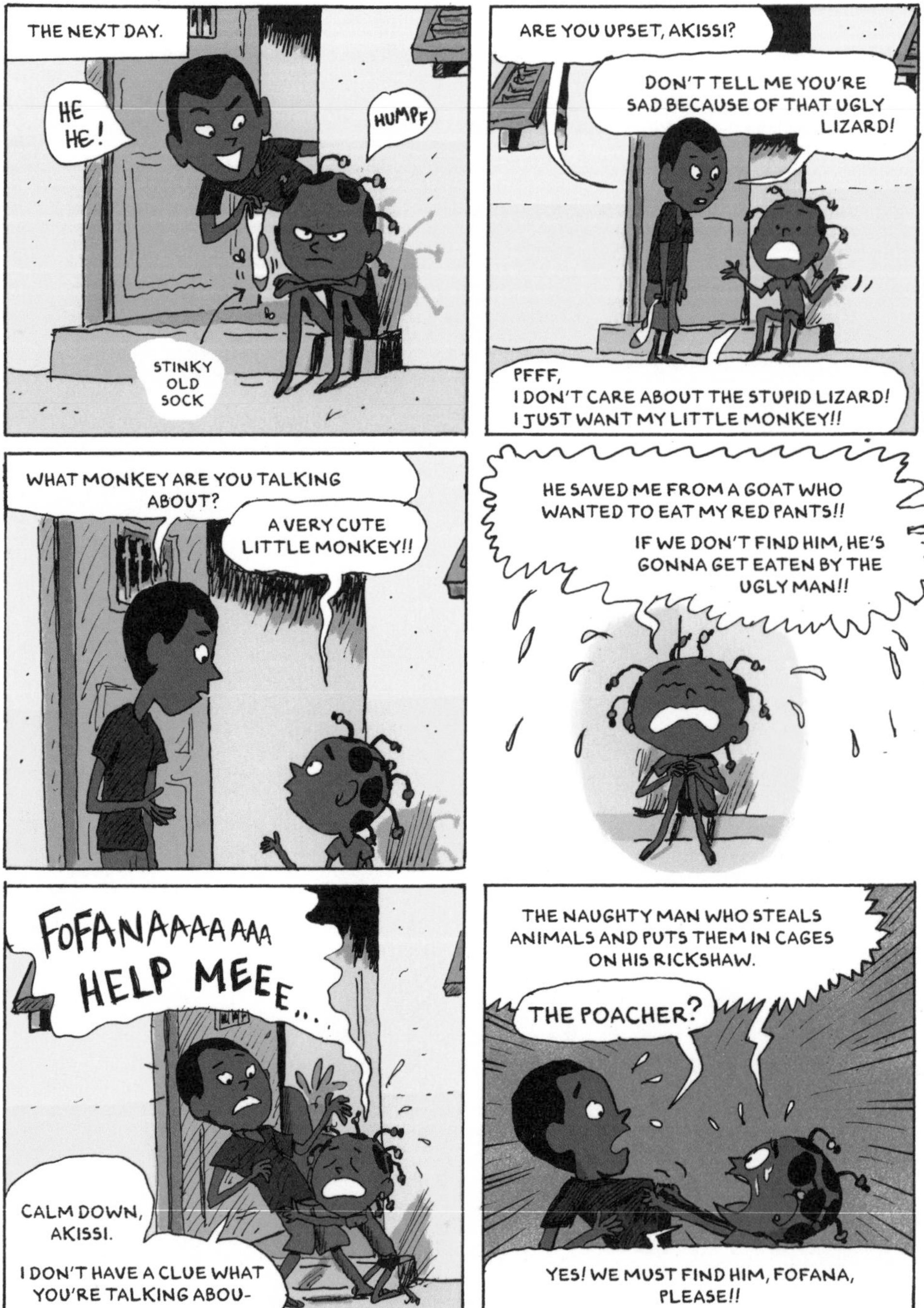
THE NEXT DAY.
HE HE!
HUMPF
STINKY OLD SOCK
ARE YOU UPSET, AKISSI?
DON'T TELL ME YOU'RE SAD BECAUSE OF THAT UGLY LIZARD!
PFFF, I DON'T CARE ABOUT THE STUPID LIZARD! I JUST WANT MY LITTLE MONKEY!!
WHAT MONKEY ARE YOU TALKING ABOUT?
A VERY CUTE LITTLE MONKEY!!
HE SAVED ME FROM A GOAT WHO WANTED TO EAT MY RED PANTS!!
IF WE DON'T FIND HIM, HE'S GONNA GET EATEN BY THE UGLY MAN!!
FOFANAAAAAAA HELP MEEE...
CALM DOWN, AKISSI.
I DON'T HAVE A CLUE WHAT YOU'RE TALKING ABOU-
THE NAUGHTY MAN WHO STEALS ANIMALS AND PUTS THEM IN CAGES ON HIS RICKSHAW.
THE POACHER?
YES! WE MUST FIND HIM, FOFANA, PLEASE!!

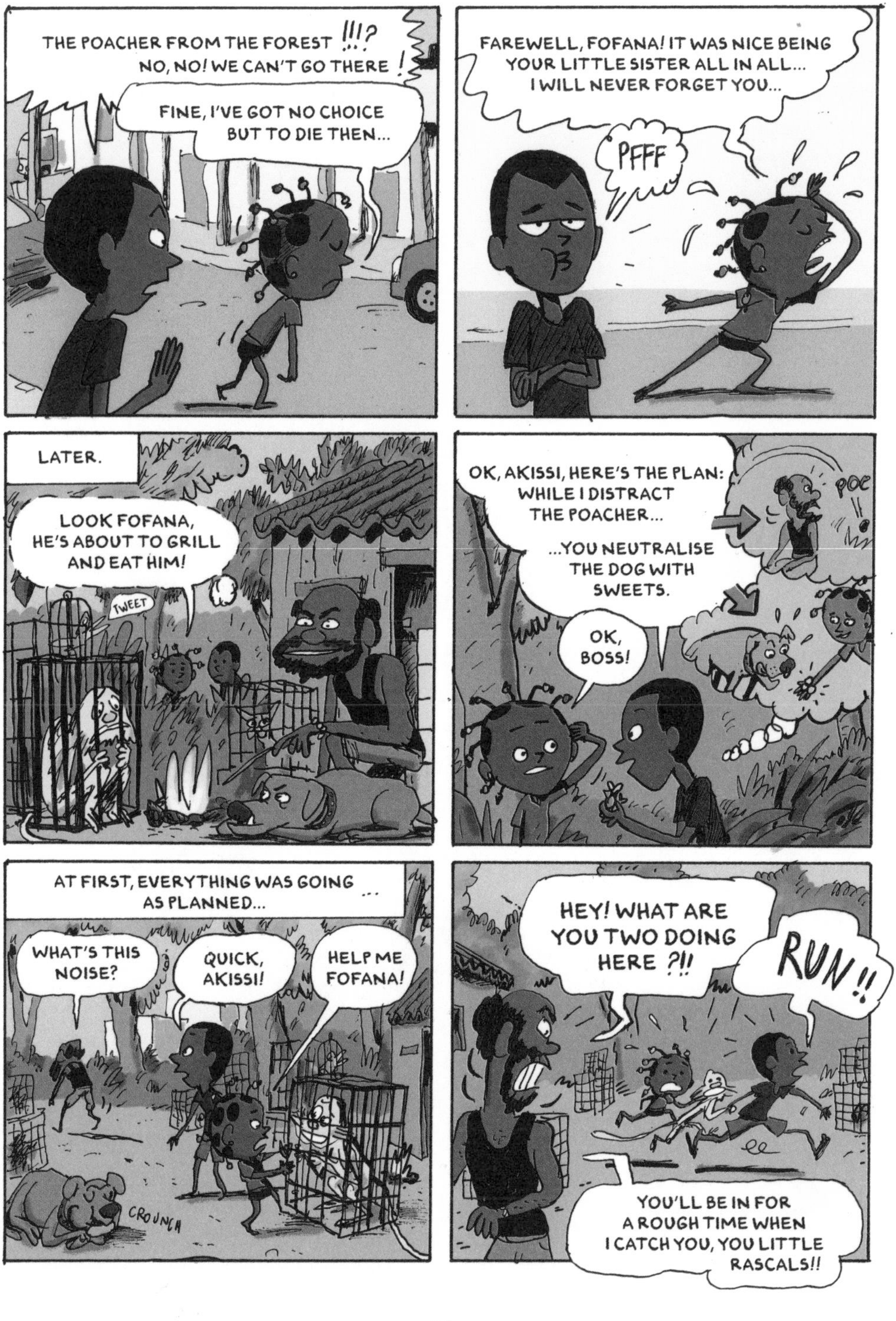

THE POACHER FROM THE FOREST !!!?
NO, NO! WE CAN'T GO THERE !
FINE, I'VE GOT NO CHOICE BUT TO DIE THEN...
FAREWELL, FOFANA! IT WAS NICE BEING YOUR LITTLE SISTER ALL IN ALL... I WILL NEVER FORGET YOU...
PFFF
LATER.
LOOK FOFANA, HE'S ABOUT TO GRILL AND EAT HIM!
TWEET
OK, AKISSI, HERE'S THE PLAN: WHILE I DISTRACT THE POACHER...
...YOU NEUTRALISE THE DOG WITH SWEETS.
POC
OK, BOSS!
AT FIRST, EVERYTHING WAS GOING AS PLANNED...
WHAT'S THIS NOISE?
QUICK, AKISSI!
HELP ME FOFANA!
CROUNCH
HEY! WHAT ARE YOU TWO DOING HERE ?!!
RUN !!
YOU'LL BE IN FOR A ROUGH TIME WHEN I CATCH YOU, YOU LITTLE RASCALS!!

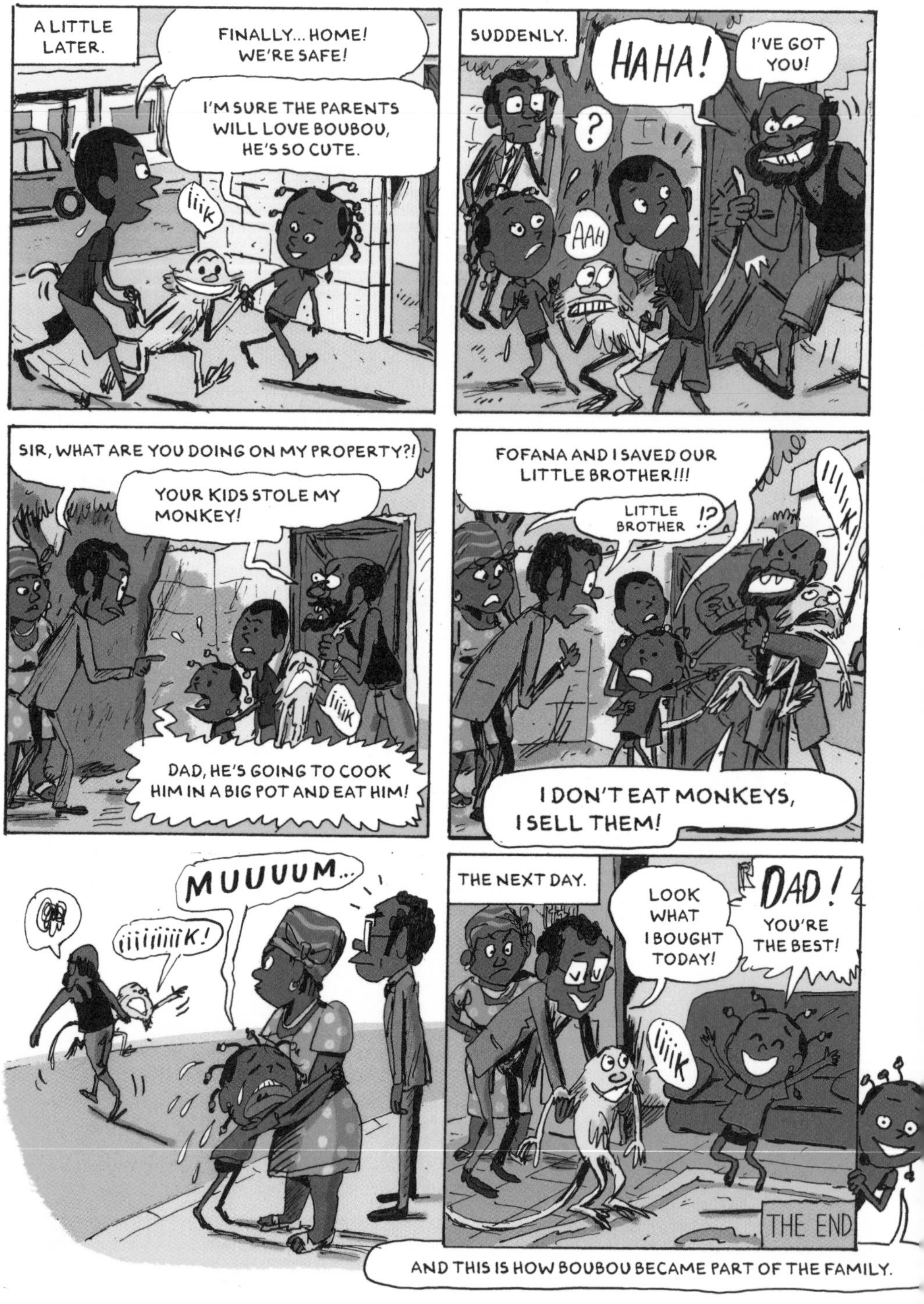
A LITTLE LATER.
FINALLY... HOME! WE'RE SAFE!
I'M SURE THE PARENTS WILL LOVE BOUBOU, HE'S SO CUTE.
IIIK
SUDDENLY.
HAHA!
I'VE GOT YOU!
?
AAH
SIR, WHAT ARE YOU DOING ON MY PROPERTY?!
YOUR KIDS STOLE MY MONKEY!
IIIIK
DAD, HE'S GOING TO COOK HIM IN A BIG POT AND EAT HIM!
FOFANA AND I SAVED OUR LITTLE BROTHER!!!
LITTLE BROTHER !?
IIIIK
I DON'T EAT MONKEYS, I SELL THEM!
MUUUUM...
IIIIIIIIK!
THE NEXT DAY.
LOOK WHAT I BOUGHT TODAY!
DAD! YOU'RE THE BEST!
IIIIK
THE END
AND THIS IS HOW BOUBOU BECAME PART OF THE FAMILY.

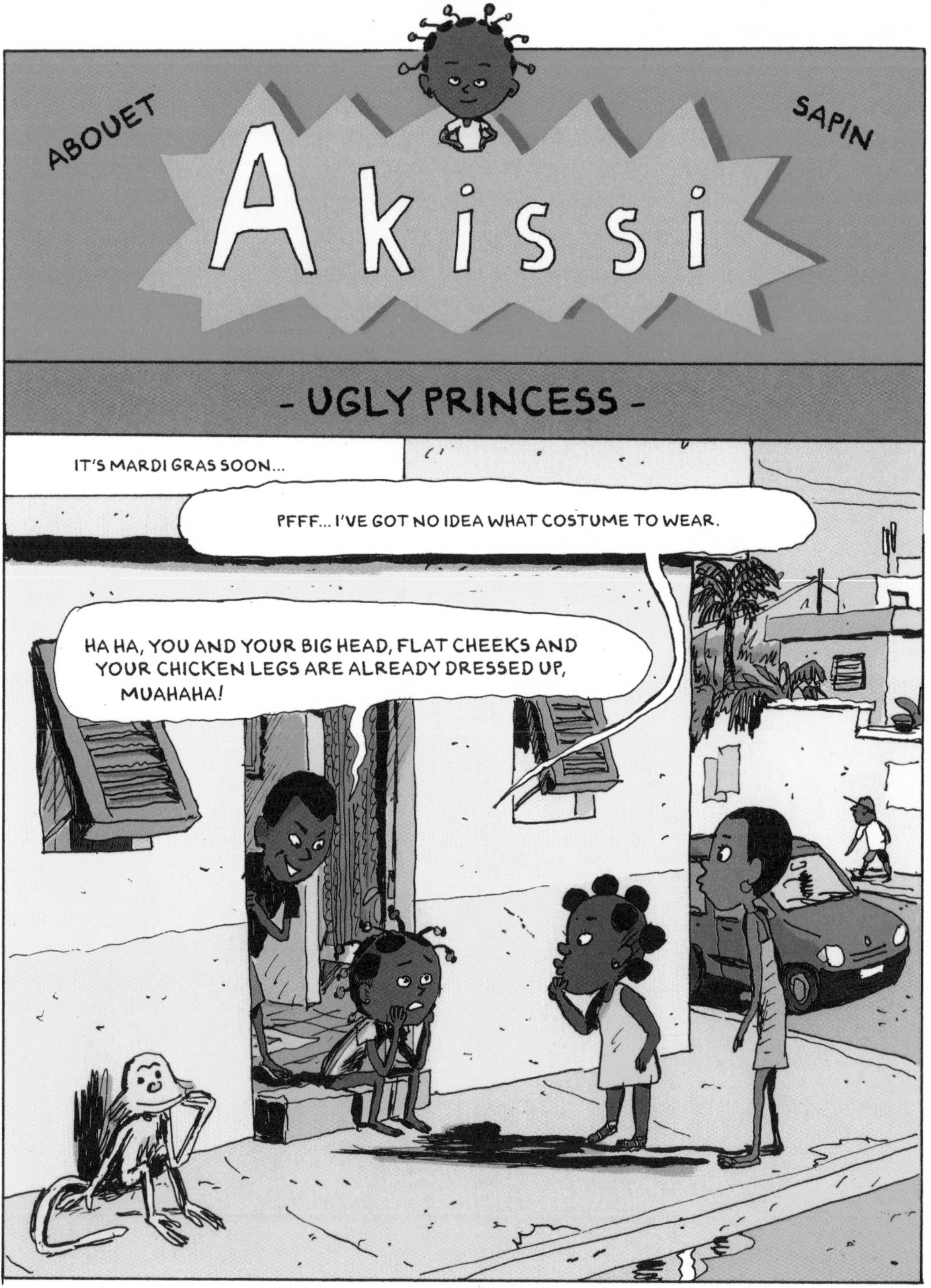
ABOUET
Akissi
SAPIN
- UGLY PRINCESS -
IT'S MARDI GRAS SOON...
PFFF... I'VE GOT NO IDEA WHAT COSTUME TO WEAR.
HA HA, YOU AND YOUR BIG HEAD, FLAT CHEEKS AND YOUR CHICKEN LEGS ARE ALREADY DRESSED UP, MUAHAHA!

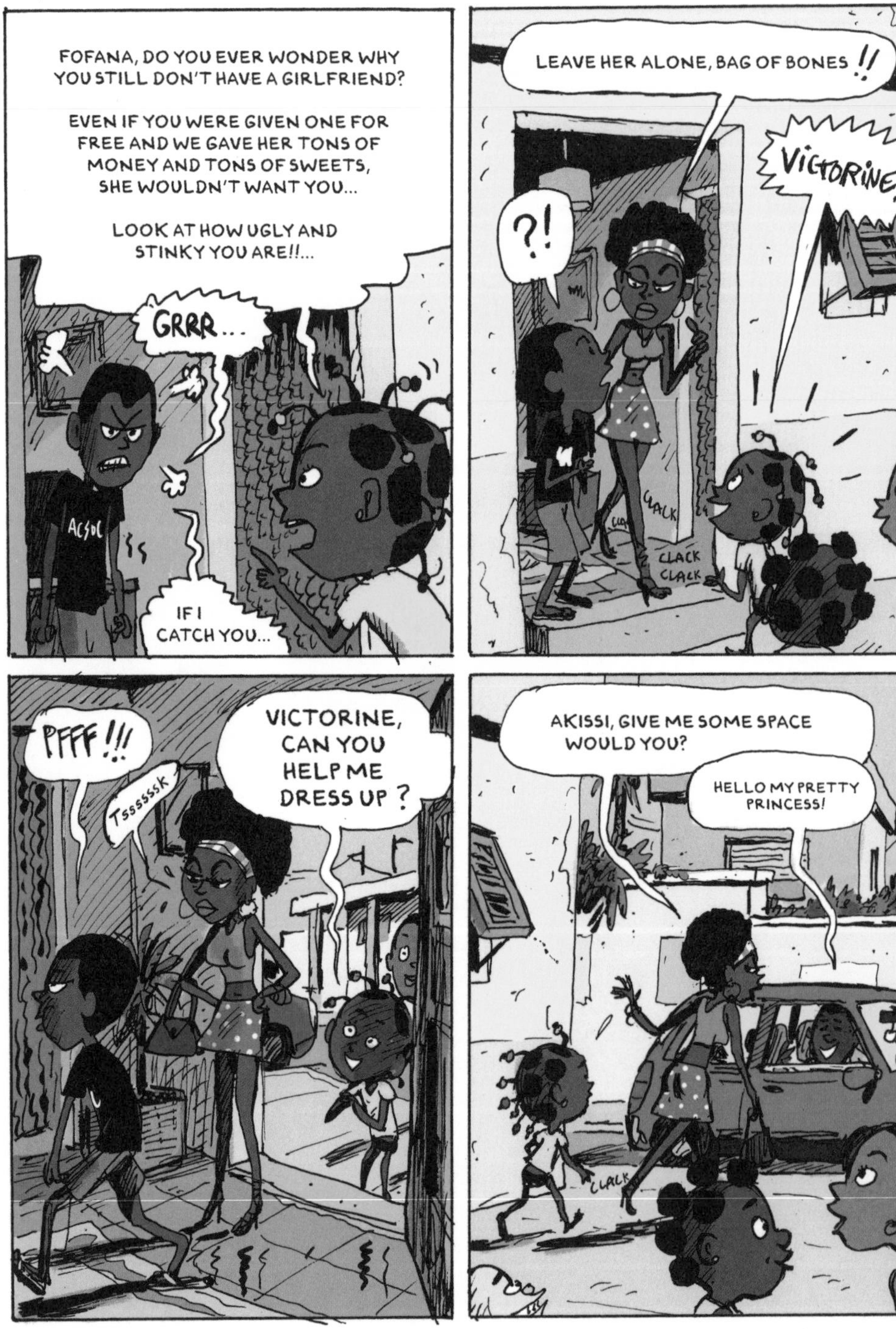
FOFANA, DO YOU EVER WONDER WHY YOU STILL DON'T HAVE A GIRLFRIEND?
EVEN IF YOU WERE GIVEN ONE FOR FREE AND WE GAVE HER TONS OF MONEY AND TONS OF SWEETS, SHE WOULDN'T WANT YOU...
LOOK AT HOW UGLY AND STINKY YOU ARE!!...
GRRR...
IF I CATCH YOU...
LEAVE HER ALONE, BAG OF BONES !!
VICTORINE!
?!
CLACK
CLACK CLACK
PFFF!!!
Tsssssssk
VICTORINE, CAN YOU HELP ME DRESS UP ?
AKISSI, GIVE ME SOME SPACE WOULD YOU?
HELLO MY PRETTY PRINCESS!
CLACK

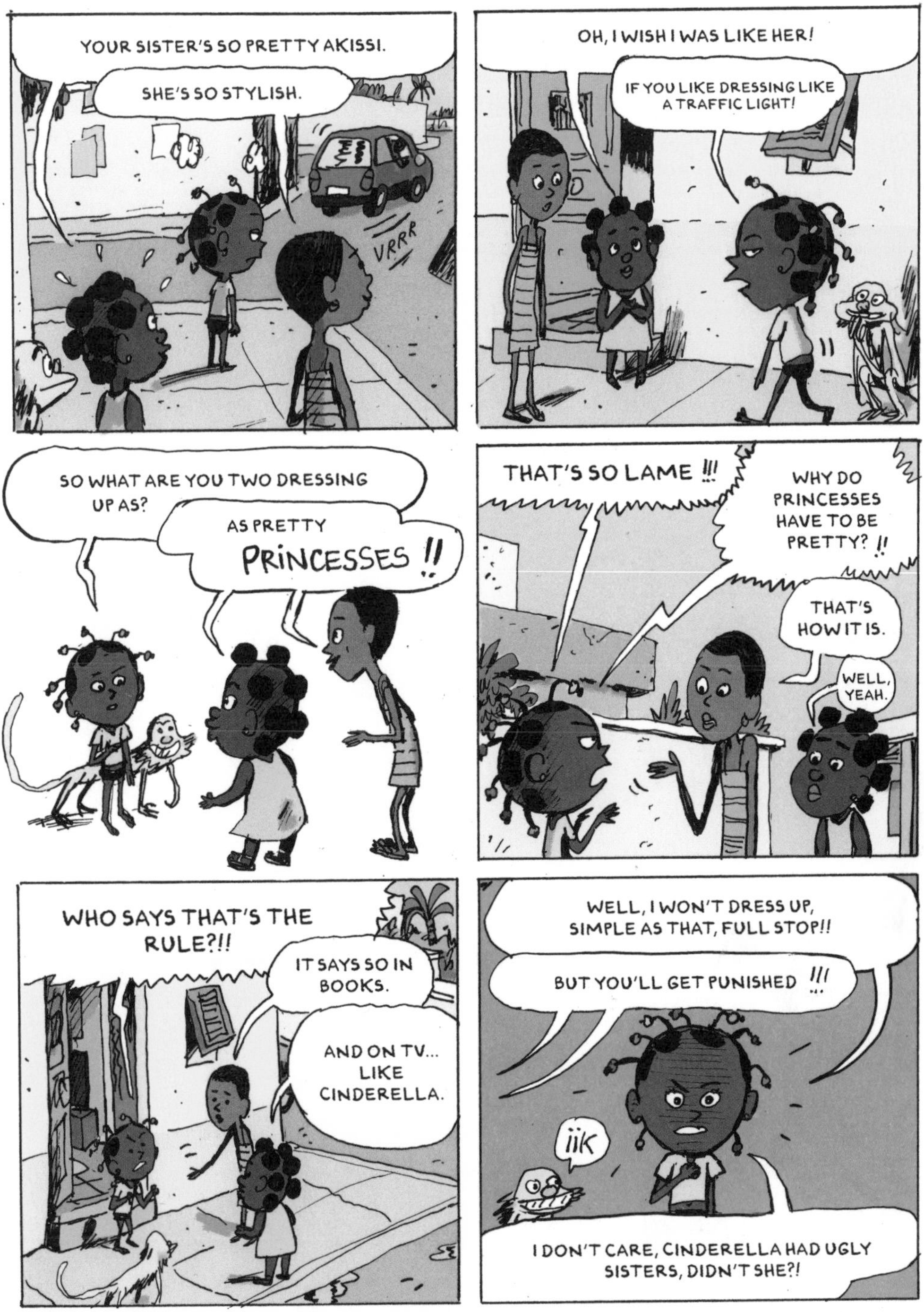
YOUR SISTER'S SO PRETTY AKISSI.
SHE'S SO STYLISH.
VRRR
OH, I WISH I WAS LIKE HER!
IF YOU LIKE DRESSING LIKE A TRAFFIC LIGHT!
SO WHAT ARE YOU TWO DRESSING UP AS?
AS PRETTY PRINCESSES !!
THAT'S SO LAME !!!
WHY DO PRINCESSES HAVE TO BE PRETTY? !!
THAT'S HOW IT IS.
WELL, YEAH.
WHO SAYS THAT'S THE RULE?!!
IT SAYS SO IN BOOKS.
AND ON TV... LIKE CINDERELLA.
WELL, I WON'T DRESS UP, SIMPLE AS THAT, FULL STOP!!
BUT YOU'LL GET PUNISHED !!!
iiK
I DON'T CARE, CINDERELLA HAD UGLY SISTERS, DIDN'T SHE?!

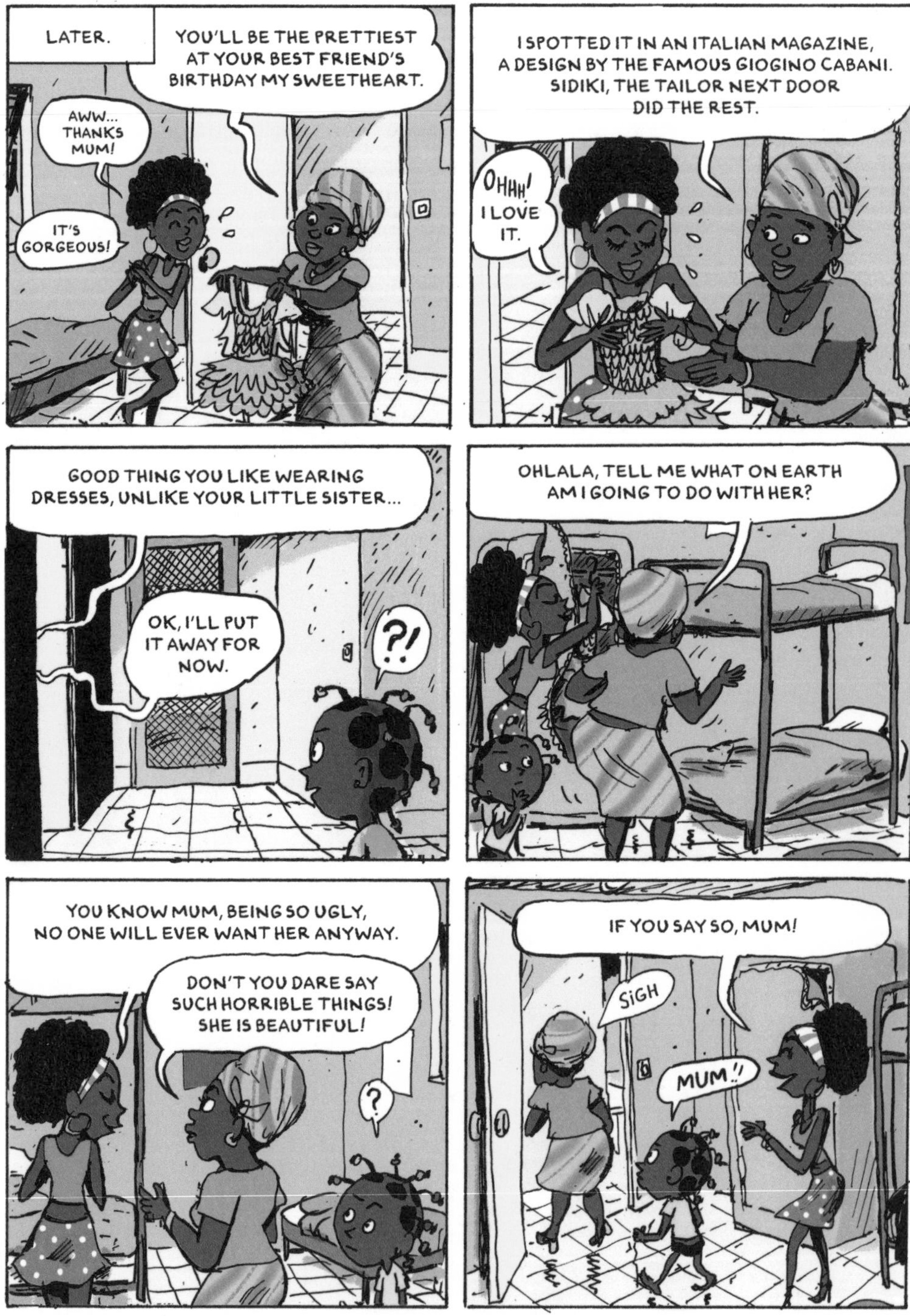
LATER.
YOU'LL BE THE PRETTIEST AT YOUR BEST FRIEND'S BIRTHDAY MY SWEETHEART.
AWW... THANKS MUM!
IT'S GORGEOUS!
I SPOTTED IT IN AN ITALIAN MAGAZINE, A DESIGN BY THE FAMOUS GIOGINO CABANI. SIDIKI, THE TAILOR NEXT DOOR DID THE REST.
OHHH! I LOVE IT.
GOOD THING YOU LIKE WEARING DRESSES, UNLIKE YOUR LITTLE SISTER...
OK, I'LL PUT IT AWAY FOR NOW.
?!
OHLALA, TELL ME WHAT ON EARTH AM I GOING TO DO WITH HER?
YOU KNOW MUM, BEING SO UGLY, NO ONE WILL EVER WANT HER ANYWAY.
DON'T YOU DARE SAY SUCH HORRIBLE THINGS! SHE IS BEAUTIFUL!
?
IF YOU SAY SO, MUM!
SIGH
MUM!!

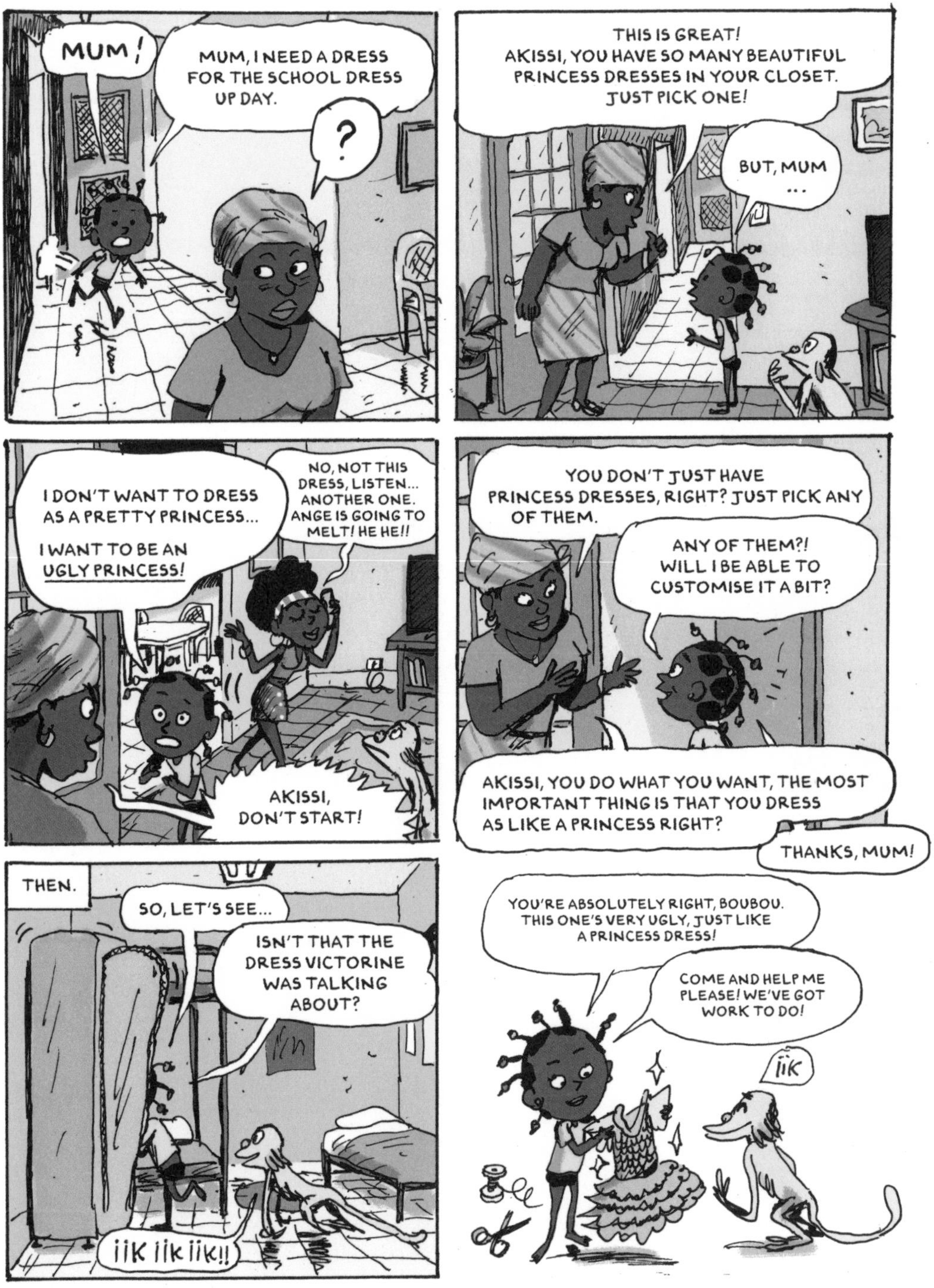
MUM!
MUM, I NEED A DRESS FOR THE SCHOOL DRESS UP DAY.
?
THIS IS GREAT! AKISSI, YOU HAVE SO MANY BEAUTIFUL PRINCESS DRESSES IN YOUR CLOSET. JUST PICK ONE!
BUT, MUM ...
I DON'T WANT TO DRESS AS A PRETTY PRINCESS...
I WANT TO BE AN UGLY PRINCESS!
NO, NOT THIS DRESS, LISTEN... ANOTHER ONE. ANGE IS GOING TO MELT! HE HE!!
AKISSI, DON'T START!
YOU DON'T JUST HAVE PRINCESS DRESSES, RIGHT? JUST PICK ANY OF THEM.
ANY OF THEM?! WILL I BE ABLE TO CUSTOMISE IT A BIT?
AKISSI, YOU DO WHAT YOU WANT, THE MOST IMPORTANT THING IS THAT YOU DRESS AS LIKE A PRINCESS RIGHT?
THANKS, MUM!
THEN.
SO, LET'S SEE...
ISN'T THAT THE DRESS VICTORINE WAS TALKING ABOUT?
IIK IIK IIK!!
YOU'RE ABSOLUTELY RIGHT, BOUBOU. THIS ONE'S VERY UGLY, JUST LIKE A PRINCESS DRESS!
COME AND HELP ME PLEASE! WE'VE GOT WORK TO DO!
IIK

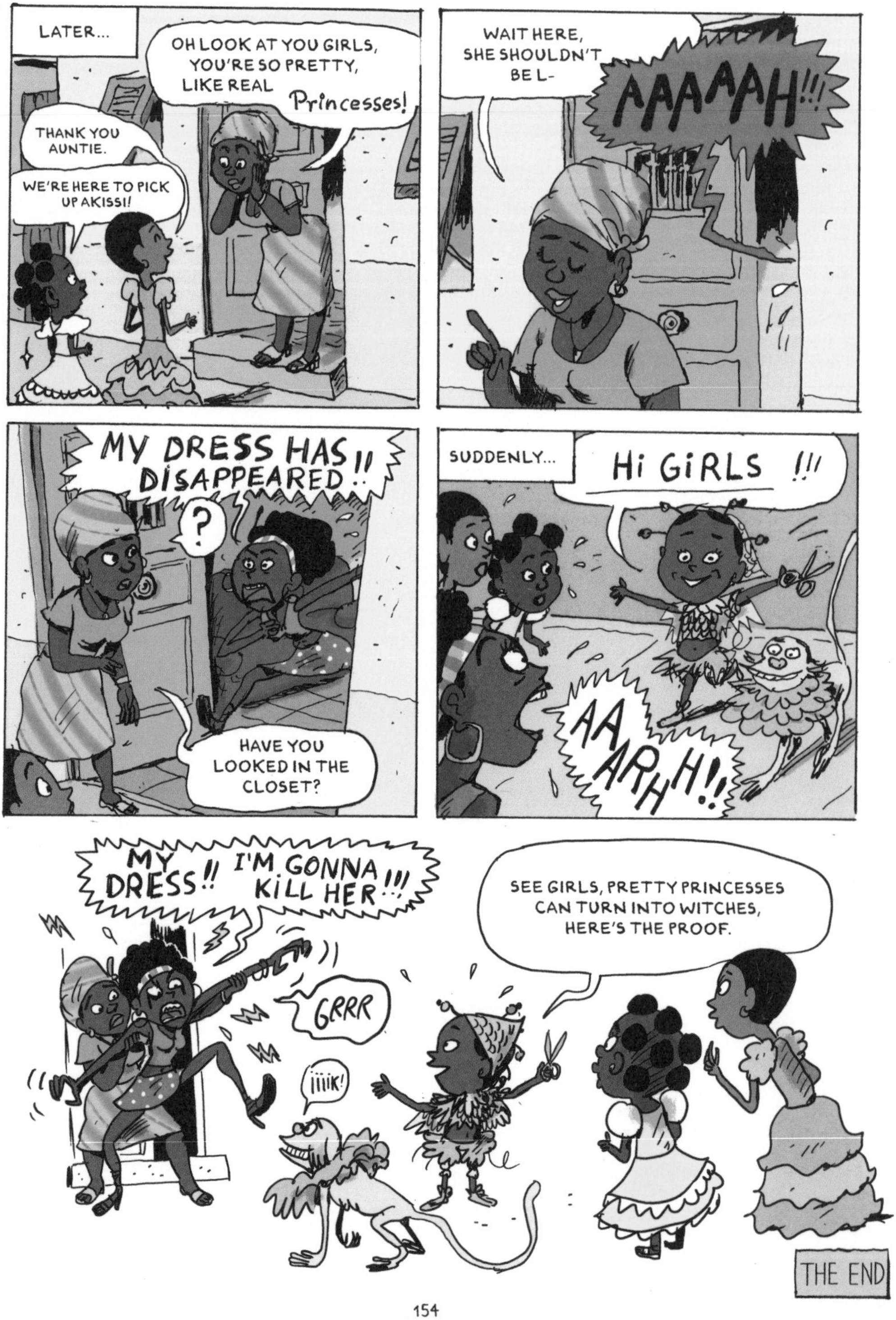
LATER...
OH LOOK AT YOU GIRLS, YOU'RE SO PRETTY, LIKE REAL Princesses!
THANK YOU AUNTIE.
WE'RE HERE TO PICK UP AKISSI!
WAIT HERE, SHE SHOULDN'T BE L-
AAAAAH!!!
MY DRESS HAS DISAPPEARED!!
?
HAVE YOU LOOKED IN THE CLOSET?
SUDDENLY...
Hi GIRLS !!!
AAARHH!!
MY DRESS!! I'M GONNA KILL HER!!!
GRRR
iiiiik!
SEE GIRLS, PRETTY PRINCESSES CAN TURN INTO WITCHES, HERE'S THE PROOF.
THE END

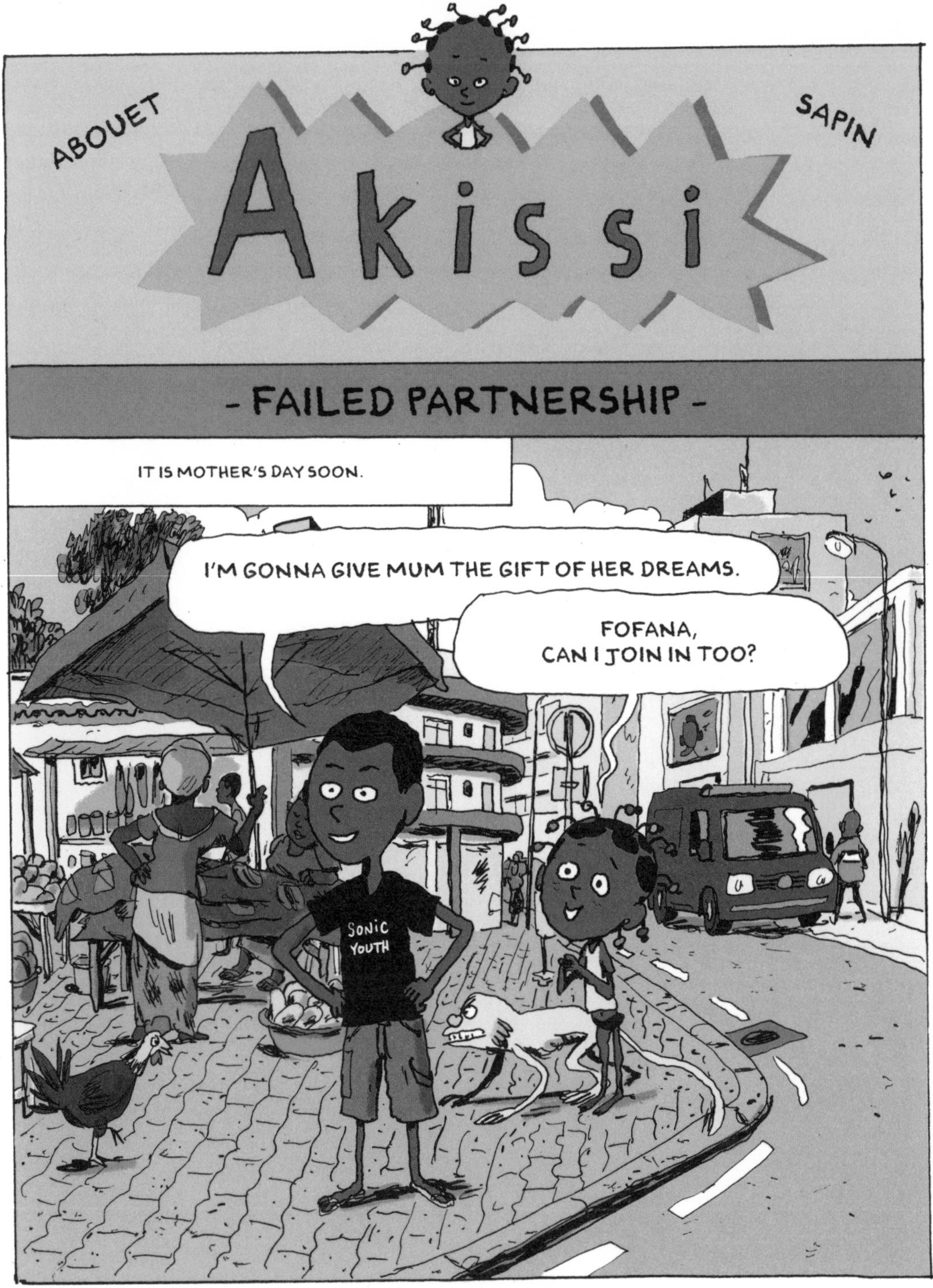
ABOUET
SAPIN
Akissi
- FAILED PARTNERSHIP -
IT IS MOTHER'S DAY SOON.
I'M GONNA GIVE MUM THE GIFT OF HER DREAMS.
FOFANA, CAN I JOIN IN TOO?
SONIC YOUTH

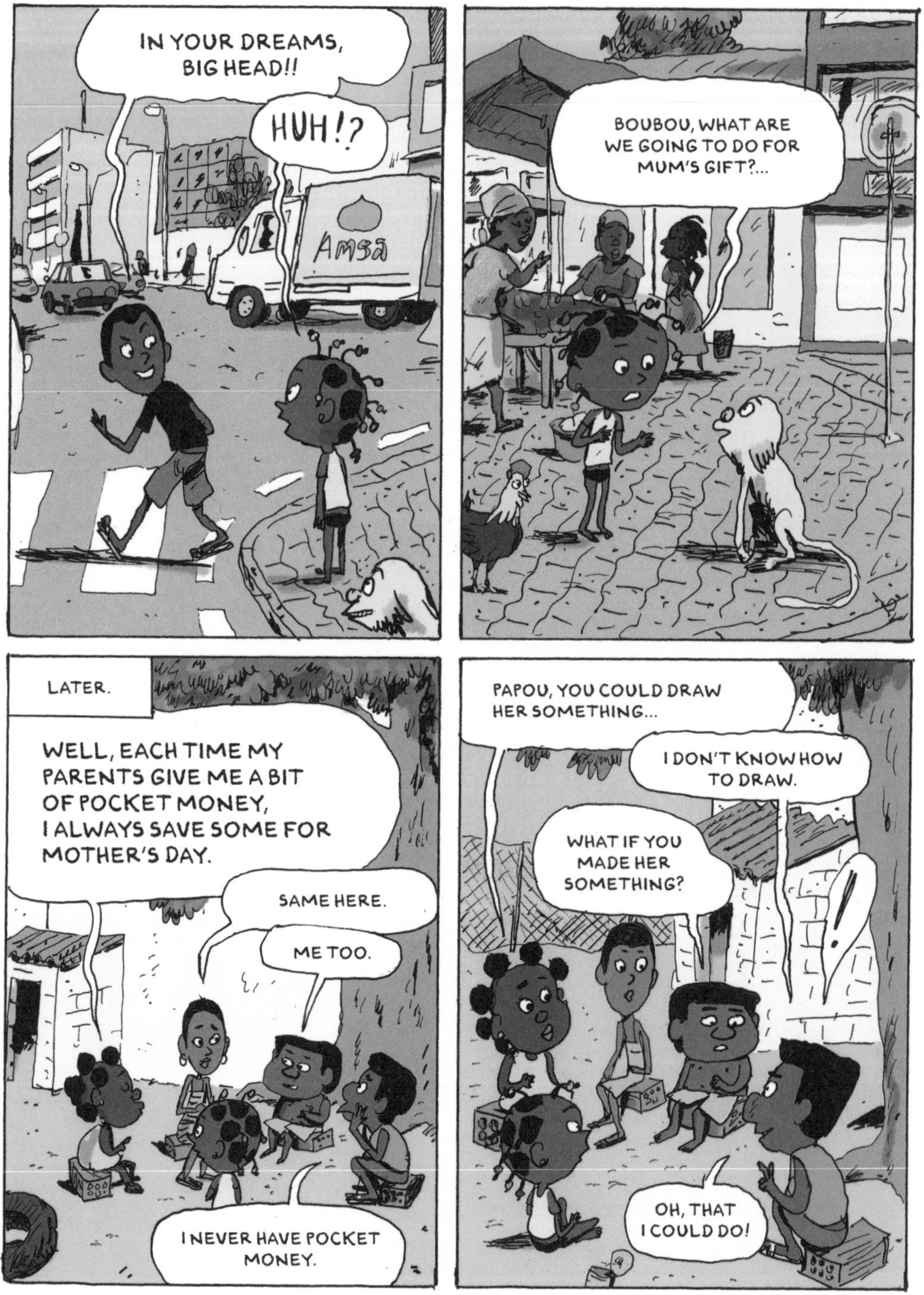
IN YOUR DREAMS, BIG HEAD!!
HUH!?
Amsa
BOUBOU, WHAT ARE WE GOING TO DO FOR MUM'S GIFT?...
LATER.
WELL, EACH TIME MY PARENTS GIVE ME A BIT OF POCKET MONEY, I ALWAYS SAVE SOME FOR MOTHER'S DAY.
SAME HERE.
ME TOO.
I NEVER HAVE POCKET MONEY.
PAPOU, YOU COULD DRAW HER SOMETHING...
I DON'T KNOW HOW TO DRAW.
WHAT IF YOU MADE HER SOMETHING?
!
OH, THAT I COULD DO!

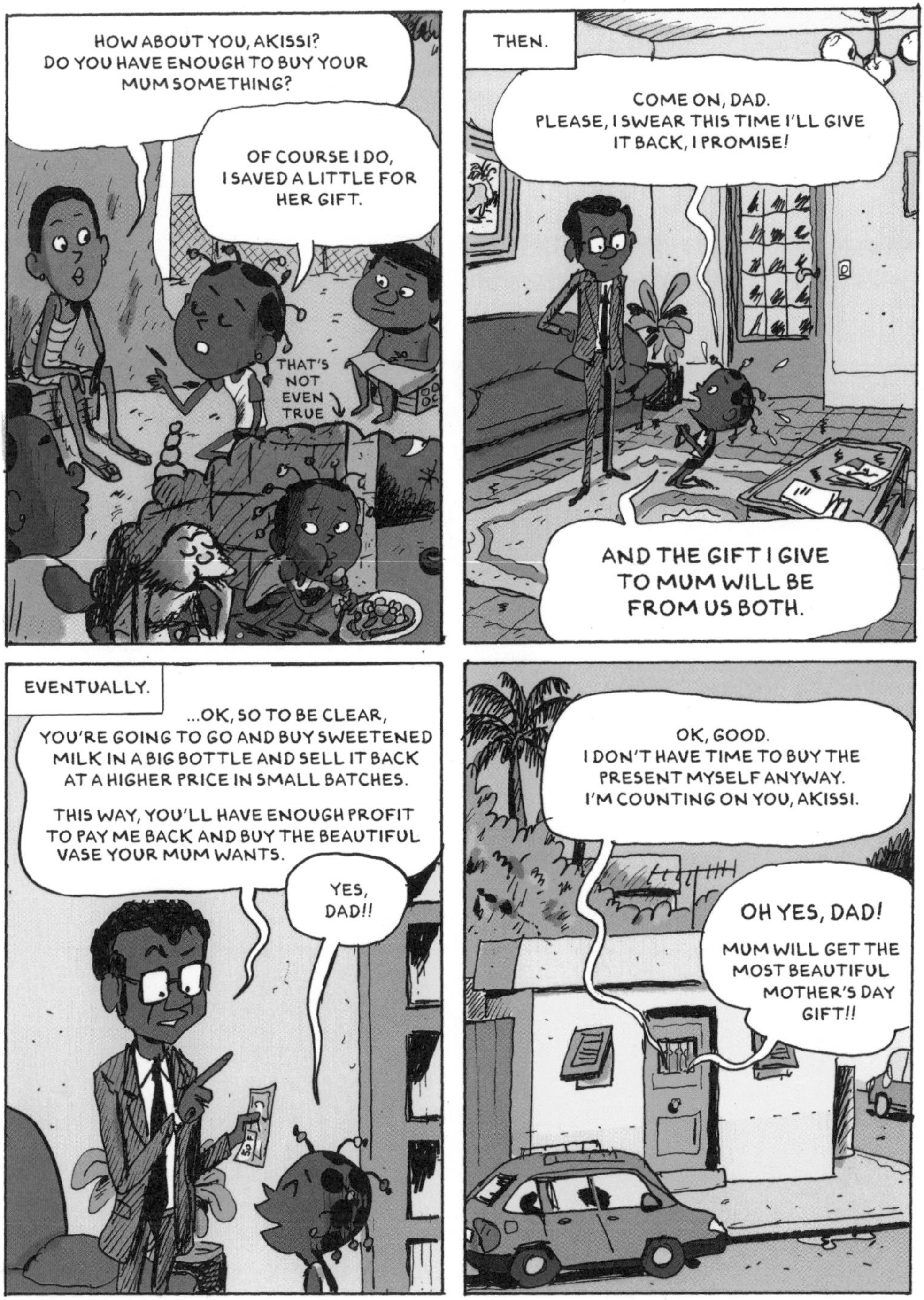
HOW ABOUT YOU, AKISSI? DO YOU HAVE ENOUGH TO BUY YOUR MUM SOMETHING?
OF COURSE I DO, I SAVED A LITTLE FOR HER GIFT.
THAT'S NOT EVEN TRUE
THEN.
COME ON, DAD. PLEASE, I SWEAR THIS TIME I'LL GIVE IT BACK, I PROMISE!
AND THE GIFT I GIVE TO MUM WILL BE FROM US BOTH.
EVENTUALLY.
...OK, SO TO BE CLEAR, YOU'RE GOING TO GO AND BUY SWEETENED MILK IN A BIG BOTTLE AND SELL IT BACK AT A HIGHER PRICE IN SMALL BATCHES.
THIS WAY, YOU'LL HAVE ENOUGH PROFIT TO PAY ME BACK AND BUY THE BEAUTIFUL VASE YOUR MUM WANTS.
YES, DAD!!
OK, GOOD. I DON'T HAVE TIME TO BUY THE PRESENT MYSELF ANYWAY. I'M COUNTING ON YOU, AKISSI.
OH YES, DAD!
MUM WILL GET THE MOST BEAUTIFUL MOTHER'S DAY GIFT!!

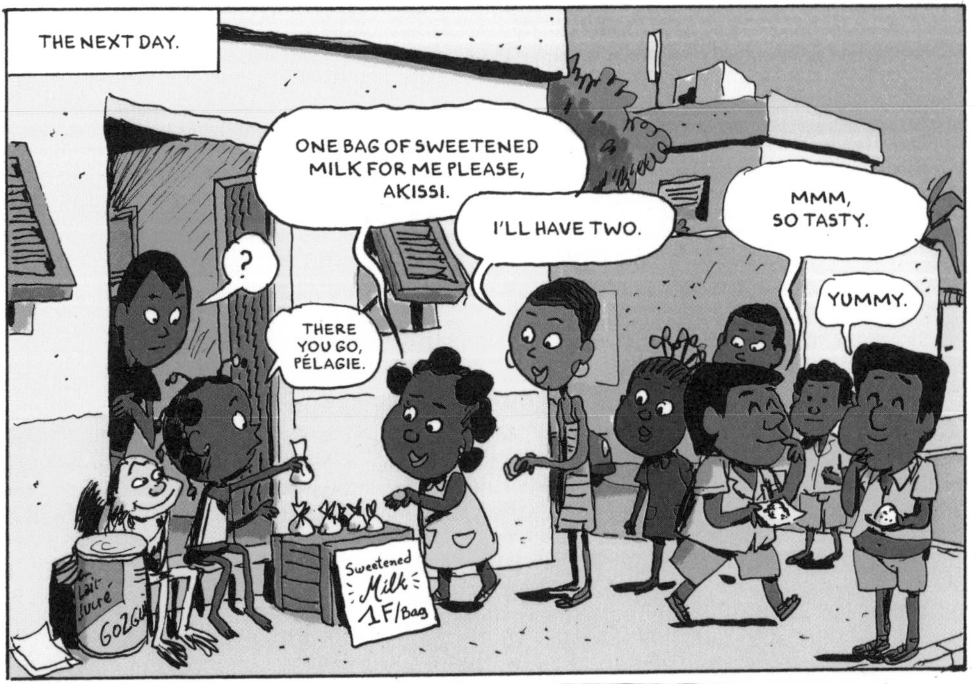
THE NEXT DAY.
ONE BAG OF SWEETENED MILK FOR ME PLEASE, AKISSI.
?
THERE YOU GO, PÉLAGIE.
I'LL HAVE TWO.
MMM, SO TASTY.
YUMMY.
Lait sucré
GOZGU
Sweetened Milk 1F/Bag

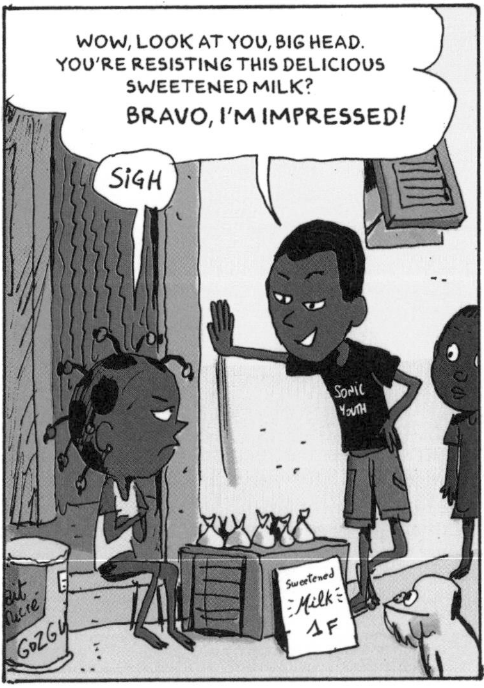
WOW, LOOK AT YOU, BIG HEAD. YOU'RE RESISTING THIS DELICIOUS SWEETENED MILK? BRAVO, I'M IMPRESSED!
SIGH
SONIC YOUTH
Sweetened Milk 1F

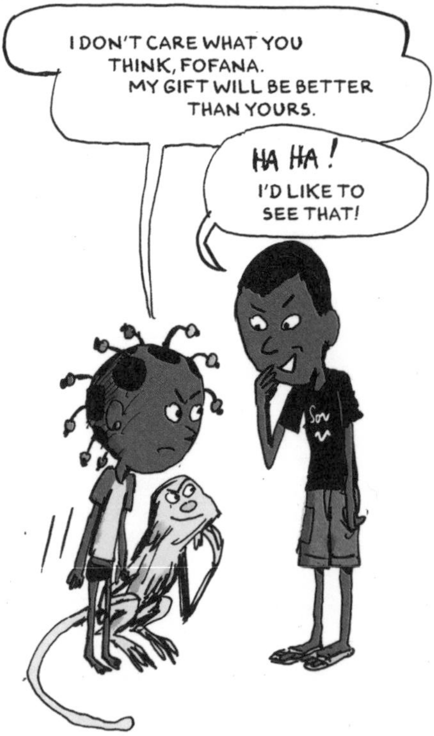
I DON'T CARE WHAT YOU THINK, FOFANA. MY GIFT WILL BE BETTER THAN YOURS.
HA HA! I'D LIKE TO SEE THAT!

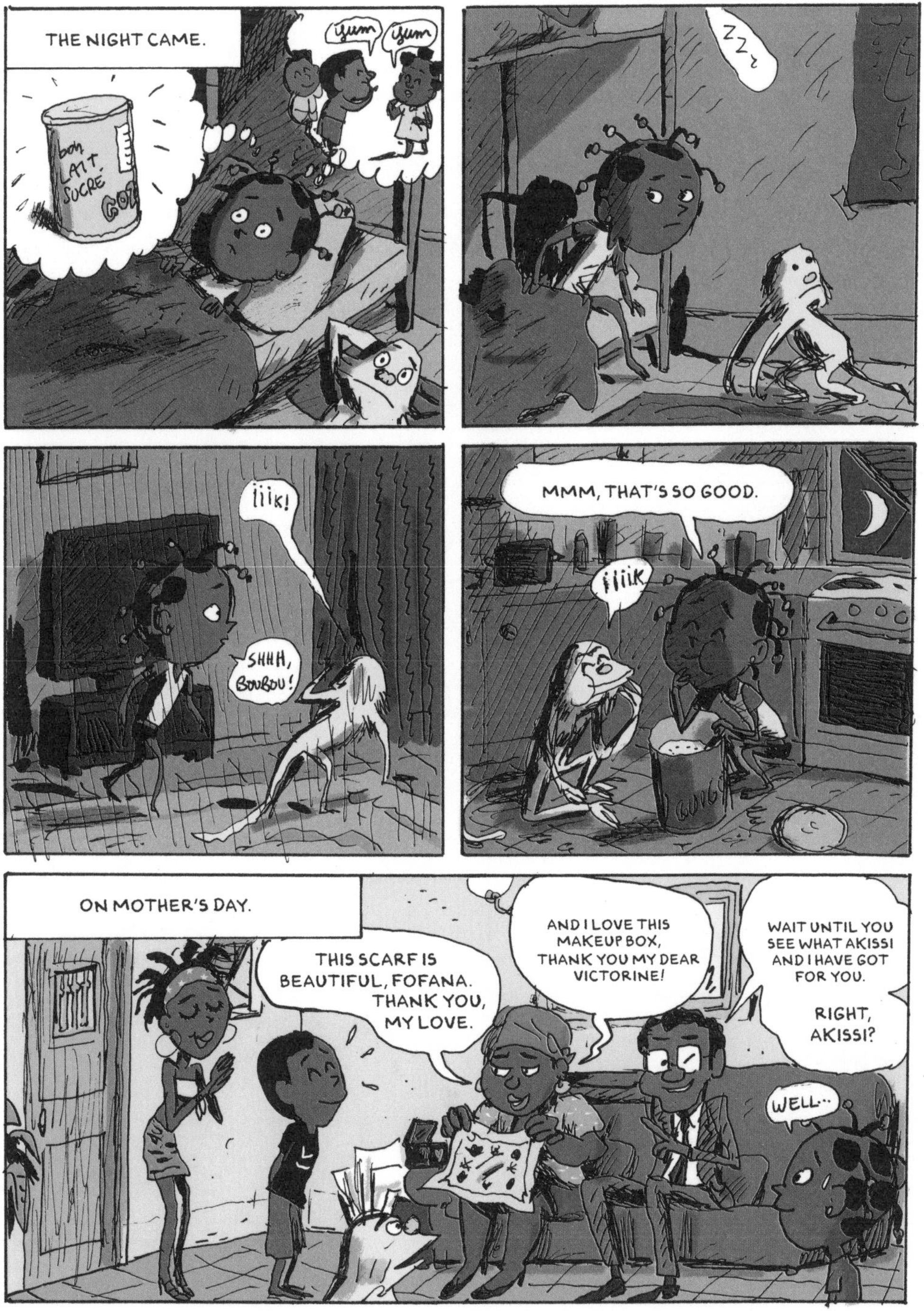
THE NIGHT CAME.
yum
yum
LAIT SUCRÉ
ZZZ
IIIK!
SHHH, BOUBOU!
MMM, THAT'S SO GOOD.
IIIIK
ON MOTHER'S DAY.
THIS SCARF IS BEAUTIFUL, FOFANA. THANK YOU, MY LOVE.
AND I LOVE THIS MAKEUP BOX, THANK YOU MY DEAR VICTORINE!
WAIT UNTIL YOU SEE WHAT AKISSI AND I HAVE GOT FOR YOU.
RIGHT, AKISSI?
WELL...

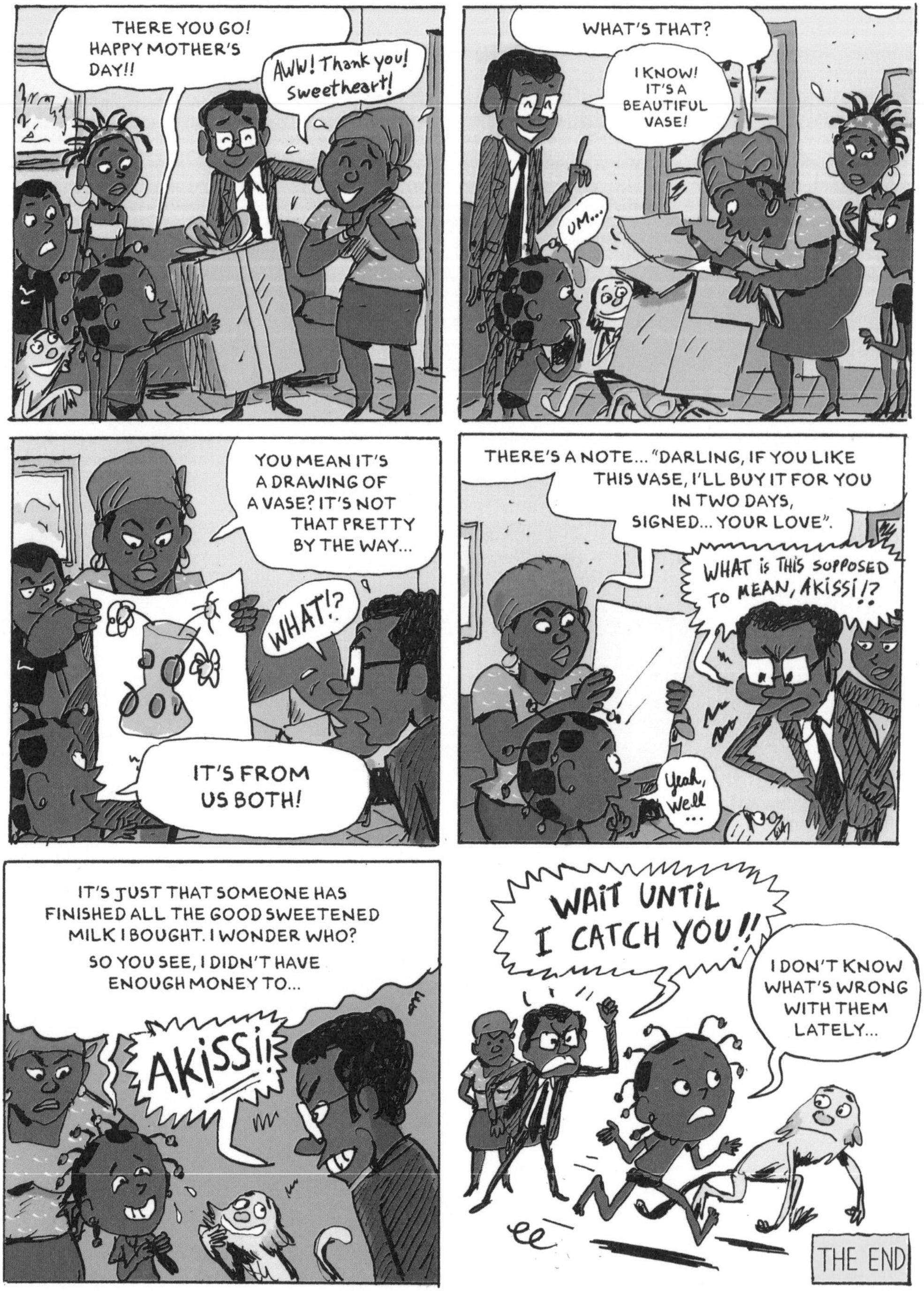
THERE YOU GO! HAPPY MOTHER'S DAY!!
AWW! Thank you! Sweetheart!
WHAT'S THAT?
I KNOW! IT'S A BEAUTIFUL VASE!
UM...
YOU MEAN IT'S A DRAWING OF A VASE? IT'S NOT THAT PRETTY BY THE WAY...
WHAT!?
IT'S FROM US BOTH!
THERE'S A NOTE... "DARLING, IF YOU LIKE THIS VASE, I'LL BUY IT FOR YOU IN TWO DAYS, SIGNED... YOUR LOVE".
WHAT is THIS SUPPOSED TO MEAN, AKISSI!?
Yeah, Well ...
IT'S JUST THAT SOMEONE HAS FINISHED ALL THE GOOD SWEETENED MILK I BOUGHT. I WONDER WHO?
SO YOU SEE, I DIDN'T HAVE ENOUGH MONEY TO...
AKISSI!
WAIT UNTIL I CATCH YOU!!
I DON'T KNOW WHAT'S WRONG WITH THEM LATELY...
THE END

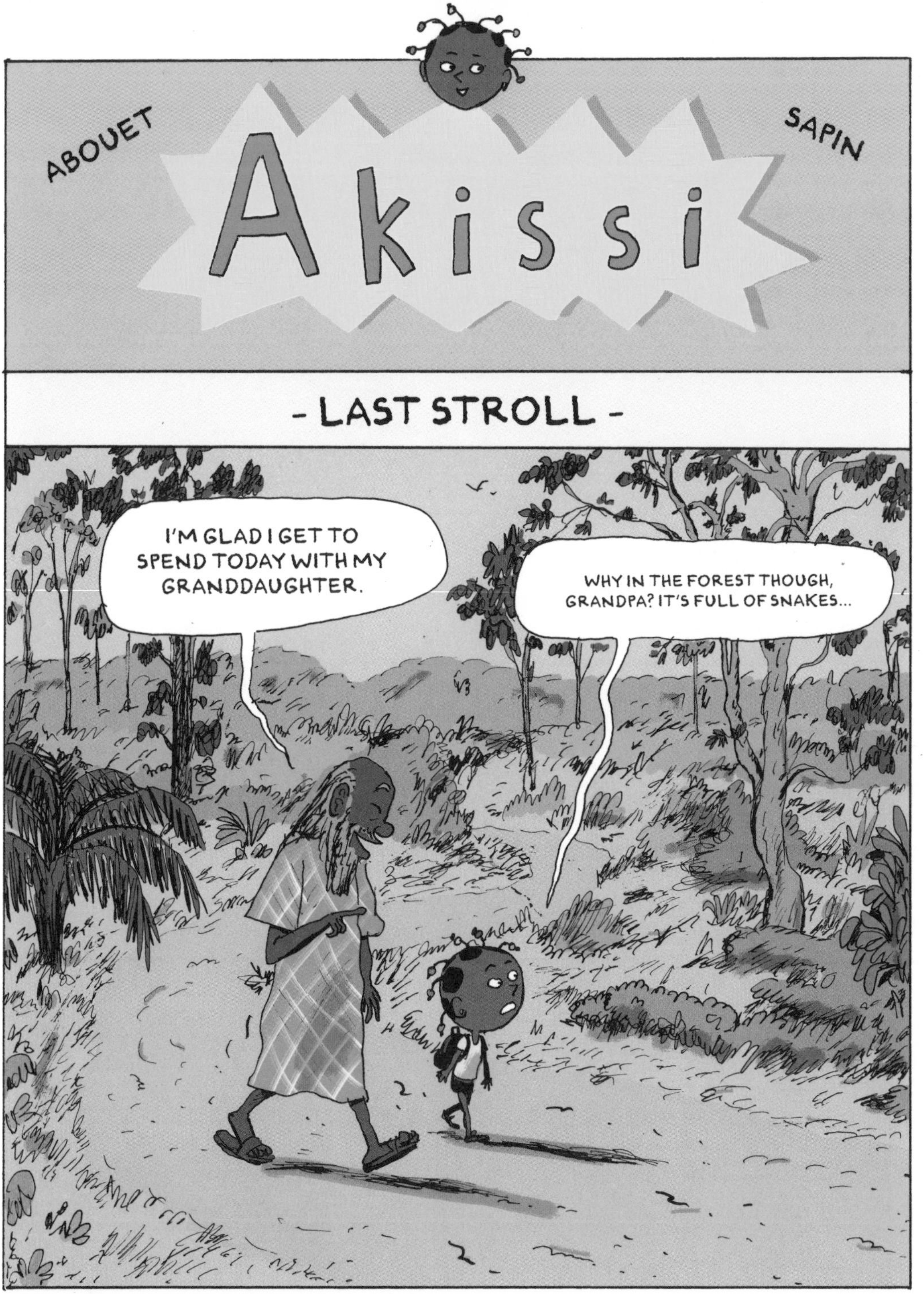
ABOUET
Akissi
SAPIN
- LAST STROLL -
I'M GLAD I GET TO SPEND TODAY WITH MY GRANDDAUGHTER.
WHY IN THE FOREST THOUGH, GRANDPA? IT'S FULL OF SNAKES...

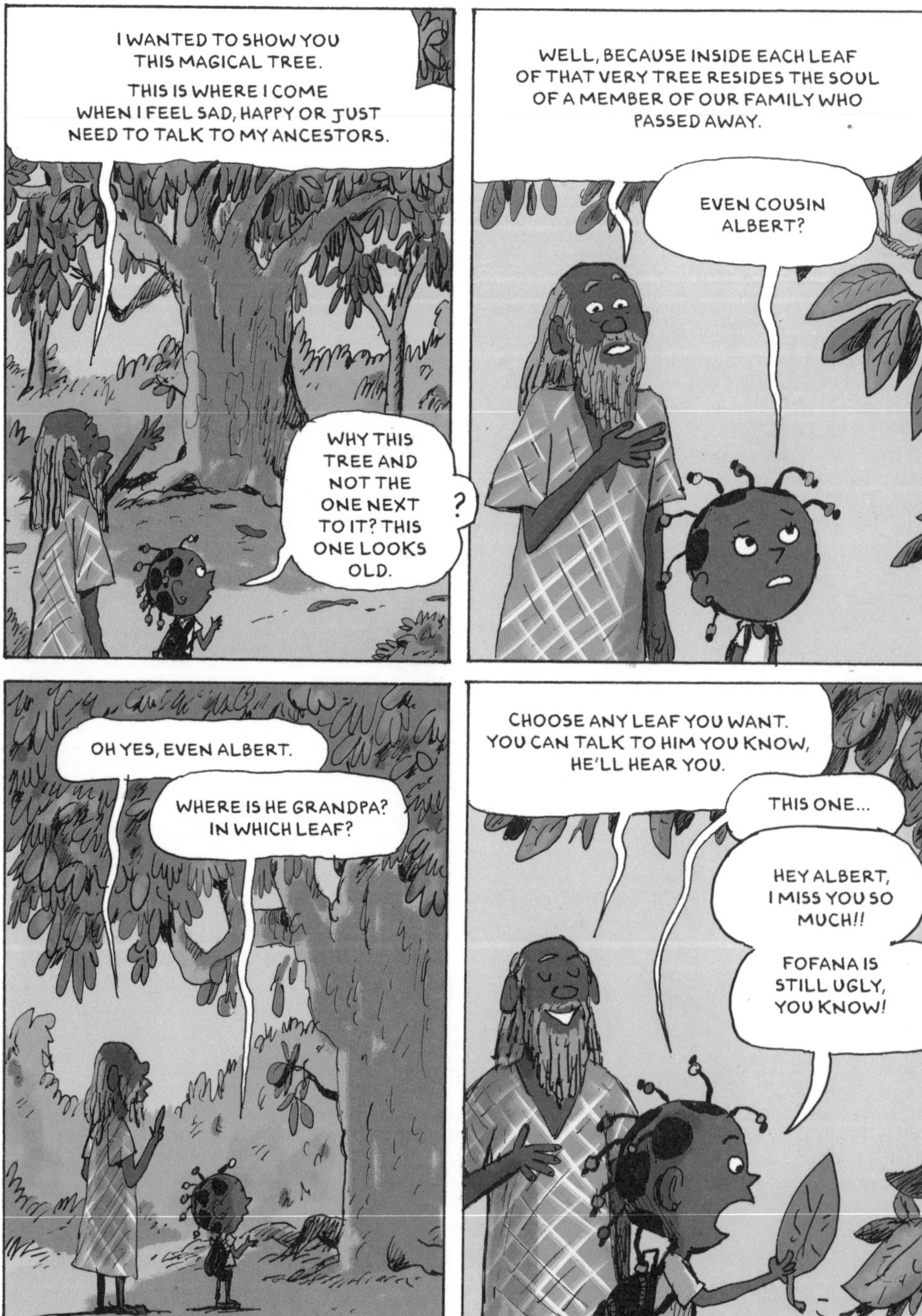
I WANTED TO SHOW YOU THIS MAGICAL TREE.
THIS IS WHERE I COME WHEN I FEEL SAD, HAPPY OR JUST NEED TO TALK TO MY ANCESTORS.
WHY THIS TREE AND NOT THE ONE NEXT TO IT? THIS ONE LOOKS OLD.
?
WELL, BECAUSE INSIDE EACH LEAF OF THAT VERY TREE RESIDES THE SOUL OF A MEMBER OF OUR FAMILY WHO PASSED AWAY.
EVEN COUSIN ALBERT?
OH YES, EVEN ALBERT.
WHERE IS HE GRANDPA? IN WHICH LEAF?
CHOOSE ANY LEAF YOU WANT. YOU CAN TALK TO HIM YOU KNOW, HE'LL HEAR YOU.
THIS ONE...
HEY ALBERT, I MISS YOU SO MUCH!!
FOFANA IS STILL UGLY, YOU KNOW!

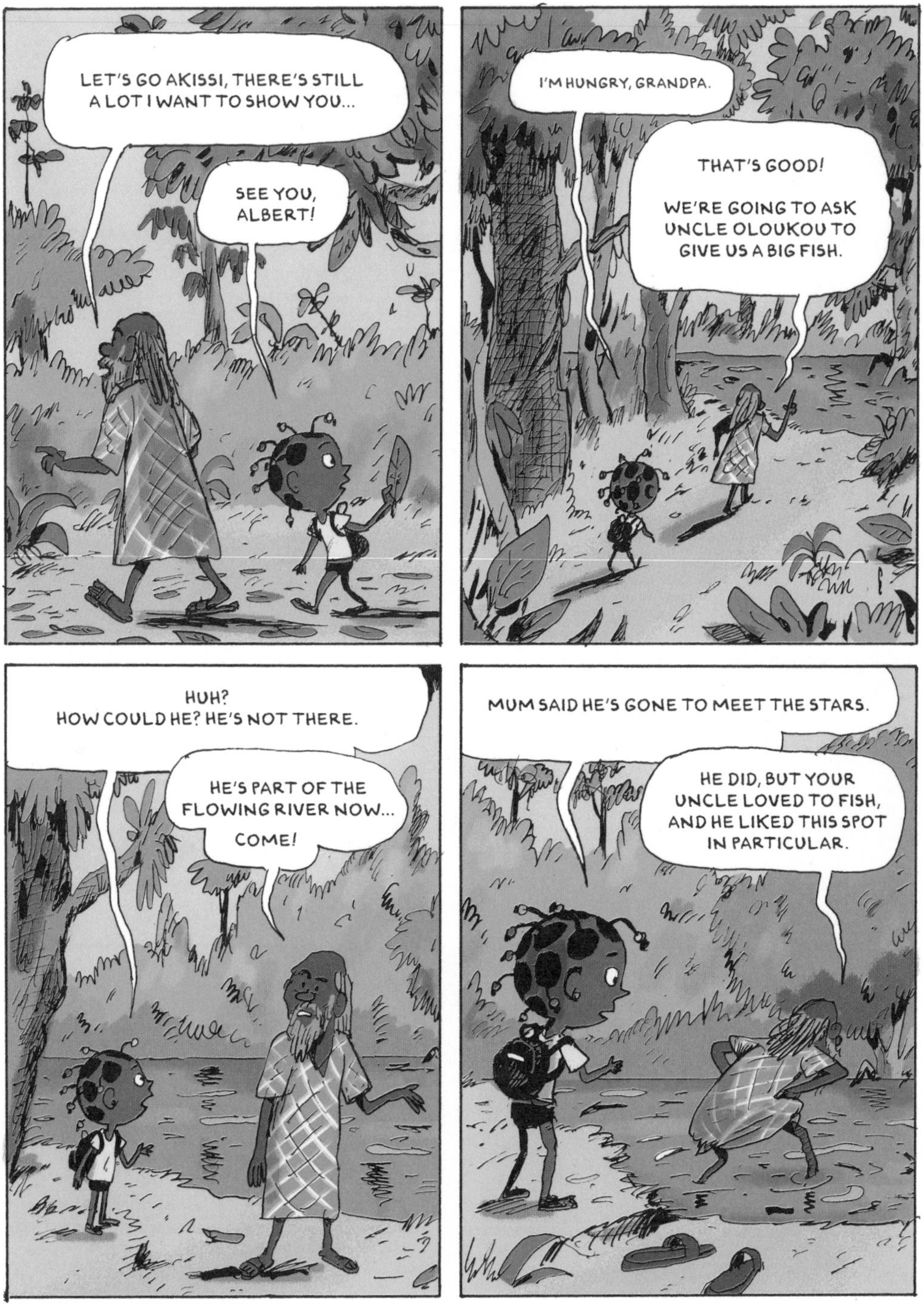
LET'S GO AKISSI, THERE'S STILL A LOT I WANT TO SHOW YOU...
SEE YOU, ALBERT!
I'M HUNGRY, GRANDPA.
THAT'S GOOD!
WE'RE GOING TO ASK UNCLE OLOUKOU TO GIVE US A BIG FISH.
HUH? HOW COULD HE? HE'S NOT THERE.
HE'S PART OF THE FLOWING RIVER NOW...
COME!
MUM SAID HE'S GONE TO MEET THE STARS.
HE DID, BUT YOUR UNCLE LOVED TO FISH, AND HE LIKED THIS SPOT IN PARTICULAR.

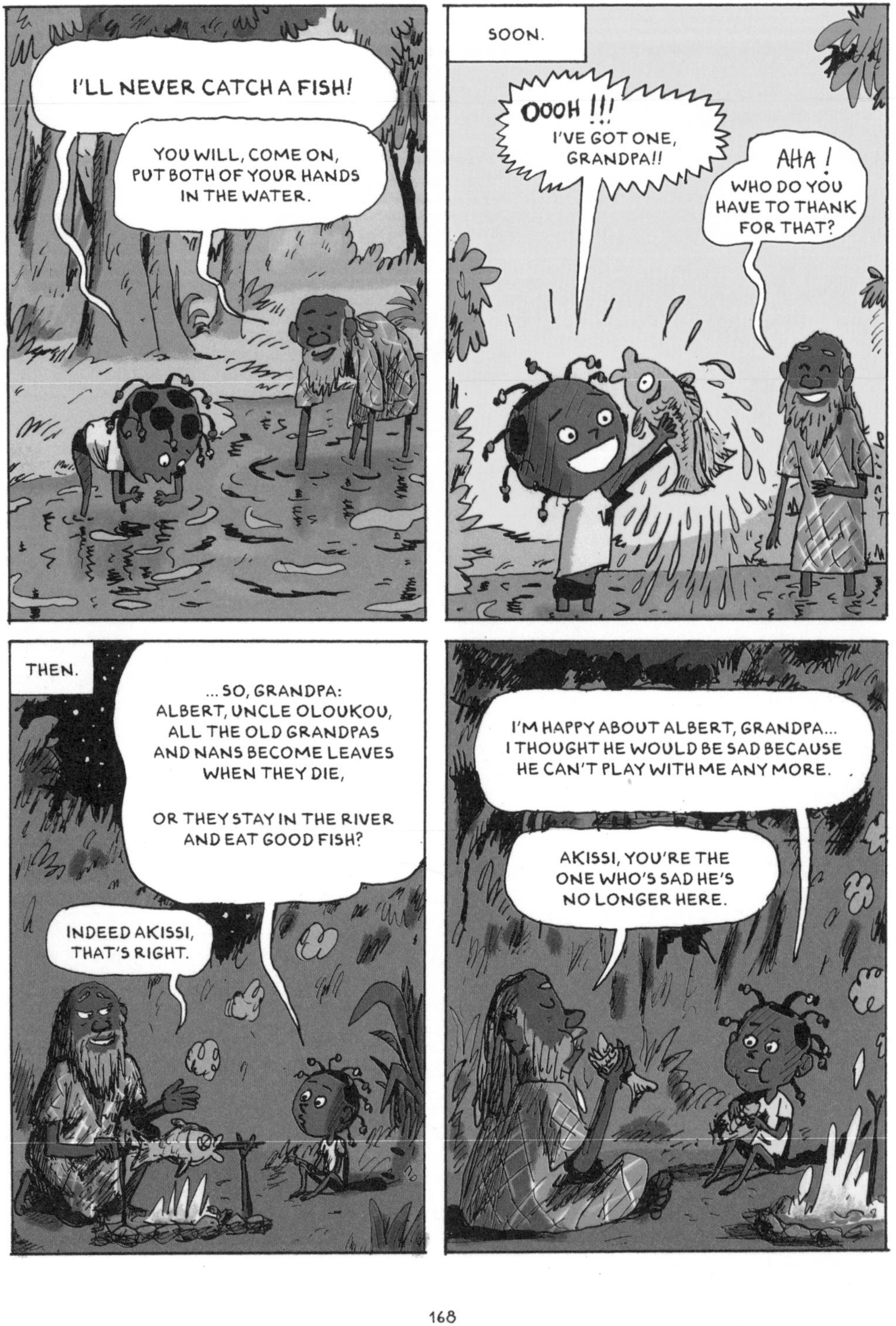
I'LL NEVER CATCH A FISH!
YOU WILL, COME ON, PUT BOTH OF YOUR HANDS IN THE WATER.
SOON.
OOOH !!! I'VE GOT ONE, GRANDPA!!
AHA ! WHO DO YOU HAVE TO THANK FOR THAT?
THEN.
...SO, GRANDPA: ALBERT, UNCLE OLOUKOU, ALL THE OLD GRANDPAS AND NANS BECOME LEAVES WHEN THEY DIE,
OR THEY STAY IN THE RIVER AND EAT GOOD FISH?
INDEED AKISSI, THAT'S RIGHT.
I'M HAPPY ABOUT ALBERT, GRANDPA... I THOUGHT HE WOULD BE SAD BECAUSE HE CAN'T PLAY WITH ME ANY MORE.
AKISSI, YOU'RE THE ONE WHO'S SAD HE'S NO LONGER HERE.

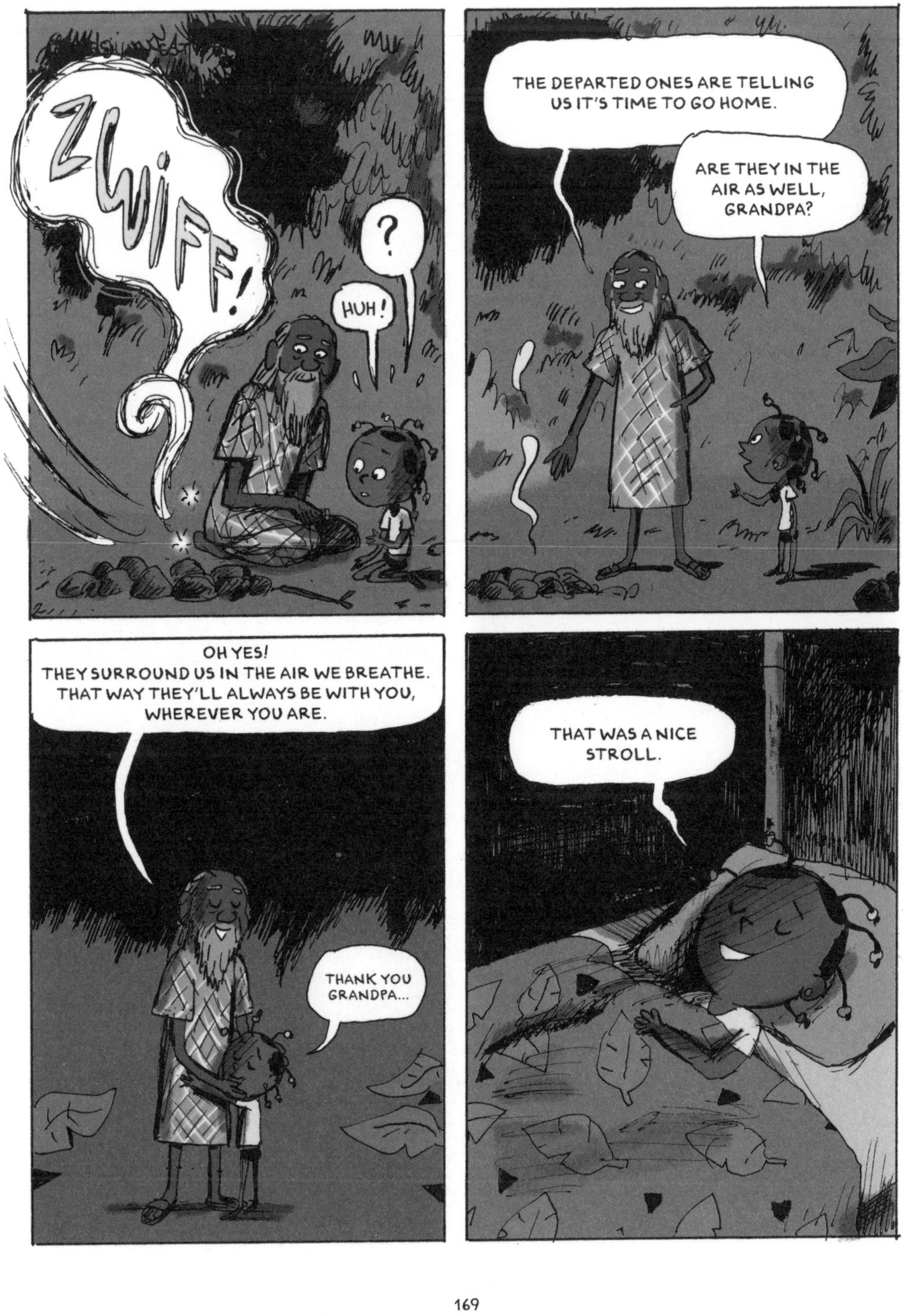
ZWIFF!
HUH!
?
THE DEPARTED ONES ARE TELLING US IT'S TIME TO GO HOME.
ARE THEY IN THE AIR AS WELL, GRANDPA?
OH YES! THEY SURROUND US IN THE AIR WE BREATHE. THAT WAY THEY'LL ALWAYS BE WITH YOU, WHEREVER YOU ARE.
THANK YOU GRANDPA...
THAT WAS A NICE STROLL.

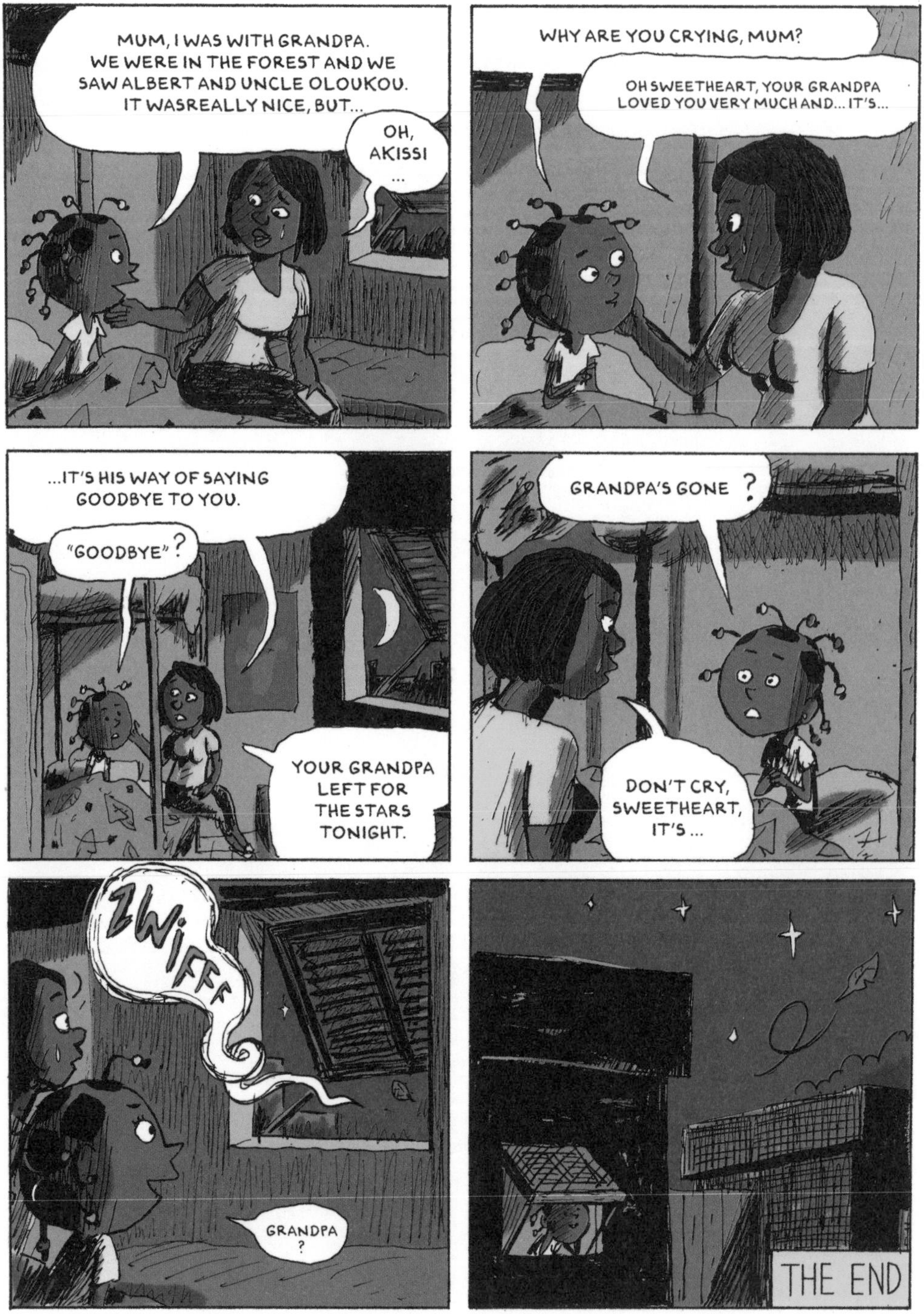
MUM, I WAS WITH GRANDPA. WE WERE IN THE FOREST AND WE SAW ALBERT AND UNCLE OLOUKOU. IT WASREALLY NICE, BUT...
OH, AKISSI ...
WHY ARE YOU CRYING, MUM?
OH SWEETHEART, YOUR GRANDPA LOVED YOU VERY MUCH AND... IT'S...
...IT'S HIS WAY OF SAYING GOODBYE TO YOU.
"GOODBYE"?
YOUR GRANDPA LEFT FOR THE STARS TONIGHT.
GRANDPA'S GONE ?
DON'T CRY, SWEETHEART, IT'S ...
ZWIFFF
GRANDPA ?
THE END

BONUS

pages

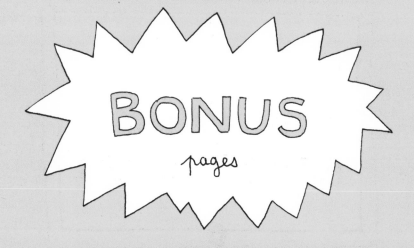

HOW TO MAKE

AN UGLY PRINCESS
FANCY DRESS

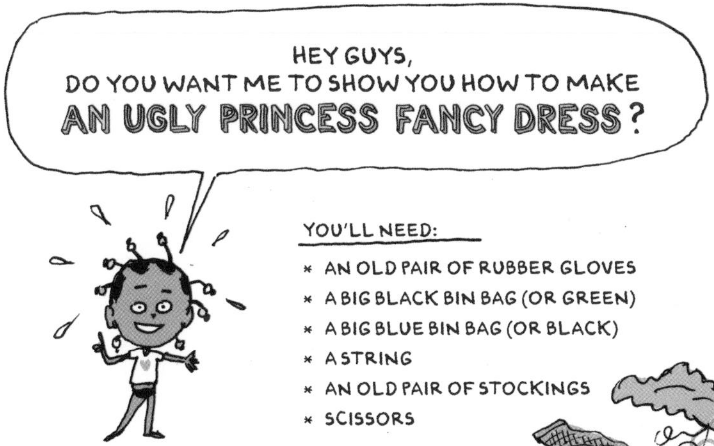
HEY GUYS,
DO YOU WANT ME TO SHOW YOU HOW TO MAKE
AN UGLY PRINCESS FANCY DRESS?

YOU'LL NEED:

* AN OLD PAIR OF RUBBER GLOVES
* A BIG BLACK BIN BAG (OR GREEN)
* A BIG BLUE BIN BAG (OR BLACK)
* A STRING
* AN OLD PAIR OF STOCKINGS
* SCISSORS

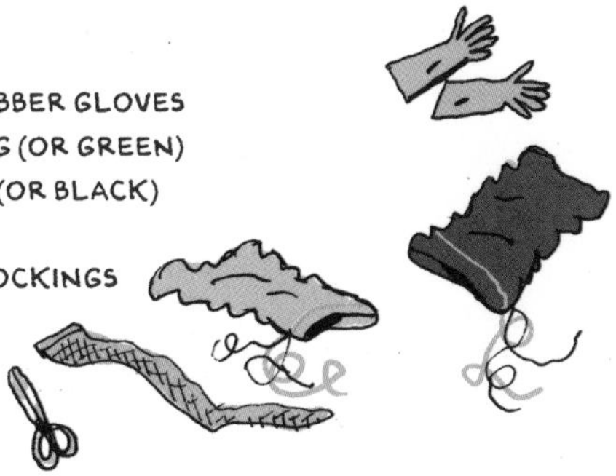

1. CUT THE BOTTOM OF THE BLACK BIN BAG TO MAKE A DRESS.

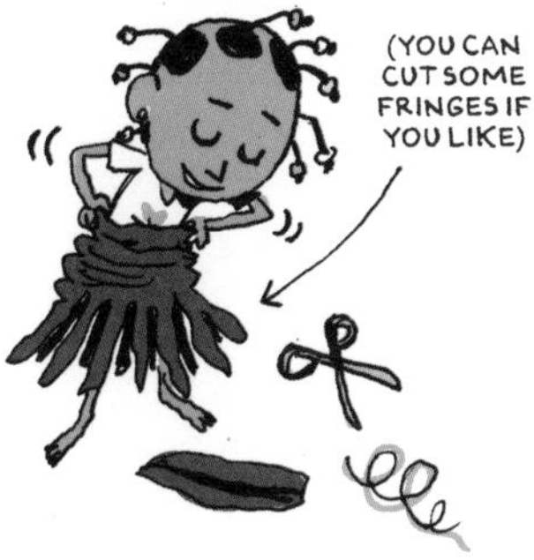
(YOU CAN CUT SOME FRINGES IF YOU LIKE)

2. TIE THE DRESS ON WITH A STRING.

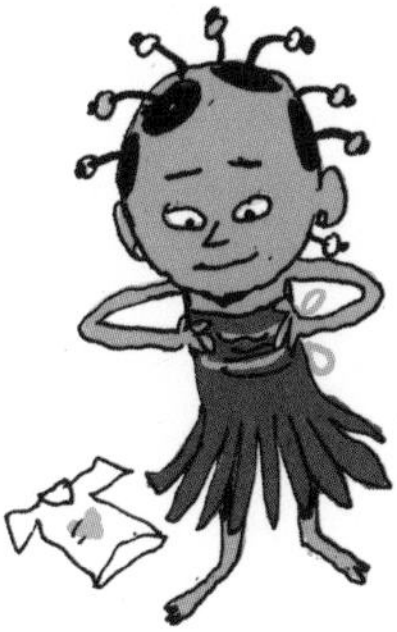

3. CUT OPEN THE BLUE BIN BAG AND TIE IT AROUND YOUR SHOULDERS (NOT TOO TIGHT) TO MAKE A CAPE.

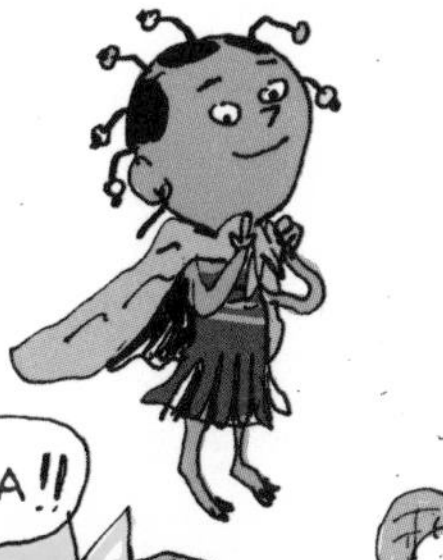

4. PUT THE OLD STOCKINGS ON YOUR HEAD.

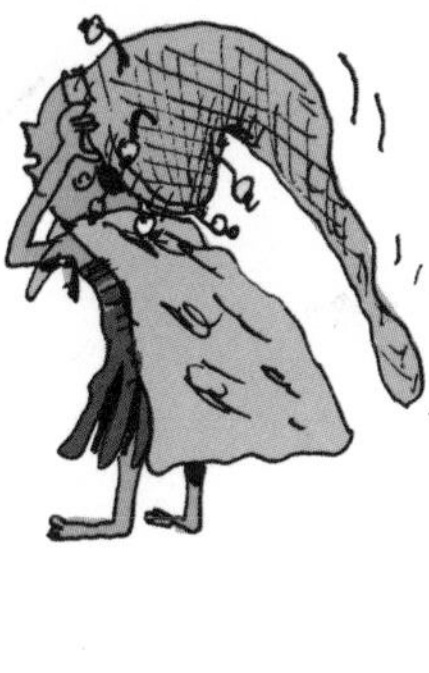

5. PUT ON THE GLOVES.

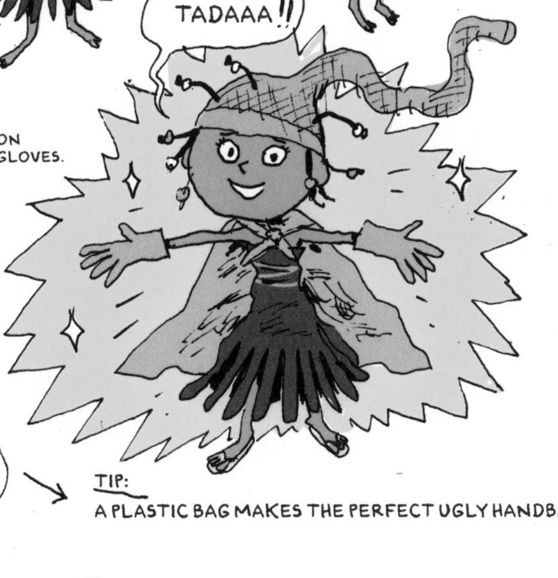
TADAAA!!

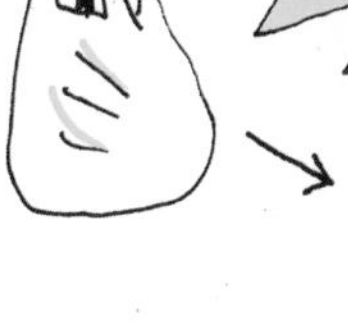

TIP:
A PLASTIC BAG MAKES THE PERFECT UGLY HANDBAG.

MAZE

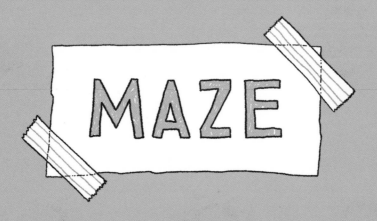

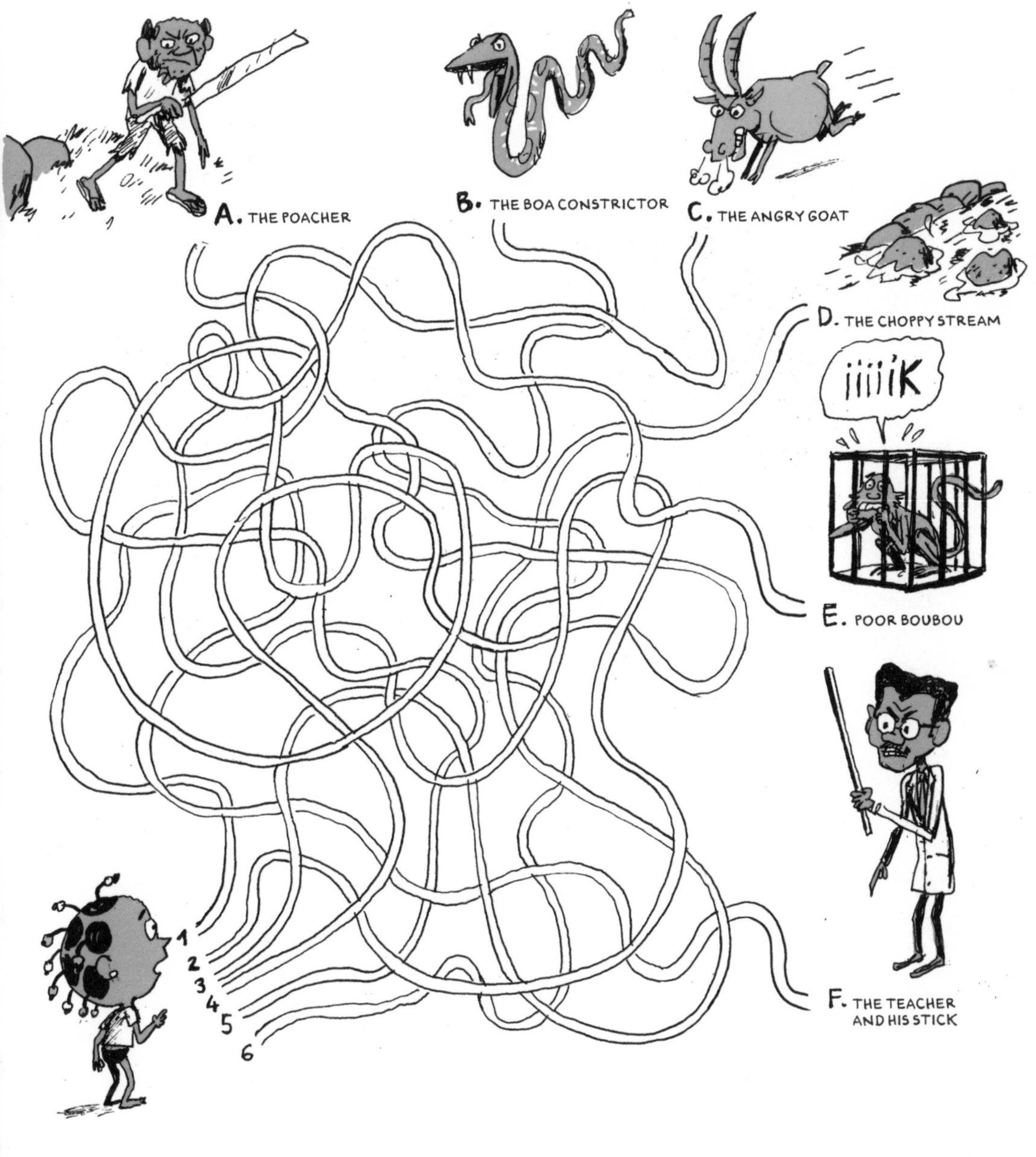
A. THE POACHER
B. THE BOA CONSTRICTOR
C. THE ANGRY GOAT
D. THE CHOPPY STREAM
¡¡¡¡K
E. POOR BOUBOU
F. THE TEACHER AND HIS STICK
1
2
3
4
5
6

SOLUTION: IT'S PATH NUMBER 2

MAPS

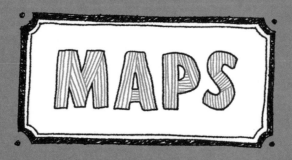

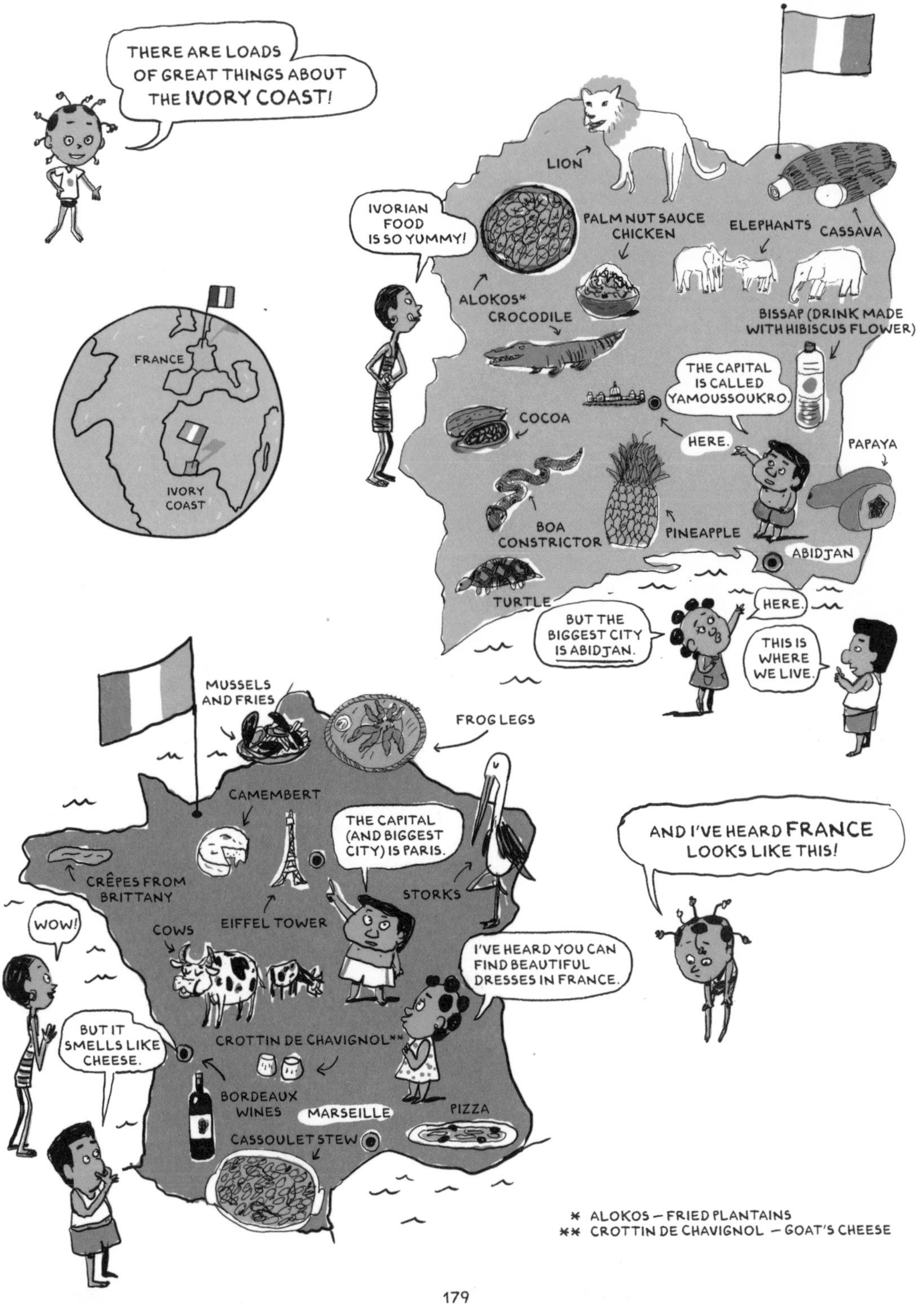

THERE ARE LOADS OF GREAT THINGS ABOUT THE IVORY COAST!
FRANCE
IVORY COAST
LION
IVORIAN FOOD IS SO YUMMY!
PALM NUT SAUCE CHICKEN
ELEPHANTS
CASSAVA
ALOKOS*
CROCODILE
BISSAP (DRINK MADE WITH HIBISCUS FLOWER)
THE CAPITAL IS CALLED YAMOUSSOUKRO.
COCOA
HERE.
PAPAYA
BOA CONSTRICTOR
PINEAPPLE
ABIDJAN
TURTLE
HERE.
BUT THE BIGGEST CITY IS ABIDJAN.
THIS IS WHERE WE LIVE.
MUSSELS AND FRIES
FROG LEGS
CAMEMBERT
THE CAPITAL (AND BIGGEST CITY) IS PARIS.
AND I'VE HEARD FRANCE LOOKS LIKE THIS!
CRÊPES FROM BRITTANY
STORKS
WOW!
EIFFEL TOWER
COWS
I'VE HEARD YOU CAN FIND BEAUTIFUL DRESSES IN FRANCE.
BUT IT SMELLS LIKE CHEESE.
CROTTIN DE CHAVIGNOL**
BORDEAUX WINES
MARSEILLE
PIZZA
CASSOULET STEW

* ALOKOS – FRIED PLANTAINS
** CROTTIN DE CHAVIGNOL – GOAT'S CHEESE

Marguerite Abouet was born in Abidjan, Ivory Coast, in the neighbourhood of Yopougon. At the age of 12, she moved to Paris, where she discovered wonderful libraries and developed a passion for books. After trying her hand at several different jobs, she became a legal assistant. In 2005, she published *Aya de Yopougon*, which won the Best Album prize at the Angoulême Comics Festival. The Ivorian series, drawn by Clément Oubrerie, comprises more than 700 pages that beautifully depict an authentic and seldom-seen side of Africa. The books are now translated into fifteen languages, and were adapted into a movie in 2013. In 2010, Abouet and illustrator Mathieu Sapin published the first volume of *Akissi*, a children's series inspired by her childhood memories. When she is not busy writing stories, Marguerite Abouet helps build libraries throughout Africa through her charity, Des Livres pour Tous (www.deslivrespourtous.org).

Mathieu Sapin was born in 1974. After attending the School of Decorative Arts in Strasbourg, he spent two years working at the International Center for Comic Strips and Images, where he illustrated children's literature for Nathan, Bayard Presse, Albin Michel, and Lito. In 2003 he began to devote himself entirely to making comics, namely the alcoholically adventurous series *Supermurgeman*. This series developed into a unique and quirky universe, rife with irony and absurdity. Today, his list of works includes over 30 titles, including the *Akissi* series.

THE MISCHIEF NEVER ENDS!
READ MORE LAUGH-OUT-LOUD TALES
IN THE WONDROUS AKISSI SERIES:

Abouet & Sapin
Akissi
TALES OF MISCHIEF
FLYING EYE BOOKS

Abouet & Sapin
Akissi
MORE TALES OF MISCHIEF
FLYING EYE BOOKS

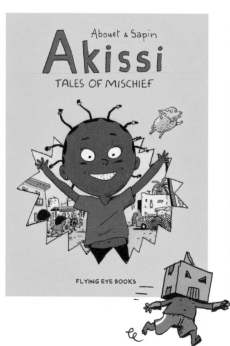

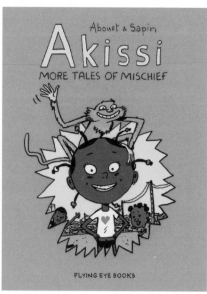

PRAISE FOR AKISSI:

"OUTRAGEOUSLY FUN - THIS INDOMITABLE LITTLE GIRL IS SIMPLY INCOMPARABLE."
- KIRKUS REVIEWS, *STARRED REVIEW*

"[AKISSI] FILLS A GAP IN CHILDREN'S COMICS FEATURING AFRICAN CHARACTERS AND SETTINGS. HIGHLY RECOMMENDED FOR MIDDLE GRADE GRAPHIC NOVEL COLLECTIONS."
- SCHOOL LIBRARY JOURNAL, *STARRED REVIEW*

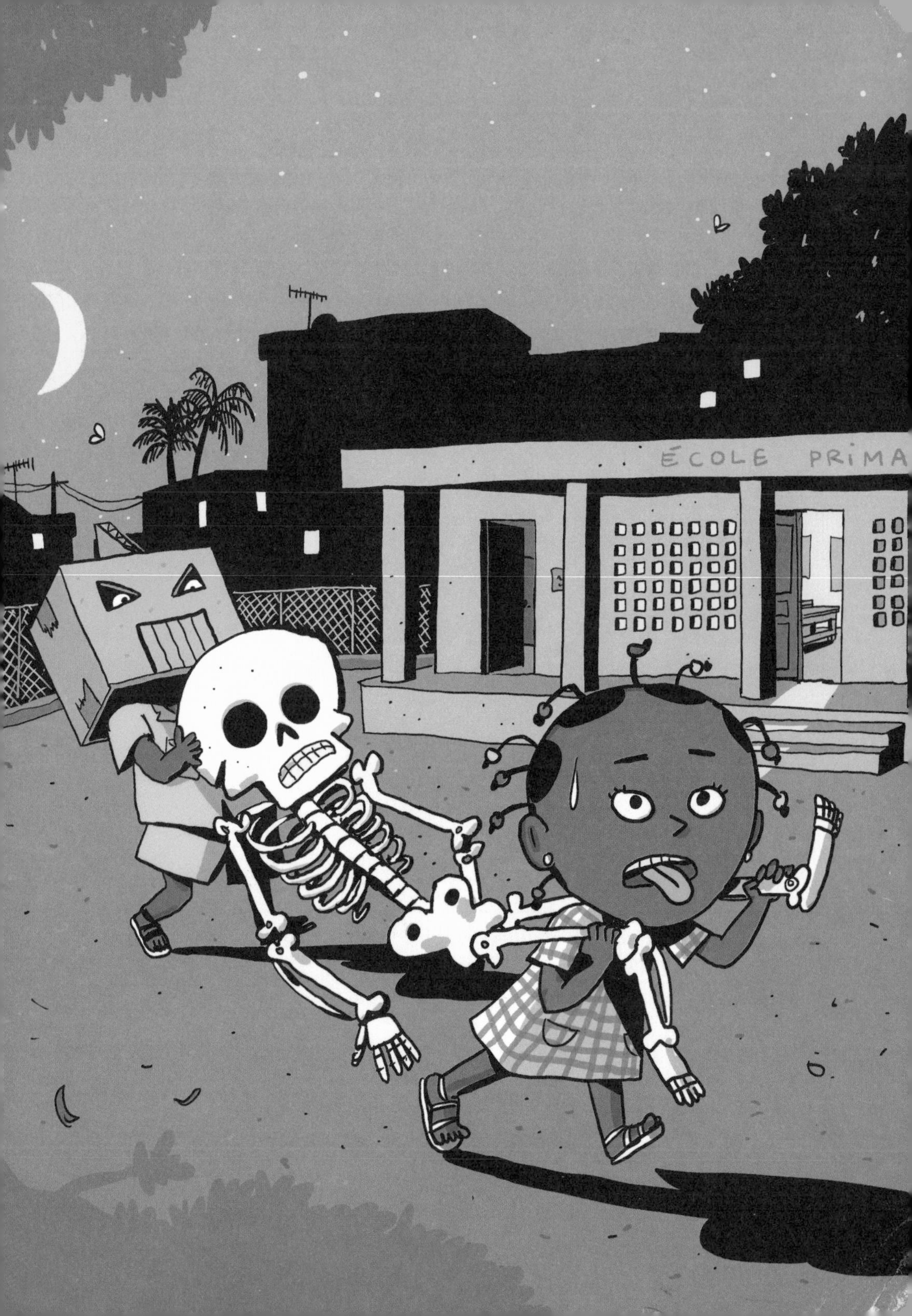
ÉCOLE PRIMA

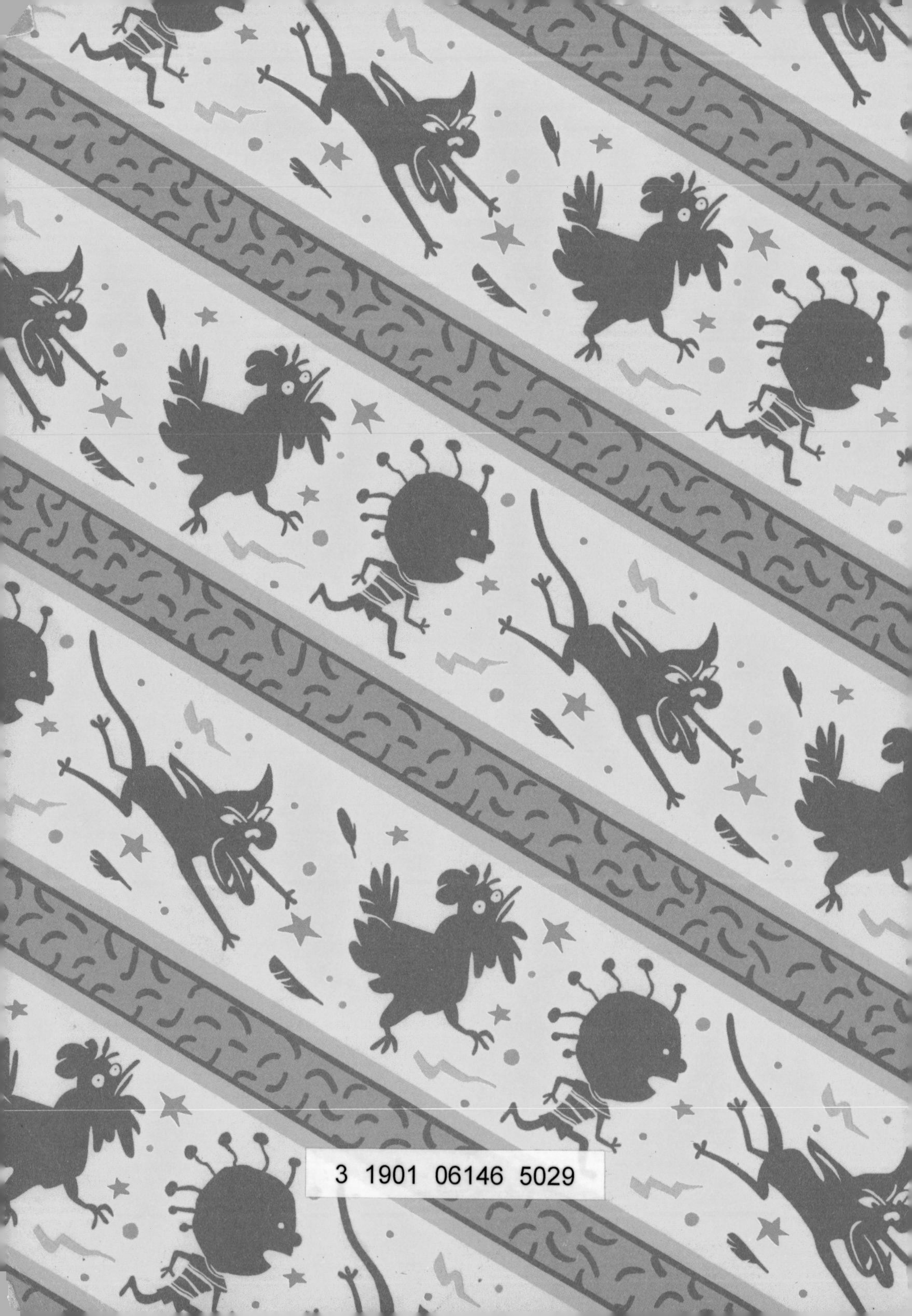